# HOLLYWOOD
# AND CRIME

# HOLLYWOOD AND CRIME

WITHDRAWN

Original Crime Stories Set During the History of Hollywood

Edited by
ROBERT J. RANDISI

PEGASUS BOOKS
NEW YORK

HOLLYWOOD AND CRIME:
ORIGINAL STORIES SET DURING THE HISTORY OF HOLLYWOOD

Pegasus Books LLC
80 Broad Street
5th Floor
New York, NY 10004

Library of Congress Cataloging-in-Publication Data is available.

ISBN: 978-1-60598-013-3

10 9 8 7 6 5 4 3 2 1

Printed in the United States of America
Distributed by W. W. Norton & Company, Inc.
www.pegasusbooks.us

To the ghosts of Hollywood

# TABLE OF CONTENTS

# HOLLYWOOD AND CRIME

# INTRODUCTION

Disneyland
Movies
The Dodgers
The Lakers
The Tar Pits
The Brown Derby
Movie stars
Famous people
sun
beach
surf . . .

That's what most people think of when they think of Hollywood. However, since I make my living as a crime writer, when I think of Hollywood I think of:

Fatty Arbuckle
The Black Dahlia
Robert Blake
Christian Brando
Bob Crane
Sal Mineo
Marilyn Monroe
O.J.
Carl "Alfalfa" Switzer
Lana Turner & Johnny Stompanato

These are some of the people involved in the most famous crimes committed in Hollywood. For years Hollywood has had a relationship with crime, and the more infamous the people involved, the more sensational the story.

However, there have been other crimes not involving the rich and famous, committed by and against people who could pass you on the street, or an intersection—such as Hollywood & Vine—and you would never know who they were, or what they had done. If their stories make the papers, it's certainly not on page one, or fodder for the gossip columnists.

I invited fifteen of today's best crime writers to craft a tale around the centerpiece of Hollywood & Vine, the most famous intersection in Tinsel Town. The tales here are representative of stories taking place in Hollywood that will not make headlines but are, nevertheless, riveting, especially when being told by these talented authors.

Here are the stories you don't hear about on the news or entertainment shows, you don't read about in the newspapers or tabloids, the stories that sometimes go unnoticed, unreported . . . even unsolved.

ROBERT J. RANDISI
Clarksville, Missouri

*Over the past decade or so a lot of writers have come along and received "the hype," and become best-sellers. In my opinion Michael Connelly might be the one who really deserved it—and still does. Whether it's a Harry Bosch book or a stand-alone thriller, he always delivers. He does it again here with a Harry Bosch flashback to the '90s.*

# Suicide Run

*by Michael Connelly*

I t was slow on night watch. They were submarining—the practice of cruising close to the station so at end of watch they could quickly pull into the back lot, dump the car, and check out. Jerry Edgar was driving. It was his idea to submarine. He always had some place to get to, even at midnight. Harry Bosch had no place to go but an empty house.

Whatever plans Edgar had, they changed when they got the call from the watch commander and were sent to the Orchidia Apartments.

"Fifteen minutes," Jerry Edgar muttered. "Fifteen minutes and we'd a been clear."

"Don't sweat it," Harry Bosch told him. "If it checks out we'll be done in fifteen minutes."

Edgar turned off La Brea onto Franklin and they were less than two minutes away. Bosch and Edgar were the night shift detectives in Hollywood Division, part of a new roving response team instituted by the commander. Captain LeValley wanted a detective team to roll to any crime of violence instead of pulling the patrol reports the following morning. It was a good theory on paper, and Bosch and Edgar had in fact cleared two armed robberies and a rape in their first four days working nights. But for the most part they took reports and did little more than pass cases off to the appropriate investigators the following day.

The air they drove through was clear and crisp. They kept the windows up and their expectations down. The call was a suicide run. They needed to make a confirmation for the patrol sergeant on scene and then they'd be on their way. With any luck they'd still make it back to the station by midnight.

The Orchidia was a sprawling pink apartment complex off Orchid and nestled into the hillside behind the Magic Castle parking lot. It was an apartment complex that had been around for as long as Bosch could remember. In the old days it was a place where studios put up the new starlets just signed to contracts. These days the people who lived there paid their own way.

There were two patrol cars with flashing blues out front. There was already a van from the Scientific Investigation Division and a station wagon from the coroner's office there as well. This told Bosch that the sergeant on scene had either forgotten about the night shift detectives or didn't think them necessary. He told Edgar to park behind the patrol car that didn't have a light bar on the roof. That would be the sergeant's car. Bosch would make sure he didn't go anywhere until Bosch wanted him to.

As they got out Edgar looked over the roof of their cruiser at Bosch.

"I hate night watch in Hollywood," he said. "All the suicides come out at night."

It was true. This would be their third suicide in four nights.

"In Hollywood, everything comes out at night," Bosch said.

There was a patrol officer at the entrance and he took badge numbers from Bosch and Edgar and then directed them to apartment six. The front door of the apartment was open and they walked into a nest of activity. It was the end of shift for everybody and everybody was in a hurry. Bosch saw the watch sergeant, who turned out to be a woman named Polly Fulton, standing in a hallway that most likely led to a bedroom.

"Detectives," she said. "Glad you could swing by. Right in here."

"What do you mean, we just got the call," Edgar said.

"Really?" Fulton said. "I called it in at least forty-five minutes ago. The watch must have his hands full."

She gestured for them to pass by her and they did. The hall ended at three doors: a closet, a bathroom and a bedroom. They entered the bedroom and saw that all the activity was centered on a naked woman lying in the bed. There were two coroner's investigators, a forensics tech, a photographer, and another patrol officer all hovering around the bed.

The woman was on her back, her arms at her sides. She was young and remained beautiful even in death. Her hair was blonde and it wreathed her face, curving under her chin. Her skin was pale white and her breasts were full, even though lying she was supine. A slight line of discoloration could be seen running with the bottom curve of each breast. Surgical scars.

There was a diamond teardrop pendant on a silver chain on her chest between her breasts. Her stomach was flat and her pubic hair was neatly trimmed short and in a perfect inverted triangle.

Edgar made a light catcall whistle between his teeth.

"Now why would she want to go and do the Marilyn Monroe?" he asked. "A girl lookin' like that."

No one answered. Bosch just stared at the woman on the bed as he pulled on a pair of latex gloves. He knew that the knee-jerk reaction was to think that beauty solved all other problems. Same thing with money. But he had seen enough suicides to know that neither was true. Not even close.

"Lizbeth Grayson," Sgt. Fulton said. "Twenty-four. Hasn't been here in the City of Angels long. Still has an Oregon driver's license in her purse."

Fulton had come up next to Bosch and spoke while they both stared at the body. There was no embarrassment about the dead woman being naked and exposed. It was police work.

Fulton held up a clipboard. Lizbeth Grayson's driver's license was clipped to it. Bosch noted that she was from Portland.

"What else?" he asked.

"She's an actress—aren't they all. She's got a drawer full of headshots over there. Looks like she did a walk-on bit on *Seinfeld* last year. You know, they film that here, even though it's supposed to be New York. Anyway, the résumé is on the back of the latest headshot. She hasn't worked a lot—at least the kind of jobs that she wanted to put on the résumé."

Bosch could almost feel Fulton's eyes drop to the small, perfect triangle of pubic hair. He knew what she was thinking. The silicone and the trim job might indicate a certain lifestyle and other means of income. Bosch looked back up at the face. Lizbeth Grayson hadn't needed anything in life but that face. He wondered if anybody besides her mother had ever told her that.

"Anyway," Fulton said, "on the side table we've got an empty bottle of Percodan left over from breast enhancement surgery last year and a good-bye-sweet-world note. It's looking pretty cut and dried, Detective. We won't be wasting your time on this."

Bosch moved his focus to the table next to the bed and stepped over.

"Thank you, Sergeant."

On the table was an empty glass with a white residue at the bottom, a plastic pill bottle, and a notepad. Nothing else. Bosch bent down to study the pill vial, which was standing up on the table. It was a painkiller prescribed to Lizbeth Grayson eight months earlier. Take as needed for pain. He wondered if that pain included the need to end it all. He took out a notebook and wrote down the name of the physician who prescribed the drug and who had presumably performed the breast enhancement surgery.

He next looked at an open spiral notebook that was on the table next to the pill bottle. There were four lines written in pencil on the page.

> There's no <u>use</u> anymore
> I give up
> I <u>give</u> up
> I <u>give</u> *up*!

He studied it for a moment, paying attention to the words that were underlined and understanding that she was putting an emphasis on a different word in each sentence. He reached down to the notebook so that he could see if there was writing on any of the other pages.

"Not yet, Detective."

Bosch turned and saw the SID photographer standing behind him. It was Mark Baron. They had worked many crime scenes together. Baron proffered his camera.

"I haven't shot any of that yet," he said. "I don't want it moved."

"Okay, hold on a second."

Bosch stooped down so he could look beneath the table. It had no drawers but there was a single shelf and it held a stack of *People* magazines. There was nothing on the rug beneath the table. He got down on his hands and knees and lifted the bed skirt. There was a pair of slippers under the bed but nothing else.

Bosch got up and stepped back to let Baron get close to take his shots. He walked back to Fulton.

"Who found her?"

"The landlord. He said he got a call from her agent and then another call from her acting coach. They were worried about her. She missed a big audition or something today. The landlord has a pass key and came in. He said the coach was very convincing."

"Was she on display like that or covered?"

"She was covered. The coroner's people did that."

Bosch nodded.

"Where's the landlord?"

"He went back to his place. He lives onsite. He was looking pretty pale."

"Get him."

"This is pretty simple, right? We're all going to get out of here in a few minutes, right?"

Bosch looked at Fulton. Even she wanted to turn pumpkin at midnight.

"Just get the landlord, please."

Fulton left and Bosch went over to the bureau where Edgar was looking through the contents of the top drawer. There were a variety of photos. There was a stack of 8x10 glossies that showed Lizbeth Grayson in varying poses and costumes. No matter what she was, wearing or what the facial pose was it was impossible to hide her beauty in character. Bosch imagined that it opened some doors but kept others closed. She would have never been taken seriously as an actress with that face.

"Man, this girl had it all going for her," Edgar said. "Why'd she want to go and waste it all?"

"Maybe she didn't."

Edgar dropped the photo he was looking at back into the drawer and looked at Bosch.

"Harry, what are you seeing?"

Bosch shook his head.

"Nothing yet. I'm just saying. I'm asking the question, you know?"

"Don't go crazy on this. You want to talk to the landlord, fine. Let's talk to him and put this thing to bed—no pun intended."

"All I'm saying is that you can't come into this with a precon-ceived idea, you know? It's infectious."

Bosch sauntered over to one of the coroner's investigators, who was putting equipment back into a tool box. Bosch knew him, too. Nester Gonzmart.

"How's it look, Nester?"

"Looks like we're out of here, Boss."

"What do you have for Tee-oh-dee?"

"We took the liver temp. I'm going to say between midnight and four this morning."

"So twenty-four hours tops. Any trauma?"

"Not a hangnail, man. This is a clean scene. Sometimes it's hard to believe but it's looking to me like what it is. We'll get the tox in about two weeks and we'll see the Perc on the screens. That'll be it."

"Make sure you get it to me."

"You got it, Harry."

He snapped the latches on the tool box and headed out of the room with it. Bosch knew he would be back with the stretcher. They were going to take Lizbeth Grayson on a ride downtown.

"Everybody?" Baron said. "Can I get everybody to step back into the hall so I can get my wide shots?"

Bosch moved toward the hall, wondering where Fulton was with the landlord.

"Thank you," Baron said.

Fulton was in the front living room with a man who was small, slight, and maybe as old as the apartment building. He was introduced as Ziggy Wojciechowski. He recounted for Bosch and Edgar his finding of Lizbeth Grayson dead. It was the same story Fulton had already related.

"Was the door locked?" Bosch asked.

"Yes. I have a passkey to all the apartments. I used it."

Bosch glanced over at the front door and saw the security chain hanging on the jamb.

"The chain wasn't on?"

"No, no chain."

"Did she pay her rent or did somebody pay it for her?"

It was always good to throw in a change-up, something unexpected at the interview subject.

"Uh, she paid. She always paid with a check."

"What about boyfriends?"

"I don't know. I don't spy on my tenants. The Orchidia offers privacy. I don't intrude."

"What about girlfriends?"

"Same answer, Detective. I don't—"

"Mr. Wojciechowski, when did you come into the apartment and find her?"

The landlord seemed a little confused by the way the questions jumped around.

"It would have been about ten-fifteen. I had watched the beginning of the news on channel five—Hal Fishman. Her coach called again and I finally said I would check on her just so they would stop calling."

"When you came in, were the lights on?"

Wojciechowski didn't answer as he contemplated the question.

"Think about when you entered. What did you see? Could you see anything or did you have to put on the lights?"

"I could see the light at the end of the hall. Her bedroom. The light was on."

Bosch nodded.

"Okay, Mr. Wojciechowski, that will be enough for now. We may have to talk later."

He watched the little man walk out of the apartment. Edgar came up close to him then so that they could speak quietly.

"I don't like that look in your eyes, Harry. I've seen it before."

"And?"

"It tells me you're in love. You want this to be something it's not."

"The chain wasn't on the door."

"So what? She was being considerate. She knew she was going to check out and she didn't want anybody to have to have to break down the door. We've seen that a hundred times before easy."

"The lights in the bedroom were left on."

"So?"

"People don't leave the lights on. They want it to be like they're going to sleep at night. They want to go easy."

Edgar nodded his head.

"All right, I'll give you that. But it's not enough. It's an anomaly. You know what that is? Something that deviates from the norm. What we have here is a deviation within the norm. It's not something we—"

There was a sudden flash. Bosch turned to see Baron coming from the hallway into the living room. He had fired off a shot at Bosch and Edgar.

"Sorry about that," he said. "Misfire. You guys want me to shoot anything else? I'm done with Marilyn Monroe in there."

"No," Edgar said. "You're clear, Mark."

Baron, a short man with a widening middle, threw a mock salute and walked out the open front door of the apartment. Bosch looked at Edgar sharply. He didn't like the junior member of the team making the call to break up the crime scene. Edgar read him correctly.

"Look, Harry, it is what it is. We're done here. Let's sign off and wait on the toxicology."

"We're not done. We're just beginning. Go out there and bring Baron back. I want him to shoot everything in this place."

Edgar blew out his breath impatiently.

"Look, partner, you may have convinced yourself of something but you haven't convinced me or anybody else here that—"

"There's no pencil."

"What?"

"On the bed table. There's no pencil to go with the note. If she wrote the note and took the pills then where's the pencil?"

"I don't know, Harry. Maybe it's in a drawer in the kitchen. What's it matter?"

"You're saying she writes a suicide note and gets up naked to put the pencil away in a kitchen drawer? Listen to yourself, Jerry. This scene doesn't work and you know it. So what do you want to do about it?"

Edgar stared at Bosch for a moment and then nodded as if conceding something.

"I'll go get the photographer back," he said.

\* \* \* \* \* \*

Bosch stared at Lizbeth Grayson on the television screen. She was tearful, beautiful, and in character.

"I've tried with him every way I know how," she said. "There's no use anymore. I give up."

"Stop it right there," Bosch said.

Gloria Palovich paused the video. Bosch looked at her. She had been Lizbeth Grayson's acting coach.

"When was this recorded?" he asked.

"Last week. It was for yesterday's reading. That's why I was concerned. She worked for almost two weeks to prepare for that audition. She got fresh head shots. She was putting everything into it. When she didn't show up . . . I just knew something was wrong."

"Did she take notes during your sessions?"

"All of the time. She was a wonderful student."

"What sort of notes?"

"Mostly on accent and delivery. How to use dialogue to convey the inner emotions."

Bosch nodded. He realized that Lizbeth Grayson's suicide note was anything but a farewell. It was the opposite. It was part of a young woman's efforts to thrive and succeed.

He looked around the acting studio. He felt uneasy, like he had missed something in the conversation. Then he remembered. The head shots he had seen in the bureau drawer in Lizbeth Grayson's apartment were not new. He had studied the dead woman on the bed and none of the photos in the drawer showed her with the same hair style. They were old.

Bosch looked at the acting coach.

"You said she got new photos. Are you sure?"

Palovich nodded emphatically and pointed over Bosch's head.

"Absolutely. She felt so good about this job that she held nothing back. She was going after it on every level."

Bosch turned and looked at the bulletin board that ran the length of the wall behind him. It was covered with a blizzard of head shots. All of Palovich's students, he assumed. He found the shot of Lizbeth Grayson and it was indeed a recent shot. Her blonde hair, curved under her chin, and the easy smile.

Bosch felt himself getting angry. Someone had picked this flower just as it had been about to bloom.

He stepped over and pulled the tack holding the photo to the board. He studied the shot in his hand. There had been no copies of this photo in the apartment. He was sure of it.

"When did she get this taken, do you know?" he asked.

"Last week, I think," Palovich replied. "She brought in the stack and gave me the first one off the top for the board."

"There was a stack?"

"Yes, usually they come in stacks of a hundred. You can never have too many photos. You have to have your head shots out there or you don't get the calls."

Bosch nodded. He had worked in Hollywood long enough to know how it worked. He turned the photo over. There was a list of Lizbeth Grayson's acting credits on the back. Also listed were her contact numbers through an agent named Mason Rich.

He turned it back over to look at the photo again.

"Why are the head shots you see always in black and white but everything they make these days is in color?" he asked.

"I think it's because the black and white better shows the contrast the movie camera will pick up," Palovich responded.

Bosch nodded, even though he didn't understand her answer and knew nothing about contrast and photography.

The picture cut off across Grayson's sternum. She was wearing an open collar blouse and Bosch could see the chain coming around her neck. The photo cut off before showing the teardrop pendant he remembered from the night before.

He turned back to check the screen. The picture remained paused and his eyes were immediately drawn to the chain around Lizbeth Grayson's neck. She was wearing an open shirt over a simple white tank top that said CRUNCH across it. But the pendant, which was clearly visible at the bottom of the chain, was not a diamond. It was a single pearl.

Bosch pointed to the screen.

"You see the pearl?"

"Yes, she always wore that."

"Always?"

"Yes, it had been her grandmother's. She believed it brought her good luck. Once in class we did some biographical sketches. She told us all about it then. In our classes we all have alter egos with alternate names. Her name was Pearl. When I called on her, if I used the name Pearl, she would respond as that alter ego. Do you understand?"

"I think so. Do you have any tapes of her as Pearl?"

"I think so. I could look."

"I don't know if it's significant or not. I'll let you know. Did you ever see Lizbeth wearing a pendant with a diamond in it?"

Palovich thought for a moment and then shook her head.

"No, never."

Bosch nodded and thanked her for the time. He asked if he could take the head shot and she said that was fine. At the door to the studio she stopped him with a question.

"Who would do this, Detective Bosch?"

Bosch looked at her.

"I don't know but I'm going to find out."

* * * * * *

In the crime analysis office Bosch sat with an officer named Kizmin Rider. He had worked with her before and knew she was one of the quickest cops on a computer he had ever seen. She was clearly going places in the department and he knew she was being fast-tracked for administration. But the last time they had worked together she had confided to him that she really wanted to be a detective.

When she was ready Bosch told her what he wanted.

"I'm looking for suicides in the last five years," Bosch said.

"Young females."

"That's going to be a lot."

She worked the keyboard and went into the department's database. In less than a minute she had it.

"Eighty-nine suicides of females between twenty and thirty."

Bosch nodded, trying to think of ways to narrow the search.

"Do you have it by method?" he asked.

"Yes. What are you looking for?"

"Pills."

"That would be overdose."

"She typed it in and had the answer in seconds."

"Fifty-six."

"What about by profession? I think I'm looking at actresses only."

"That would be a catchall—entertainer."

She typed and had the answer before Bosch took his next breath.

"Twenty-six."

"White females?"

She typed.

"Twenty-three."

Bosch nodded. He could think of nothing else to narrow it down to cases similar to Lizbeth Grayson's phony suicide.

"Can you print out the names and case numbers for me?"

"No problem."

Thirty seconds later Bosch had the list and was ready to go down to the archives to pull the files.

"You need any help with that, Harry?" Rider asked.

"You mean like you might want to do some detective work?"

She smiled.

"I wouldn't mind," she said. "It gets kind of boring up here looking at the computer all day."

Bosch checked his watch. It was almost lunchtime.

"Tell you what. I'll go pull the twenty-three files and then meet you in the cafeteria for lunch. We can look through them then. I could probably use the help because my partner thinks this is the wildest goose chase I've ever been on. He's working on our backlog while I do this. And he's losing his patience."

She kept her smile.

"I'll get a table and see you down there."

Bosch opened his briefcase and pulled out the Grayson file.

"Start with this."

＊　＊　＊　＊　＊　＊

In the cafeteria, Bosch put the stack of files down on the table Rider had commandeered. She had half a tuna fish sandwich on a plate and was looking through the last few documents in the Grayson file.

"Are you sure you can do this?" he asked her.

"No problem. What are we looking for?"

"I don't know yet. But if you read that file you know there are inconsistencies in the Grayson case. The suicide note was a plant and a piece of jewelry is missing. A silver chain necklace with a single pearl on it."

Rider frowned.

"What about the autopsy?"

"That was yesterday. We're waiting on the tox."

"Was she raped?"

"No abrasions. No DNA recovered."

"What do you think happened, Harry?"

"What do I *think* happened? I think somebody drugged her and had his way with her when she couldn't resist. And then he let her OD. Now ask me what I can prove."

"What can you prove?"

"Nothing. That's why I pulled these files."

"Looking for what?"

"Sometimes you don't know what you are looking for until you find it," he explained. "But I'm convinced Lizbeth Grayson was murdered with such careful planning that it wasn't the only time this happened."

"The guy hit before."

Rider nodded at the stack of thin files.

"That's what I'm thinking," Bosch said. "So I am looking for anything that is a commonality between her and any of these other suicides."

Rider frowned.

"And we'll know it when we see it," she said.

"Hopefully."

They got to work. Bosch split the stack in two and they both began working through the files. When one of them finished with a file they put it on the stack for the other to read. This way they each looked at every file. Because the cases were suicides, the files were thin and largely filled with autopsy and toxicological reports. All contained photos of the victims in death and most contained a photo in life as well.

Hollywood has always ground up a good share of the young women who come with their hopes and dreams. Ever since the actress Peg Entwistle gave up her celluloid dreams and jumped off the H on the Hollywood sign, many others have followed suit—but in less attention-getting ways. It is the dark secret of the industry. It grinds many of the fragile ones to powder. The powder blows away.

The files contained tragically similar stories. Young women whose lives collapsed when they didn't get the part and realized they never would get the part. Young women taken advantage of by those who could. Men mostly, but not always. Young women who were clearly fragile before even getting to Hollywood, who had come like moths to the flame, seeking to fill the empty spaces inside with long-shot fame and fortune.

But there were also files that contained only questions. Suicides without explanation, involving women who had growing credits and reason to be hopeful about their lives and careers. A few left one-or two-line notes but Bosch could not tell if these were possibly lines from auditions or parts they were playing.

Bosch studied the photos, many of which were professional head shots, and the lists of credits. He found nothing in common with Lizbeth Grayson other than that they had all been young and hopeful. There was no shared acting school or common agent. No showcase play or work as an extra on the same movie. He didn't see the connections and began to think that maybe Jerry Edgar was right. He was chasing something that wasn't there.

He was on the second-to-last file when Rider spoke up.

"Harry, are you finding anything?"

"No, not yet. And I'm running out of files."

"What will you do?"

"I have to decide whether to drop it or continue on. If I continue I'll have to work it on the side. In homicide they call it working a hobby case. You work it when you have the time. The next step is to conduct a field investigation—go out and talk to the people who knew these women, check their apartments, see if anybody has any of their belongings still. I can tell you right now my lieutenant isn't going to let me go off and do that. I'll have to work it like a hobby."

"Who's the lieutenant in Hollywood? Is that Pounds?"

"Yep. Pounds. He's not much of an expansive thinker."

Rider smiled and nodded.

"Look, I'm sorry I wasted your lunch break," Bosch said.

"Not at all," she said. "Besides, I'm not finished yet."

She held up the five remaining files she needed to look through.

He smiled and nodded. He liked her confidence. They dropped into silence and dove back into the files.

In ten minutes Bosch was finished and had found nothing that would bump the case up higher than a hobby. He asked Rider if she wanted a cup of coffee but she said no. He got up to get a cup for himself. The cafeteria was thinning out and getting quiet after the lunch rush. When he got back to their table Rider was standing. Bosch thought she had finished and was about to go. But she was standing because she was excited.

"I think I found something," she said.

Bosch put his coffee down on the table and looked at what she had. She was holding two head shot. They were of two different women.

"This first one is from a case last year," Rider said. "Her name was Nancy Crowe. Lived on Kester Avenue in Sherman Oaks. This other one is Marcie Conlon. Died five months ago. Also an overdose. Lived up in Whitley Heights."

"Okay."

Bosch looked at the head shots. The women had entirely different looks. Crowe had short dark hair and pale white skin. Conlon was blonde and tan. Just by looking at the photos Bosch would have guessed that Crowe was a serious actress and Conlon was not. He knew that would be subscribing to a sweeping generalization so it was not something he would say out loud.

"Look," Rider said.

She put the photos down on the table side by side.

"What's the same?"

Bosch immediately saw what had been there all along and simply gone unnoticed in his survey of everything contained in the files. In the Crowe photo she was posed, looking around the corner of a brick wall. Bosch guessed that she was supposed to look mysterious, the photo showing depth of character and perhaps making up for her not being a knockout beauty. In the Conlon photo she was posed with her back leaning against a brick wall. Her pose was meant to be alluring, even sexually intriguing, and the soft beauty of her features was set off against the hard brick wall.

"The brick wall," Bosch said.

Using her finger, Rider pointed out bricks in each photo that were the same. They were either chipped or scuffed in some way that made them unique. It was clear that each actress had posed at the same brick wall.

"But now look," she said.

She flipped the photos over and below the list of credits was the name of the photographer. The names were different but each name was followed by a matching location. Hollywood & Vine Studios.

"So you have different photographers using the same studio," Bosch said.

He was thinking out loud, trying to take it to the next step.

"Did you look through the other files where there are head shots?" he asked.

"No, I just discovered this connection."

"Good work."

Bosch quickly went back to the stack of files and soon they were pulling the head shots out of files where they could find them.

"Every actress in the city needs head shots," Rider said as she worked. "It's like death and taxes. You walk down Hollywood Boulevard and there are ads for photographers on every light pole."

In five minutes they had six head shot photos of dead actresses with photo credits from six different photographers but all from Hollywood & Vine Studios. Lizbeth Grayson's photo—the shot Bosch had borrowed from the acting coach—was one of the six.

Bosch spread the six shots out side by side and stared at them.

"Could this just be a coincidence?" Rider asked. "Maybe Hollywood and Vine Studios is a place all the photographers use."

"Maybe," Bosch said, continuing to stare at the photos.

"I guess we could check out wheth—"

"Wait a minute," Bosch said excitedly.

He picked up one of the photos and looked at it closely. It was a shot of an actress named Marnie Fox. She had supposedly committed suicide by overdose six weeks earlier. He nodded and put it back down. He then went to the Grayson file.

"What?" Rider asked.

From the file he pulled one of the photos of Lizbeth Grayson in death and placed one down next to the shot of Marnie Fox. Now it was Bosch's turn.

"What do you see that is the same?" he asked.

Rider moved in to look closely at the side by side photos. She got it quickly.

"The pendant. They are both wearing the same kind of pendant."

"What if they are not duplicates?" Bosch asked. "What if they are wearing the *same* pendant? A diamond pendant the killer takes from one victim and then puts on his next victim. And from that victim he takes her pearl necklace and puts it—"

"On the next victim," Rider finished.

Bosch started putting the files back into a stack he could carry.

"What's next?" Rider asked. "Hollywood and Vine Studios?"

"You got that right."

"I'm going with you."

Bosch looked at her.

"You sure? Do you need to get an okay?"

"I'll call it a long lunch."

\* \* \* \* \* \*

On the way, Rider made a list of the photographer's names and handed it to Bosch. When they got to Hollywood they parked in the lot by the Henry Fonda Theater and Bosch found a pay phone to call Jerry Edgar. He brought him up to date and his partner seemed miffed that he was working the case with an analyst, but Bosch reminded Edgar that he hadn't been interested in Bosch's hunch about Lizbeth Grayson. Properly cowed, Edgar said he would meet them at Hollywood & Vine Studios.

The photo studio was on the third floor of an old office building at the northeast corner of Hollywood and Vine. The building had been updated in recent years, each floor being gutted and turned into lofts. This was attractive to the creative industry. Most of the listings on the building directory in the lobby were production companies, talent management offices, and various other enterprises from the fringe of Hollywood. Bosch assumed that having an address that was as steeped in myth as Hollywood and Vine was a bonus to them all.

They waited ten minutes in the lobby for Edgar and then Bosch grew annoyed. Hollywood Division was less than five minutes away. He pushed the button and told Rider they weren't waiting any longer. They worked out how they would handle the visit to the photo studio on the ride up. They stepped out of the elevator and to a counter where a young man his head down had reading a script. He got to the bottom of the page before looking up at them.

Bosch badged him and asked his name. He said Louis Reineke and he spelled it for them. Bosch asked to see a photographer named Stephen Jepson and Reineke told him that Jepson wasn't there. Bosch proceeded down the list of the six photographers. None was there and none could be reached, according to Reineke. The counterman became increasingly nervous as Bosch asked about the photographers.

"So none of these photographers are here and you have no contact information for them either," Bosch said.

"We rent space by the hour," Reineke said. "The photographers come in, pay for an hour or whatever time they want and then they split. There is no need for numbers. Are you guys from Internal Affairs or something?"

Bosch was getting annoyed that the lead was hitting a dead end.

"We're from homicide," he said. "Where is the manager of the studio?"

"He's not here. I'm the only one here."

"All right, when was the last time any of these six men were here taking photographs?"

"I'll have to check the books."

He moved down the counter and opened a drawer. From it he took a large accounts book and opened it. The book appeared to list rentals of studio space by date, time, and photographer. Reineke ran his finger backward over the columns and finally stopped.

"He was here last Friday," he said. "Shot for an hour."

"He? Which one?"

Reineke looked back down at the book.

"That would have been Stephen Jepson."

There was something off about the conversation with Reineke. It was like they were missing each other.

"So how would that have worked?" Bosch asked. "He just came in and said he wanted some space to shoot?"

"Yeah, like that. Or he might've called first to make sure we weren't booked up. Sometimes that happens."

"Did he call?"

"I don't remember."

"Can we go back and look at the studio space?"

"Sure. We're empty right now. I've got a three o'clock and then a four."

They went around the counter and through a door into the loft space. There were three different photo setup areas with light stands and pull down backgrounds. There were a few pieces of furniture to use as props. There were wires running across the ceiling and black curtains that would allow the different photo areas to be partitioned for privacy. Bosch saw the brick wall from the photos running the length of the space. He guessed that Stephen Jepson's session on Friday had been with Lizbeth Grayson.

Bosch was staring at the wall when he remembered something that had been wrong about the conversation with Reineke. He turned and looked at the young script reader.

"Why did you ask if we were with Internal Affairs?"

Reineke stuck out his lower lip and shook his head as he looked over at the doorway back to the counter.

"Did I? I don't know. I guess I was just wondering."

"Why would you wonder if we were with Internal Affairs?"

Reineke did not look at him. The classic act of a liar.

"I don't know. I was just guessing."

"No, Louis, you were just lying. Why did you ask about IAD?"

"Look, man, I just was goofing. I was trying to think of something to ask."

"Call the manager, Louis. Tell him he better get here for the three o'clock because you are going to the station with us. We sit you down in a room for a while and when you're finished *goofing* and want to tell us the truth then we'll talk."

"No, man, I'll lose my job here, man. I can't go to the station now!"

Bosch made a move toward him.

"Let's go."

"Okay, okay, I'll tell you. I don't owe the guy anything anyway."

"What guy?"

Reineke shrugged off any further hesitation.

"The guys you asked about. They're all one guy. He's a cop."

"A cop?" Bosch asked.

"I think so. He says he is. He takes photos for the police. All the crime scenes."

"He told you this?"

"Yeah, he told me. He said that's why he uses all the different names when he comes in. Because it's like moonlighting and that's not allowed. When you came in asking about all those names I thought you were like Internal Affairs and you were onto him."

Bosch looked over at Rider and then back at Reineke.

"Louis, call the manager. You still have to come to the station to look at photographs."

"Ah, come on, man! I told you everything I know. I don't even know the guy's real name."

"But you know his real face. Let's go."

Bosch took him by the arm and started to lead him toward the door to the counter. As they approached, Edgar stepped into the studio.

"About time," Bosch said.

"Where's the crime scene?" Edgar said.

"There is no crime scene," Bosch said. "We're taking Louis here back to the station to look at photos."

"That's weird."

"What is?"

"I just passed Mark Baron, the crime scene guy, coming out of the elevator. He was in a hurry. I thought he was going to get his camera."

\* \* \* \* \*

They found police photographer Mark Baron in his apartment in West Hollywood. The door was unlocked and open two inches. Bosch called his name and then entered. Edgar and Rider were with him.

After listening to Reineke tell Bosch and Edgar about the police photographer who used phony names to take Hollywood head shots of young women, Baron had rushed home, gone into the bedroom, and took out the gun he kept in a shoebox under his bed. He sat on the edge of the bed and put the muzzle into the fleshy spot under his chin. He pulled the trigger and blew the top of his head off.

Bosch didn't look too long at the body of the dead photographer. Instead his eyes were drawn to the walls of the bedroom. Three of the four were covered floor to ceiling with collages of crime scene photos. All were of dead women. Next to each photo of death was a photo of life. The same woman alive and posing for him.

"Oh my God," Rider murmured. "How long was he doing this?"

Bosch scanned the room and all of the photos of all of the different women. He didn't want to guess.

"I better call this in to the captain," Edgar said.

He left the room. Bosch continued to look. Finally, he found the headshot photo of Lizbeth Grayson on the wall. A photo of her lying dead on the bed was taped to the wall next to it.

Bosch wondered which of the photos Baron had prized the most. Dead or Alive?

"I better call my office and tell them where I'm at," Rider said.

Bosch nodded his approval. She left the room then and only Bosch remained.

"Do you still want to be a detective?" he asked, though he knew she was gone.

*Bill Pronzini has been at it for ages, and just gets better and better. He's one of the most prolific writers of our time, and the thirtieth book in his "Nameless" series,* Mourners, *was just published by Forge. Number 31,* Savages, *will mark the fortieth anniversary of the Nameless series in print. (from the first published N. short in 1967). His new stand-alone,* The Crimes of Jordan Wise, *was published by Walker in July 2006. Here he takes us back to the Hollywood of the 1930s, a time of Prohibition, Packards, rods, and rubouts.*

# I Wasn't There

*by Bill Pronzini*

They had the car ready when the cab dropped us off at Brady's Garage in West L.A. It was a Packard touring car, shiny black, the side curtains already buttoned up. Nick walked around it a couple of times, kicked the tires, stuck his head inside.

"New, huh?" he said to Brady.

"Nineteen thirty model, only been available a couple of months. Fit right in where you're going."

"Yeah?"

"Yeah. It's the older models stand out up there."

"Take your word for it," I said. "What about this finger man?"

"Fenner."

"Yeah, Fenner. Dependable?"

"Hundred percent," Brady said. "Been hanging on Macklin's coattails ever since he spotted him."

"So there won't be no slipups tonight?"

"None. Count on it."

"Okay. Take your word on that too."

"You boys know how to get to the Hollywood Plaza? I got some maps in my office."

Nick said, "You think we ain't looked at maps already?"

"Just making sure."

"We're the best Renzo's got. He must've told you."

"Sure, he told me."

"We don't make mistakes. We don't overlook nothing."

"That's what he said. I wish I had a couple like you in my outfit."

"You ain't the first to say it, Mr. Brady."

"Come on," I said to Nick, "we're wasting time. Let's get rolling."

Nick liked driving the new Packard. He kept grinning and smacking the wheel with his hand. He was crazy about cars. He'd rather have a car to play with than a woman. There wasn't a better wheel man on a job like this. Or for a fast getaway when you need-ed one, like the time the Feds ambushed us while we was helping offload a shipment of Canadian whiskey up by Bodega Bay. Hadn't been for Nick that night, we'd've both been in a federal pen now.

It didn't take us too long to get to Hollywood. "Hey," Nick said, "hey, Joey. Hollywood Boulevard, huh?"

"Yeah."

"Look at the people, everybody dressed up fit to kill. And the cars, nothing but the best. Rolls, Bugattis, Duesies—that Duesen-berg J over there, that's the third one I seen already. Yeah, and all the neon. One a.m. and everything's lit up like New Year's Eve."

"Too many lights."

"Won't make no difference. Remember what Brady said?

Everybody minds his own business down here, no matter what time it is."

"Yeah."

"It'll go easy, no sweat."

"You ever see me sweat? No, and you never will."

"Man, I can't get over the traffic this time of night. And so many of the flash crowd out partying. Bet most of 'em are in the moving picture racket."

"Couldn't prove it by me."

"Maybe we'll recognize somebody."

"Yeah. Macklin."

"No, I mean somebody famous. Actors, actresses. Chaplin and Buster Keaton, them two I'd like to meet. Find out if they're as funny in person, you know? They make me laugh every time I see 'em on the screen." He laughed to prove it and smacked the steering wheel again. "Norma Shearer, Joan Crawford, Greta Garbo. Yeah, Garbo. And Mary Pickford and that gee she's married to, Fairbanks."

"I wouldn't know any of 'em if they jumped on the running board."

"Don't you never go to the pictures, Joey?"

"No."

"You must've been sometime."

"Once or twice, years ago. Make-believe don't interest me."

"What does, besides the skirts?"

"Speaks. Hot jazz."

"Yeah, sure," Nick said. "But I like the pictures too. The silents, they were good, that Chaplin kills me, but the talkies, they're even better. You don't have to read them subtitles. And the actresses, they all got voices like they're whispering in your ear in bed, you know what I mean?"

"I never heard an actress whisper."

"I wonder what they'd be like in bed. Garbo, Crawford, Thelma

Todd, swell dames like that."

"Like any other dame with her clothes off."

"Nah, better. Tits, gams, asses—all better or they wouldn't be actresses. Give you the ride of your life, huh?"

"*You'll* never know," I said.

He laughed and smacked the wheel. "Hey, there's Musso and Frank's Grill. Plenty of movie stars hang out there. Too bad we ain't got time to go in, look around. Bet they got some real good liquor in their speak."

We been working together three years now, me and Nick. If I got any friend in Renzo's outfit it's Nick Coletti. He's a good boy, but that's the trouble, he's a twenty-five-year-old boy don't seem able to grow up all the way. Gets himself excited about things that don't matter. Cars, horse races, poker, baseball. And now this Hollywood crap. Like he was some goddamn hayseed from Iowa. He grates on my nerves sometimes.

"Kid in a candy store," I said.

"Huh?"

"How much farther to the hotel?"

"Vine Street's just up ahead. Plaza's around the corner."

"Don't park right in front. Or under a street light."

"You think I don't know better than that?"

"Yeah. Okay."

"There's the Melody Club," he said. "Brady's finger man . . . what's his name again?"

"Fenner."

"He better be inside that joint with Macklin."

"Getting him primed. Macklin likes his hooch."

"Better not let him leave too early."

"He won't. Brady wouldn't steer us wrong about Fenner. Him and Renzo go way back."

"That Macklin," Nick said. "Pretty stupid bird, huh?"

"He thought he could get away with it."

"They always think that. But nobody ever does."

"That's right," I said. "Nobody ever does."

We turned the corner onto Vine Street and Nick found a place to park. "Hey, Joey, Hollywood and Vine, huh?" he said and started rattling off more names that didn't mean nothing to me. Sardi's Diner, Brown Derby, Hollywood Playhouse, some fancy theater they were putting up on the corner, some building where Chaplin had his offices. The only place I cared about was the Plaza Hotel. It was right down the block, big neon sign all lit up on the roof, doorman, three or four cabs lined up in front. But we were far enough away and it was dark enough here. Just some night lights behind a store window across the sidewalk.

"The It Cafe," Nick said.

"The what?"

"It Cafe. In the Plaza Hotel."

"What the hell kind of name is that, the It Cafe?"

"Clara Bow owns it. You know, the It Girl."

"Another actress."

"No, she's something special. They named her right. That dame's got it and then some."

"Yeah? Somebody give her a shot of penicillin, then she won't have it no more."

He laughed hard enough to cough and thumped the steering wheel. "That's good, Joey. That's rich. 'Somebody give her a shot of penicillin, she won't have it no more.' I got to remember that."

"What time is it?"

"Must be close to midnight."

"Check and make sure."

He opened his pocket watch, held it up close and squinted at it. "Eleven fifty. Won't be long now."

It wasn't too long. Less than twenty minutes. I spotted them first, crossing the street at the corner. Macklin and a tubby little guy with an arm around his shoulder, steering him. They came down the sidewalk on the side we were on. Macklin looked pretty steady on his feet. He always could hold his liquor.

"Here they come," Nick said.

I got my rod out, slid it into my coat pocket. They were about ten paces from the car when I opened the door and stepped out. Brady's finger man, Fenner, did a fast fade as soon as he saw me. Macklin didn't know what was happening until I stepped in close and jabbed the gun into his belly.

"Stand still, Mac."

"Joey!" He knew then and his eyes bugged. Their eyes always bug when they see you and feel the rod. They know right away their number's up. "Oh Jesus, no."

"Get in the car."

"Listen, listen . . . "

"In the car or you get it right here."

He sagged a little and I had to hold him up, prod him over to the Packard. Nick had the motor running. A couple went by on the sidewalk, the woman draped in furs, but they didn't pay attention to us. I opened the door, shoved Macklin inside, crowded in after him.

Nick said, "Hiya, Mac."

"Oh Jesus," Macklin said.

Nick got us rolling. Macklin slid over against the far door. I could see the whites of his bugged eyes in the darkness.

"What's the idea?" he said. "Joey, Nick?"

"Don't play dumb," I said. "It won't do you no good."

"Renzo sent you? All the way from Frisco? Why?"

"San Francisco," Nick said. "You lived there long enough, you know we don't like it called Frisco."

"What'd I do? What's Renzo think I done?"

"Tell him, Nick."

"Oakland warehouse raid," Nick said. "Six weeks ago."

"What's that got to do with me?"

"Somebody tipped the Feds about the load of jackass brandy coming in. You, Mac."

"No! It wasn't me." He was sweating now. You could smell the liquor he'd been drinking, the fear that came oozing out with the sweat. "Why would I tip the Feds?"

"Forty grand, that's why."

"The payoff money? The Feds got it along with the shipment."

"They didn't get it."

"They must've. How you know they didn't?"

"The same way we know you tipped 'em," I said. "Renzo's got a pipeline. Not direct, so it took a while, but the word come through. You didn't figure on that, did you?"

"I tell you, I didn't take that dough. You think I'm crazy?"

"You and Garza were the bag men that night."

"Then Garza must've took it. It wasn't me."

"Garza didn't take it."

"How you know he didn't?"

"He stayed home," Nick said. "You hung around a while and then quit and come down here."

"I didn't quit," Macklin said. "I fell into a better deal. I told Renzo and he said it was okay."

"It ain't okay anymore."

"Yeah, a better deal," I said. "Some boys from Encino."

"That's right."

"That's wrong. Nobody in Encino ever heard of Frank Macklin."

"You talked to the wrong people. This is a new outfit, they got a deal worked out with some Mexican shippers. I'll give you their names."

"Buy a lot of lies with forty grand."

"I tell you, I didn't take that dough. It must've been Garza."

"It wasn't Garza," Nick said. "Garza lived in a roach trap in the Tenderloin, same like always. Didn't change nothing in his life. You live high on the hog in the Hollywood Plaza Hotel."

"What you mean, he *lived* in a roach trap? He's not there anymore? He must've took a run-out powder. You found me, can't you find him?"

"Sure we can. We know right where he is."

"Whyn't you go after him then? Take him for a ride?"

"We can't do that."

"Why can't you?"

"He's down in Colma, six feet under."

"Dead? Garza's dead?"

"Hit and run on the Embarcadero, right around the time you blew town."

"You think I done that too? I didn't!"

"Might've been an accident," Nick said. "Or somebody with a grudge. I figure it was a gee named Macklin trying to protect his ass."

"It wasn't me. How many times I have to say it!"

"Let's have your wallet, Mac," I said.

He didn't move. I reached over with my left hand, opened his overcoat, yanked the wallet out of his pocket. Fat. You could choke a cat with the wad of greenbacks in there.

"How much you got here? Couple grand?"

"The boys from Encino, they pay big. Thousand a week."

"Sure they do," Nick said.

"I'll cut you in. Five, maybe ten grand apiece. How's that sound?"

"Sounds like what's left of Renzo's forty."

"No, no—"

"Might as well tell us where you got it stashed. We'll find it anyway."

"All the dough I got's in my room at the Plaza. Maybe fifteen grand. But it's Encino money, I swear it. Those boys out there--"

"Yeah, we know. They pay big."

"That's right. Big."

"Not as big as tipping the Feds when you're a bag man for forty grand."

"I didn't take it, I didn't!"

"Nobody else at the warehouse that night," Nick said. "Except Garza and he's out. That leaves you."

"Wait a minute," Macklin said. "Wait a minute now."

"We're all through waiting."

"No, wait a minute. Listen. Garza and me, we weren't the only ones there that night. Somebody else was there too."

"Yeah? Who?"

"Joey. Joey was there."

"Bullshit," Nick said.

"No, it's true. I just remembered. I remember now."

"I wasn't there," I said.

"Nick, listen, Joey was there. He showed up right after Garza and me got to the warehouse. Right before the Feds broke in."

"Bullshit."

"I wasn't anywhere near Oakland that night," I said.

"He come in, I saw him, and then all hell bust loose and me and Garza powdered. The satchel was on the desk in the office. Joey must've took it."

"Bullshit," Nick said.

"Joey, you son of a bitch, you took that money, not me!"

I slapped him across the mouth, hard. "Shut up, Mac."

"You're the one run over Garza too. Sure, sure, shut him up so he couldn't tell that you was there—"

I clubbed him with the gun this time. The sight opened up a gash on his cheek that spurted blood. He yelled and cringed back and his head smacked into the side curtain, made it jiggle.

"You say another word, I'll give it to you right here. In the belly, where it hurts the most."

He started to moan.

"Cut it out," Nick said, "for Chrissake."

Macklin didn't cut it out. He just cowered over there against the door like a kicked dog, whimpering.

We were climbing into the hills now, up behind Hollywood. Narrow twisty roads, hardly any traffic. Down below there were plenty of lights, big dazzle spread out wide, but it seemed pretty dark up here.

Nick said, "Man, look at that view. This Hollywood's really something, hey?"

"Find a spot," I said.

Macklin moaned and whimpered. He kept saying, "Oh Jesus," over and over, like he was praying. In the glow from the dashboard, blood gleamed black on his cheek and hand. Brady wasn't going to like it when we brought the Packard back with blood on the seat.

The hell with Brady.

"Dirt road up ahead," Nick said.

"Houses?"

"No houses. Just trees."

"Pull off there."

The Packard bounced and slid a little as he turned off the pavement. Once we were in among the trees, you couldn't see the light dazzle any more. Real dark except for the headlights.

"Looks good right here."

"Leave the headlights on," I said.

"You think I don't know that, Joey?"

Macklin was holding his face in both hands now. "Oh Jesus," he said between his fingers.

The tires crunched over something and we stopped. Nick set the brake, left the engine running and the lights on.

"All right," I said to Macklin. "Get out."

"No. No! Nick, you got to listen to me—"

"Shut up. Get out."

"No. Please."

Nick got out and opened the back door. Macklin almost fell out. Nick pulled him the rest of the way, shoved him up against the side of the car. I slid out alongside. It was dark as hell up here, woods closed in tight against the road. If it weren't for the headlights, you couldn't've seen ten feet in front of you.

Macklin started to slide down the side of the Packard, like he didn't have bones in his legs anymore. Nick hauled him up again. "Come on, Macklin," he said. "Stand up and take it like a man."

"You got to believe me—it was Joey, it was Joey!"

"I'm sick of listening to him," I said. "Let's get it done."

Nick backed off a few steps. He already had his rod out.

All of a sudden Macklin yelled and shoved off the car and tried to run into the trees. He ran like a woman, all floppy arms and legs, yelling the whole time.

He didn't get ten yards before I shot him. Three times, fast. All the slugs went in under his shoulder blades. I never miss at that range—I wouldn't've missed even if he hadn't been running right through the headlight beams. He flopped down on his face and lay there with one leg twitching. Nick went over and put two more into him to make sure.

I frisked him for his hotel room key and we got back into the Packard. Neither of us said anything until we were out on the paved road again. Then I said, "I wasn't there that night, Nick."

"Sure, I know," he said.

"Macklin was just trying to buy time, drive a wedge between us."

"I never believed him for a minute."

But he was wondering just the same. I could hear it in his voice.

* * * * *

Next afternoon we rode a cab to Union Station and caught the Coast Flyer for San Francisco. Nick had been real quiet all day—no more Hollywood talk, not much talk about anything. Couple of times I caught him looking at me with a funny look on his pan. And he wanted to hold the fifteen grand cash we took out of Macklin's room at the Plaza, be the one to hand it over to Renzo. "You know, Joey, just to have the feel of that much dough for a while."

He was wondering, all right.

On the trip down we'd had meals together, played euchre in the smoker. Not this trip. He went to his compartment right after we got on board. Said he wasn't feeling so hot and didn't want dinner.

You could see what would happen once we got to San Francisco. He'd do more than deliver the fifteen grand, he'd tell Renzo what Macklin said about me being at the warehouse that night. Probably Renzo wouldn't believe it. But maybe he would. I couldn't take the chance.

Sometime during the night I'd have to bump Nick off.

Make it look like an accident. Catch him off guard, sap him, toss him off the train. People get drunk on bootleg hooch, fall off trains all the time. Nobody'd figure it for anything else. Renzo wouldn't.

It was a dirty shame. I liked Nick, he'd saved my bacon that time up at Bodega Bay, he was the only friend I had. But what else could I do?

I wasn't at the warehouse that night. I didn't tip off the Feds, I didn't take the payoff money, I didn't run over Garza on the Embarcadero, I didn't have anything to do with any of it. But that bastard Macklin had planted a seed in Nick's head, and if I let Nick plant it in Renzo's, then maybe it'd be me got picked up next for a one-way ride. I just couldn't risk it.

You got to look out for yourself in this business. Yeah, you do. Nobody else is gonna do it for you.

*Max Allan Collins has long been considered the king of the historical crime novel. Here he shows why, when he takes Moe Howard—one third of the Three Stooges—and turns him into a detective. Who else would even think of that? He recently completed the* Road to Perdition *trilogy with the prose novel,* Road to Paradise; *and is currently working on a novel about Wyatt Earp in the twentieth century.*

*This is one of several short stores he has recently collaborated on with his young writing partner, Matthew Clemens. They also continue to work together on tie-in projects, including* CSI *and* Bones. *Like the Stooges, this seems to be a partnership made in heaven—even if there are only two of them.*

# Murderlized

*by Max Allan Collins & Matthew V. Clemens*

The early lunch crowd at Sardi's seemed thin even for a Monday. *Okay*, Moe Howard thought, *so it's only two days after Christmas . . . but where the hell is everybody?*

Sitting alone in a booth near the front, the little man wore a dark suit, white shirt, and conservative shades-of-blue tie, his trademark Three Stooges soup-bowl haircut slicked back and parted in the middle. Although the haircut was part of the act, Moe cultivated a different look offstage—when you played an idiot, you had to make sure the role didn't follow you into real life, particularly business.

On the table in front of him rested a four-day-old L.A. Times and a cup of coffee from which he sipped only occasionally, to help him maintain this little piece of linen-tablecloth-covered California real estate.

Outside, the morning sun gave Hollywood Boulevard that golden aura that drew the dreamers, schemers, and desperate souls who served as sustenance for the Hollywood magic machine. Traffic glided slowly by, but both the famous Hollywood and Vine intersection and the eatery itself seemed uncharacteristically quiet.

Right now Moe shared the joint only with the staff, a handful of tourists, and the array of caricatures famously lining the walls of the restaurant. Nursing his cup of coffee, he glanced idly up at the drawings.

Many—hell, most of them—were friends and acquaintances, none of whom treated Moe and his brother Jerry and their partner Larry like second-class citizens, even if the Stooges were relegated these days to short subjects, not features. Looking at these familiar faces—Crosby, Gable, that sweet kid Shirley Temple and the old standbys like Wallace Beery and Marie Dressler—Moe felt a wave of melancholy nostalgia wash over him.

The caricature sketched by Alex Gard that had summoned these feelings—creating the kind of expression on Moe Howard's face that usually preceded the delivery of a slap to a fellow Stooge—was of Ted Healy, the well-known vaudevillian and film comedian, and the reason Moe found himself in Hollywood occupying a booth in Sardi's this bright December morning.

A Texan transplanted to Brooklyn, Charles Ernest Lee Nash— a mouthful that somehow became the stage name "Ted Healy"— had in his (and their) youth made close friends with the Horovitz brothers, especially Moses and Samuel. The three show biz aspirants palled around Coney Island doing anything they could to elicit laughs, and maybe the odd donation, from passersby.

Though the fire for fame already burned in the bellies of Moses and Samuel Horovitz, Nash had fanned those flames, nudging, nagging, encouraging, challenging. Eventually the boys changed their names, Marx Brothers–style, taking family nicknames (Moses and Sam into Moe and Shemp) and changing their last name to Howard. Eventually, the baby of the five Horovitz boys, Jerome, would become Curly Howard and take his turn in the act.

But the real beginnings had been in 1923, when Healy was working a vaudeville show in Brooklyn only to inadvertently change the history of show business by having his two friends Moe and Shemp Howard join him on stage as his foils.

His stooges.

The act had bumped along for a couple of years in various incarnations until they met a young Philadelphia comic/musician named Larry Fine, who joined up and gave Healy a third stooge to slap, providing visual variety with the similarly visaged Howard brothers. Like the rest of them, Fine—who had an unruly wreath of wiry hair giving no quarter to a fast-receding hairline—had shortened his name (from Feinberg).

Healy, however, was always the star of the show, and—friend or not—made sure they all knew that. He paid each stooge a hundred dollars a week while he was making a cool thousand. Known to be a hard-nosed businessman, Healy could be foe more than friend, particularly when, as they traveled on the road together, he turned into a mean, belligerent drunk.

But bastard boss or not, Healy had been the one who got the Stooges to Hollywood—no question, he had almost literally made them. They had shot their first film together, *Soup to Nuts*, in 1930, and from there, things had simultaneously gone downhill and taken off.

The film, a ramshackle episodic affair designed to bring the cartoonist Rube Goldberg's vision to the screen, had flopped; but Moe, Shemp, and Larry had shone. Soon Shemp had his own movie contract, playing Knobby Walsh in the "Joe Palooka" shorts, and brother Jerry had come aboard as one of the Three Stooges—sans Healy—appearing in occasional features and a continuing series of popular shorts. (Jerry's family nickname, Babe, was replaced with "Curly" when Jerry shaved his head to bring yet one more distinctively wacky hairdo into the act.)

Yet Ted Healy remained a presence in their lives, warmly congratulatory when they ran into him when he was sober; and bitterly resentful when he was in his cups.

And Healy—the man who had done the Stooge slapping before Moe took over—was why Moses Howard sat in this booth on a lovely sunny day that he should have been spending with Helen and the kids, Joan and Jeff.

Instead, he waited for Henry Taylor, a screenwriter who had written several B westerns in the earlier '30s. The two were to have lunch to discuss the untimely death of Moe's mentor, friend, sometime adversary, and former boss, Ted Healy.

This year, 1937, had been a good one for the Three Stooges, three years out from under Healy's oppressive thumb. They had made another eight shorts for Columbia, headlined shows on the East Coast, and were making far more money than they ever had with their abusive boss. Things were good, things were great; but Healy's death had cast a depressive pall over Moe. Their split from their mentor had been acrimonious and bitter, and many an insult, even a threat, had been traded; and yet down deep, Moe still counted Healy a friend. Had loved the lousy son of a bitch.

Catching movement out of the corner of his eye, Moe looked up to see a short man come in and stop at the hostess stand; the unprepossessing gent had thinning silver hair, a doughy complexion, and eyes made buggy behind thick-lensed glasses as he cast his gaze around the restaurant.

Henry Taylor finally saw Moe waving at him, smiled, waved back, and shambled over. The screenwriter's slightly threadbare suit was gray, his shirt white, and his tie blue with red flecks, and although Moe was hardly a clotheshorse, Taylor's entire outfit probably cost about as much as Moe's small custom-made shoes.

Moe half-rose in the booth and extended a hand. "Henry, how have you been?"

Trembling slightly, Taylor shook hands with Moe. Despite his shaky condition, his grip remained firm. Shrugging, he said, "Up and down—you know how this town is."

Indeed, Moe did. Though he and his brothers had suffered the vagaries of show business, their careers seemed blessed compared to Henry Taylor's. Screenwriter on a series of westerns for John R. Frueler's struggling Big Four Film Corporation, Taylor seemed to have hitched his wagon to a slowly falling star.

Though Big Four had done all right in the early '30s, the film company was now on the verge of bankruptcy, and Moe had no idea how the scribe was making ends meet. Moe counted on picking up the check today, just as he had whenever he and Taylor had gotten together over the last couple of years.

Moe managed to maintain his patience through small talk and lunch, but once the waitress—a pretty blonde whose smile of recognition told Moe she was either a fan or an actress—cleared the dishes and refilled their coffee cups, he could wait no longer.

Grabbing the L.A. *Times* from December 23, Moe pointed at the story about their mutual friend. "What the hell happened to Ted?"

"Papers say he died of 'acute toxic nephritis.' "

Shaking his head, Moe said, "That's what they said on the twenty-third. On the twenty-second, the day after he died? They were printing a different story—about Ted being in a brawl."

"That does sound like Ted."

"Doesn't it?"

"Early reports often get it wrong."

Moe frowned. "Early reports often predate the fix going in."

"What can you do?" Taylor said noncommittally. He obviously meant this generally not specifically.

"C'mon, Henry," Moe said, his voice rising slightly. "Ted was your friend, too."

Taylor shrugged again. "Yes he was. And he was also a fourteen-karat son of a bitch."

"When he drank."

"When he drank," Taylor admitted. "And we both know he drank a lot."

Moe could hardly deny that. "Was he drunk the night he died?"

"Moe, you knew Ted. You surely know the answer to that question."

Ted was drunk most nights.

Taylor shifted in his seat. "Look, Moe, the coroner's already ruled, Ted's already in the ground. You need to let this go."

For the first time, Moe thought he saw apprehension in Taylor's eyes, perhaps exaggerated by the thick lenses; but it was there. "What is it, Henry? What's really going on?"

Shaking his head vigorously, Taylor said, "Nothing. Nothing! If you want to swap war stories about our rambunctious, lovable, hatable old pal, I'm your man. But if you want to stir up trouble, well . . . . You just need to let Ted rest in peace, Moe."

"I can't," Moe said quietly. "He was my friend. He gave me and my brothers and Larry Fine our careers. And now something's out of kilter where his death's concerned. And I want to know what!"

Quickly Taylor rose, a wad of bills appearing from his pocket. "Gotta get going, Moe. Let me grab this, for a change."

Staring at the roll of bills, as his friend peeled off a five and dropped it on the table, Moe had a sinking feeling. "Where'd you get the moolah, Henry?"

Taylor seemed not to hear the question, already heading for the door.

Picking up his paper, Moe trailed after the writer, finally catching the older man outside, at the intersection of Hollywood and Vine.

"Come on, buddy!" Moe said. "What's going on?"

"I just can't talk about it anymore," Taylor said, his eyes darting. This was not a good corner for lying low.

"What aren't you *telling* me?" Moe pressed.

Taylor shrugged. "Look, Moe—there's no good that can come from you digging into this sad situation. Ted's gone and maybe he's, well . . . finally out of his misery."

"Henry. . . you can do better. Ted deserves better."

Henry drew in a deep breath, most of it bus fumes; then he let it out and said, "Well . . . if you must, check out the list of pallbearers. *That* will tell you everything you need to know."

Before Moe could speak again, Taylor slipped between two cars, crossed the street, and sped along pretty well for a man of his age as he disappeared into the group of pedestrians strolling Vine Street during the lunch hour.

Standing on that legendary corner, Moe wondered what Taylor had meant by his "pallbearer" remark. After a shake of the head, he walked quickly in the opposite direction, climbed into his parked Ford roadster, and opened the newspaper on the steering wheel.

He skimmed the article down to the last break headlined "Services Today." The funeral had been at ten on the morning of the twenty-third, at St. Augustine's Catholic church across the street from the MGM studio. Father John O'Donnell had presided, burial had been at Calvary Cemetery, where Ted had been laid to rest beside his mother. Then, finally, the list of pallbearers.

Ray Mayer was another comic, a friend of both Ted and Moe. Dick Powell, the actor, had recently appeared in a movie with Ted. The directors Busby Berkeley and Charles Reisner had both worked with Ted over the years. His manager, Jack Marcus, had been there too. Did Taylor think Ted's manager was up to something?

Moe considered that. He knew that Marcus, a former actor himself, was devoted to Ted and had done his best to take care of him, both personally and professionally. Moe found it impossible to believe Marcus was in any way connected to Ted's death.

The final two pallbearers were MGM execs, Harry Rapf and E. J. Mannix. Rapf, generally considered a good guy throughout the industry, had produced over forty films, worked as an executive at Metro-Goldwyn-Mayer, and was credited with having discovered a Texas beauty named Lucille LeSueur, a little lady now working as Joan Crawford. Known as "The Anteater" by anyone who had ever seen his face, Rapf had been making money off MGM's employee Healy, who been working regularly in comedy support roles.

E. J. "Eddie" Mannix, on the other hand—a bespectacled, balding guy who looked more like a high school science teacher than a movie exec—was known throughout the industry as one of MGM's chief "fixers." A fixer's job was simple: if a star stepped in shit, the fixer cleaned the shoe and sprinkled on perfume—sometimes very expensive perfume. More than once, Ted's drinking had forced MGM to call out one of their top fixers, either Howard Strickling or Eddie Mannix.

When Moe read the name Mannix, there was no doubt in his mind where Taylor had been pointing.

The question was, how did the notorious fixer figure into whatever was going on with Healy's death? Mannix's presence screamed coverup—but covering up *what*?

Folding the paper, Moe saw only one way to find out.

Spotting a phone booth across the street, he decided to let someone know just what was going on, and where he was headed. Eddie Mannix had a reputation for making problems disappear, and Moe knew the rep to be well-earned. Digging all his spare change out of his pocket, he called Larry, who was still on the East Coast, and explained what he had learned and where he was going.

Larry's voice reverted to its familiar whine. "What happened, Babe hit you too hard with that pipe wrench, last shoot?"

"No," Moe said, his patience wearing thin.

"You know this guy Mannix's rep. He *knows* people."

By "people" Larry meant gangsters.

"I know his rep," Moe said. "Do I sound scared?"

"No. You sound terrified. This Mannix, there's talk he divorced his wife the hard way. Or maybe that's the *easy* way."

Larry was referring to Mannix's wife, Beatrice, who had died a few months earlier, in a car accident that whispers said might not have been all that accidental.

"Yeah, I heard the talk. Talk is cheap in this town."

"This could be expensive, this time. And you're still going?"

"Of course I am. Ted and me, we were friends for a long time."

"Are we talking about the same prick?"

"Larry, I owe him. You owe him."

"Yeah, well, he still owes us thousands for what we did for him, and do you think we was in the will?" He paused. "You want me to go with you?"

"No," Moe said, "but I, uh . . . appreciate it, pal, your concern."

"You need somethin', pucker up and ask."

"Well, uh . . . how 'bout this. If you haven't heard from me by midnight, call somebody."

There was a long silence.

Finally, Larry said, "By midnight, you could be . . . what time is it where you are?"

"A little before noon."

"Okay. By midnight, you could be dead for twelve hours. So I'll call an undertaker."

"Thanks for the vote of confidence, Porcupine," Moe said.

"Oh, do I have a vote? I vote you don't go."

"I *have* to."

"You'll go when you're good and ready . . . and you're ready. Well, what should I tell Babe when you don't come back?"

"Tell him," Moe said dryly, "I'm a victim of circumstance."

"Why can't you be like Shemp? Scared of your own shadow?"

"Just not my style, Chowderhead. See you in the funnies."

He hung up.

Back in the roadster, Moe drove the seven or so miles to Culver City to the Metro-Goldwyn-Mayer studios. Funny, Moe thought, that Hollywood's biggest studio wasn't even *in* Hollywood.

A pole gate barred the entrance, and when Moe pulled up and stopped, a cement block of a guard lumbered out of his small shack. The midday sun was behind the guard and Moe couldn't make out anything about the man other than his formidable build.

"Moe Howard!" the guard said. "How've you been?"

Putting a hand to his brow to block the sun, Moe recognized the guard. Tommy Flatley had occasionally been used by the studio as a babysitter for Ted Healy, and Moe had met him through Ted. Short, wide, with a flat face and perpetual grin, Flatley had a sunny disposition for a strongarm, and Moe had hit it off with the guy, though he hadn't seen the guard in nearly a year.

"Tommy, life is good. Me and the boys are kings of Poverty Row.

How about you?"

The Stooges' studio, Columbia, was the biggest of the smaller studios that had been collectively dubbed Poverty Row.

Flatley shrugged. "Can't complain. Or if I did, it wouldn't get me a raise, is for sure."

"Terrible news about Ted," Moe said.

Nervously, the guard glanced toward the offices on the lot to his left. "Yeah. Terrible. Goddamn shame."

"He could be a monster, Ted, but a talented man. Say, I'm here to see Eddie Mannix—is he in?"

"Appointment?"

"Naw. But I think he'll see me. We're friendly."

This was not quite a lie.

"Let me find out." Flatley disappeared into his shack, made a phone call, then came back out. "Mr. Mannix can spare you a few minutes. He's in building twenty-three . . . they're working on the new Gable picture. You know where twenty-three is?"

Moe nodded. "Think I'm a dope? Right after twenty-two!"

"Smartass," Flatley said good-naturedly, then he raised the gate for Moe to drive through.

Building twenty-three, a large soundstage, loomed on the back-lot of the MGM grounds. Parking next to the massive structure, Moe noticed that the big thirty-foot doors were closed, as were the few windows and the small door just to the left of the large ones. The whole building seemed to be saying, Stay away.

He strode to the small door.

A sign on it read: **IF RED LIGHT IS ON, DO NOT ENTER. "TEST PILOT" SET—DO NOT ENTER!**

Moe had heard about the production through the grapevine and knew it to be a drama starring Clark Gable, Spencer Tracy, and Myrna Loy. He glanced above the door at a small red lightbulb, which was glowing. But even as he looked at it, the light winked off.

He opened the door quietly, stepped inside, and closed it after him. For a few moments, he stood motionless while his eyes adjusted to the interior darkness. Perhaps fifty feet away across the huge floor, from around and above, lights and cameras were trained on a set decorated as an office. A large crew was gathered around, and only when he got closer did Moe begin to recognize some of the people.

Laughing as they stood around a desk on set, Gable, Tracy, and acting legend Lionel Barrymore all waved when they caught a glimpse of Moe. He returned the gesture and saw a heavy-set fellow, his back to Moe, turn to follow the actors' eyes.

Eddie Mannix.

When he saw Moe, Mannix grinned and walked over to greet the head Stooge. Mannix had close-cropped dark hair and dark, bird-like eyes behind rimmed glasses. He wore a tan shirt under a darker tan jacket, and a chocolate brown tie. Five or six inches taller than Moe, and maybe thirty pounds heavier, he nonetheless moved with an easy grace. If anything made him seem less like a science teacher and more like the cutthroat Hollywood exec he was, the gait was it: He walked with a swagger that said he was King Kong in this particular jungle and damn well knew it.

Extending a hand, he said, "Moe Howard! What can I do for you? Ready to come back and work at MGM again? Our shorts department could use some funny fellas like you boys."

"You're too kind, Mr. Mannix," Moe said, still shaking the man's hand as Mannix steered him on a course that led back to the door.

By the time the handshake ended, they were outside and the door was closed again.

"I thought Wallace Beery was up for that part," Moe said, jerking a thumb toward the building. "Not that Barrymore's exactly a piker."

Mannix shrugged. "Things change, and it's not like Lionel isn't a major player."

"The best," Moe said.

"Besides, Beery went to Europe for the holidays."

Moe nodded. "Lucky guy."

Mannix grinned but his eyes were growing suspicious. "I don't remember you being Beery's agent, Moe. What can I do for you?"

"Mr. Mannix, I—"

"Please. Eddie. The name's Eddie. We're all street kids here."

"Eddie. Thanks. I . . . I want to talk about Ted."

"A fucking tragedy," Mannix said instantly, his voice ice-cold. "I was a pallbearer, you know. god-awful thing. Tragic loss of talent. You were out of town, weren't you?"

"Yeah," Moe said. "We were in Grand Central Terminal, waiting for a train to Boston, when I heard the news. It was all I could do to get through those last few days of our engagement, and get back here."

Mannix patted Moe's shoulder. "Well, Ted was a dear friend to many of us."

"Uh . . . evidently not." Moe's voice was now as cold as the fixer's.

Behind the eyeglasses, the dark bird eyes grew smaller, harder. "What do you mean?"

"No offense meant, Mr. Mannix. We both know what you do around here, around town. I want to know if you covered up Ted's murder."

Mannix took a step back as if he'd been punched, his mouth dropping open, a hand going to his chest. "Murder?. . . Now that's not funny, Moe."

"Not meant to be, Eddie. Ted gettin' in a fight was in the paper, one edition. Next edition, it's dropped. That smells of your invisible byline, Eddie."

"Careful, Moe."

"The doctor who treated Ted the night he got beat up refused to sign the death certificate, but suddenly the coroner does—writing off the beating as superficial. You couldn't get to the *Times* before they printed it, but everybody else fell in line, didn't they?"

"First of all," Mannix said, his voice thin and brittle, a hand raised as if in benediction, "I have no idea what you're talking about. Second of all, you are way the hell out of line, little man."

"Am I? This whole thing reeks of studio coverup. You know it, I know it."

"That's a strong accusation."

"Which I notice you're not denying."

Mannix shook his head. "All right, if that's what you want, I'll deny. I deny it. Now, do you mind if I get back to work?"

Moe stepped between the bigger man and the door. "I have an idea you do your best work after hours, and off the lot."

The fixer's eyes were as hard now as they were dark; a very small tic twitched at the corner of Mannix's left eye. "Moe, you do not want to do this. Ted is dead and buried. You know what a brawler he was, and what a drunken troublemaker he could be. If anything, you and I are both surprised he didn't stumble into the grave he dug himself years ago. You've confronted me and gotten this off your chest—fine. Now let it go."

"You're the second person to tell me that today . . . in so many words."

"However it's phrased? Good advice."

Moe drew in a deep breath and let it out slowly, watching Mannix's tic work. Then he said, "Just tell me the truth, Eddie, and I will let it go. I'll go back to being a dumb little bastard who doesn't know up from down . . . I promise."

Mannix took a long, appraising look at Moe. He, too, took in a deep breath, let it out slowly; and then the eyes softened, and the man's entire manner shifted.

"All right," Mannix said. "I know he was like another brother to you, but if I give you the straight dope, will it end here?"

"I just want to know, Eddie. Mr. Mannix."

The exec gave the lot a quick, furtive glance, making sure no one was within earshot. "It happened at the Trocadero on Sunset. Ted was in there, drunk as a skunk, but happy. He had already been to Clara Bow's and the Brown Derby. He was really tying one on to celebrate the birth of his son."

Moe sighed. "Yeah, I know he just had a kid. Makes this thing even sadder. Then what?"

"Ted started up an argument with these three college kids."

"College kids?"

Mannix nodded. "Ted offered to meet them outside and take them apart, one at a time. But when they got into the parking lot, the three kids jumped him and beat the everloving shit out of the poor soused-up bastard."

Moe frowned. "And *that's* why you covered it up? To protect some college kids?"

"One of them has a father who's a good friend of Mr. Mayer."

"That doesn't—"

"Moe, Ted started the thing, and an inquiry would only blacken his memory. Anyway, Mr. Mayer says keep a lid on it, that's what I do."

"And I thought I was a stooge," Moe said.

Shrugging, wincing, Mannix said, "Think what you will of me, Mr. Howard, but I get slapped around a lot more than you and your pals. Okay? We done here?"

Getting into his car, Moe felt unsatisfied. Something still didn't sit right. Why would a major movie studio give two shits about three college kids when they'd beaten to death a personality who was an asset to MGM?

The more Moe mulled it over, the thinner Mannix's explanation seemed.

When he got back to the gate, Tommy Flatley came out of the shack and waved him down.

"Find out what you wanted?" the guard asked.

Moe shook his head. "I don't think so."

"Hmmm. The college kid story?"

"Yeah, Tommy, why? Don't you believe in fairy tales either?"

"Doesn't matter what I believe, Mr. Howard." He leaned close, like a car hop taking an order; he was almost whispering. "but if you stop by the Hollywood Plaza Hotel, you might talk to someone who has a different story."

"Really."

Tommy nodded. "Ever hear of a fella called Man Mountain Dean?"

Moe had indeed.

Driving back to Hollywood and Vine, Moe pulled up in front of the Hollywood Plaza Hotel at 1637 North Vine Street and parked.

Inside, he went straight to the desk clerk, a tall reed of a man with slicked-back blond hair and a crisp dark suit.

"Man Mountain Dean, please," Moe said.

The clerk nodded and without looking at the register said, "Room 1624. . . . Aren't you the Three Stooges, sir?"

"Just a third," Moe said, handing the guy a buck, and headed over to the elevator.

A gray-haired attendant in a faded uniform asked, "What floor?"

"Sixteen."

The ride was quiet and fast. When they got to the floor, the old guy opened the door and said, "Thank you."

Moe, wondering what he'd be doing at the fellow's age, slipped the "boy" two bits and strode down the hall until he got to room 1624.

He knocked and waited.

Nothing.

He knocked again and waited some more. He was just about to walk away when the knob rattled. A moment later, he heard the chain slide back, and the door opened. Moe found himself looking up into the face of a bleary-eyed giant with a mane of wild dark hair and an equally untamed beard, clad in bib overalls and a T-shirt, and barefoot.

"Frank Simmons Leavitt," Moe said with a sly smile, "how the hell are you?"

The man ran a hand over his face, then looked down, grinned, and picked Moe up off the floor in a bone-popping bear hug. "Moses Horovitz! You little bastard!"

The big man was playing, but Moe had the sudden feeling his chest might explode at any second. "Puu . . . puuuu . . . put . . . me doow . . . down!"

Man Mountain Dean did as directed but gave Moe an extra squeeze as he did so, completing the impromptu chiropractic adjustment. "It's goddamn good to see you, Moe! How long has it been?"

Moe shrugged, partly in answer, partly to see if his body still functioned. "Couple of years anyway. Where did we run into you last?"

"Kansas City, I think." The big man was leaning against the door jamb. "You boys was there the night before we went in to wrestle. You, your brother Shemp, and Larry was leaving, while the other wrestlers and me were coming in."

"Kansas City," Moe echoed. "A long way from home for us New York kids."

Dean nodded shaggily. "You ever get back to the city? The old neighborhood?"

"Yeah, we were just there last week! You?"

"Naw. I'm pretty much a California kid when I'm not on the road.

I've been gettin' some movie work." He smiled. "Not like you guys, though. The Three Stooges! Big stars, you little fellas became."

Moe grinned back. "We're eating regular."

The wrestler's face turned somber. "Sorry about that horse's ass Ted. I know you was good friends."

"Thanks, Frank. Actually, that's why I'm here."

"Thought it might be." His eyes lost their spark. "You want to know what I know, right?"

"If it's not too much to ask."

Dean nodded. Shrugged. "Come on in."

Moe did, Dean shut the door and waved for Moe to take a seat. The room was home to a metal-frame, unmade, single bed, a small radio on a nightstand with lamp, a bureau with no mirror, and a table with two chairs. Not a shabby room exactly, but no suite at the Waldorf-Astoria.

Moe took a chair facing the bed, figuring Dean couldn't have fit in one of those chairs on a bet. And indeed the wrestler sat rather gingerly on the edge of the bed.

"I suppose," Dean said, "you heard about the college boys."

"Yeah," Moe said.

"Well, it's bullshit. That fixer Mannix, more of his bullshit."

"So I figured."

Dean took a deep breath and let it out. "I don't know what good it'll do, telling you."

"Neither do I. But I need to hear it."

Dean shrugged again and the bedsprings squeaked. "Okay. I'll tell you what I know, but nothing else."

Moe was still trying to make sense of that when his old friend launched into his story.

"It wasn't no fucking college kids. At least that's not what Ted said, when he come around."

"He came here?" Moe asked, sitting forward.

"Yeah. He got the shit kicked out of him at the Trocadero by three guys—not college kids. He said he offered to fight them one at a time, outside; but when they got to the parking lot, they jumped his ass and wailed on him pretty damn good."

"Why would he come here, then?"

"He stumbled in wanting me and Joe Frisco to go back out with him and make it a fair fight. He wanted us to pick up Doc Stone, too, then go back to the Trocadero so he could get 'even and a half.'"

"You didn't go?"

"Hell no! You know I'm not afraid of a fight, Moe, but Ted was beat up worse than a redheaded stepchild. I got the hotel sawbones to patch up his broken ass."

"How did Ted get here?"

"Joe brought him."

Joe Frisco, another Los Angeles comedian, was a good friend of Healy's. The other guy Dean had mentioned, Doc Stone, was a small-time actor and part-time boxer.

"So . . . what happened?"

"Ted told me while the doctor patched him up. He was at the Trocadero celebratin' his kid bein' born when he got into an argument with this guy."

"What guy?"

Dean shrugged. "Ted didn't know the guy's name, but the guy isn't alone—turns out he's a cousin of Pat DiCicco, who is also present."

Moe felt the words like a blow to the gut. "DiCicco the hoodlum?"

"Is there another? Anyway, they're not the only ones. DiCicco and this other guy are there with Wallace Beery."

Everyone in Hollywood knew that Beery hated Ted for stealing scenes in a movie the pair had done earlier in the year, *The Good Old Soak*, which had not exactly taken Hollywood by storm, but word around town was Beery still had it in for Healy.

And Beery could be a brawling brute, with or without liquor, not nearly as lovable as his screen image.

Nodding, Moe said, "So that's why Beery 'spent the holidays' in Europe—he's lying low. What about DiCicco?"

"I heard he took a run-out power to Mexico. But nobody seems to know why."

"And we don't know who the third guy is," Moe said quietly.

"Doc might," Dean said.

"Doc Stone?"

"No! No, sorry. Too many docs. I mean Doctor Wyannt LaMont, hotel doctor here. I'll take you down to his office, and you can talk to him."

After Dean took time to put on a pair of clodhoppers, the big man and the little man took the elevator to the first floor and by the front desk cut down a short hallway. The door had the doctor's name painted on it in black block letters.

Dean knocked but opened the door without waiting for a response, and led the way in.

The room was an examining room with a central metal table and wall-hugging cabinets of medicine and a counter with bandages and more. At a small desk off to one side, reading a medical journal, sat a squat, heavy-set man of fifty or so with graying hair and pink chipmunk cheeks. He wore a white doctor's smock over a white shirt and what Moe could barely make out as the knot of a blue tie.

The doctor put down the journal as they entered, obviously not offended by the intrusion.

Man Mountain Dean said, "Dr. Wyannt LaMont, I'd like you to meet Moe Howard."

Rising, beaming, the doctor extended a hand. "Mr. Howard, it's truly a pleasure. I enjoy your work immensely. Splendid absurdity."

"Well, it's silly, all right. Nice to meet you, too, Doctor."

Dean filled the doctor in.

LaMont said, "Once I saw how badly beaten Mr. Healy was, I sent Frank here to call the police and an ambulance. Then I was alone for several minutes with my patient. And he told me that this other man was DiCicco's cousin, a New Jersey kid named Albert Broccoli, who just moved out here to try to get into the movie business."

"Did he tell you what happened?"

"Oh yes. Ted freely admitted to starting the fight. He said there was something he didn't like about Broccoli's face, so he just hauled off and clocked the guy. That was how the altercation began."

"What about the ambulance?" Moe asked. "The papers said nothing about an ambulance."

"By the time it got here, Ted and Joe Frisco had left. Ted said his friend—Joe, was it?—was just going to take him home."

"Thanks, Doc," Moe said.

In the lobby, he said his good-byes to Man Mountain Dean, then used the phone booth there to make some calls. Finding Broccoli took a bit of doing, but an agent friend prompted Moe to try a bar Broccoli frequented on West Sunset.

A short drive later and he was inside the club, his eyes adjusting to the dim lights, one of those chrome and mirror cabarets, but a junior job. On the stage some underclad, overly cute female dancers were rehearsing for the night's show, and around the bar maybe four patrons otherwise had the place to themselves.

A fellow matching Albert Broccoli's description sat at the bar, an empty stool on either side, his back mostly to Moe.

Settling in next to him, Moe said, "Buy you a drink, friend?"

A rugged-looking guy with dark, wavy hair and piercing brown eyes turned toward him. The eyes widened, a finger pointed. "Hey, you're . . . "

"Yeah, I am. Let's not advertise it."

"Sure, sure. Well, hell, you can buy me a drink any time, Moe. The laughs you boys have given me . . . "

He waved the bartender over and got another bottle of beer for his new friend and a cup of coffee for himself. "You Albert Broccoli?"

"Yeah, I'm Al Broccoli. How did you know? And, uh, no offense, but. . . what's it to you, Moe? Or should I say, 'Mr. Howard'?"

"Moe is fine. We have mutual friends."

"Call me Cubby, then. Most everybody does. Mutual friends, huh? Like who?"

He was just a big gregarious, likable kid—more like one of those imaginary college students than the brutal Beery—and Moe wondered what Ted had said to piss off the young man; or maybe Ted had pissed off DiCicco and the kid had just jumped in on his cousin's side.

"Mutual friends like Ted Healy," Moe said. "For one."

Broccoli's face sagged. ". . . uh. I don't know . . . didn't know Healy. I hear he passed away. You used to work with him, right?"

Moe leaned in a little. "Cubby, don't play stupid with me. I'm an expert at playing dumb and you don't make the grade. We both know you know exactly what I'm talking about."

Broccoli put up his hands as if surrendering. "Okay. But I wasn't in on it."

"In on what?"

"The fight."

"I heard you were. I heard Ted popped you."

"Well, yeah, he did pop me, but that's not a fight. That's one-sided. Hell, that's assault. All I did was, I tried to congratulate him on the birth of his son and got socked in the snoot for my trouble."

"Then what?"

"Then nothing. I knew the guy was drunk. Celebration got away from him—we all know guys who booze makes nasty. So I let it go."

"Somebody didn't let it go."

Broccoli shrugged. "Well . . . my cousin Pat saw me with a hand-kerchief to my bloody nose and wanted to know what happened. After I told him, him and Beery started giving Healy a bunch of lip. That's when Ted said he'd meet us outside. We were a bunch of cow-ardly bums and bastards if we didn't. So, anyway, when we got out there, Beery and Pat, they . . . hell. They just beat the hell out of him. It was . . . it was horrible. Way out of line. Jesus."

"And you did . . . nothing?"

The young man sighed and swigged some beer. "I did at the start. I kicked him once, just to get even for what he did to my nose, you know? But when those two got carried away, I just kinda froze. Backed up and froze." He shrugged and sighed somberly. "That's it, Mr. Howard. Moe."

"So, then—the three of you beat him to death."

Broccoli held up his hands again. "No, we didn't! I swear. He got up. On his own steam. He was tough in his way, Healy. Him and that friend of his, Frisco, who come along at the end there, they left. He was beat to shit, but I swear he was walking. He seemed okay. Just another guy got the wrong end of a barroom brawl."

"What did you guys do next?"

"Ah, hell. That asshole Beery panicked. He called the studio. Pat and me, we had another drink inside the Troc, then Pat drove me home."

"And where did Pat go?"

Shrugging elaborately, Broccoli said, "Home, I suppose. How would I know?"

Moe shook his head. "I hear you want to get into the movie busi-ness."

Broccoli nodded glumly.

"Well, kid, it better not be as an actor, because a good actor is a good liar, and you're not that good. Where did Pat go that night?"

The kid called Cubby tried to hold it together, tried to look tough, but eventually, the roof caved in. He was trembling and his eyes had teared up. "Pat was still pissed and thought Healy might rat us out to the police. I think maybe . . . I don't know for sure and I ain't about to ask . . . I think maybe Pat went over there and had another little . . . 'talk' with Ted."

A second beating on top of the first was probably enough to kill Healy. For twenty-four hours Healy fought the effects of the beating or beatings before his heart finally gave out.

Moe knew that there was no way anyone would be doing jail time for Ted's death, not in this one-industry town with a star like Beery involved; but at least he thought he had gotten most of the truth.

He could go to the cops with his circumstantial case, but where would it end up? Most likely in the porcelain filing cabinet where a flush from the fixer would take the careers of himself and the other Stooges with it. Still, Ted had been a friend and mentor since they were kids back in Brooklyn. Moe felt he had to try something.

"Cubby," Moe said, at last. "I want you to tell this story to the cops."

"No way. I shouldn't have told you. Three beers ago, I wouldn't have."

"*Somebody's* going to have to tell the truth, kid. You can do it, and paint yourself in a good light. Or I can do it. Take your pick."

Moe watched Broccoli carefully to see if the bluff was working.

"All right, I'll come forward. I'll tell the cops what happened."

Moe drew a breath and let it out. "Good. And you better."

"Or what? You going to come back here and slap me around?"

Rising to leave, Moe managed a weak smile. "Me? Why, Cubby—haven't you heard?"

Broccoli frowned.

"That," Moe Howard said, "is just not my style."

> *NOTE FROM THE AUTHORS: Numerous books on the Three Stooges were consulted, in particular* The Three Stooges: An Illustrated History *(1999) by Michael Fleming, as well as newspaper files of the day. Though essentially sticking to the facts, this story should be viewed as fiction.*

*Bob Levinson writes about Hollywood with an insider's knowledge after years as a journalist and a publicist. He was on* Esquire Magazines *first "Hot 100" list of music industry headliners and the first "Publicist of the Year" honored by* Billboard *magazine. That knowledge is never more obvious than here, where he covers the business of gossip in the early '50s, with a story containing both Hedda Hopper and the famed gangster Mickey Cohen.*

# And the Winner Is...

By Robert S. Levinson

T he little guy strutted into my boss lady's suite in the Guaranty Building on Hollywood Boulevard like he owned the world. He briefly checked around for signs of life before shouting for attention in a growl straight out of a Warner Bros. gangster movie, and at once was captivated by the three-deep bank of framed and autographed photos of movie stars gracing the side wall of the modest reception lobby.

He stepped over and, with his body angled so that his red-and-blue-veined bulb of a nose almost touched the frames, alternated a rubber-lipped smile between big and bigger while tracing faces with an index finger and reciting inscriptions in an accented voice filled with awe, acting as if he'd discovered a long-lost chapter from the Old Testament.

"*With all my love, Jimmy Stewart,*" he said. "*I love you like anything. Clark Gable.* Here, look. Barrymore. *With much love for her old and trust valued friend. Jack.*" He shook his head in disbelief and stepped away, calling, "Anybody home? Anybody?" Moved to the other side of the room to inspect the framed photos of Marie Dressler and Grace Moore, the only women Hedda Hopper allowed in her rogue's gallery of glamour boys of the silver screen.

He gave his nodding approval to an original sketch of a ballroom gown by Janet Gaynor's husband, Gilbert Adrian, and lingered over Bugs Bunny and Tom & Jerry cartoons until irritation got the best of him. "I said friggin' anybody here or what, for Christ sake?" he said, his hooded eyes down to squints, taking in the walls one by one while he dug out a wafer-thin gold cigarette case from a jacket pocket of a wide-lapeled, double-breasted blue pinstripe suit that belonged on someone getting ready to shoot craps in *Guys and Dolls*.

He powered up a filter-tip with a flip-top Ronson and was filling the air with balloons of smoke as I emerged from behind the filigreed iron grille that separated the lobby from the narrow area I shared with the boss lady's secretary, Treva, and which wouldn't have been out of place in a pawn shop. Hedda's business manager and her secretary occupied private offices to our right. The door to the left of our desks fed into Hopper's sanctum sanctorum, a space befitting the town's queen of the Hollywood gossip columnists among those who didn't owe more fear or allegiance to her aging alcoholic rival, Louella O. Parsons.

Overall, the office suite blended the worst features of a messy city room, like Hearst's *Examiner* downtown, a dressing room at the Biltmore Theater or the El Capitan, and any junk shop anywhere, with Hedda's trademark predilection for bizarre hats in evidence everywhere, chapeaux in shapes and styles as outrageous as a Carmen Miranda fruit bowl on view or in hatboxes stacked seven and eight feet high on the faded linoleum flooring or piled on the sagging visitors' couch. Shelves stacked with books and full of bric-a-brac. A broken lamp. An old, beat-up wooden desk pushed in a corner now the repository for piles of business mail and fan letters, notebooks, paste pots, magazines, makeup jars and accessories, and a pair of silk stockings with runs that had been there since the day I first came to work here, three years ago, a star-struck kid as wet behind the ears as the ink on my bachelor's degree from UCLA.

I said, "Something I can do for you?"

My voice startled him. His hand was halfway inside his jacket as he wheeled around to face me. I was ready to bet it was after a shoulder holster that would explain the tight fit and the bulge. I threw up my hands in surrender. He shot me a puzzled look to go with an insincere smile as he pulled back his hand and wagged an envelope. "Got this message for Miss Hedda Hopper, private-like, so I got to deliver it to her in person." He checked over his shoulders. "She around?"

I held out my hand. "Miss Hopper is gone for the day, Mr. Feldman, but I can take it and personally see that she gets it tomorrow."

"Tomorrow's too late," he said, drawing the envelope out of reach. "My instructions, it got to be today." Then, suddenly realizing I had addressed him by name, he said, "How'd you know me, kid? I know you from someplace? We met before?"

I shook my head. "I have a memory for names and faces," I said. "I've seen your picture in the newspapers."

He couldn't disguise his pleasure at being recognized, even though the only times he'd been mentioned in print dealt with crimes the cops had attributed to his boss, the mobster Mickey Cohen, including the recent disappearances of two or three Cohen rivals and one dead gangster found floating facedown in Echo Park Lake, over by Aimee Semple McPherson's old Angelus Temple.

Feldman wasn't on the same level as Happy Meltzer, Lou Schwartz, Dave Ogul, or any other of Cohen's lieutenants, the "Seven Dwarves," or even the up-and-coming Aaron Lodger. He was a low-level gofer who chased after coffee, picked up the laundry, and handled other chores that required more obedience than brain-power when he wasn't stocking shelves at the swank haberdashery on San Vicente Boulevard that Cohen operated as a front for his less savory underworld operations.

"The newspapers?" he said. "Like what newspapers?" I rattled off names. "The *Mirror*, that's the one ran the best picture of me. When I was over to McNeil Island to welcome Mickey back to free-dom after he finished doing his time on the bum income tax inva-sion rap cooked up by that bum Kefauver Committee."

"Income tax *evasion*."

"What?"

"Never mind."

"I never done no hard time myself," he said, wearing his words like a badge of honor. "A traffic ticket once or twice, as far as it goes. Mickey, he gets blamed for anything bad happens, nobody ever out to give him a break." Then, remembering what brought him here, protecting the envelope with both hands, he said, "Anyways, what's your story?"

"I'm Miss Hopper's leg man."

"I'm an ass man myself," he said. "Her gams that special, kid, say compared to Grable or Hayworth?"

"Leg man means I do her running around town. I check out the stories and gossip items fed her by the studios and press agents. Hit the soundstages by day and the club scene at night. Ciro's. The Mocambo. The Slate Brothers on La Cienega. The Coconut Grove. Opening nights and parties she's either too busy or too important to show up for. Mornings, when she's putting it together against an eleven-thirty deadline, her steno notebook full of the exclusives she's pulled for herself in one phone call after another, I run inter-ference for her. You have to be a Zanuck or a pal like Duke Wayne to get by me."

"I don't look it, but I'm fifty-one years old, and since the age of eight

I've been getting by everyone I damn please. Capeesh?" He checked the Rolex he wore on the inside of his wrist. "It's already a long time since eleven thirty, so where is she, so I can get this envelope to her, Leg Man?" He gave me a look that seemed to say my kneecaps were an endangered species if he didn't get the answer he was after.

I weighed that against the possibility of the boss lady excising my gonads were I to do anything to interrupt her lunch a half mile away at the Brown Derby, where she was conspiring over a Cobb salad to save the United States from communism with her fellow superpatriot, all-American defenders of democracy and Beverly Hills property values, Ward Bond and Adolph Menjou. This time, they were framing the statement that would lead off her column if anything smacking of Red Menace reared its ugly color tomorrow night at the Academy Awards.

"I wish I could help you out, Mr. Feldman, but she doesn't always confide in me," I said, trying to sound as sincere as Gary Cooper in *Mr. Deeds Goes to Town*. He studied me for the lie, but it was hidden inside a deep breath I was too nervous to exhale. He took a year field-stripping what was left of his smoke and pocketing the paper ball and filter tip before deciding. "My man needs to hear this straight from the horse. You got a jacket or something?"

"I can't leave the office until Treva or—"

"You got a jacket or something?"

I got my jacket.

\* \* \* \* \* \*

The Frolic Room was a brisk five-minute walk from the office, a dump of a bar hiding between the Equitable Building and the RKO Pantages Theater on the boulevard, about twenty yards east of the Hollywood and Vine intersection. Its distinguishing features were a wallpaper mural of old-time movie stars and the possibility of discovering a famous face hiding away from the spotlight for a bit of boozing or the kind of naughty sexual encounter that my boss lady loved to expose, always hankering for a repeat of the kind of attention she got breaking the news about Bergman and Rossellini running off to cook pasta together in unwedded bliss.

Foot traffic was light compared to what was expected tomorrow, when the Oscar show would bring out a mob of fans armed with autograph books and shooting off flashbulbs every time a favorite pulled up to the Pantages and stepped onto the red carpet now being rolled out and taped in place. It was a small part of the prep work in progress inside the theater and in the adjacent parking lot, in the process of being tented for the hundreds of working press who didn't merit a seat, unlike the boss lady, of course, who'd be sharing an armrest with one of the major names, most certainly an acting nominee like Chuck Heston or Liz Taylor, maybe Jack Lemmon or Audrey Hepburn.

A flack for the Motion Picture Academy would be letting her know before the end of the day.

If she had an objection, there'd be a hurried shifting of seats.

Nobody wanted an upset or angry Hedda Hopper.

Ever.

Any more than my escort, Arthur "Irish Artie" Feldman, wanted his boss upset or angry, but that's the message I read on Mickey Cohen's puss after we stepped through the Frolic Room curtain and my eyes adjusted to the day-for-night lighting. He sat facing the entrance, at the last booth opposite the bar, somebody twice his size with shoulders that stretched a mile end to end by his side, a stare as cold as witches' milk.

Cohen motioned us forward and indicated the seats across from him, tilting his moon-pie face and studying me from the corners of eyes the color and size of Raisinets. He took a swallow from the can of Lucky Lager he was rolling between his palms and shook his head, signaling his displeasure over some conclusion it took him another minute to share. He settled the beer can on top of the water ring that marked its place on the scarred surface of the table, carefully, until he'd made a perfect fit. Ran his thumb and fingers down his deeply rooted five o'clock shadow. Said, "Irish, how kindergarten can it get? I give you a simple letter to deliver to the Hopper broad for her to read. All you're supposed to come back here with is her answer, a yes or a no. Who's this? A singing telegram from Western Union?"

"I can explain, Mick."

"Right after you figure out what two plus two equals." Cohen eased his lazy squint back to me. "See what can happen if you got a Jewish poppa, but not your mama?" He made a circular motion at his temple with an index finger. I had no answer for him beyond an uneasy shrug. "Not that I got anything against the Irish. Except the ones who grow up to be cops."

"Mick, the Hopper dame wasn't there, just him, and since you said not to give the letter to anybody else, I brought it back." Feldman patted his breast pocket. "Him with it, in case you had use for him. He's her leg man."

Cohen leaned forward for a closer look at me, his arms resting on the table. "I'm a tit man myself," he said. His look dared Shoulders and Irish Artie Feldman not to equal his hearty laugh, but accepted my tense tight-mouthed grin. He smelled like he bathed in expensive aftershave. It could not, however, dim the odor of cigars clinging to his butter cookie brown silk suit and rust and burgundy Countess Mara tie punctuated by a stickpin diamond twice the size of the diamonds in his cufflinks.

"Candy Barr, now there's my shining example," he said. "When we was going out regular together, it was impossible to miss her delicious bazooms. Winchell himself once wrote how she walked into Ciro's five minutes before she walked into Ciro's." Shoulders and Irish Artie laughed like he had just invented humor. Milton

Berle was using the line regularly in his Vegas act, only about Marilyn Monroe, but I managed a smile that satisfied Cohen, who said, "John Stompanato and me had us a running bet over whose were bigger, Candy's or Lana's, but we never got around to proving nothing before he was stabbed to death. I still think she did it, Lana, not that daughter of hers, no matter what the coroner's jury decided. Justifiable homicide, my fat Jewish ass. Was the first time I ever heard of a guy being convicted of his own murder."

He silently reflected on the thought over another drag of Lucky Lager, again careful in returning the can to the table. "And speaking about murder . . . " He aimed a chubby manicured finger at Irish Artie Feldman, then swung it in my direction. I pushed back and began sweating April showers, like the flop sweat that hits a lot of actors before a performance. "Irish, you did good for a change," he said. "Give this kid the letter. You go on and read it, kid, then we'll gab some more."

Irish Artie was feasting on the compliment as he dug after the envelope. If he were a dog his tail would have been in perpetual motion.

I tore away an edge of the envelope, crimped it open, eased out and unfolded a sheet of expensive stationery bearing Cohen's laced initials engraved in gold. There was nothing funny about the message written in ink in a schoolboy hand and signed by him.

I locked onto Cohen's eyes.

He understood the disbelief radiating in mine and nodded.

"Like it says in black and white, kid," he said. "I'm tipping Hopper to a murder that's set to happen tomorrow night at the Academy Awards shindig. Exclusive, the way Hopper likes it."

It took me another minute to find my voice. "Mr. Cohen, is this some kind of April Fool joke?"

"Kid, it may be April, but murder is one thing I wouldn't ever fool about."

"Who? Who's going to be killed?"

He planted an elbow on the table and turned his palm parallel to the cottage cheese ceiling. At once, Shoulders filled it with a six-inch Cuban and gold guillotine. Irish Artie was ready with his Ronson. Cohen finished preparing the cigar, accepted the light, ran a string of smoke rings, and said, "Let's us take a walk. It's good for the ticker, you reach my age."

* * * * * *

Cohen avoided the subject as we strolled along Vine, his henchmen dutifully trailing six feet behind us, past the Broadway-Hollywood Department Store and the Huntington Hartford Theater to Sy Devore's menswear shop across from the NBC radio studios, where he criticized the suits, sports jackets, and shirts in the windows and condemned Devore's status as "Tailor to the Stars."

"Frank, Dean, Sammy, that whole Rat Pack thing—Sy gets his reputation from them, when no question I got superior merchandise and no swindle on the price," he said. "It's only they don't want to be seen in my company, have the government come down on them the way they done me with the friggin' IRS. Can't say I blame them, although Frank never gives me a straight answer when I bump into him and bring up Momo Giancana and his other Eye-talian mob connections. Your boss, Hopper, another story entirely."

Despite my polite nudging, Cohen wasn't ready to share it yet, if ever, instead surprising me with his knowledge of local history, like he was auditioning to be a Chamber of Commerce tour guide. Crossing Selma on our way back to the boulevard, he pointed out where DeMille and Lasky had filmed *The Squaw Man*, the movie that brought the industry to Hollywood, in a barn they bought for twenty-five dollars; mentioned how CBS broadcast the *Lux Radio Theater* show from the Hartford, when it was the Vine Street Playhouse.

Passing the Brown Derby, I wondered if my boss lady was still inside saving America or, worse, would pick this moment to leave and spot me with Cohen, whom she openly detested and never mentioned in her column. He was among the many who had somehow drawn her enduring wrath, most often by giving some choice tidbit to Parsons instead of her, a hanging offense.

Cohen, meanwhile, was consumed with memories of the Hollywood Plaza Hotel, saying, "The It Girl, you know, Clara Bow? Had her It Café there when she was on top of the business, back in the silent days. Stuttering Joe Frisco, you know, he lived there. A wit faster than Hope. He'd hang out under the canopy and his comic pals would toss him straight lines. He'd come up with a belly-buster of an answer, which they'd work into their act and pass off as their own. Joe didn't care. Maybe that's why he died broke. That and the ponies. I helped him out a few times, covered his markers. Nothing I'd want broadcast."

Approaching Hollywood and Vine, he directed me to the top of the Taft Building on the southeast corner. "Was the first building on the boulevard they let climb high as a hundred and fifty feet," he said. "Use to be an electric sign up there during the war years, not as grand as the sign on the *New York Times* building. Wrapped around the corner of the building, scrolling out the news in light bulbs."

He studied the building for another few moments, sighing appreciation at the mention of former tenants like Charlie Chaplin and Will Rogers. "The Motion Picture Academy had offices there for ten years, thirty-five to forty-five," Cohen said, and shifted his attention to the activity outside the Pantages Theater.

The marquee now announced the 32nd Annual Academy Awards Presentation of the Academy of Motion Picture Arts and Sciences in bold, black capital letters. Workmen were installing sidewalk bleachers on both sides of the theater's lobby entrance. Giant rotating klieg lights had been rolled into position. NBC-TV trucks were lined up across the boulevard in front of the Taft Building, where a production crew was laying cable and building platform towers for the cameras that would capture the crowd's infectious excitement at the arrival of one movie star after the next tomorrow night.

Cohen draped an arm across my back and pointed at the theater. "That's where it's going to happen, kid, the murder," he said. "Unless Hopper can do something to stop it. You be sure to tell Hopper that when you give her my letter."

"What else?"

"Like what?"

"Like I asked already. Who? Who's going to be killed and who's going to do the killing?"

"Whaddaya think, I know everything?"

"Don't you?"

\* \* \* \* \* \*

"You smell the gas fumes?" Cohen said, tweaking the broken nose he'd worn since his early years in the ring. "Too many cars clogging up the streets and more to come; I know what I'm talking. Getting around L.A. ain't been the same worse—since they got rid of the Red Line streetcars on this boulevard and every other street-car made sense. Politicians paying back the influence peddlers, the car industry—and they call me and mine crooks and thugs and worse."

Walking back to the Guaranty Building and waiting outside for Shoulders to bring around his Cad from the Capitol Tower parking lot on Vine, he repeatedly resisted my efforts to get him to reveal more about the impending murder. He talked tour jive, like he was satisfying a need to convince me—and himself—Mickey Cohen was smarter and better than how the press regularly portrayed him, as a Boyle Heights elementary school dropout and third-rate boxer who owed his success as a two-bit mobster more to muscle power than brain power.

Now, he found something about the Beaux Arts façade of the building that brought on a smile. He gave the brick facing a hand polish and said, "I'm laying odds it's something you don't know about the Guaranty, kid, what it has in common with City Hall, Shrine Auditorium, and the Griffith Observatory." He waited out my silence like a quiz show host before announcing: "John C. Austin is what. He's the architect what architectured those landmarks. Helped make this town something special."

I couldn't contain my frustration any longer. "Is John C. Austin also the person who'll be architecturaling the killing tomorrow at the Academy Awards?"

Cohen made a kind of *Are you crazy?* face. Got as far as saying, "He's been dead himself since—" before catching my meaning and the grammatical insult I'd attached to my question. He angled his head at me. "You're one friggin' brave kid talking at me like that. I don't take kindly to anybody talking at me that way, once being one time too many."

Irish Artie looked to be reaching after the bulge inside his jacket.

Cohen stopped him with a hand on his arm as a musical horn honk signaled the arrival of his Cad.

Irish Artie stepped over to open the rear door for Cohen, who said, "Hop in, kid, you first. Artie, you up front with Nathan."

Swell.

Just great.

The hood many believed was behind the murder of his friend and benefactor Benjamin "Bugsy" Siegel was taking me for a ride.

I started pleading deadlines, phone calls that needed returning, an interview I couldn't be late for at Musso & Frank'.

Cohen smirked. He wasn't fooled. He knew where I was coming from. He said, "You got guts, kid. They'll either get you ahead or dead, so watch yourself. Now, get in before my patience expires, and we'll finish the business what brought us together." I hesitated. "What do I gotta do, count to ten?"

\* \* \* \* \* \*

The Cad smelled of stale tobacco and sweet perfume.

Cohen wedged himself between the door and the back leather cushion, told Shoulders aka Nathan to drive around until he heard otherwise, and said, "The letter I sent over for Hopper was me trying to make nice-nice, even the score between us, get on her good side—supposing she got a good side—and maybe score a favorable mention for myself once in a blue moon in her *Times* column. What do you think? Does she?"

"I can't complain, Mr. Cohen."

"Smart. Complaining gets you dumped on. Playing along gets you raises and promotions and the chance to improve your lifestyle. She's had a hard-on for me ever since her queer buddy Joan Edgar Hoover turned his bloodhounds loose on me, she ever say that to you?"

"No."

"After that Turner bitch took a carving knife to my man John, me and her were on the same side for a while, Hopper out front calling Turner a hedonist who passed off the blame on her kid, Cheryl. Hedonist, that's a person who's only out for pleasure."

"Yes."

"Then Joan Edgar goes and squeals to her that I'm the guy who maneuvered for Turner and John to meet in the first place and even paid for the deluxe motel suite where they done the dirty for the first time. It was all downhill after that, so here I am two years later, trying to make it up to Hopper by tipping her off to what could earn her a Pulitzer Prize for her bookcase, don't you think so?"

"It's for her to say, Mr. Cohen. I'm only a leg-man."

"Tits and ass both for me," Shoulders called from behind the wheel, a buck-toothed smile filling the rearview.

"Strictly ass for me," Irish Artie said.

"Can it, both of you," Cohen said, then to me: "And seeing as how it happens tomorrow night at the Academy shindig, I needed to get the word to her in a hurry, so she can get the law turned on, because sure as shit they ain't about to ever give me the time of day where she can get right through to Joan Edgar at the FBI or that *momser* Bill Parker downtown at the LAPD."

"How did you say you find out about this, Mr. Cohen?"

He turned coy, tried to hide the flicker of a grin from me as we made another right turn at Las Palmas on our merry-go-round of a drive. "I didn't. My pop taught me I was a kid, you gotta stay in the game to get ahead in the game, so let's say I learnt it from a reliable source who learnt it from an even more reliable source."

You spend enough time on the phone confirming news items or at an interview trying to pull sensitive information out of someone, you can't help developing a sixth sense. His caution with words and his body language, the way he quit looking me in the eye and started gazing out the smoked glass window, convinced me Cohen was holding back.

I said, "It's a damn shame you don't have an inkling of who's out to do the killing or who the target is. My boss doesn't go for blind items from unnamed sources. She says it's like buying a pig in a poke."

"I promise this-here pig I'm donating is strictly kosher, tell her." Cohen dug into my eyes and swept at his nose. Gave Irish Artie a tap on the shoulder. Received a Cuban and a light in return. Filled the cabin with smoke that immediately coated my throat with a bitter taste, and spent a minute consulting with the cigar. "Okay, kid," he said. "You ran the spike high enough up my ass for me to get the point. Here's the rest of what I know."

Less than fifteen minutes after Cohen dropped me back at the building, my boss lady swept into the suite in her usual mad-dash fashion, an easterly wind that threatened to destroy everything in its path, and motioned for me to follow her, calling over her shoulder in a husky voice that bordered on baritone, "We hear from the Academy yet?"

"Your usual row, off the center aisle, next to Janet Leigh and Tony Curtis. Arthur Freed has them presenting in the two writing categories."

"Don't know who's prettier, her or him . . . My money's on Billy and Iz for *Some Like It Hot* and Ernie Lehman for Hitch's *North by Northwest.*" She settled behind her desk and picked up the phone receiver, started dialing. "What seat are they pouring Parsons into?"

"Same row, other end of the aisle, by Natalie Wood and Robert Wagner, who're handing out the sound award. Boss, I have a letter I need to show you, something we have to talk about."

"*Ben-Hur* in a walk, and I hope Arthur's warned Nat and R. J. about the sounds that'll be emitting from Parsons, her deafening belches, and farts strong enough to stop an elephant in its tracks." Her boisterous laugh bounced off the walls. Hopper was her own best audience. "Sheilah Graham?"

"Ten rows farther back. Next to George C. Scott, unless he's good as his word and doesn't bother to show up."

Hopper dismissed him with a wave. "Those Broadway types with their method," she said. "He came across in *Anatomy of a Murder* only because my dear Jimmy underplayed brilliantly." She put a finger to her lips, wheeled around in her chair, and dropped her voice to a whisper. The phone conversation ended after a minute. Turning back to me, she scribbled something in a steno notepad that was never out of reach. "Bruce Cabot," she said. "I filled him in on the lunch. Now there's someone who could have done real justice to the Scott role in *Anatomy*. Bruce. Twice the actor George C. Scott can ever hope to be." She shook her head and flung her tailored eyebrows to the sky. "Show me what?"

I held up Cohen's letter.

"Hand it over and sit," she said, pointing at the chair alongside her desk that Treva used whenever she was taking dictation. She read it, reared back in her seat, and looked up at me with an expression bordering on amazement. "And I'm supposed to buy what this little creep hoodlum is selling?"

"There's more."

"Make it snappy. I promised Cukor I'd skedaddle up to his place and show my face at this cockamamie cocktail party George is hosting for the foreign-film nominees, as if I'd give a damn if our best-director nominees weren't also going to be there."

"George Lincoln Rockwell."

"All the *Saturday Evening Post* covers. What's he have to do with the cocktail party?"

"Not the artist, boss. The anti-Semitic nut job who founded the American Nazi Party last year, calling Hitler a visionary and advocating destruction of all the biologically inferior Jews running and ruining our country."

"There's a moron for everything." Her nails started doing an anxious dance on the table. She removed the hat Mr. John had created exclusively for her and settled in on the desk, began fussing with the fur feathers and stuffed raccoon decorating its broad sombrero brim. "So what about this George Norman Rockwell?"

"He's inspired two or three of his followers, maybe more, to stake out the Awards show tomorrow night. The plan is to kill someone associated with *The Diary of Anne Frank*—"

"Eight nominations."

"—hopefully someone who wins an Oscar, the more famous the better, as a statement to the world that the American Nazi Party means business and is here to stay."

"Shelley Winters, that precious Ed Wynn, and, of course, George Stevens, but my egg money is on Willie Wyler for *Ben-Hur*." She rattled off the names of some of the other *Anne Frank* nominees and reached for a phone, then just as swiftly pulled her hand away. "What else did Mickey Cohen want you telling me?" She planted her elbows on the desk and her laced fingers under her sagging chin, listened patiently while I replayed the entire conversation in as close to word-for-word detail as I could come.

When I finished, she slapped the desk and said, "That dirt-mouthed gangster has some nerve talking that way about a great patriot like Edgar Hoover."

She pushed up from her chair and traveled the office with the lightning pace of a woman half her seventy-five years.

"Lana? The part about arranging her motel tryst with Johnny Stompanato? He forgot to tell you he had the room wired for sound. He made two thousand copies of their moaning and groaning, Lana begging for more in what got to be known on the Bel Air circuit as her finest performance. He sold them for fifty bucks a copy. He pressed more copies and raised the price after his guy was dead."

Hopper paused to catch her breath, slightly bent, using the wall for support.

"The worst part?" she said, tossing her hand against her broad forehead and running it over the upswept bun of bottled brown that added two or three inches to her five-seven height, the old actress in her rising to the surface, her voice rising in a crescendo. "I had to find out by reading it in the papers. That lousy son-of-a-bitch bastard didn't have the smarts to call me first. Now, Mickey Cohen wants to kiss and make up with me? Hah! Whatever he told you, forget it. Everybody knows he's a liar as well as a crook."

"Boss, what if it's true about Rockwell and—"

"And if it's not, he's made me out to be a fool and robbed me of my credibility. Mickey Cohen can go tell it to the Marines. Then, he can go to hell."

She tossed away Cohen's letter and eyed the phones like she was commanding them to ring and rescue her from our conversation. I'd seen the look many times before. It was a dead issue with her.

* * * * *

Oscar night.

Klieg lights roaming the cloudless sky.

My press credential got me out front of the Pantages, where a cadre of parking attendants in rented tuxedos dealt with limos and status cars that wore their price tags like license plates, as famous, equally expensive faces stepped out to the manic screams of the adoring fans filling the modest sidewalk bleachers and lined up three and four deep behind wooden horse barriers across the boulevard.

Once the ceremonies began, it allowed me admission to the press tent that connected to the theater and was divided into sections that collectively and irreverently had come to be called the Stations of the Cross. Upon leaving the stage, winners and presenters would be moved to an area reserved for newspaper and wire service reporters and photographers working against a tight deadline. Next came areas for other photographers; journalists who'd be out-shouting one another for attention in one after another brief, impromptu press conference; other news correspondents and magazine photographers; radio interviewers armed with wire and reel-to-reel tape recorders.

I hung out in the largest section of the tent, available to everyone, ringed with television monitors and full of typewriters and telephones on tables organized cafeteria style; buffet tables filled with hot and cold dishes from Chasen's, including the chili the restaurant was famous for, but which for me never measured up to the chili poured on top of a Pink's hot dog.

Outside, my nerves had been doing a St. Vitus dance any time a car delivered someone nominated for *The Diary of Anne Frank*, like the cinematographer William C. Mellor or Charles LeMaire, the costume designer; Ed Wynn, when he tottered in on the arm of his son, Keenan; especially Shelley Winters, who answered the urgings of the fans by crossing over to pose for Kodaks, sign dozens of autographs, and shake hands with two boisterous women, who swore they'd driven all the way from Shelley's hometown, Brooklyn, in hopes of seeing her. If there was some Nazi nut case hanging back in the crowd, Shelley had made herself an easy target, but—

It wasn't only the crowd I feared.

There could be a high-powered rifle aimed at the arrivals from one of the windows of the Taft Building across the street. Or the building roof. Why not the roof? No reason. No reason at all. No reason why not. Easier than breaking into an office, hoping it offered a workable sightline.

My B-movie imagination grew more intense in the tent, where I helped myself to a beer from the self-service tubs, then another brew, then popped the lid on a third, watching the monitor wondering if Nazi sharpshooters were hiding somewhere in the upper reaches of the second balcony or in the projection booth, having somehow slipped past the heavy security posted at every Pantages entrance and exit, or—

Maybe—

Maybe—

They had managed to infiltrate the press tent.

They could strike anywhere, starting with the deadline room.

A heat rash had turned the backs of my hands as red and raw as my nerves and my bladder was begging for relief by the time Bob Hope brought Olivia de Havilland onstage to reveal the winner for Best Supporting Actor.

Ed Wynn's palsy was never more pronounced as she gave an elegant reading to the list of nominees and bravely put on a clown's smile when de Havilland followed a dramatic pause with the name of Hugh Griffith. I wanted to share the great comedian's disappointment, but I knew the loss made him a less likely target.

I unbridled my thighs and raced for the row of discreetly curtained portable toilets posing as a men's room, returning as Yves Montand completed a song-and-dance routine that confirmed he'd never be a threat to Fred Astaire, and Hope introduced Edmond O'Brien, to present the award for Best Supporting Actress.

Shelley Winters scrambled up to the stage when her name was read.

She finished reciting her phone book of thank yous with loving words about Anne Frank, "who wrote with such depth and perception about human beings," and headed for the Stations of the Cross with O'Brien.

I was the first to reach the entrance to the deadline room.

Two six-footers in their mid-to-late thirties, wearing rented tuxedos with outdated lapels and deadpan expressions, barred me from entering. I protested, pointing to the all-access badge hanging from my neck. They weren't impressed. I tried shoving past them. The one with a blond butch haircut shoved back and inched me down the corridor as Shelley and O'Brien approached from the other direction. I called out to her and got a smile and a wave back, Shelley hoisting her Oscar like it was Lady Liberty's torch and I was another fan sending congratulations.

The one with neatly trimmed black hair pushed the curtain aside for Shelley and O'Brien and followed them into the deadline room.

I planted both hands on Blond Butch Haircut's arm and struggled to push him aside.

He had twenty or thirty pounds on me and wasn't going anywhere.

Except for the revolver in his belt holster.

He brought the barrel down on my shoulder blade to release my grip, then swung it hard against the side of my face.

Then—

There was no *then* then.

* * * * * *

I woke up the following morning to the mother of all headaches and a radio news report about an exclusive story on the front page of the *Examiner*. How FBI agents had thwarted plans of the American Nazi Party to infiltrate the Academy Awards ceremony. No further details would be forthcoming for reasons of national security, according to FBI Chief J. Edgar Hoover.

The lead item in Louella O. Parsons's *Examiner* column, carried as a front page sidebar, revealed how she had been the one who tipped off the FBI after information about ANP leader George Lincoln Rockwell's plot was brought to her attention by a confidential source with unimpeachable credentials.

The balance of her column was devoted to the celebrities who attended the Oscar show and the party afterward at the Beverly Hilton Hotel, noting how many men were handsomely attired in tuxedos and tails acquired from the well-known Beverly Hills "Haberdasher to the Stars" Mickey Cohen.

The phone call I was expecting came within the hour.

Hedda Hopper declaring me a traitor and firing me, effective immediately.

Slamming down the phone in my ear before I could thank her for our time together or mention I'd be starting next week as Louella's leg man.

I replaced the receiver thinking how right Mickey Cohen had been when he said, *You gotta stay in the game to get ahead in the game.*

*Terence Faherty was an obvious fit for this anthology because of his Scott Elliott series, which has garnered him two Shamus Awards. His Elliott novels and stories are set in historical—and storied—Hollywood, and here he moves Elliott into the '60s, when he is asked to search for yet another would-be Hollywood starlet.*

# Closing Credits

*by Terence Faherty*

## ONE

Hollywood Security, the company I'd served for the better part of twenty years, occupied a building on Roe Street, not far from the Twentieth Century Fox lot. When I'd signed on fresh from the army, the ersatz hacienda with the red tile roof had been too small for us. On those rare occasions when all the operatives had been in the bullpen at the same time, it had been like playing musical chairs in the Notre Dame locker room.

That was then. By 1966, business had tapered off and then some. My boss, Patrick J. Maguire, Paddy to almost everyone, had designed his firm to serve the old-boy network that had run Hollywood in its heyday, men who'd paid generously to keep their valuable actors safe from bad influences and out of the crime beat section of the newspaper. These days, though, the studios all had revolving doors on their head offices. The current title holders didn't know Paddy, except by his reputation, which was not without its gravy spots. Worse, they were inclined to look on the occasional scandal as nothing more than free publicity.

All of which meant that Paddy and his business-partner wife, Peggy, had space to rent. They'd rented it to a telephone answering service, Jordan's Jingles, which provided about every service you could provide over a telephone line, from wake-up calls to fronting for nomadic producers and writers and whatevers who lacked offices but liked to keep that sad fact quiet.

I arrived at our subdivided building one February morning and found Mary Jordan, owner of Jordan's Jingles, seated in Paddy's inner sanctum. She and Peggy Maguire were in the visitor chairs and the great man himself was behind the desk, looking, as he usually did, like Buddha's Irish cousin. I thought I'd stumbled across a tenants meeting and started to back out, but Peggy, rising, waved me in.

My boss's wife was spare and dark and a little stooped. As she slipped past me, she said, "It's you they want," and prodded me toward her vacated seat.

The way she'd delivered the line started me thinking of alibis. Jordan's telephone jockeys were all would-be starlets awaiting their big breaks, and Jordan wasn't the whimsical person the name of her firm might lead one to expect. She ran her little troupe of goddesses-to-be like a YWCA from a 1930s movie: no smoking, no drinking, no dating the customers. I suspected the last rule was tough to enforce, all her girls having telephone voices that, for sexual promise, were just on the safe side of Jayne Mansfield's. I'd been warned by Peggy to stay in our end of the building, and being a happily married guy, I'd done it. But innocent men had been hung before.

Paddy's opening remark told me I was worrying over nothing. "Our friend Mary has a problem she'd like our help with. One of her girls has gone missing."

He leaned back then to chew on an unlit cigar, giving Jordan the floor.

"Her name is Dorothy Marling," Jordan began. She was a forty-ish, squarely built woman who had reacted to living in the epicenter of a looks culture by adopting early the outward trappings of old age: hair in a bun, half glasses, plain suits long in the skirt, practical shoes. She adjusted the glasses on her shiny nose before continuing. "Dorothy's been with me for six months. You've probably noticed her as you're a . . . ah . . . detective. She's quite a pretty girl. Twenty-one. Five-five, slender, fair hair and complexion. She reminds me of Cathy O'Donnell."

This last item was a form of shorthand popular around Hollywood, the classification of a person according to the screen personality he or she most resembled. O'Donnell had once specialized in girl-next-door parts, notably in *The Best Years of Our Lives*.

I knew by then the one Jordan meant. The telephone girls used their own entrance, but I occasionally saw them coming and going. And as I was a man, as Jordan had almost said, I'd noticed Dorothy Marling. Any man would.

"She's a sweet girl," Jordan added. "But a little naive. She's from Iowa. Ames, Iowa."

"Scotty here is from the Midwest, too," Paddy said. "You wouldn't guess it to look at him now, but he used to leave hayseeds behind whenever he sat down. And he was a young hopeful once."

Something else I had in common with Marling, I realized, when Jordan nodded.

"Yes," she said, "Dorothy wants to be a star. She's taking the usual acting classes taught by the usual failed actors. That's how I get most of my girls and how I lose most of them, when they get discouraged and go home."

"Maybe that's what Dorothy did," I said.

"Ah, no," Paddy said. "At least, Mary doesn't think so. Dorothy has a paycheck coming to her, and her things are still in the place she rents."

"I have Dorothy's spare keys," Jordan explained. She produced a key ring in case I was the skeptical type. "She's the kind that loses things. I went by her place the first day she didn't come in. That was yesterday."

"The police?" I asked.

"Not much interested," Paddy said. "Not yet."

They wouldn't be, young transients being more common in greater Los Angeles than sunburn cases. I would have asked next why Hollywood Security was interested, but I knew better than to inquire in front of Jordan.

So I asked instead if her other girls had any ideas on the subject.

"Dorothy didn't have any special friends at work," Jordan replied, which I might have guessed from the fact that Jordan held her spare keys. "But one of the girls seemed to think Dorothy had a man in her life. An older man."

She said "older man" the way she'd earlier pronounced "failed actor," like she was listing types of snake. I was both a failed actor and, by the Dorothy Marling measure, an older man. But I kept the hurt feelings out of my voice as I said, "One of your clients, maybe?"

Paddy sat up, finally. "A delicate area that, as Mary was explaining before you came in. She doesn't want to scare off her paying customers with any heavy-handed inquiries. I thought you might start with Marling's apartment. There might be something there that will help us narrow the field."

Jordan was still holding the key ring, which made me think the apartment search was her idea and not Paddy's. But a boss was a boss was a boss, as my literary wife might have paraphrased it.

I held out my hand and said, "I'll get right on it."

# TWO

I asked Jordan for a photo of Marling, but she was reluctant to give up the only one she had, a group shot from the office Christmas party. She told me to take one from Marling's apartment. Then she stood and nodded to Paddy.

I stood, too, but after Jordan had marched out, I sat back down. "What's next?" I asked. "Getting cats out of trees?"

"I wish I knew what was next," Paddy said. "Or maybe I don't."

He paused to light the cigar he'd been teething on. "I know this isn't exactly in our line. Five will get you ten this Marling has just moved in with some guy and forgotten her job, her dreams, and everything her mother taught her, except how to yank a zipper. But business is slow, and Mary's a good tenant.

"Her nibs," he added, referring to Peggy, "thinks this telephone racket is the coming thing. We put a little money into it, did you know that? Mary may be supporting us in our golden years, if we ever get there."

The Maguires were there already, according to the Social Security people, but I didn't point that out, as I was still waiting for Paddy's real reason.

After blowing a smoke ring or two, he said, "Peggy likes the way Mary looks after her flock. Strikes a chord with her, as you'll understand."

I did. Peggy had all but adopted me back when I was still leaking hayseeds. She now considered my kids to be her grandchildren.

"How long do we give it?" I asked.

Paddy pushed an index card my way. On it was typed an address. "Let's see what you find. Then we'll discuss it."

\* \* \* \* \* \*

I mentioned sunburn cases earlier, and generally speaking, L. A. is a good place to wear a hat. But I drove to Dorothy Marling's apartment through a steady rain. The apartment was in a subdivided house on Fremont Street that had once been a mansion and was now a maintenance headache. It had five mailboxes. The box belonging to Marling held a couple of bills and nothing else. I carried them to the front door with me.

There were five electric buttons next to the door, each identified only by an apartment number. I pushed Marling's first, got no answer, and then tried the other four. I didn't need the front door opened for me—one of my borrowed keys unlocked it—but I wanted a witness, someone I could question about Marling and who could later testify that I hadn't snuck or broken in.

What I got was a man dressed in undershirt and pajama bottoms and no smile whatsoever. His name was Crowe, and he was a second-shift printer at the *Los Angeles Times*. Crowe got less irritated when I told him I was looking into the disappearance of one of his neighbors. He knew Marling by sight and liked her, mainly because she worked days when he was trying to sleep. He was less fond of her noisy roommate, but he thought she had moved out a week back, or maybe two. He didn't know the roommate's name or anything about her, except that she was unlight on her feet. Nor had he noticed any male visitors, but he guessed that they would have come by while he was at work. I guessed that, too.

I asked after the landlord. Crowe said he lived in Encino. He gave me a name and a phone number. In exchange, I promised to do my looking around on tiptoe.

After knocking on Marling's door, I let myself into her second-floor apartment, which consisted of front room, kitchenette, bedroom, and bath, all small, all smelling of a perfume or powder I couldn't place.

I started in the bedroom, wanting to confirm that Marling's things were still there. The closet's shelf and hanging space were both more than half taken up. Its floor held a neat row of shoes with one small gap. The row was punctuated by a pair of fuzzy pink slippers complete with rabbit ears. The drawers of the small dresser were also well stocked, the lingerie suggesting Ames, Iowa, more than Hollywood, California.

I checked the bath and kitchen next. Both looked like they'd been left by someone who expected to be back. There was a tooth-brush in a glass by the bathroom sink. The kitchen counterpart held a coffee cup, rinsed.

That left the front room. It was furnished with a convertible couch, an old console television, and a student desk that bore a telephone and two framed photographs, one James Garner's and the other Paul Newman's. Neither was autographed, so I was saved those social calls.

There was a jam jar near the phone containing pencils and ball-point pens, but there was nothing to write on, no pad or blotter. That made me curious enough to crouch down and examine the desktop at an angle. Its light coating of dust was broken by a rect-angular outline to the right of the phone. It was about the size of a desk diary.

I sat down at the desk and searched its drawers for the missing address book or whatever else might have rested next to the phone. I found no candidate, and not finding one made me fairly certain that I'd find nothing else of interest in the desk. It also heightened my interest in the case. Either Marling had taken some odd things away with her or someone had been there before me.

I was about to give up when I noticed a square of paper behind Newman's portrait. It was a piece of notepaper folded around a pho-tograph of a knockout wearing a feathered headdress, a sequined bikini, and high heels. The undated note read: "What would they say in Des Moines? Send my bunnies. It's cold out here at night. Love, Sally."

I went back into the bedroom and held one of the pink slippers against another shoe from the line. The slipper was much bigger, far too big for the five-five Marling but just right for a rookie showgirl who appeared to be seven feet tall in her headgear and heels.

If I was guessing right, Sally was the roommate who'd moved out a week or two earlier. Unfortunately, I couldn't find her full name or her new address written down anywhere in the apartment. She wasn't the addressee on any of the mail, and there was no sign of the envelope the note had come in.

Finding that photo reminded me that I was supposed to be collecting one of Marling. It also made me realize that I hadn't seen one. Not one of the professional portraits a starlet-in-training would likely have. And no snapshots with mom and dad that a girl away from home would surely have.

Using Marling's phone, I called the landlord's office and spoke to his secretary. She told me that Marling's name was the only one on the lease. Her rent was paid up, and she hadn't mentioned moving out. Her lease ran through July.

I put down the phone and immediately picked it up again, dialing a more familiar number this time. My wife, Ella, answered.

"I'm driving to Las Vegas," I said. "Want to go?"

"Too busy, Scotty. Way too busy. Who are you kidnapping this time?"

"Nobody. I'm trying to trace a showgirl. All I have to go on is a photo of her legs. Do we still have that tape measure?"

"I'll be ready in twenty minutes."

# THREE

Before I left the apartment, I made one more call, to Paddy, to let him know about the Vegas trip. Peggy answered the Hollywood Security phone and immediately approved my plan without consulting her husband. When she heard Ella was tagging along, she hung up fast so she could get first dibs on babysitting our daughter.

I locked up after myself and drove to Doyle Heights in my still-new Oldsmobile Toronado. I'd wanted to try a front-wheel-drive car ever since Cord had introduced one in my home state of Indiana, back when I was too young to get a driver's license. My Olds was a gold fastback coupe with a four-hundred-twenty-five-cubic-inch V-8 engine and a floor-mounted four-speed manual transmission, the latter a particularly silly option for someone who drove in L.A.'s stop-and-go traffic, as Ella hadn't tired of reminding me.

Today she didn't mention the gearshift when she joined me on the "strato-bench" front seat, perhaps because we spent the first minute or so kissing. That was a long kiss for a couple who'd been together as long as we had, but Ella liked to remind me what a lucky guy I was whenever I was about to mix with actresses or chorines.

It wasn't necessary. One look at Ella's faded blue eyes, her blonder and shorter than-usual-hair, and her knowing and not-giving-a-damn smile was enough to remind me of my luck. But I played along.

"You should have saved that for the Nevada line. My memory's not what it used to be."

"It's the rest of you I'm worried about," Ella said. "Let's go, Parnelli."

The rain became spotty by Bakersfield. At Barstow, where we stopped for a sandwich and where I filled Ella in on the case, there wasn't a cloud in the sky. After lunch, I gave the Olds its head. Ella held on with one hand and edited her latest script with the other, pausing only to read me a letter from our son, who was away at military school. We rolled into Las Vegas around four o'clock.

When Ella had joked on the phone about me kidnapping someone, she'd been referring to a job Paddy and I had pulled off several years earlier, one that had gotten us banned from Vegas for a time. That ban had only recently been lifted, and this was my first visit under the armistice. I was struck by how much the town had grown and said so.

"You'll be saying that every time you come here for the next thirty years," Ella predicted. "They'll still be building this place when Gabriel gets his solo. How do we do this? You going to have every show pony in town try on the glass slipper?"

She meant the fuzzy pink slipper. I'd brought the pair along with me, and Ella had noticed them sitting on the backseat. They were hard to miss.

"We won't need them with this," I said, producing another souvenir from Marling's apartment, the photograph of the underdressed Amazon. "I once wrote a monograph in which I identified one hundred and forty varieties of sequined brassiere."

"Give me a man who loves his work."

My actual plan was to show the photo around the first casino we came to on the theory that each one knew what the others were doing by way of entertainment. We started at the Sands.

The dance director there, a guy who looked like he knew his way around a sequin if not a brassiere, glanced at the photo, sniffed, and said, "Stardust. If you can't afford designers, use scissors. That's their motto."

At the Stardust Casino, Ella surprised me by finding a seat at a slot machine and leaving me to it. The showgirls, I learned, were just gathering for their evening shift. I worked my way backstage, using twenty-dollar bills to light my way. Eventually, I met someone who actually knew the woman in the snapshot.

"New kid," this person, herself a very old kid, said. "Sally something. Sally Reed, I think."

I interviewed Reed in the little room where they glued the feathers back on the headdresses and made other costume repairs. She left the door to the busy hallway open when she came in and declined the room's only chair. She wasn't as tall as her picture had led me to believe, but she was a full order, and eye-catching, even in the jeans and cowgirl shirt and Keds that were her street clothes. There was still a wisp of the Hawkeye State about her, in the broad, freckled face and the cornflower-blue eyes and the tomboy arrangement of her hair.

She spotted the slippers I carried as soon as she stopped trying to place me. Her face lit up.

"My bunnies! Dot sent you?"

"Not exactly," I said. I told her about Mary Jordan's concern for Marling, half hoping—despite the time and gas I'd invested—that Reed would laugh those worries off. She didn't.

"Something must have happened to her. She'd never miss work, not without calling in. Not that farm girl. I knew it wasn't safe for her to be alone. She's too trusting. She offered me a place to stay just 'cause we happened to be from the same state. That's just the way she is."

Reed confirmed that Marling had kept a phone diary on her desk and that she'd had photos of herself around the apartment. When I told her that the photos and diary were gone, she changed her mind about not sitting down.

I tried Paddy's theory. "Could she have moved in with somebody? A friend?"

"A man?" Reed asked, in exactly the scandalized way Doris Day might have asked it in one of her bedroom comedies. "Not unless she changed her spots. A goodnight kiss was a big deal for her."

"But she was seeing someone. An older man."

"You must mean Lawrence Wray. He's not that old. No older than you," she added, so winningly that I was glad Ella was handy.

"Who is he?"

"Dot's big Hollywood contact, the one who's supposed to get her into the movies. Larry's an art director. You know, the guy who designs the way a picture's going to look. It's a very important job. At least, he made it sound important."

I'd never heard of Larry Wray, but I didn't know many art directors by name. Reed didn't have an address for Wray or a very high opinion of him.

"I never thought he was going to do much for Dot. I think maybe he's a has-been."

"Maybe he's a fake," I said, thinking aloud. "Maybe he's not even in the business."

Reed shrugged. "He mentioned a couple of pictures he'd gotten screen credit for. The only one I remember is *Gunfight at Yuma*, a western. I'm a sucker for westerns.

"He made it sound like a big deal, getting a screen credit. Dot seemed to understand that. I guess it's part of that dream, the chance to see your name up there on the screen."

I asked for a description of Wray, and she based it on me. He was shorter and thinner, with a longer, more delicate nose and less hair, the hair black, maybe bottle black.

I handed her the slippers and thanked her. She told me to wait and dug in her purse, eventually producing a little metal-edged photograph, the kind you get from an arcade photo booth. The subject was a smiling Dorothy Marling.

"Maybe that'll help," Reed said.

"I'll tell Dot you said hello."

"I hope you can."

# FOUR

Ella had packed us an overnight bag, but after an early dinner at Tony Cento's, we headed back. She could see I was anxious to follow up the Larry Wray lead, though, by the time we rolled into L.A., it was too late to do much.

I did check the phone book for Lawrence Wray. There were none listed. And I contacted Mary Jordan through Jordan's Jingles to see if Wray was a customer. A down-on-his-luck art director easily could have been, but, according to Jordan, he wasn't.

The next morning, at Ella's suggestion, I drove to the office of the guild, or union, the motion picture art directors shared with the television art directors, which was located west of town, in Century City. It was bright and early, or at least early. The rain was still falling, and the newspaper I'd scanned before leaving the house had warned of mud slides up in the canyons. At the guild office, things were just wet.

Those things included the records clerk at whose desk I landed, a young guy with long hair that had absorbed at least a quart of the rain and seemed reluctant to give it up. I told the clerk I was trying to trace a Lawrence Wray. He rolled up the sleeves of his madras shirt and asked me why.

"Rich aunt of his died out in Ames, Iowa. Left him a packet. I'm working for her lawyers."

"How rich?" the kid asked.

I held up the last of my twenties, wondering as I did so if Paddy would cover my expenses. "So rich she uses these for mattress ticking."

The clerk looked at the twenty, shrugged, and got up. He left a trail of water drops on the floor between his desk and a card file and doubled it on the return trip.

"Didn't recognize the name, but here he is: Lawrence Wray. Been a member of the guild since 1953. First picture he got a credit on was *Gunfight at Yuma.*"

"That's the guy," I said. When he looked at me inquiringly, I added, "The rich aunt was a sucker for westerns."

He pushed the card across to me and held out his hand. I ignored the upturned palm.

The card contained Wray's address, 6 Esel Street, and the names and release dates of four motion pictures, beginning with the western Sally Reed had remembered, which had come out in 1953, the year Wray joined the guild. The other three titles were vaguely familiar, though none had been big hits. Wray had worked on a World War II submarine picture made in 1957, a Judy Holliday comedy from 1959, and one of the many imitations of *Peyton Place.* Wray's version had been released in 1962. Not a large body of work, but an eclectic one.

Beside each notation were the letters AAD. I asked the soggy clerk about them.

"Means he was credited as an associate art director. That's a fancy way of saying assistant."

So Wray had lied to Marling about his job title. That wasn't uncommon. I usually tried to keep mine out of the conversation altogether.

The clerk was musing. "Funny, this Wray never moved up, except that he doesn't seem to work much. You'd think a guy who didn't get more movie work would do some television. He doesn't seem to like TV at all."

That was another thing Wray and I had in common. We could discuss it when I found him, which should have been easy, now that I had his address. But there was something about that address I didn't like. I'd gotten to know Los Angeles street names fairly well over the course of a misspent life, and I'd never heard of Esel Street. I decided to hedge my bets.

"How about the name of the art director Wray assisted?"

"He inherit money, too?" the kid asked.

I pushed Wray's file card and the twenty across the desk. "Just wanted to invite him to the celebration."

The clerk left a fresh trail of dewdrops to a different filing cabinet. He rooted around for a while and came back whimsical.

"Better reserve an extra table at your party. Wray worked for a different art director on each of those movies. Some top guys, too."

He handed me a card on which he'd scrawled four names: Leon Spencer, Robert Brattain, Edmund Daeger, and James Sheehy. Next to Brattain's name was a phone number.

"No charge for the number," the kid said when I thanked him. "I just happen to know it. Bob Brattain was president of the guild last year. Just don't mention me when you call him."

# FIVE

My hunch about Wray's Esel Street address turned out to be all too solid. No such street appeared in the index of my timeworn Los Angeles map. I checked a newer map at a newsstand and got the same result. I even consulted specialists, by which I mean cabdrivers. All I got from them was a tip on a wrestling match.

It was time for Plan B. I called the number I'd been slipped for Robert Brattain and got his secretary, a woman who would never land a job at Jordan's Jingles. She sounded less like Jayne Mansfield than anyone I'd ever heard, Paddy included. Something in her Death Valley voice told me she wouldn't tolerate any fairy tales about rich aunts in Iowa, so when she asked me to state my business, I gave her Wray's name, period. She asked next for a phone number. I read her the one on the pay phone in the lunch wagon where I'd gone to dry off.

I returned to the coffee I'd left cooling on the counter. Before I'd drained the cup, the pay phone rang. It was Brattain's defensive line. She told me her boss could see me in thirty minutes at the Paramount lot, where he was working. When she asked if I needed directions, I smiled to myself, said no, and we parted friends.

I'd smiled the secret smile because I knew the Paramount lot better than any other corner of Southern California, except my own house. I'd been a contract player for Paramount before Pearl Harbor. During the war, I'd visited the lot often in memory. I still dreamt of the place some nights, though I seldom mentioned those dreams to Ella. In them, Dorothy Lamour was often having problems with her sarong.

Brattain received me in an office in the same building as the little theater where I'd first seen myself on the screen. He had one of the windows cranked open, and our conversation was accompanied by the patter of raindrops on the stucco sill.

The art director had been built by nature to play beefy British baronets in Ealing Studio comedies. He had a square, ruddy face slightly inclined toward jowls, heavy black brows, and wavy hair to match. He wore a white polo shirt and a rumpled tweed jacket whose breast pocket was so distended from hard use that it looked like the pouch of a cartoon kangaroo.

He'd been in the process of lighting a pipe when I entered. He asked if I minded the smell. When I produced my own pipe to prove that I didn't, Brattain offered me some of his tobacco, which he claimed was blended for sailors, or maybe from sailors, it was that strong.

"What's all this about Larry Wray?" he asked when we were puffing away like fellow clubmen.

"I'm trying to find him."

"Why?"

"He's been seeing a young woman who's gone missing." I took out the do-it-yourself portrait of Marling and handed it to him. She's the one I'd really like to find. But I'm starting with Wray."

"You'll need your passport. He's in Italy."

"Working on a picture?"

"No. He's buried there. He was killed at Monte Casino in 1943."

For a second I thought I was on the trail of the wrong Larry Wray. Then I remembered *Gunfight at Yuma*, the movie Dorothy Marling's beau had worked on, as assistant to the man seated across from me.

"Wray's pretty active for a dead guy," I said. "He's done at least four pictures since the war."

"How could you know about those?" Brattain asked, his black brows knocking together like rival storm clouds.

The short answer would have involved the records clerk who had asked me to keep him out of it. So I gave Brattain a long answer and a slightly dishonest one. I told him about my efforts to date to find Marling. To shield the clerk, I said that Sally Reed had remembered Wray mentioning four movies he'd worked on. And Brattain's name.

"Whoever this guy was," Brattain said, "he wasn't Larry Wray. You'll just have to take my word for that."

"I might. But the woman who hired me isn't going to. Neither will the cops, when they finally get interested in this."

Brattain poured out smoke for a time like the Cannonball Express. Then he said, "Okay. I'll have to level with you. But I'm telling you this in confidence. You'll understand why. Before the war I was an apprentice art director at MGM. One of a group of apprentices working for a guy named Wilhelm Wichman. You've probably never heard of Wichman, but he was maybe the best art director in the business, a genius who'd learned his craft in Germany in the twenties. It was the chance of a lifetime to study under him, even though it was also the beating of a lifetime. He called us apprentices his five donkeys and he worked us like donkeys."

I interrupted. "You remember the other donkeys' names?"

"Besides me, there was Jimmy Sheehy, Leon Spencer, and Ed Daeger."

The names I carried in my pocket, along with Brattain's own. "That's only four."

"The fifth was Larry Wray. He was a great guy, idealistic, enthusiastic. He worked as hard as any other two of us. The five donkeys used to share a bottle sometimes in a little pull-off up on Mulholland Drive, the kind of spot you'd take a girl if you didn't have a room. We'd get drunk and look down on the lights of Hollywood and dream about the work we were going to do.

"Larry's big dream was to see his name in the credits of a picture. That was his idea of making his mark on earth. It was no small dream in those days, when hardly anybody got a screen credit. Things have loosened up a lot since then. Twenty years from now, they'll be giving a credit to the kid who goes out for coffee."

"Back to our story," I said.

"Right. World War II came along and put a lot of people's dreams on hold, including Larry's. He was the only one of our group to enlist. Like I said, he was idealistic. Two years later, he was dead.

"The night we heard about Larry, we drove up to Mulholland Drive, to the old spot, and split one last bottle. And we made a pact. We each swore we'd share a screen credit with Larry. He'd be listed as our associate. And we each came through for him."

"How did you pull it off?"

"It was easy enough to get his union card renewed. I've always been active in the union. I walked the paperwork through myself. After that it was only a matter of convincing whoever was producing the film to go along. They always did, when they heard Larry's story."

Which meant that any number of people around Hollywood could know about the scheme. I decided to stick with the men who'd hatched it. "Which one of your old friends might be using Wray's name?"

Brattain paused in the process of relighting his pipe. "What makes you think it's not me?"

"Marling's roommate described her Wray."

"I see. Well, it isn't Ed Daeger. He died in a plane crash in Mexico two years ago. And it's not Jim Sheehy. He's been in North Africa for the past six months, working for Sergio Leone. That leaves Leon Spencer. He's a big guy, as tall as you and heavier than me. That fit your description?"

"No," I said, "but I'd like to talk with him anyway."

"Of course. I'll give you his number."

# SIX

"And that's it. It was a sentimental thing we did for a guy who went off to war. We were drunk when we made the pact, but I'd make it again right now."

That was easy to believe, since the speaker, Leon Spencer, was drunk again. Maybe not as lit as he'd been on a certain night in '43, but well along toward it.

Spencer was exactly as Brattain had described him: too tall and too fond of his mashed potatoes to be the runt Sally Reed had met. And the story he'd just told me, in the bar where Spencer had insisted we meet, the Intersection Lounge, at the fabled crossing of Hollywood and Vine, was exactly the same tale Brattain had trotted out.

In fact, the match was so good I was convinced Brattain had gotten hold of Spencer before I had and coached him.

I bought us another round—straight bourbon for him and straight Coca-Cola for me—on the off chance Spencer would get careless under its influence. The Intersection's piano player, a woman with a slow left hand, banged out ballad after ballad. Spencer matched her, story for song. All of his were about the legendary Willy Wichman, and none mentioned Wray or any of the other five donkeys.

Finally I decided I'd get tooth decay before Spencer made a slip. So I paid our tab and reached for my hat.

"You've no idea who the phony Wray might be," I summed up as I vacated my stool.

"It could be anybody. Bobby Brattain thinks this is another Manhattan Project for secrecy, but it's not. We each had to whisper it around to get Larry his credits. We made the people we whispered to take an oath, but you know how it is with a good story. Hell, I've probably spilled it once or twice myself under the influence."

I thanked Spencer and walked to a corner pharmacy that still had an old-fashioned indoor phone booth. I used it to call Hollywood Security for the second time since my visit to Paramount. My first call had contained a long overdue progress report for Paddy and a request that he verify Edmund Daeger's death and James Sheehy's absence from the continent.

I was expecting bad news when I called back and I got it. Daeger was really dead and Sheehy was really elsewhere. That word was passed to me by Peggy, who asked if I was giving up.

"No," I told her. "Not yet."

I drove around with no destination in mind, the Olds' wipers dragging every time the rain slackened, reminding me of the pianist in Leon Spencer's favorite bar. What he'd told me there—that the story of Larry Wray's posthumous screen credits could have worked its way around town—held together up to a point. It was the kind of story that would get around. But I couldn't buy Spencer's conclusion, which was that the false Wray could be anybody, any stranger who'd happened to hear the tale.

It made no sense to me that someone wanting to fool a farm girl like Dorothy Marling would choose Larry Wray's identity. He could have picked any one of scores of better-known names or made one up and Marling would have swallowed just as hard. And why pick an obscure category like art director? Why not claim to be a film director? The guy could have worn an eye patch and told Marling he was Raoul Walsh or even John Ford.

It was no good arguing, as I briefly did with myself, that Mr. X had taken the name because he knew the real owner wasn't going to show up and claim it. His kind of masquerade wasn't meant to age well. It only had to work for as long as it took him to separate Marling from her virtue.

All of which left me convinced that the man who had impersonated Wray had to have some special interest in the pact of the five donkeys. Unfortunately, I was out of donkeys and out of ideas.

Not so the Toronado. It had found its way onto Canyon Boulevard, one of the roads that climbed up from Hollywood into the Santa Monica Mountains. There Canyon met Mulholland Drive, the road that figured so prominently in the story of the five apprentices. Having nothing better to do, I decided to try to find the spot where the five had done their drinking.

Mulholland snakes along the very crest of the range that separates Los Angeles from the San Fernando Valley. As such, it features spectacular views of both the valley and the city, most of which have to be glimpsed from a moving car or while trespassing on private property. There are two or three public overlooks, one offering a great view of Universal Studio and another of the Hollywood Bowl. But Brattain had described something less formal, a site that may or may not have survived the decades of development since the war.

When I reached Mulholland, I turned right, Brattain having specified a Hollywood view. I took my time on the wet asphalt, slowing even more whenever the road threatened to develop a berm. Once I stopped at an actual pull-off. I found empty beer cans, but no panorama.

I almost passed up the right spot because the turnoff was partially hidden by some undergrowth. I decided to risk the Toronado's golden paint and was rewarded with a level parking space and a rain-obscured view of Hollywood and the sprawling city beyond.

So that part of Brattain's story was true or at least plausible. I climbed out of the car to stretch my legs, my hat and topcoat already being damp. Scattered around were more beer cans and that other residue of modern romance, condom wrappers. I walked as far as the edge of the dropoff, thinking about mudslides and what my insurance agent would say if the Olds ended up in somebody's swimming pool.

Then I saw something a few feet down the slope. It was a woman's shoe, hung up in a bit of brush. I started down, straddling a little rivulet that was cutting a new canyon in the side of the mountain. I reached but didn't touch the shoe, a plain black pump about the size of the one I'd compared to the pink slipper in Marling's apartment. From my new vantage point I could see something else, something that lay across the slope and had collected a little of the soil and stone washing down from above.

It was a woman's body, partially clad.

## SEVEN

Ten minutes after I'd climbed back up to my car, I was in a filling station phone booth, talking with Paddy. The booth had a leaky roof, but it was private.

"You're sure it was Marling?" Paddy asked.

"Positive," I said.

"Dead how long would you say?"

"A couple of days, for whatever my guess is worth."

"Your guessing's been great so far. I'd love to know what made you go mountain climbing."

"So would I. But right now I need to know how to call this in to the cops, straight or anonymously."

I could hear Paddy scratching one or more of his chins. "I'd like to get the creep who did it," he finally said.

I seconded that.

"Then do it anonymously. That'll give us a little room to maneuver."

"A little is right," I said. "There's a guy at Marling's apartment who'll remember me."

"We'll just have to work fast. Any thoughts on how to proceed?"

I had one, as a matter of fact. On the drive down to the filling station, it had occurred to me that there was one other person I could question about the five donkeys: the man who had once ridden herd on them, Wilhelm Wichman.

I asked Paddy if he knew Wichman.

"Not to borrow money from. But I remember him."

"Is he still alive?"

"God knows. He'd be old enough to call me sonny. He worked for MGM, didn't he? Then I know just who to ask. First, though, I've got to break the news to Mary Jordan. Come in after you've made your call."

By the time I reached the office, Paddy's web of contacts had produced the welcome news that Wichman was still alive. Even better, Paddy had come up with a phone number and an address in nearby Pasadena. We tried the number but got no answer. The same thing happened when I drove to Pasadena and knocked on Wichman's door.

The evening newscasts all mentioned the discovery of a body off Mulholland Drive. The morning papers carried Marling's name and photograph, the photo cropped from Mary Jordan's Christmas group shot. On instructions from Paddy, she'd called the police, but only after the first bulletins about the body had been broadcast. She'd further protected our lead by not mentioning Hollywood Security.

At eight o'clock the next morning, I tried the Pasadena number and got a woman who identified herself as Wichman's niece and live-in housekeeper, Thelma.

"Sorry you weren't able to reach us yesterday," she said when I mentioned the attempt. "It was doctor day for Uncle Willy."

I told her I wanted to interview Wichman about his time at MGM and asked if I could come right over. She put me off until eleven.

## EIGHT

I was knocking at the door of the neat white bungalow at ten forty-five. Thelma didn't call me on it. She looked like the kind of person who never called anyone on anything. She was small and almost as bent as Peggy Maguire, and she walked with a limp that wasn't quite corrected by her shoes, one of which had twice as much sole as the other. She left me in a sunny room with "Uncle Willy" and hurried off to make coffee.

Wilhelm Wichman was propped up in a chair that occupied a patch of sunlight. He was wearing dress trousers, a white shirt, and a bow tie, their formality undercut by his flannel robe and carpet slippers. I took one look at his very complete inventory of white hair—white fringe around the head, white eyebrows, white goatee—and his slack mouth and decided I was wasting my time.

Then he said, "You used to be an actor." He held up a hand. "Don't tell me. Before the war. For Goldwyn. No, Paramount. You did some movie with Paulette Goddard. She was something, that Paulette Goddard."

"You've got a great memory," I said.

"Think so? Ask me what I had for breakfast." Wichman's voice was strong, with only a trace of an accent. "Sit down, sit down. What's your name?"

"Scott Elliott."

"Sorry. I don't remember the name. May not have known it. I remember thinking of you when we were making a service picture. I thought you were a natural for a soldier."

"You and my draft board," I said. "I came to ask you about another soldier. Larry Wray."

Wichman brought his withered hands together. "Larry? He was a sweet boy. Not a born art director though. You know what an art director is? He's an artist who never touches a brush. Imagine an artist who works by doing some sketches, showing them to fifty or so other people, and then letting each one pass by his canvas and daub on some paint. That's an art director. He works through directors, cameramen, costume designers, actors, whoever. Those are his brushes. A crazy way to work, but he's still an artist.

"Larry Wray wanted to be an artist. He worked hard at it, harder than I ever did. But whether he would have made it in the end, we'll never know. That's the worst of sending youngsters off to be killed. You never know what you're losing, what Michelangelo, what Goethe."

"You had other apprentices besides Wray."

"Did I?" Wichman asked, causing my heart to miss two beats.

"Yes. You called them your donkeys."

"Right, right. I was running a little school back then for MGM. Training the next generation of art directors. It was an experiment we tried for a few years. After the war, they dropped it. Things changed after the war."

"Do you remember the donkeys?" I was looking for a loophole, some crack in Brattain's story I could squeeze through. Wichman gave me a barn door.

"Don't say donkey. That sounds too mean. Say *Esel*. That means donkey in German, I know, but it doesn't sound so bad."

It sounded great to me. I recognized the odd street name from Larry Wray's address, the phony one Brattain had made up when he'd slipped a dead Wray onto the union rolls.

Wichman was chattering on. "They were all just boys. Each one a genius in his own mind. Part of my work was taking them down a peg. You can't teach a genius. An *Esel* you can teach."

"There were six of them, weren't there?" Not five, as I'd been told. Six, the house number the sentimental Brattain had used for Wray's address.

"Right. *Meine sechs Esel.*"

"Larry Wray and five others. Do you remember the others?"

"Like I remember Paulette Goddard in a cashmere sweater. She could do marvelous things for a sweater, that one. Single-handed, she could justify the entire wool industry. Let's see, there was Eddy Daeger, who died, like Larry. And Bobby Brattain and Leon Spencer, both big successes. So is Jimmy Sheehy, my Irishman. You should have heard him sing. Like Dennis Day, he sounded."

"One more," I said.

"Oh yes. That would be Morris Molchan, my black sheep. Or red sheep, I'd guess you'd say."

"Molchan was a Communist?"

"Yes, but I don't know how political he was. Mostly he was just angry. I knew his kind in Germany after the first war. Men who were mad at everything, who wanted to tear down everything. They joined the party that promised them the most things to wreck."

"What happened to Molchan?"

"He was blacklisted in that ugliness in the fifties. I don't know what happened to him after that. Wherever he is, I bet he's still angry."

## NINE

I struck out again with the phone book: no Morris Molchan. I had the same luck with the city directory I borrowed in the Pasadena library. Before leaving the library, I used its phone to call the Century City office I'd visited the day before, the one maintained by the art directors guild. I asked for my friend the records clerk, not by name but by hair length.

He remembered me. His reply to my hello was, "Who's dead today?"

"Funny you should ask," I said. "I need the last known address of a Morris Molchan. He was blacklisted in the fifties. If he's using another name, I need that, too."

"I don't think so," the kid said. "I dodged a bullet yesterday. Twenty bucks isn't worth losing my job over."

He didn't hang up, however, signaling a willingness to negotiate.

In the old days, Paddy had often threatened to write a handbook for his employees, one describing the pitfalls other operatives had tumbled into, usually me. The book would also have contained Paddy's maxims, one of which was, "Pay once, own forever." It meant that once you got a person to accept a bribe, the threat of exposure often made paying him again unnecessary.

I could certainly have used that threat with the clerk. Instead, I asked him if he'd read the morning paper.

"Yeah," he said.

"Did you read about the body they found up on Mulholland Drive? It was a woman about your age named Dorothy Marling. You would have liked her, if you like them innocent and sweet. I think this Molchan killed her. I'm going to get him, with or without your help."

He told me to hold on, and I did, for what seemed like an hour. He came back apologetic.

"The only thing we have on Molchan is a card in our lapsed members file. It doesn't look like he ever got a screen credit. There's a name written on the card in pencil, Bill Smith, and an address, but it's at least ten years old."

"I'll take it anyway," I said.

The address was in Temple City, not far from the Santa Anita racetrack. The specific house, a tiny carport-with-attached-bedroom model, was on a dead-end street. The mailbox had a name painted on the side: Smith.

I parked a house away. I spent a minute collecting my Colt 1911 A1 from the Toronado's glove compartment and another minute separating it from the holster I hardly ever wore. I didn't wear it now. I figured my coat pocket could handle the weight of the automatic for the short walk to Molchan's door.

His carport held a five-year-old Pontiac, which was leaning as though taking a curve. That was odd, since the carport's concrete looked perfectly level. I investigated and found that both right side tires had been slashed.

I knocked on the front door with my left hand, my right being full by then of Colt. When no one answered, I tried the door. It was unlocked, yet another thing about the setup I didn't like. Even so, I eased the door open and slipped inside.

Right away, I knew I was too late. The little front room was heavy with a very distinctive odor, one that was part gun smoke, part fresh corpse. The corpse itself was front and center, sprawled across a desk that faced the front door, which I closed behind me.

The body fit Sally Reed's description of her roommate's big Hollywood contact. It wasn't exactly warm, but it wasn't that cold either. Its right hand held a snub-nosed revolver that was more or less pointed at a hole in the narrow head. There was a corresponding though larger hole on the other side of the skull.

I checked each room of the house before I put my Colt away. Then I searched more carefully, looking for a suicide note and not finding one. Nor did I find Marling's missing phone diary or her photographs, though there were some suspicious ashes in the backyard grill. My theory was that Molchan had taken the diary because he was listed in it and the photos to delay the identification of Marling's body, in case it was discovered while the face was still intact. But those didn't sound like the actions of a guy contemplating suicide.

I ended up back in the front room. I was gazing at a blank square of wall beneath an empty picture hook when the phone rang.

I picked it up but didn't say anything. The person on the other end didn't speak either. I heard breathing and, in the background, someone playing a piano with a slow left hand. Then the line went dead.

I wiped my fingerprints off the phone and headed for the door. Before I got there, an idea stopped me. I took out the photo-booth portrait of Marling, wiped off its metal edges, and propped it on the desk facing Molchan's shattered head.

# TEN

I broke every traffic law in the book on my drive from Temple City to Hollywood and Vine. Even so, I didn't expect my anonymous caller, Leon Spencer, to still be at the Intersection Lounge. But he was. As a bonus, Robert Brattain was seated next to him.

Their backs were to the door, so they didn't see me come in. The bar's pay phone, in a nook by the coat rack, commanded a view of the exits. I settled in and called Paddy.

I told him what I'd learned at Wichman's and what I'd found in Temple City, leaving out details I thought might muddy the water, like the slashed tires and the empty picture hook.

"So that's that," he said when I'd finished. "I'll phone it in to a friend on the force. A little tit for which we'll collect a later tat. First, though, I'll tell Mary Jordan. I may imply that you helped this Molchan reach his last decision, which will make for a more satisfying ending. If she looks at you with newfound respect, don't be surprised."

I didn't mind the embellishment. I didn't expect Jordan to take it too seriously. And I agreed with Paddy's esthetic judgment. Molchan getting a helpful push did round off the story nicely. I was pretty sure that two other guys, men who'd been trained to add the artistic touch, had seen it exactly that way.

I hung up the phone and went to ask them about it. The piano player, whose characteristic style I'd recognized when I'd picked up Molchan's phone, was doing serious damage to a Duke Ellington number, "All Too Soon." Luckily for her, I'd left my forty-five in the Olds.

Brattain almost swallowed his meerschaum when he saw me. Spencer was much more impassive, probably a benefit of his having had more to drink. They occupied the last two seats on the long side of the L-shaped bar. I took the first seat on the short side, so I could watch their faces. I'd stuck to soda when I'd last been in the Intersection, but I ordered a Gibson now, a double. A lot of drink for that hour of the day, but then we had a lot to drink to.

Spencer got the conversation rolling. "Did we leave some unfinished business when we talked yesterday? I didn't think so."

"I've come about the unfinished business you left in Temple City. I wanted you to know that it's all wrapped up, except for the paperwork."

"We don't know what you're talking about," Brattain said, getting that formality out of the way.

"Let's review. You lied to me yesterday when I came to ask you about Larry Wray. You told me that Wally Wichman had five assistants back when Wray decided to enlist. His five donkeys. Actually, there were six. Wichman told me that this morning."

I left out the bit about Wray's phony address—6 Esel Street—being the vital clue. It would have been nice to have rubbed Brattain's nose in that, but it might have gotten my friend the filing clerk canned. I'd covered for the clerk once before, and it had been a lucky move. If I'd told Brattain at our first meeting that I knew the Esel Street address, he never would have lied about the number of Wichman's flunkies. He would have thought of some other way to throw me off.

"Wichman even remembered the name of the sixth man: Morris Molchan. No news to you two, of course. You also won't be surprised to hear that Molchan's been living in Temple City under the name Smith, probably since he was blacklisted in the McCarthy purge.

"One or both of you were out at Molchan's this morning. You'd read the story about Dorothy Marling and you knew the significance of the spot where Molchan left her body. So you paid a call on Molchan and persuaded him to drill a hole through his head for the good of the regiment.

"You trusted him to do it, but only so far. You slashed the tires of his car in case he had second thoughts. Then you called from here to see if he was dawdling. You got me."

"You can't prove any of that," Brattain said. For an artist, he was a pretty conventional guy.

"Who drove here?" I asked.

"I did," Spencer said.

"Then how about I arrange for the cops to search the trunk of your car? I'm betting they'll find a framed photo matching a clean spot on Molchan's wall. I'm guessing it's a group shot of Wally Wichman and six smiling young men."

Spencer said, "Damn," and drained his glass. As Paddy had observed, I was riding a great guessing streak.

"What do you want?" Brattain asked.

"I want you to convince me that you didn't know Marling had been murdered when you lied to me yesterday. I'll give you exactly one chance to get it done."

Brattain had lost his resemblance to a bumbling baronet. The sweat on his unstiff upper lip had spoiled the effect. "We'd never cover up for a murderer. We'd never heard of Dorothy Marling before you came around yesterday. If we had, we would have warned her off Molchan. He was always a goat. And his tastes always ran toward young women fresh from the flatlands. Spoiling them was his great hobby. Even twenty years ago it was hard to stomach."

"Then why did you cover for him?"

"We didn't. We were protecting ourselves. And Larry Wray. As soon as you told me somebody was using Larry's name to go after women, I knew it was Molchan. But I thought Leon and I could handle him, quietly. I had no idea how far he'd gone."

"Why did he use Wray's name? Why didn't he pretend to be one of you or your dead pal Daeger?"

Spencer spoke up. "He hated us, that's why. We'd moved heaven and earth to get screen credits for a dead soldier but we'd never done anything for Morris when he was blacklisted. He thought Larry's credits should have gone to him. He took them by taking Larry's name."

"Did he tell you why he'd killed Marling? Was that part of his revenge?"

"Not a conscious part," Brattain said. "He said it was an accident, that things just got out of hand. Molchan took her up to that Mulholland lookout the way he'd taken dozens of women before. Only this woman yelled rape when he started to paw her. Molchan claimed he was only trying to quiet her down. They struggled. The next thing he knew, she was—"

"He told us he didn't mean to kill her," Spencer cut in. "And we believed him."

I didn't. There was too much symbolism in the place where Molchan had left Marling's body, a spot sacred to her killer and to the two men now staring holes in the bar.

"Why didn't you help Molchan ten years ago?"

"He wasn't an easy man to like," Brattain began.

Spencer cut him off again. "We should have helped him."

"It's more complicated than that, Leon. Morris always wanted so much. First he wanted to change the world. Then he wanted us to undo all the mistakes of his life. It was simpler with Larry. All he ever wanted was to see his name on a movie screen."

"Funny," I said, tossing some bills down next to my empty glass. "That's a lot of what Dorothy Marling wanted. She's had to settle for newsprint."

# ELEVEN

I thought that was it for the Marling story, but it turned out to have a postscript. About a year after I walked out on Brattain and Spencer, I got a call from Brattain's gravel-voiced secretary inviting me to attend a preview of a movie out in Glendale.

"Stay for the closing credits" was all the explanation she would give me.

Ella and I drove out after dinner, collected our tickets and comment cards, and watched Lee Marvin deadpan for two solid hours.

When the credits finally rolled, I looked for Larry Wray to be listed under Brattain, but he wasn't. Nor, I was relieved to see, was Morris Molchan. Instead, at the very end of the extended cast, the name Dorothy Marling appeared. Her part was described as "hopeful newcomer."

Ella saw it, too, and said, "Sweet of them. Only there weren't any hopeful newcomers in this epic."

"Every picture has at least one," I said, and we called it a night.

*Ken Kuhlken is a past winner of the PWA/St.
Martin's Press Best First Private Eye Novel
Contest, with his novel* The Loud Adios, *which
first introduced P.I. Tom Hickey. The stories are
historically set, and in this new Hickey tale Ken
takes Tom into the '60s. In the latest Hickey novel,*
The Do-Re-Mi, *the year is 1971, and detective
Tom Hickey interrupts his retirement to protect his
sons, one a folk singer, the other a fugitive.*

# Too Sweet

*by Ken Kuhlken*

lvaro Hickey had a wild streak. For
three years, beginning at age six, he'd
made his way as a Tijuana street kid,
living off theft and running errands for prostitutes.

Now, at seventeen, he had vanished without even telling his
brother Clifford.

His adoptive parents, Tom and Wendy Hickey, doubted he was
gone for good. Still, Wendy worried. Tom, a private investigator,
promised to go hunting for the boy if didn't show up in a week.

One Sunday evening in June, after Tom and Wendy had gone to
bed, Clifford spotted his brother on television.

He was watching *The Steve Allen Show*. During the part when
Steverino led the audience out of the theater, across Vine Street,
and up and down the aisles of the Hollywood Ranch Market, Alvaro

brought up the end of the line. He was holding hands with Melody Sweet, but he didn't look as happy as a guy holding hands with his first love who was now a celebrity ought to look.

Her real name was Melanie Sweedler. Sweet had been her mother's stage name. It fit Melanie. She had a voice so pure, even when she was in fourth grade, when Tom first heard her sing, even some of the rowdiest kids in the auditorium sat bug-eyed or with their jaws gone slack. Seven years later, Tom still remembered her song, "Greensleeves," and the way Alvaro glowed with admiration. The boy had survived off his wit and charm. At eight years old, he'd been crafty and bold enough to pick the lock on the trunk of Tom's old Chevy, stow away, and smuggle himself across the border. But sitting next to Melanie while they drove her home, Alvaro looked as if a hangman had just slipped the noose on him. And he couldn't talk except in peeps.

Melanie's father had died long ago. She and her mom lived in one of the flimsy duplexes that had risen up on Grand Avenue in Pacific Beach during World War II. Her mom had done time as a Hollywood dancer and Vegas showgirl. Now she was a drunk who supported her habit with jobs like waitress and sales clerk. She rarely lasted a week. Their rent and food came from the V.A. pension Melanie's father had earned them by crashing a Coast Guard helicopter during a rescue mission.

When his brother appeared on television, Clifford rushed to the door of his folks' bedroom. He knocked and opened it a crack. Wendy was sleeping.

"It's Alvaro," Clifford said in an excited whisper.

Tom jumped up and hurried to the living room, still wearing his glasses and holding a book on Chinese history. On the television, the line of tourists tagged behind Steve Allen. Tom and his son watched the procession file out past the coffee and hamburger bar where a trio of would-be starlets wiggled and beamed and a teen-aged boy and girl who slumped against the counter gave the camera their James Dean looks. Tom and Clifford watched until the last of Steve Allen's tourists had crossed Vine and gone into the theater. No Alvaro.

"Okay, Pop," Clifford said, "I'm not on drugs, I'm not hallucinating. They were there."

Tom nodded.

Clifford stared at him for a minute and said, "I'm going with you."

"Nope."

"Look—"

"We don't leave your mother alone, right?"

"Yeah but—"

"And who's got school?"

"Me but—"

"And who's the family bloodhound?"

*　*　*　*　*　*

Tom caught a few hours sleep. By dawn, he was racing through San Clemente, trying to keep his foot still when it wanted to floor the pedal. Tom loved driving, the faster the better. If anybody asked why he kept the ten-year-old Chevy station wagon now that his boys were grown, he told them police aren't as likely to chase and ticket a faded green four-door.

He slipped off his shoe so his accelerator foot wouldn't be quite so heavy. He tuned the radio to the first L.A. jazz station he could find. Brubeck, Monk, Ramsey Lewis and João Gilberto accompanied him past orange groves and Disneyland and into the city, while he thought about Melanie, mostly about her breakdown three years ago.

He didn't know all the facts. He knew that Melanie's mom and some boyfriend of hers had gotten into a spat. The boyfriend landed in Emergency with a kitchen knife in his belly, but he wouldn't press charges. And the judge looked unkindly upon woman beaters, which kept Brenda Sweedler out of jail and Melanie out of the foster home Tom and Wendy offered.

Melanie cracked up at school, during eighth grade English class. She was a model student. She loved books and all kinds of art and pleasing her teachers, but after the fight in her apartment, nerves overpowered her brain and will. When Alvaro walked her home or through the halls, she might say a few words but never could finish a sentence. A month passed, then the teacher asked her to present her report on *Great Expectations*. Instead of admitting she hadn't finished, she collapsed. She slipped from her seat, fell to the floor and wept, wailing and thrashing around while Alvaro knelt beside her and pushed desks, chairs, and people out of the way until the school nurse and her aide came. They picked Melanie up and led her off.

After six weeks in a county mental health facility, she returned home and to school. But she wouldn't sing anymore, or read aloud, or even stand with a group in front of the class for a spelling bee.

So, three years later, after Melanie sang, accompanied by Paul Case on guitar, in a talent program at Pacific Beach High School, people considered Case a miracle worker.

He taught junior English, American literature. The girls in his classes worshipped him. After all, he moonlighted as a folksinger and had cut a record with a trio called The Wanderers. And the shaggy hair and beach-boy tan helped him look younger than his thirty-some years.

\* \* \* \* \* \*

Tom exited on Firestone and pulled into a Richfield station next to a diner where long ago he and other L.A. police officers used to meet for coffee. A Mexican fellow was on the pay phone. When he saw Tom approaching, he hung up and hustled away, perhaps wary of a guy in a sport coat, hand-painted tie, and fedora.

At 7:30, Tom called Melanie. After two dozen rings he gave up and called Brenda Sweedler's number. He let the phone ring about fifteen times.

"What?" She yawned into the receiver.

"I saw Mel on TV last night. Steve Allen."

"Big deal. She's on TV at least once a week. This Tom Hickey or who?"

"It's Tom. Alvaro was with her."

"So what?"

"I told you a week ago, he ran off."

"Oh, yeah, well now you got him."

"First I need Melanie's new address."

\* \* \* \* \* \*

The boarding house was on Selma near Gower, midway up a block of California craftsman bungalows shaded in poplar and eucalyptus. The old mansion looked like it came from Pasadena, with the Spanish tile and balconies.

On one of the balconies a pretty girl stood, leaning on the rail. She smiled and waved to Tom as if he had come to serenade her.

A sign above the archway read, "Maude Sinclair's Home for Ladies." When Tom was a boy, he saw plenty of those places, meant as sanctuaries, where the girls who migrated from Iowa and Kansas to become starlets often made their first stop, partly because they feared the local wolves, partly to comfort their worried moms and dads.

He passed beneath the archway and into a courtyard that featured tall agave and pillars of bougainvillea climbing the walls. He hadn't yet passed the cactus garden on his way to the stairs that led to the second-floor rooms when a high voice trilled, "Mister, oh mister."

When he turned, he saw a buxom woman of around his own sixty years. She had a pale face except for the splotches of rouge, and yellow hair in tight curls. Her long, flouncy skirt was the same yellow.

He greeted her, introduced himself, and said, "Melanie Sweedler will want to see me."

"Be that as it may," Maude Sinclair told him, "no men are allowed in the ladies' rooms. I'll go myself and ask if in fact she does care to see you."

She strode to the staircase and limped up, using the side rail. At the top, she rested, then turned right toward the street-facing rooms, went to the third door, and rapped on it. After a minute or so, she knocked again, and waited before she turned and came back.

Tom met her at the foot of the staircase. She gave him a look of dark chagrin. He asked, "You think she didn't come home last night?"

"If she didn't, I'm not surprised. She's the flighty, wayward sort."

Though the Melanie Tom knew was reserved, cautious to a fault, and always respectful of authority and rules, he nodded and listened for more.

"She drinks, I'm rather certain, although I haven't yet put my hands on her liquor."

Which meant, Tom thought, the woman had used her key and gone snooping. "But you're certain she drinks. How's that?"

"I see it in her eyes and in the rubbery way she walks. I hear it when she speaks, just the hint of a slur."

"How about men?"

Sinclair looked as if he'd made her bite a lemon. "I caught her trying to sneak that folksinger into her room."

"Folksinger, you say?"

"The one who struts around behind his big guitar, on that silly *Hoot and Holler* show."

"You know him?"

She was staring at his tie. "Are you a policeman?"

"A friend of the family."

Sinclair staged an expression of woe. "The girl told me she has no father. What a trial such a rebel must have been to her poor mother."

"The man," Tom said. "Paul Case, correct?"

"If that's the name of the leader and elder of that troupe of hers. The one who drives a brand new Lamborghini."

"Any others?" Tom asked.

She placed a finger to her mouth as though to assure him gossip was beneath her. "Not three days ago, I happened upon her on this very path brazenly holding hands with a Mexican boy. They were going to her room. Oh, I'll admit he was handsome. Still, I believe that shows how far she's fallen."

Tom nodded. "Two men. Any others?"

"Not that I saw, but surely an older man and a Mexican are two too many."

"How about girlfriends?" Tom gestured toward rooms that surrounded the courtyard.

She held up both hands as though to stop him from disturbing any of her ladies. "I believe she's too busy with her troupe, her men, and gadding about. Still, I shall inquire. You may call me at this number." She pulled a card out of a pocket in the folds of her skirt.

Tom shook her hand and walked past the cactus garden and out of the courtyard. He meant to move his station wagon farther down the block, watch for and intercept Melanie or any of Maude Sinclair's girls on their way into or out of the home through the archway, the only passage to the courtyard. But the blonde was still on her balcony.

She gave him a droopy grin. "Hi'ya handsome. Ol' Maudey give you the boot?"

He smiled. "Yes ma'am." Then he risked Sinclair's wrath by crossing her lawn to stand beneath the blonde's balcony. "I'll bet you're a friend of Melanie's."

"You bet right. Who are you?"

"Tom Hickey."

"Hickey, you say." She leaned so far toward him, to study his face, Tom got ready to break her fall. "Like Melly's dreamboat. Only you don't look like him."

"He's my son. I need a word with him. Help me out, would you?"

"What day's this?"

"Monday."

"Okay, right. Let's see, is it Monday mornings The High Country Singers record? Yeah, it is."

\* \* \* \* \* \*

Paul Case had recruited a dozen singers, including a few guitar strummers. They were mostly kids. Melanie, Tom believed, was the youngest. Case named the group, promoted them around the L.A. folk clubs, landed them a spot on a weekly variety show called *Hoot and Holler*, which won them a contract with Capitol. If they were recording today, it would be in the Capitol Building, an eyesore that looked like a dozen dinner plates stacked upside down, a block up the hill from Hollywood and Vine. He parked curbside across Vine and fed the meter. If he'd been looking for Melanie, he might've gone to the Capitol front desk and asked for admission to the studio. But he was looking for Alvaro, who could be loitering anywhere in the neighborhood, waiting for her session to finish, or running errands, coming and going to fetch the group's cough drops and sodas.

So he sat in his wagon and thought about Melanie. Maybe the Sinclair woman was right and Melanie had turned her problems over to liquor, like her mother. And like her father, from what Tom had heard about the man. Tom supposed Melanie could've been nipping at her mama's sauce since she was a baby, and caught the habit that way. But he still couldn't feature Melanie as a drunk. Of all the drunks he'd known, which were plenty, none had been so guarded or self-controlled as Melanie. As a sometime jazz musician, Tom had known more than his share of guys and girls who reminded him of Melanie. Gifted introverts. The kind most likely to become junkies.

His Timex read 11:15, and he was thinking about a sandwich, when he spotted a dark-haired, wiry fellow on a bus stop bench down the hill past Hollywood. He crushed the fire in his pipe with a golf tee he kept for that purpose, and left the pipe in the ashtray. He jumped out of the car. While he walked, he watched his son cross Vine and go a few steps east then stop and stand still looking down at the sidewalk. He stood there the whole time Tom waited for the light at Hollywood Boulevard to change, and while he crossed the street.

When Tom reached him, the boy was still gazing down, at the star that commemorated Mary Pickford, Tom saw. She was an actress his mother had done seamstress work for and about whom he'd told his boys a few stories.

He said, "She was one of the good ones."

Alvaro looked up, with a weary and mirthless smile. "Let's see. I'm on TV last night, you find me this morning. About twelve hours. Not bad."

Tom hung his arm across the boy's shoulders. "You didn't tell us where you were going because . . . ?"

"See, at first, when Mel called, I figured I'd just come up for the day. Then, you know."

"Nope," Tom said. "I sure don't."

Alvaro pointed across the Boulevard. "Here they come."

A gang of young folks had poured out of the Capitol Building. All but two of them walked down Vine, and as they came closer Tom recognized the bunch he had watched every Thursday for the six or eight weeks since they landed the TV spot. They looked wholesome, fresh, unlike most folk singers. Tom had no passion for blazing banjos, the strums of relentless guitars, or for any kind of foot-stomping number except those of gospel choirs. But Melanie's every song threatened to break his heart. Last week she soloed on "Barbara Allen," a ballad about a dear girl who dies from shame and lost love. For the first time in maybe thirty years, a tear had dribbled out from the corner of his eye.

With some hugs, backslaps and victory waves, the group dispersed in three directions. Paul Case and Melanie stepped into the crosswalk at Hollywood and Vine at the same time a guy in jeans and an L.A. Angels ball cap ambled up behind Paul Case. Tom didn't see him pull the gun.

They were halfway across Vine. A second after what could sound to the untrained like a distant backfire, Case lurched forward and staggered head-first toward the curb in front of the Taft Building. He touched down a few yards from Tom, his head ramming straight into the ridge of the curb.

Tom should've kept his eye on the shooter. But he didn't. He couldn't pull his eyes off Melanie, who had stopped cold in the middle of Vine and stood long enough for Alvaro to dash to her. Then she collapsed into Alvaro's arms.

Wedged between Tom and son in the front seat of the Chevy, Melanie quaked. Her wavy, honey brown hair rippled. Her sobs were like gasps so deep they choked her and made her gasp again for air. They turned her pale cheeks to red.

"Not as wild as that time in eighth grade," Alvaro said.

"Is she using?"

Alvaro turned away, toward the hills. For a minute, he kept her secret. "Yeah, but not like you think, not off the street. Pills, capsules actually. Sometimes, like before a show, when she needs a real jolt to stay cool, she pours it out of the capsule and snorts it."

"Morphine?"

"I guess. Melanie doesn't even know. They just give it to her."

"Who's they?"

"Whoever's on duty at this place we're going to."

As they turned onto Primrose, a half mile up from Cahuenga, Alvaro said, "Dad, who do you think shot that Case?"

"A pro, for sure. One shot, with a silencer, then disappears."

"I wonder why."

"The music business is dirty," Tom said.

Alvaro nodded and started petting Melanie's hair. "So's the dope business."

The clinic was a '30s mansion Tom remembered well, as the playhouse of Eleanor Boone, a silent-movie vamp. Her favorite seamstress was Tom's mother, who would come home from fittings and rave at Tom and his sister about all the boozing and fornication that went on at Eleanor's house.

Melanie took a few steps on her own while Tom and Alvaro lifted and bolstered her between them, taking her into the clinic. She felt bone-thin and seemed to weigh almost nothing.

Whoever owned the clinic must be an Eleanor Boone fan, Tom thought. The house was a ringer for the one in his memory. With it's murals of mythical goat-men chasing plump wood nymphs, the decor seemed more likely to drive patients mad than help heal them.

On the wall behind the ebony desk hung a layout of at least a dozen photos in gilded frames. Each of them featured a famous actor, actress, politician, or athlete standing or sitting beside the same fellow, a guy who made Orson Welles look gentle and trim.

A girl in a short-skirt nurse outfit came around from behind the desk. Her name tag read "Lilly". She had skinny legs and smeared crimson lipstick. She rushed to open a door, which the men helped Melanie through, into a room of burgundy leather couches and a single well-padded executive's chair. When they seated her on one of the couches, she quit sobbing long enough to gaze around. And she gave Tom a look he believed meant "Save me."

So he kissed her cheek and said to Alvaro, "Call your brother. If I don't get back here by, say, suppertime, we'll use him to relay messages."

"You don't need my help, Pop?"

"Not like Melanie does. But, yeah." He looked to make sure the girl in the nurse outfit had left. "Snoop around. Find out all you can about this place."

Alvaro nodded. "Pop, Mel's no junkie. It's just, she hadn't sung ever since eighth grade. And Paul Case, he knew the key, he had the stuff. Mel still thinks he set her free."

Tom reached out and squeezed his son's shoulder then let go and started to leave. But he stopped and turned back. "Mel called you every week or so. What made you come up this time?"

"She was crying, and spooked. Paul Case was acting scary, she said. Like Brett, remember him? The guy her mom stabbed. And he'd snatched a bottle of her pills, she told me when I got up here. But a couple days later, before she ran out of her stuff, he gave her two bottles. And he didn't look scary to me."

In the lobby, Tom leaned on the nurse's big desk.

"She'll be just fine," Lilly said.

"Who's the boss here?" Tom asked. "That guy all over the wall?" He pointed to the layout of photos.

"Doctor Worth. He owns the building and everything," she said, sounding impressed as if her employer owned California.

"I need to talk to Doctor Worth. Soon."

She reached for an appointment ledger and found the right page. "Perhaps Friday at four p.m. will work for you."

"Perhaps not. Where is he now?"

"He's in Las Vegas," she said, as if that chintzy town were Paris.

"That'll do," he said. "Which hotel?"

* * * * * *

Tom only left Melanie in that place because the very sight of it had calmed her, and now wasn't the time for her to kick any habits.

He found a payphone outside a newsstand on Cahuenga. Twenty-five years after he left the LAPD, not many of his pals were still cops. But a switchboard operator helped by reading names off her roster. She connected him to Pete Battaglia. He only remembered Pete as a rookie. Now he ran a team in homicide.

The Paul Case murder had gone elsewhere, but Pete had heard talk about it.

"Who's got it?" Tom asked.

"Let's see. That'd be Gonzo. Gonzales to you."

"Say, Pete, what do you know about one Doctor Worth, psychiatrist, has a clinic on Primrose?"

"Just he's been known to produce a few movies, or so say the gossips."

"Movies, huh?"

"Nothing that's going to win him an Oscar," Battaglia said. "The kind you don't want to send your kids to. Why? Paul Case into the doctor for something?"

"You tell me."

"I got my own challenges, Tom. Talk to Gonzo."

*　*　*　*　*　*

It was Tom's first trip to the City Hall, new since his L.A. years, that towered above its surroundings like some gothic cathedral in the plaza of a humble village.

He located Gonzales on the third floor, in a long, narrow room crammed with matching gray desks. To the rookie who stood up and greeted him, Tom said, "Tell Lieutenant Gonzales I can describe the Paul Case murderer, would you?"

The rookie fetched his lieutenant from an office sectioned out of the back corner of the room. Gonzales was young for a lieutenant and either a fighter or not much of one, judging from his flat, bent nose.

Tom spent a minute describing the scene and the shooter. Gonzales set his note pad on the nearest desk and folded his arms. "How old are you?"

"Old enough."

"Well, in all that time nobody told you to stick around a crime scene, talk to the officers, tell them what you saw?"

"What do you think?" Tom asked. "Music or dope?"

"Dope, you say?"

"Just a thought."

Gonzales unfolded his arms. "Dig a little." He rolled his hand. "Just where did that thought come from?"

Tom shrugged. "Say I stumble across a dope pusher with M.D. after his name, who do I deliver him to?"

"How about you give me the name and we do the stumbling?"

"There's an idea," Tom said, as he turned toward the elevator.

\* \* \* \* \* \*

Tom preferred to drive fast especially when he was mad or more fed up with the world than usual. His favorite drive was the road to Las Vegas, the part beyond the state line. In Nevada, the only speed law was, don't crash into anything. His station wagon hadn't the muscle or weight of the Cadillac he'd long threatened to buy, but it ran the big motor, a 350-cubic-inch V-8. The tires were new, the front end steady.

He got stalled by an overturned semi in Pomona. He rolled up the windows and smoked his pipe all through the San Bernardino Valley, preferring to gag on smog of his own making. Once on the open highway, he only managed to drive within ten m.p.h. of the speed limit by telling himself he'd make up for the aggravation once he reached Nevada. He pulled through the Bun Boy in Barstow for a couple of hamburgers with plenty of soggy bread and bit-sized patties of meat he didn't want much of anyway.

He crossed the state line at 4:10 p.m., did the fifty miles left into Vegas, and checked into the Desert Inn, all before 5:00.

\* \* \* \* \* \*

He found Dr. Worth beside the pool, greased and brown and lying on his back. His fingers tapped like a frantic pianist's on his medicine ball belly.

Tom sat across the pool, ordered a Dewar's from the leggy bar runner. He tipped her big and got an inviting smile.

Dr. Worth couldn't lie still. Every minute or so, he hoisted his bulk up with his elbows and looked both ways and as far around back as his beefy neck would allow. The temp had to be a hundred plus even after six p.m. And fat guys could sweat plenty. Even so, the sweat pouring off him looked excessive. The drinks he bought were tall and icy and looked like Tom Collinses. They gave him something else besides his belly to drum his fingers on.

Tom knew from the photos in the clinic that Worth could look imposing, tough as a gorilla, in the right outfit. But neither his swim suit nor his fright flattered him. Today he looked half as menacing as Pooh Bear.

The last wedge of sun dipped behind the far mountains. Worth picked up his towel and yellow-and-orange Hawaiian shirt and padded on small feet with legs half the length of the bar runner's, to the sliding door of a room that opened onto the lawn that bordered the pool deck.

Tom counted the rooms from the end of the wing to the one Worth had gone into. He strolled to the end of the wing, entered the interior corridor, and walked the length of it, counting doors until he reached the doctor's.

From a comfortable chair in the lobby, he kept an eye on the door to Suite 118. When a bellhop passed, he requested a phone, and tipped the bellhop well. The fellow whispered, "You don't know who to call, I could give you some numbers."

Tom shook his head and called home. When Clifford answered, Tom apologized for taking so long to check in.

Clifford said, "Alvaro's called four times already."

"Is Melanie okay?"

"She still isn't talking, but she's not shaking so bad. He said to tell you he's monitoring the dosage. When did he get to be a medic?"

"I'd rather not ask."

"Yeah, and he said to tell you some nurse called Lilly flipped out when he told her about Paul Case getting shot. She was blubbering when Alvaro called me one time and still blubbering the next time he called. She told him Case was her first boyfriend, and they made some movie together.

"Pop, Alvaro's as worried about you as he is about Melanie. He says you're chasing a murderer."

"Tom said, I leave murderers to the police these days."

"Where are you, anyway?"

"Vegas. The Desert Inn. My room's 167, but I'm in the lobby now."

"Why'd you go there?"

"If your mama asks, just tell her I'm fine and due home tomorrow, maybe by afternoon. Clifford, you and Alvaro will need to share a bedroom for a while. Make your room or Alvaro's up for Melanie, would you?"

"No, how about I let her sleep in with me. I mean, I'll sleep on the floor, promise."

"I guess a son like you is what I get for being a smart guy."

"Hey, Pop . . . Don't get shot or anything. Okay?"

"I'll see you tomorrow."

* * * * * *

A room service cart that passed by Tom and made him salivate with its broiled steak smell continued on to room 118. When the cart was on its way back, he stopped the waiter and asked for a steak sandwich and a Dewar's.

"To what room, sir?" the waiter asked.

"Just bring it back here, I'll take it out by the pool."

When the meal came, he ate it in the lobby and stepped outside for a smoke in a place where he could watch room 118 through the glass doors. Then Worth lumbered out of his room.

He wore white slacks and a red and blue Hawaiian shirt. His moist face glistened. Tom backed around a corner, suspecting the doctor would come out past him-on-his way to the parking lot. When he didn't, Tom went back to the lobby and saw the man half-way down the wing that led to the casino.

Worth lumbered straight to a cashier's window, where he scribbled on a house check or an I.O.U. He carried his new stack of chips to the closest roulette table. Minimum bet $10.

Tom wasn't much of a gambler, but he'd spent a couple of years as chief of security at Harry's Casino in South Lake Tahoe, so he knew losing bets when he saw them. Every spin, the doctor would lay a stack on a single number and make a play of covering the long-shot with another stack on black or red. He kept repeating the bet on different numbers and different colors, and hardly paid attention to the ball or where it landed.

When his chips ran out, he returned to the cashier, all the time shooting glances right and left and over his shoulders.

He lost another stack of chips on baccarat, came back to the cashier for more, then settled at a blackjack table, $20 minimum, across an aisle from the table where Tom sat watching and playing one-dollar bets. For a while, luck overthrew the doctor's carelessness, and he gathered a mountain of chips. But he either didn't notice or care when a mechanic with giant paws and sunglasses came in as relief, though anybody half wise to casinos would know he was there to sneak looks at the second card, deal whichever of the two suited him, and break the winner's spell. Four players knew, and left the doctor and a diamond-studded older woman to get robbed.

Shortly after midnight, the doctor's chips ran out once again. He started back toward the cashier, shooting glances everywhere, but veered off and stumbled toward a dark place with tables and food servers who doubled as keno runners. When one of them tapped the doctor on his shoulder and he leaped a yard off his chair, Hickey decided he'd seen enough.

As he neared, the doctor's small white hands shot up and clutched the edge of the table. Hickey nodded and sat down. "What's up, Doc?"

Worth's cheeks became balloons. "Huh," he said, as all the breath he'd held spewed out.

To get the doctor's reaction, Tom said, "I mean, is Paul Case the first guy you've had killed?"

The doctor let out a frail squeal and started to rise. But when Hickey touched his side where a gun might've been if he'd worn one, the man sank back into his chair and began to quiver. "I don't know anything about—"

"Shh. Let's take it out by the pool."

While they walked down the wing toward the lobby, with Tom steadying him the way he would help a drunk, the doctor asked three times, "What are we doing?"

Tom didn't answer. He was thinking how he'd changed over a lifetime. Once, the thought of what he meant to do now would've horrified his sense of justice. In the old days, he'd thought the world needed guys like him, to hold it together. He didn't know what the world needed anymore, so he didn't go looking to fix it. He didn't look much further than his family.

Melanie was family.

The doctor said, "You're not a cop, are you?"

Tom didn't bother to answer. Worth didn't seem to notice or care that urine dribbled out of his pant leg and onto the floor while Tom led him through the hotel lobby and out to the pool deck, and parked him on a lounge chair poolside. On the far deck, a couple smooched between giggles and coos.

"Did Paul send you to kill me?" the doctor whimpered.

"Never mind that," Tom said. "I might not kill you if you'll do me a little favor."

The relief on the fat man's face made Tom want to kick him into the pool, dive in behind, and drown him.

"A favor?"

"We take a ride," Tom said. "We go to L.A., you talk to Lieutenant Gonzales, tell him how you prescribed a little girl who never had a physical pain in her life all the morphine she could swallow. That's it. You find a new occupation. I go away. Deal?"

The doctor had fallen to panting so hard, Hickey needed to slap him. Which he enjoyed.

"How about it?" Tom said.

"Yeah, sure," the doctor stammered. "Sure, it's a deal."

\* \* \* \* \*

Standing beside his Chevy, Tom said, "You're not getting into my wagon soaked in piss." He pointed to the doctor's white trousers. "Take those off."

Worth unzipped, unsnapped, and let them fall then stepped out of them, all the while watching Tom's hands.

"Those, too." Tom pointed at the man's silk boxer shorts.

The doctor's mouth opened but snapped shut as he glanced up at Tom's face. He peeled the shorts down and stepped out of them, already trying to cover his privates with his small hands.

Tom opened the trunk, grabbed a blanket and threw it at Worth. "Get in back."

The doctor left his clothes on the asphalt and climbed in. Tom slid behind the wheel, then reached over and opened the glove box. The pistol he pulled out he showed to the doctor before laying it on his lap.

The old Chevy wagon behaved like a family car until they left the strip for the highway and passed the city limits. Then it roared into the desert.

After a few miles, Worth yelled over the hot wind through the open front windows "Paul Case was going to kill me"

Tom rolled up the windows. Let me guess. You saved Case from going to the streets for his fix. He paid you by playing the stud in a movie or two. When he struck it rich, you offered to sell him the prints. Fair enough. But he disagreed and threatened you."

The doctor's silence backed up Tom's speculation.

After a long minute Worth mumbled, "Who told you those lies?"

"Hush," Tom said. He switched hands on the wheel, grabbed the .38 off his lap, threw his arm around and aimed the pistol at Worth's head. "Sit still and keep quiet, Doc. Let me forget you're still alive."

\* \* \* \* \* \*

The speedometer bounced between 110 and 120. Feeling a slight pull to the left, Tom wondered if he needed a wheel alignment. And he wondered how much this exploiter of the troubled and the too-sweet-to-survive-in-a-crass-and-violent-world could handle. How much fright would it take before the fat man's heart caved in?

Worth had lifted the blanket to shield his sweaty face from the wind. A truck blasted by going east. A little squeal issued from his mouth.

They were almost to the state line when he peeped, "Could we please slow down?"

Tom jammed the accelerator so hard he thought he might've dented the floorboard.

*All Christine Matthews has ever wanted to do was write short stories. She'd like to make her living that way. Alas, there are few who can. She's written three novels in the "Gil & Claire Hunt" series, but her short story production far outweighs her book production. The short form is sacred to her; she chooses every word carefully. And she likes to try new things. Here is a new voice for her, straight from the streets of Hollywood.*

# And Then She Was Gone

*by Christine Matthews*

High-risk lifestyle, my ass. I supposed she thinks them dudes over to the firehouse are high-risk, too? They out there 'cause they bein' paid to be out there. They gets to wear them uniforms, all clean an' nice, a fancy place to live for a few days a week. They don't live in them houses every day, ya know? And the food. You ever been 'roun' one of them station houses when it's dinner time?"

"No, and I know you ain't, neither," Rita shot back.

Victor acted like he hadn't heard her, but she knew it was only an act.

"Well, it's like Christmas every damn day. But you think they eat leftovers after they get back from a fire? No way, they just cook them up some more."

Rita leaned back in the front seat, fishing around in her purse for the lipstick she'd bought last Saturday, waiting for Victor to finish griping. He was always carrying on about how much everyone in the world had except for him.

"An' po-lice? How can you say that's high-risk when them muthas carry guns, for Chrissake? At least they got a fightin' chance. But miners . . ." He shook his large head back and forth slowly, "Now there's some high-risk for ya. All the trouble them poor suckers havin' down in some hole in some shanty town? Goin' down into hell wearin' raggedy clothes, their lungs all black. Hardly makin' no money at all. Now that's what I consider high-risk."

"Well, every one of them jobs, every single one of them is high-risk, no matter what you think."

Victor jammed his right hand on the horn, yelled out the open window of the limousine, "Yo! Shit for brains. Ya retarded or some thin'?" then continued the conversation. "You're right, Rita, that's my point. We takin' all the risks while every asshole out there looks at your sorry ass thinkin' how dangerous ya got it when that ain't the truth, at all."

Victor and Louie lived in their own macho world, stumbling through days drunk and coked up. Somehow they had convinced themselves that the girls they sold day after day, night after night, were safe because of them. Cared for. Even loved.

"Me and the King, we knows how to work it. First we check out the johns, an' then deliver you real classy, first class in a lim-o-zeen. We always pick ya'll up later, don't we? Have you or any of my other ladies had to wait in the cold? Or the rain? No street corners, no alleys for my girls. Clean sheets, clean business, that's how I does things."

"She musta been talkin' 'bout them girls, the ones on the corners with their tits hangin' out, those girls that ain't lucky like me an' Tanya or Contrelle," Rita lied.

"Yeah, maybe."

Victor stared straight ahead and Rita looked at his profile against the tainted glass. No hat for this limo driver, he wasn't anyone's servant. Victor had what the girls all called the three B's. He was bi, black, and bald. Handsome, vain about how he looked. A large diamond stud glistened in his earlobe. It was the first thing Victor had bought himself with the first dollar he'd earned pimpin'. Only Victor didn't never call it pimpin', he considered himself a "businessman." His girls were his "staff," and the johns, they were "clients." His motto: "If ya thinks proud an' walks proud, you is proud," would have been engraved on a plaque, hanging on his office wall . . . if he had an office.

"So where are you s'posed to meet her?"

Rita put her lipstick back. "Look, I don't hafta go—"

"Oh yes, you do. I tol' you it's good PR."

"For Chrissake, PR for what? We're fuckin' breakin' the law here. We're doin' shit here that makes me an' you, both of us, lowlifes."

"Lowlifes is somethin' you're puttin' on yourself there. Now, you're gonna meet her at her hotel an' do that interview."

Rita glared out the window, wondering how the hell all the decisions she'd made in her life had led her here? Sittin' next to this jackass, ridin' in this stinkin' limousine, livin' an' workin' in fuckin' Hollywood, California? Why was she bein' punished just for bein' a little stupid?

"Did you brush your teeth?"

She turned and gave him a big toothy grin.

"Ya got on that underwear I bought ya?"

"What the hell does that matter?"

"It's respectable. It'll make ya feel like a lady."

That one cracked Rita up. "Lady, my ass."

Victor squealed to a stop for a red light. "An' don't be talkin' trash like that. We want this Miss Whatzername to take notice of Victor's work force."

The light changed and he turned onto Sunset Bloulevard.

"It's just that I hates that bitch. I hates everything about her."

"You don't even know her, baby."

"She comes into the diner the other day swishin' her Louis Vuitton like she owns the place and every damn thing in it. Tanya an' me sit there askin' each other just who the hell does this bitch think she is?"

Victor patted the bag in Rita's lap. "You got your own Vuitton, girl, so what you gripin' about?"

"I seen you, Victor. Me an' Giselle watched you sneakin' out of that Chink girl's apartment, buyin' this here knockoff. Who the hell you think you're foolin'?"

If he hadn't been driving he would have hauled off and smacked her. But instead, Victor just gritted his teeth. "No one knows the difference."

"I do. Giselle do. Even that stupid bitch Connie do."

"That Daisy Mae from buttfuck Nebraska? I'll have to teach that hillbilly somethin' about respect."

Shit. Now Victor was mad and Rita's big mouth would probably be the cause of Connie getting knocked around. The poor kid couldn't help being so ignorant. Rita never told anyone how much she liked the girl . . . especially Victor. She was smart enough not to let him know she had feelings for anyone or anything. And now she was even smarter, sitting back and letting his anger run its course.

He pounded the steering wheel several times, hollered about how ungrateful every single one of his whores were, until Rita couldn't stand it anymore. "Look, you want me to do this interview thing? So, tell me what to say."

That got him going. There wasn't anything Victor loved more than talkin'. Talkin' *at* her, talkin' *to* her, repeatin' every word, turning them over and inside out, sure she'd die without his expertise on everything in the whole frickin' world. That and money. Victor loved to hear himself talk and he loved money. The only thing Rita wasn't sure of was which he loved more.

* * * * * *

Liz Petkus didn't think Rita would show. As she sipped her water she wondered if the coffee shop was too casual. She'd rethought her choice of meeting places for days. The first place she'd considered was far too formal, too intimidating. The second place, too dirty. The last thing she wanted was for the hooker to think she was treating her with contempt. Even choosing her clothes had seemed difficult. After three changes she finally settled on jeans and a blue pullover sweater. A watch was the only jewelry she wore but it was the Rolex her father had given her when she'd graduated from film school. And now here she sat, so very proud of herself, making notes for her first documentary.

She checked the clock on the wall, behind the counter. If Rita didn't show up she would order lunch without her. She was starving.

"Are you sure I can't get you anything?" the waitress asked for the second time in ten minutes. "How about some iced tea, at least? A cocktail? Maybe some soup to start off with?"

The soup sounded good and Liz was just about to give in when she saw Rita walk through the door.

"My friend just arrived. Give us a few minutes."

The waitress was one of those too-much women. Too much bleach on her too-short hair. Too much shiny lips gloss making her lips look way too big. Too much perfume, too much cleavage, and way too much glitter on her claw-like fingernails. When she turned to look over her shoulder and saw Rita strutting toward the table, she asked Liz, "That's your friend?"

"Yes, you know her?"

"I don't associate with her kind."

"Well, it's a good thing then that I'm only asking you to bring us some lunch and not be our friend, isn't it?"

Rita smiled as the waitress huffed off. Sliding across the black plastic seat on her side of the booth, she wiggled out of her jacket. "Tiffany givin' ya trouble? 'cause if she is, I'll tell Victor an' he'll—"

"No, it's okay."

"If that old queen been insultin' ya, Victor'll have to have a little talk with her, know what I'm sayin'?"

"Queen? That wasn't a woman?"

Rita laughed. "Nuthin's what you think it is in movieland. This here is Oz, Dorothy, an' that bitch is the Wicked Witch."

Liz hated feeling naive. It shifted power to Rita, and she had to stay in control if the project was to get done.

Liz leafed through notes scribbled on a yellow legal pad.

Rita sat across from her, calm, hands folded on top of the table.

Liz glanced up. "Are you hungry? Should we talk now or while we eat, or after . . ."

"It don't matter to me. But I gotta be out front at two. Sharp. Victor's drivin' me to a date at LAX, some dude has a two-hour layover an' wants to spend it with me." Rita smiled proudly.

"Okay, that gives us almost two hours."

"For what, exactly? When you made this date . . . an' it is a date . . ."

"Don't worry. I'm going to pay you for your time," Liz assured her.

"Good." Rita held out her right hand. "Two hours, two hundred."

"Now? Before we talk?" Liz asked.

"Get business outta the way first. That's how it's done."

Liz pulled out her checkbook.

"Cash," Rita said. "How dumb are you, anyway?"

Liz counted out two hundred dollars, leaving her with only thirty in her wallet.

After counting the bills again, Rita stuffed the money down inside her cowboy boot. Then she straightened up, folded her hands, and asked, "So, what you need?"

Tiffany came back and threw down two menus. After they ordered, Liz started right in. "I'm making a documentary about working girls, such as yourself. I want to find out how you got hooked up with Victor, why you . . . need him. What makes you—"

Rita played with a small pearl button on the cuff of her blouse, listening until she couldn't take anymore. "That the best you can do, girl? You tellin' me you takin' up my time askin' the same tired-ass, bullshit questions everyone been askin'?"

"I know there've been documentaries abourt prostitution . . ."

"Bet your sorry little self they done hundreds an' thousands of 'em. All the time showin' some bitch with her eye swelled up, dirty alleys, cars bouncin', parked on some street while they tape gruntin' and groanin'. An' every time, they say, 'never-before-seen footage, shocking, the untold story.' " For the last part Rita sounded as good as Barbara Walters ever had. "I seen 'em, you seen 'em. Everybody who's got a TV set seen 'em. They be on the news, HBO, Showtime, all over every channel. So why does a girl like you from the middle of nowhere—"

"Lincoln, Nebraska. Then on to Iowa City where I studied film. I graduated at the top of my class, with honors, I am working on a grant, now. I think I know what I'm doing just a little bit better than some—"

"Hooker? Whore? Will it make you feel smarter to think I'm not as good as you? I can be anyone you wants me to be. You wants a druggie? I'll shake all over, scream for a fix. You wants me to tell you I come from a home where my Daddy raped me? Beat me? I'll gets me some scars to show you. I can be anybody you wants. But you. Look at you." Rita sniffed like she'd just smelled a pile of shit. "Just startin' out, tryin' to make a name for yourself. For the life of me, I can't figure out why you don't wanna do somethin' better. Why you wanna waste your time an' film on the same ol' crap?"

Liz didn't get angry. How could she? The woman sitting across from her had just said everything she'd been thinking for months. But she'd kept it to herself. Her first important project and it had come too easy. Late at night, when she sat up, doubled over with doubts, a thought had started taunting her, asking her if maybe her father had pulled some strings? Her idea wasn't original. She knew it then and she knew it for sure now.

"Okay, let's suppose someone dropped a camera in your lap. What would you make a film about?" she asked Rita.

Their burgers arrived and Rita took a big bite. After a few moments of chewing and thinking, she said, "The men. I'd tell the truth about them."

"You mean pimps? It's been done."

Rita nodded. "They likes to think of theyselves as royalty, you know?"

"I've seen films about the Pimp Ball. That big party they have, all of them arriving in limos, dressed in the ugliest suits, girls catering to them, fussing over them like they're movie stars."

"An' why you think that is?"

Liz shrugged. "I don't know. I've always wondered why anyone needs them for anything."

"It's the fear. They have the fear."

"Fear of what?" Liz asked.

"Bein' nobody. They knows they can't make it without us girls an' that scares 'em. Scares 'em big time. Then they pass the fear down to us. All the time sayin' how worthless we is, how we'd be nowhere without 'em."

Liz wiped ketchup from the corner of her mouth. "Work with me, Rita," she said. "Help me. Instead of interviewing you, I'll use you behind the scenes. I'll pay you a salary, you can be my production assistant."

"Uh-oh, here come the fear again," Rita said.

"What do you mean?"

"I'm afraid you couldn't pay me enough to make it worth my while. An' Victor would never let me do anything like that. Are you crazy? He'd kill us both."

Liz tried to understand how one minute this woman could seem so educated, so self-assured, and in a heartbeat collapse into helplessness.

"You think Victor would kill someone? For real?"

"I ain't sayin'; I just knows better than to cross Victor." Rita picked up her burger and continued eating.

*  *  *  *  *  *

When Victor came to get her, King Louie was sitting in the back seat of the big black limo. The gaunt, pale pimp thought of himself as a full-time rock star and a part-time "businessman." He had a cell phone in one hand and a glass of champagne in the other. When she got into the front seat, Rita ignored their passenger.

"So, what happened? You didn't tell that bitch too much, did ya?" Victor asked.

"What kind of a fool you take me for?" Rita worked up an innocent look.

"I'm just lookin' out for you . . . an' all my staff. A man can't be too careful in this line of work."

"I know," Rita assured him, "I know you is."

King Louie snapped his phone shut. "I don't like this. Not one single, tiny bit."

"Shut up, you hillbilly," Victor shouted. "We needs to show our respectability. Rita show up there all classed up, no boobage hangin' out. She look like a model. Better than any those bitches in them magazines. Good enough to be in the movies. No damaged merchandise here, just prime cut—Grade A. Did you tell that woman you went to college? Do she know that? You tell her no one makin' you do nuthin' you don't wanna do? You what they calls a free agent. I just actin' as your manager, so to speak."

"I told her," Rita lied.

"Good."

King Louie pushed himself forward, stuck his face closer to the back of Rita's head. "We gonna be in her movie, then? All of us?"

"Maybe. She still got a lot of interviewin' to do."

"You sure she's gonna make us look good?" Louie asked. "Not like some derelicts in them cheap-ass pornos. Make us look respectable. High-class?"

Rita stared straight ahead. "Sure."

\* \* \* \* \*

"Say you love me," the john demanded as Rita spanked his fat ass.

"I loves ya, baby. I loves ya soooo much it makes me wanna hurt ya good an' hard."

"I still don't believe you."

Rita picked up the magazine spread out on the night stand. He wants Halle Berry, she thought, he gonna get her. Rolling the magazine tight, she smacked his butt until he screamed. "Does ya believe me now, sweetheart? Can ya feel the love?"

She waited for an answer but he was too busy jerking off. It was times like these that she felt so totally in charge of her life. Better than any big-shot CEO. Just this dip-shit an' her in one of the best rooms in the Beverly Hills Hotel. Five hundred dollars stuffed deep in her bag. Thirty minutes of workin' off the anger. That same anger those Botox wives carried with 'em to their fancy psychiatrists. It don't get much better, she thought.

Lifting herself off the bed, she stood in front of her date, letting him take in her nudity. "Are we done or do ya wanna fuck me?"

As he lay there, she could see where the sprayed-on tan had dripped down his left thigh. "No, baby, we're done. That was great. I'll call Victor next time I'm in the neighborhood.

"You do that."

She slowly walked across the room to the glorious bathroom. After emptying a bottle of bath salts into the tub she lowered herself into the hot water and settled in for a leisurely soak.

Winter in Hollywood. Plastic Christmas trees, plastic snow, plastic credit cards makin' everybody nice an' happy.

It was always about the money. She mentally calculated. The money she'd taken from that Petkus chick topped off her private account at fifty grand. Victim, my ass, she laughed. Victor an' his idiot friend might scare the other girls but Rita was different. Rita had a plan and stayed focused. Rita was goin' to Paris. Get herself a little place, buy some new paints, study real hard. They liked black girls over there. Color didn't matter in Gay Paree.

She looked out the window at the lush surroundings. Everything seemed to be washed with gold today. The jasmine-scented room made her feel as though she were on an island planted in the middle of a sea bluer than blue. No need to rush. The dirtbag in the other room had an appointment and the room was hers for the rest of the day . . . or until Victor called.

She was thinking how she needed a pedicure when her cell phone rang. Then a knock.

"Should I answer it?" he asked from the other side of the door.

"Would you be sweet an' bring it in to me?"

Half dressed, he skittered across the tiled floor with the phone held at arm's length like it was a snake. "Cool ring tone. Prince rules."

What a dipwad, she thought. "Thanks."

He stood there for a moment, waiting for her to flip the phone open. Before speaking she dismissed him, watching him practically skip out of the room.

"Hello, Victor."

"I'm comin' for ya. Be out front in five."

She laughed. "Hell, I'm not even dressed here. You're gonna hafta give me—"

"Get your bony ass downstairs or I'll give ya up ta the cops. Does ya want that? Does ya wanna end up in fuckin' prison?"

"Is this another one of your lame jokes?"

"Listen up. That white girl? The one makin' the movie?"

"What about her?"

"She got herself killed, stupid bitch."

"What that gotta do with me?"

"They found her in your crib, spread out on your bed. Dressed in your Gucci."

"Goddamn."

* * * * * *

"Why'd ya'll go an' tell that cunt anything? Anything at all?" King Louie whined. "She was our ticket, man. Our free pass."

"What the hell you talkin' 'bout?"

"The cops have her for the crime, let her put in the damn time. How dumb are ya, man?" Louie reached up to rap his partner on his shiny skull.

Victor grabbed the man's wrist, nearly snapping it in two. "How many times I gotta tell ya? Never touch me. Never!"

"All's I'm sayin' is we don't owe that bitch nuthin'. Not one fuckin' thing."

"She's one of my girls an' I takes care of my girls. That's what Victor do. Besides, she innocent. You knows that as well as I do."

"Who the fuck cares?" Louie smiled, wiping at his nose. The doper was always wet somewhere. "She takes the heat off us, keeps the cops off our ass."

"How do you figure?"

"What the hell do ya mean, how do I figure? What's wrong with you, man?"

"Rita knows lots of stuff that could get both of us locked up for a long time. Stuff worser that some murder. Stuff that gets ya killed in the joint."

Louie squinted up at his partner, "Murder's the worse. Dude, ain't nuthin' worse than that."

"Ya think?"

* * * * * *

Rita was waiting in front of the hotel when Victor pulled up. Her hair, limp on her head, damp; she held a pair of gold metallic stilettos in her right hand. In her left she swung the tote bag containing her bra and panties as well as the usual. When she saw the limo pull up she ran, beating the doorman to open a back door.

Trying to be calm, Victor waved. "Fuck."

"What?" Rita asked from the back seat. "What now?"

"That's Freddie. You know, Four-Way Freddie?"

"From Glendale?" Louie asked. "So what?"

"So he seen Rita, all undone. An' he gonna remember, 'specially when he looks at TV, sees the news. Make him put two an' two together, know what I'm sayin'?"

"I ain't done nuthin', Victor. Ya believe me, dontcha?" Rita asked, trying to hold it together.

"'Course I do, baby."

"So where we goin', then?"

Louie looked up, suddenly aware he was in a moving car. "Yeah, man, where we goin'?"

"We gotta stash Rita someplace safe."

"But Victor . . . I —"

"Shut up, girl, I knows what's best. Just trust me."

Now he'd gone and done it. Asked for the one thing she'd used up long ago. The one thing she didn't have to give. Not to him—not to anyone. Trust.

He braked for a red light and that's when she jerked open the back door.

Louie opened his door, unsure of what to do.

As Rita cut through a parking lot she could hear Victor shouting for her to come back.

* * * * * *

The good thing was, Rita didn't have any friends. She hung out with Victor's girls, but they didn't count. And she liked it that way. No family, no friends. No one cryin' or bitchin'. No guilt, no waitin' 'roun for some half-assed promises to be kept that tender lovin' relatives or best friends passed out like they was free samples down at the grocery. She considered herself smart and lucky. Most the time. But now . . . well . . . she wasn't feelin' neither. There was no one to trust. Nowhere to go. No one to help her out. An' that sucked royally.

Her hair had dried and now stood out all kinky. Ducking into a gas station bathroom, she washed her face, pulled off her skirt, took a pair of shorts out of her bag and yanked them on. She'd left her shoes in the limo but always kept a pair of Nikes with her. Bending, she hastily tied the laces. Without makeup she could pass for someone at least five years younger than her twenty-four years.

Now what?"

She stood there, listening to voices outside, traffic, stood there just wondering. Then a knock at the door.

"Are you almost done? My kid's gotta go."

She'd have to leave sometime. Might as well be now.

A cab rolled by and she waved for it to stop. The driver, a burned-out hippie type, smiled. When she got in, he turned down the music coming from some Moldy Oldie station. "Where to?"

She had no idea.

He patiently waited for her to say something but after a full minute he asked, "Just get into town?"

What was wrong with her? Lying was her business. If they gave out trophies she'd be in the fuckin' Hall of Fame.

A car honked but the driver ignored it, still waiting. "I bet you're an actress," he finally said. "We get busloads of 'em every day. Come to La-La Land to get a million-dollar contract. Right?"

"No."

"Then you gotta be a tourist. Here to look at all the stars."

"You're good. Damn good." The bullshit kicked in and she smiled. Thank you, Jesus.

"So, what do you wanna see first, then? I can be your guide." He leered at her from the front seat. "Show you what's what, if you know what I mean."

She watched him lick his fat, ugly lips and POW! Just like that, she was back in charge. "Sure." This could buy her time till she figured something out. "Maybe I can show you a few things, too." Flash them pearly whites, she told herself, an' keep movin'. Use the dude to hide behind. Douchebag wanna play the big man, let 'im.

He must have heard her stomach growl. "How about some lunch for starters? There's a great place over 'round Hollywood and Vine called Joseph's Café. Greek food. Sound great?"

"Let's do it."

* * * * * *

Rita expected it to be like in one of them black-an'-white movies Victor was watchin' all the time. She really thought when she walked into the restaurant there'd be a newspaper on the counter with them big ol' black headlines. And those headlines would be about that Petkus chick gettin' murdered. And there'd be a TV up over the bar or in a corner. They'd shoot a close-up of an anchorman, lookin' real serious, talkin' 'bout the murder. An' neighbors she might recognize from her building. All sayin' what a surprise it was they didn't hear nuthin', considerin' a woman was bein' murdered.

But it wasn't like that, at all.

"By the way," the cabbie extended his hand, "name's Perry."

"Rita," she said as he held the chair out for her.

Before the waiter could say anything Perry waved him off. "The lady and I will need a few minutes. But while we're decidin', you can bring us a couple of beers."

"Ain't you drivin'?"

"It's okay," he said. Then to the waiter, "Two Buds."

He started tellin her about every fuckin' thing on the menu like he had the damn thing memorized. While she pretended to be listening her eyes kept track of every part of the room. How long did she have? was all she could wonder. How long until Victor or Louie went to the cops to cover their own be-hinds?

Perry was still yappin' when the waiter came back. She just nodded when he asked if it was okay for him to order somethin' foreign.

Then he stood up. "I gotta go wash my hands. This town's a cesspool, know what I mean?"

"Sure do."

He hadn't even cleared the dining area when she heard a rapping on the window near her. Then another, until she was curious enough to walk over to have a look.

"Yo, Rita."

The sun was bouncing off the glass and she couldn't get a really good look.

"Come outside."

A lot of men in Hollywood had long hair but not like his. The Beatle cut was his trademark.

She tried shushing him through the glass, but he kept calling for her to come out. Jumpin' up an' down like a fool idiot. The waiters outnumbered the customers, and those not in the kitchen were real busy ignoring her. So, she grabbed her stuff an' took off. Weird as he was, Rita knew she could trust Crazy John Lennon.

But by the time she hit the sidewalk, he was gone.

"Over here."

Rushing past the large window of the café, Rita ducked behind the bushes where Crazy John was hiding.

"You're in big trouble, Rita."

"No shit. Tell me somethin' I don't know, fool."

"That's why I ran over here soon as I saw you go in there. Don't worry—I'm gonna take you home. To my house. You'll be safe, an' I got something really, really important to show you."

She'd never thought he had a home—well, not a real one. Now she tried picturing him in a regular house with furniture an' shit. Hell, the only time she ever saw him was on Hollywood an' Vine, where he was all the time cleanin' an' polishin' that star they laid down in the sidewalk for John Lennon. She and some of the girls had even started calling him Crazy John Lennon after a while 'cause that's all he ever talked about. A crazy fan but nice enough. Just some poor bastard with nuthin' better to do, who'd never done nuthin' worse than smile at her. Soon she started looking for him when she had a date nearby. She'd even make Victor stop so she could bring him coffee or a taco every now and then, thinking poor ol' Crazy was homeless.

"How far is it?"

"Long Beach."

He had to be kiddin'. "How the hell we suppose to get there? That's all the fuckin' way over there somewhere."

"Don't worry. I have a car."

A car? Who the hell was this maniac? "You got a car? I'm supposed to believe you got a house an' a car? All to yourself?"

Before she had a chance to get an answer he was slinking off toward a parking lot.

What else could she do but follow? Hell, man had wheels an' a place to crash. Best offer she'd had all day.

Then Crazy John Lennon all of a sudden straightened up all proud like an' took a set of keys out of a front pocket of his bell bottoms. Three keys, all attached to a chain with a small guitar made up of letters spelling out the words: IMAGINE. Then he put the biggest one of them keys into the lock of the whitest, sleekest sports car Rita had ever seen.

"Oh man," she whispered, "you gotta be shittin' me."

\*  \*  \*  \*  \*

"Here we are." He pulled into a circular driveway.

"I still don't get it," Rita said. "You live all the way out here? You got beach right outside your back door an' you get in your fine car an' drive all the way to Hollywood for some ol' piece of sidewalk?"

"No, I do it to honor the greatest human being to have lived in my lifetime. I owe him that, at least."

"You don't owe no one nuthin', baby."

Crazy John unlocked the front door and Rita felt like she was in one of them magazines all 'bout style the movie stars have in their houses an' clothes—shit like that.

"Come on, Lovely Rita Meter Maid, I'll give you the tour."

"How many times I tol' you not to call me that?"

"Eight times. You told me eight times."

"So why you still call me that, then?"

"It fits."

The formal living room was painted white. A white piano was the only piece of furniture and it stood in the middle of the room.

"John Lennon once owned this," he told her.

Dumbest thing she'd ever seen. A whole room just for one lousy piano. She was not impressed.

They walked down a long hallway and then he stopped.

"Before I open this door, I have to tell you I've never shown this part of my collection to anyone. Ever. You're the first."

She didn't know how to feel about any of it.

He took out the keychain again and inserted a small gold key into the lock. When he opened the door, Rita couldn't help but be impressed. Even if she didn't know what the hell she was lookin' at.

The room was huge. And like everything she'd seen so far, it was white. Walls, carpet, every shelf, even the two leather chairs. Glass had been mounted in front of every shelf. Dude lived in a fuckin' museum.

"Let me get this right so's I understand what's happenin' here. You drive me all the way out to fuckin' Long Beach to show me all this very important shit while I'm runnin' for my life. My fuckin' life! You get that? Tell me I have this wrong. Tell me you're not standin' there in them raggedy old clothes—"

"Vintage, they're vintage clothes. From the sixties. And they cost a hell of a lot more than any of the knock-offs you wear."

"Well, excuse me all to hell." She shook her head, still not believin' all this crap. "So, you're standin' like an idiot in some vintage clothes, expectin' me to cream my pants because you showin' me a buncha posters an' ol' records? Shit, I wasn't even borned when that Lennon dude got hisself shot. Am I supposed to care? You crazy, man. Really crazy if you think I care 'bout any of this shit."

His hands started to shake. "No, you're crazy," he said. "You're looking at a collection any museum would kill to have. You're standing in a house worth more than two million dollars; that you got to in a car driven by a genius. A brilliant man who would have been kind and loving to you, like I'm trying to be."

He walked over to the other side of the room. Behind a portrait of John Lennon and Paul McCartney was a safe. Crazy John twisted the dial and reached in. After closing it back up he walked over to her and handed her a plastic bag.

"What's this? More of your sixties shit?" She could tell she was pissin, him off and didn't care one bit.

He bit his lip, trying to hold back anger caused by her disrespect. "No, it's a present . . . it's your freedom."

She held the plastic bag up and immediately recognized the Rolex. The one that Petkus bitch had been wearing. It wasn't easy to forget somethin' as big an' expensive as that. No way.

When she started to open the bag he jumped at her. "Don't touch it! It's got prints on it. I bagged it—like they do on *CSI*. You can take it to the police."

Rita didn't like what she was thinkin'. Backing away, she threw the watch to the floor. "You killed her?"

"No, listen, that's not what happened. Why would I kill someone I don't even know? I'm a pacifist . . . like John was . . . like he wanted the world to be. Love, baby. Peace and love." He made that dumb-ass peace sign. It was the first time she realized how small his hands were. How gay he looked.

Bending to pick up the watch, still sealed in the sandwich bag, he took her arm and led her out of the room.

"Where ya takin' me?"

"To the kitchen. I'm thirsty."

\* \* \* \* \* \*

"So you saw Victor? You saw him kill that dumb bitch?"

Crazy John poured her another glass of iced tea. Carefully, up to the top line of the design on the crystal. Then he put a slice of lemon in the glass, carefully, so as not to splash on the white countertop.

"Like I said, I was down, cleaning the star, and I saw Victor and that friend of his—"

"King Louie?"

"Skinny? Sounds like a real shit-kicker."

"Yeah, that's him."

"They were talking real loud. I couldn't help but hear. And then that woman shows up. I didn't recognize her. Figured her for a tourist until I saw her holding up a recorder, asking questions like she was interviewing him."

"Bet Victor ate that up."

"No, he seemed upset. Louie tried calming him down but Victor got angrier, especially when she kept calling him a pimp."

"It was getting dark and they started pushing her. Louie on one side, Victor on the other. I looked down for a minute, one tiny minute . . . and then she was gone. They all were. Victor came back after about five minutes; Louie was running after him, brushing his pants off."

"An' they was nowheres near my apartment?"

"What's your apartment got to do with anything?"

"Victor says they found her in my place. In my fuckin' bed, for Chrissake."

"You must 've heard wrong. After I was sure they were gone I went down the alley. First I spotted her watch by the Dumpster and then I see her foot sticking up. Carefully, I picked up the Rolex, figurin' it would nail those bastards.

"You see the news?"

"Yeah. Why?"

"An' they don't say she was found in my place?"

"Rita, Lovely Rita, where are you getting all this from?"

"So Victor lied. Why he do that?"

"'Cause you're holding' out on him. Something about you cheating him out of money that belonged to him. 'Cause he wants to teach you and the other girls a lesson."

Rita hugged her bag close. It never left her side. It held her life, her fortune, her fifty grand. How the hell had Victor found out?

Crazy John asked if she wanted another glass of tea.

"No. I gots ta figure this out."

"What's to figure? You take the watch to the police, they have Victor's prints on it—"

"How do you know that for sure?"

"I watched them grab her, the way they led her down the street— they have to be there."

"You go, then, you so sure. Why I have to be involved at all? You go, Victor don't know you. You just a witness. A rich, white witness. Everybody believe you."

A phone rang from somewhere in another room. Crazy John held up a finger, cutting her off. "I gotta get that."

After he left, Rita crept behind, listening, trying to figure out who was tellin' the truth an' who the hell was jerkin' her around.

There was an office at the end of a long hallway, carpeted in white shag. That ugly shit oughtta be burned, she thought. As she stood close to the doorway she heard Crazy John yelling something about money an' promises. Rita leaned in closer.

"I delivered—you owe me, man. I'm not takin' no more crap from you, understand? I've carried you long enough. You an' Victor better be nice to me 'cause I got something here that can put both of you away. All I gotta do is make one call to the cops."

Liar. So he did know Louie. Was there one fuckin' man alive who didn't lie?

"That's better. You want the big rush—you pay. Good. I'll bring the stuff by around six."

Drugs. That was the only thing she wasn't into. King Louie was all the time tryin' ta get her high, but she told him to blow the blow out his ass.

Rita didn't move fast enough. The door opened and she stood, frozen. "You dealin', an' you dealin' ta Louie? Is that what's happenin' here?"

"Come on, whose side are you on? I keep you safe—"

"An' just why you be doin' all this for me? Just 'cause you queer for some dead Beatle? Is that it?"

His fist went into her face before he realized what happened. Just a reflex. But when her head banged against the wall, she dropped hard. Blood spattered across the glass of his autographed White album, hanging beneath a single spotlight.

\* \* \* \* \* \*

The sun was shining brightly, making John Lennon's star at Hollywood and Vine almost glow. But then, he was one of God's favorites.

A grubby family of tourists walked over the star, Crazy John swore as they left dirty marks behind. "Have some respect, here!" Bending down, he squirted Windex across the metal and rubbed.

"Calm down." It was a cop. "We've been getting complaints. You harassing the tourists again, John?"

"No, man, I wouldn't do that. Love and peace. That's what I'm about. You know that, Pete."

"Yeah, I know what you're about. I heard you were down at the station yesterday. Word is you had some evidence regarding that girl found in the Dumpster. Better watch out or Geraldo will be coming out here, making you famous." Pete laughed.

Look at him, one of the little piggies they sang about. And now ol' Crazy John was their hero. Brilliant. Bringing that watch in himself really made him look like a concerned citizen. John Lennon would have approved big-time of the way he tried to help Rita out. No kissing up to the establishment, just one on one. Love and peace. But maybe this one time, just to get the piggies looking the other way so he could keep his sources from drying up.

"Have you seen this girl?" Pete held up a picture of Lovely Rita.

"Rita. Wow, I used to see her around here almost every night. Then all of a sudden—nothing. One minute here, and then she was gone."

"Well, if you see anything, hear something, let me know, will you? Some of Victor's girls got together a reward for information. They're scared. You know how dangerous their line of work is. Hookers get thrown away all the time."

"Yeah, I'll let you know, Pete."

As the cop walked away, Crazy John looked at the flyer the cop had given him. Ten thousand dollars. Shit, he'd made more than that just yesterday. But it wouldn't last long. No one had any idea how much money it took to keep up the house, the collection . . . his life's work.

Love, love, love. All you need is love.

And Lovely Rita's fifty grand.

*Another obvious fit for this book was the grand master Stuart Kaminsky, because of his long- running series featuring Hollywood detective Toby Peters. Interestingly he employs none of his four famous series characters in this story, preferring instead to introduce us to yet another. When this one gets his own series, only time will tell. Even as a stand-alone, though, this clever, surprising tale is a standout.*

# Evangeline

*by Stuart M. Kaminsky*

D ouglas Kvival was from out of town, way out of town, somewhere in great America where people were sure President Dick Nixon loved his dog.

People like Doug came to Los Angeles certain that if they camped out at Hollywood and Vine they would eventually see Lorne Greene, Dan Blocker, or one of the actors on M*A*S*H. They would more than settle for Jamie Farr.

It was 1972. People were dying that year, including William "Hopalong Cassidy" Boyd, J. Edgar Hoover, and Harry Truman. It looked as if Douglas Kvival was likely to join the funereal march.

My name is Gerald Perault. It used to be Gerald Bosmanian. Then, for two years, 1966 to 1968, it was Lightfoot, just Lightfoot. For those two years, I lived in a one-room just outside Venice beach with a girl named Evangeline. She didn't have a last name either, at least for those two years. We spent a lot of time sitting on the floor or the Pacific Ocean shore. Good years, couple of years. We got married, I think, by Ranger Dew, a preacher who also did tattoos and cashed money orders in a shack near Muscle Beach.

Evangeline got a tattoo. It was on her thigh. It was in blue and red script and read, "Lightfoot". I didn't get a tattoo. My mother was Jewish. She said I couldn't be buried in a Jewish cemetery if I had a tattoo. I found out later she got that not from a rabbi but a Lenny Bruce album.

Evangeline and I had a television: old, color, small screen, images too red. Then, one April morning, the day after I stepped on and got stung by something on the beach that might have been a jellyfish, Evangeline got off the floor and went back to Kansas City from whence she had sprung. I don't think it had anything to do with my stepping on the jellyfish. The television broke down the next day.

That's how Doug Kvival got my name, from Evangeline.

I was pissed and flattered. Pissed because she gave him my name, flattered because she remembered my name. I think I had told it to her twice. I think on those two occasions I spoke of Gerald Perault in the third person. I wasn't him. I was Lightfoot.

In addition to my name, Evangeline had also remembered that I had, off and on, been a cop. Not a real one. Not for long stretches and not for any good reason other than that it had seemed like a good idea.

Now it was 1972. I was now a security guard again, this time for a chain of drugstores in the Valley. Their standards were low and I was cheap. When I worked, I wore a uniform. I had become one of the creatures from which I had run. I was no longer in the third person.

I no longer held Evangeline's hand.

Now, I was standing at the corner of Hollywood and Vine, an

intersection I knew well. Douglas Kvival had picked the spot. Someone, he had said over the phone, wanted to kill him.

I told him to go to the police.

Douglas Kvival had picked not only the spot but the time, noon. I was there. He wasn't. Plenty of time to take in the slouch of zombie drug addicts, the kids in cutoff T-shirts with words like 'Shit' and 'Hate' Magic markered on the front. There were tourists too. Clean. Walking in protective packs, trying not to step on Clark Gable's or Lou Costello's star, or into the most recent spot where someone had vomited.

Shopping was not upscale on Hollywood Boulevard in 1972. Clothing stores for men, women, and freaks stood between places that sold knives, photographs of movie stars, and very greasy hot dogs and dangerous burgers, guaranteed to have been touched and served by questionable human hands. There was also a movie theater which showed triple-feature porno films and which served as a gathering mecca for gay pickups.

The sweet, acrid smell of decay and indifference was the aroma of Hollywood and Vine.

There was no mistaking Douglas Kvival when he arrived, primarily because he had described himself concisely.

"I'll be wearing a red baseball cap. It has the word 'Beef' on it in blue letters. I'm a kind of big guy."

That was so I could tell him from all the other people who were wandering the street in red baseball caps with the word 'Beef' on them.

I was leaning against a wall next to the newsstand on Vine from which I could watch the slowly passing parade of gawkers and gawked-at.

Then I saw him, above the crowd, head turning left and right to take in the sights of the street and to look for me.

Beneath the baseball cap, Doug Kvival stood a hefty six and a half feet tall. He stopped at the corner. A pair of willowy kids, one male, the other female (maybe), approached him bare-bellied. Doug nervously declined whatever they were offering and looked around some more.

I rescued him.

"Doug," I said moving next to him.

"Gerald?"

He sounded relieved.

"Gerald," I confirmed.

"You're the first person I've met who's called me anything but Beef."

"It's the hat," I said.

"I know. The hat's KC. Steak town. Lots of people have hats like this at home. No one calls them 'Beef'".

"Interesting," said. "You said someone is trying to kill you?"

"Yes," he said, looking around.

"Who? why? Why don't you take it up with the law?"

"The law?"

"The police," I explained.

"Can't do that," he said. "Jessica said they wouldn't believe me. She said you would know what to do."

"Jessica?"

"Oh, right. She said you wouldn't know her real name. Jessica Shtoltzman. She said you were married to her."

A trio of female tourists teens walked by, whispering and gawking at Beef as if he were one of the sights that had to be seen and talked about when they got back to their hotel room. I doubted they would talk about me. I was an average-looking thirty-one-year-old in jeans and a blue no-logo polo-style shirt with a pocket. There was nothing in the pocket.

"Jessica Shtoltzman," I repeated. "I was married to someone name Jessica Shtoltzman?"

"Still are, officially, she said."

Evangeline.

"Who's trying to kill you?" I asked.

"Them," he said pointing down the street at two men walking toward us.

The two men didn't seem to be in a hurry. They were both in their fifties, maybe. One was wearing tan slacks, a brown T-shirt and a brown zippered jacket. The other was wearing black slacks, a blue shirt with buttons, and a navy, colored zipper jacket. The guy in brown looked a little like Broderick Crawford on a good *Highway Patrol* day. The other guy looked a little like Dennis Weaver on a bad Chester Goode day.

"Why do they want to kill you?"

"Something I found out in Kansas City last week," he said. "Something I shouldn't have found out. Something I didn't want to know. Something that made me talk to Jessica, pack a bag, and get on a plane."

"To L.A. Why here?"

"Part of what I found out," he said.

"Want to share it with me?"

We were both looking down Hollywood Boulevard at the two men coming toward us.

"Maybe later," he said. "You don't want to know. I just need you to keep me from getting killed. I can pay."

In 1972, I was living alone in a one-bedroom in Van Nuys. I could see the hills through the smog from my apartment window. I had a four-year-old paid-for Volkswagon bug with a few small scratches and a Category Four dent in the right fender. I had a girlfriend named Sharon Bain, a loose-fitting security guard uniform, a television set with acceptable reception, and food in the cupboards and refrigerator. I was reasonably secure but unwilling to pass up an opportunity for a fast payoff, especially since it was presented in the context of a favor for a woman who might still be my wife.

"How much?"

"I don't know," he said taking off his hat and blinking tightly. "What's a reasonable price for saving a life?"

"What the market will bear," I said.

The two men in zippered jackets were next to a narrow jewelry store about twenty yards away. The huckster owner was trying to hail and haul them in with the promise of a golden deal.

"A thousand? Two thousand?"

"Two thousand," I agreed.

He nodded his agreement, and I said, "Come on."

The duo in zippered jackets had shucked the huckster. I could see their faces, eyes, Broderick Crawford–Dennis Weaver eyes. All they lacked was sunglasses.

My car was parked two blocks away on Argyle. I walked Doug around the corner and said, "Run."

We ran. Doug was right at my side. I jumped over a man or woman lying in a doorway, feet outstretched. So did Doug. He followed me onto a parking lot. We wound through a jumble of packed-in cars, made it to the alley, and kept running.

When we got to my car, I opened the door and paused for a few seconds to catch my breath and look back to see if the two men were behind us. They weren't. Doug drooped to the car, put one hand on the roof, and puffed animatedly.

"Let's go," I said.

He didn't look up or answer. He did raise a hand with one finger extended to let me know he needed a little more time looking down at the small array of used condoms, candy wrappers and cigarette butts on the street.

When we did get in the car and were moving, I said, "You have an idea of how I might get rid of them?"

Doug was looking down at his cap, which now sat on his lap. He teased the stitching "Beef" logo with his fingers and said, "I thought you might kill them,".

I looked at him. "Kill them?"

He shrugged. "I don't know. I just know they'll keep coming. They'll find me, kill me. You can't be with me for the rest of my life."

"I don't kill people," I said, missing a light on Franklin.

No police. No sirens.

"You have a gun?" he asked.

"No. You?"

"I wouldn't touch a gun," he said.

Tell me your story now, "Doug."

He puffed out some air and took a deep breath as if he were about to spew out a nonstop string of words.

He told me his story.

"Let's say this guy got. . . mixed up with this girl," he said.

"This guy? You?"

"Let's say. So he gets mixed up with her. He even marries her. He's happy, makes a living."

"But . . . ?"

"But," Doug went on, "one day this guy finds out his wife is making it with her boss."

"Her boss?"

"The guy she works for is a politician," said Doug. "A politician with a future, a politician who just came out of nowhere to get elected to Congress, a politician who is starting to get talked about as a strong young candidate for the Senate."

"So . . . ?"

"She wants a divorce. Our guy says he wants to think about it. She starts thinking her husband is considering blackmail or just coming out and embarrassing her."

"Ruin her future," I said.

"Ruin her future, exactly," said Doug. "He says he won't do that. She doesn't believe him. Gets him to say that he's shared their secrets with no one else. He wouldn't share his secrets, would you?"

"No," I said.

"So, she hires two men with guns to kill the husband."

"To kill you," I said.

"Yeah, let's say it's me." he paused. "I'm hungry."

"Burgers?"

"Sure."

"I know a good place on Ventura," I said. "We get some burgers. You give me two thousand dollars. I figure out a way to stop those two from killing you."

Cyril's on Ventura. Bright sun through the window of a two-seat round table just big enough to hold our Mr. Pibbs, our large order of fries, and one Cyril Special—a Gorgonzola burger with honey-fried onions, mushrooms, tomatoes, and a slice of lettuce.

Before we were served, Doug found the phone near the rest rooms and called his mother in Kansas City while I sat imagining two stick figures in various stages of distraction or disposal.

Back at the table, Doug sat and announced, "Mother's worried about me. She says Jessica called her, wanted to know if I was all right."

"Are you?"

"No," he said reaching for his Cyril Special. "But I will be when you tell me what you're going to do."

"Two thousand dollars," I said.

He took the top half of the bun off his burger laid four thin fries evenly spaced on the exposed lettuce and added more ketchup. Then he put the top of the bun back.

"You've got a plan," he said with a smile.

"Two thousand dollars," I repeated. "Before my Gorgonzola congeals."

"Check?"

"Cash," I said.

He puffed out air, put his burger down, shifted his considerable bulk, and took his wallet from his back pocket. The tables were close together. Cyril's was almost full. People talked softly but voices drifted.

No one paid attention as Doug counted twenty one-hundred - dollar bills from his bulging wallet. I took the money and stuffed it in my pocket.

"So?" he asked.

"It won't do you any long-term good to get rid of those two," I said.

"It won't?"

"No. Your wife will just find two or three others to get rid of you."

I took a bite of burger. It was still reasonably hot.

"Then . . . ?" he said, mouth full.

"We stop your wife, get her to call off the killers. Good burger, huh?"

"Not bad, but they're bigger, better in Kansas City. Angus. How do we get her to stop?"

"You call her, tell her you've written a letter, made six copies, signed them. They're with a friend who will send them to selected media and to the political opponents of your wife's boyfriend if you turn up dead."

"What if I accidentally get hit by a truck or lightning?"

"That'll be her bad luck."

"Mine, too."

"Yours, too," I agreed.

"And these letters, what do I write in them?"

"All the things your wife doesn't want the world to know. You can even create a few things. I'll be happy to help."

He attacked his burger and the fries, jaws moving.

"Might work," he said. "But what if she still says she won't call off those guys?"

"Then I go to Kansas City and I kill her," I said.

"No," he said.

His jaws had stopped grinding. His mouth was full.

"Yes," I said.

"You'd kill her?" he whispered.

"You don't have to whisper," I whispered. "Everyone thinks we're talking about a movie script or a television episode. They always think you're talking about the movies or television. It's the Grand Illusion. Real can only be real if it's about a story and a deal. We have a deal?"

"I've got to think about this," he said.

"Not much time," I said. "They're bound to find you."

"You'll want more money won't you?"

"Ten thousand and expenses," I said. "I'll fly economy and I'll eat inexpensively."

"If you go to Kansas City, you've got to have steak."

"I will," I promised. "Now, do you have anything smaller than a hundred-dollar bill?"

"Yeah," he said.

"Good. Put thirty or forty dollars on the table."

He got his wallet out again, found the right combination of bills and put them on the table.

"Let's go," I said.

"We're not finished."

"Your two friends just parked across the street. They are walking slowly but purposefully toward us."

We got up and Doug followed me back through the restaurant to the rear exit. There was a small lot in back of Cyril's where regulars like me who knew about it parked. We got into the car and I drove, this time west, toward Van Nuys.

We didn't say much. Doug had put his cap back on. I was sure he was thinking about who he would like to see dead.

Normally, I don't like it when people say things like "To tell the truth" or "Frankly." Hadn't they been telling the truth before? Hadn't they been frank before?

This was an exception, because I hadn't been telling Doug the truth. So, to tell the truth, I didn't plan to kill anyone. The call to Doug's wife should be enough to make her call the whole thing off, but if it didn't, I'd advise him to just release the letters. Once they were public, he should be safe.

We got to my apartment house on Roscoe at about three in the afternoon. My plan was to type the letter, take it to the nearby Rexall to make copies, have Doug sign them, and then make the call.

At this point I confessed. I confessed to myself that I wasn't doing this just for money or to help Evangeline's friend. I was doing it because it was on the edge. I could get used to it.

I was on the third floor. We took the elevator. Inside the apartment, I locked the door while Doug found the sofa, dropped himself into it, took off his cap, and closed his eyes. I went to the window. The mountains hadn't moved. The only thing new and interesting on the other side of the window were the two guys again. They were leaning against their car looking up at my window.

Couldn't hide, too late. I gave them my very best warning glare. They didn't buy it. I hadn't expected them to.

I took my blue Olivetti out of the closet and placed it on the kitchen table along with about ten sheets of paper. I moved to the refrigerator, opened it, and cursed.

"Damn thing's broken again. Just had it fixed and . . . "

Then I picked up the phone, looked at the collection of business cards magneted to the refrigerator door, and dialed.

Doug looked at me and shifted his weight.

"Yeah," I said when I got an answer. "This is Gerald Perault. My refrigerator is broken again. It's a simple fix. If you can't get it right, you should give serious consideration to blowing out your brains because it has ceased to function. Yes, I want an appointment. Okay, that's acceptable. I'll be home all tomorrow morning. Good-bye."

I hung up and turned to Doug.

"I'm going to go ahead and do the letters."

I moved past him on the sofa and took another look down at the street. The car was there. The two men were not.

"Sure," he said.

"Okay, then you get on the phone right now and call your wife. Tell her the letters are already in the hands of the man who'll distribute them if she doesn't call off the guys who are on the way up here right now."

Doug was suddenly flapping and trying to get out of my sofa.

"No," he said.

"Yes," I said. "Phone's over there on the wall. We can keep them out of here for a while. I'll try to get them to call her from the phone booth down at the corner after you talk to them."

"What if she's not home?" he asked.

"We'll stall," I said.

"This isn't the way it's supposed to be," he said.

His voice was different, steadier, more calm. I turned from the table where I was frantically trying to get a sheet of paper into the reluctant typewriter.

Doug Kvival stood about eight feet away from me. He had a gun in his hand. There was a knock at the door.

Doug shook his head no. I said nothing.

Another knock. Another. Six in all.

Voices through the door.

Gravely voice.

"All right. Now what?" High male voice at the door.

"We know you're in there. We just saw you. You saw us."

I said nothing. The gun in Doug's hand was in charge.

Creaking outside the door. Voices moving away. I turned to Doug.

"Don't tell me," I said. "You're the young Kansas politician."

"I won't tell you," he said. "You figure it out."

I had, but I didn't like the way it was scheduled to end.

"Evangeline's the wife," I said. "I'm the husband. You want me out of the way. She doesn't want me to see her picture in the papers and give a tell-all interview somewhere. End your shot at the Senate and who knows where after that."

"That's about it," he said.

"Easier to kill me than to take my word," I said.

"Not easier," he said. "Just more certain."

"What about the two guys at the door?" I asked.

"Actors," he said. "I hired them to follow me, look tough."

"The phone call you made from Cyril's was to tell them where we were."

"Right, the show was for you."

"Why not just find me and shoot me?"

"I wanted you to tell me if anyone else knew about you and Jessica. You told me. Remember you said in the car you wouldn't share your secrets if you were the husband."

"I remember."

"Well, you are the husband."

"Why kill me if you believe I wouldn't say anything about me and Jessica?"

"Ah, you haven't told anyone up to now, but if you came across her picture . . . "

"Different ball game."

"Different ball game," he said.

"Shooting me will make a lot of noise."

"You have a better plan?"

"Trust me."

"Can't," he said. "I'm a politician."

"I lied," I said.

"Lied?"

"Well, not a lie. I deceived."

"What are you talking about?" he asked.

"That wasn't the refrigerator repair people I called," I said. "I hit 911 and then four other numbers. My guess is the police will be here any second."

"Now you're lying," he said.

"No. I saw the gun in your pocket when we were at Cyril's. You told me you had no gun."

Doug lowered the gun and shook his head.

"You're the one who should be running for public office."

"I don't have your ambition or your sterling record," I said.

"You win," he said. "I don't want to be here when the police arrive—if, in fact, they are going to arrive."

"Stand outside and see," I said.

"I will."

He put the gun back in his pocket, adjusted his cap, and went to the door.

"I'm going to sit right down and write myself a letter," I said.

"I'm sure you will," he said.

And he was gone.

I locked the door and moved to the window. About a minute later, Doug crossed the street and began talking to the two waiting actors.

There was nothing wrong with my refrigerator, but I had called the number on the refrigerator repair business card, not 911. I had left my message on their machine. I'd worry about it tomorrow.

I picked up the phone and dialed long distance.

When the operator answered, I said, "Kansas City, Kansas. The number for Jessica Shtoltzman. If there's no Jessica, I'll take the number for any Shtoltzman in Kansas City, Kansas."

I spelled 'Shtoltzman' for her.

"We have a listing for a J. Shtoltzman," she said.

"Great."

"I'll connect you."

Five rings and a voice I knew from the past.

"Evangeline," I said. "This is Lightfoot. I'm afraid I have some bad news."

*That Lee Goldberg fits in this anthology is a foregone conclusion. He has written for the TV series* Diagnosis: Murder, Monk, *and* Missing, *among others. So when he writes about Hollywood, he knows whereof he speaks. Here he writes the best story I've read—or seen—about a star on the Hollywood Walk of Fame since Lucy and Ethel stole John Wayne's star on* I Love Lucy. *(Okay, it was his footprints, but you get the idea.)*

# Jack Webb's Star

## by Lee Goldberg

*"The story you are about to hear is true; the names have been changed to protect the innocent."*

When it comes to sex, everyone is wired differently. You just can't predict what will get some people excited. I knew a guy who got a hard-on any time he licked an envelope. He couldn't tell you why it turned him on, it just did.

For my wife Carly, it's Jack Webb. He was an actor who played this cop named Joe Friday on a TV show called *Dragnet* that ran in the '50s and '60s. Later, they made a Tom Hanks movie out of it that sucked, and another TV series, with that Al Bundy guy from *Married With Children*, and it also sucked, but I'm digressing.

Jack Webb had a turtle face and moved like he was in a full body cast. The cop he played was just as stiff, physically, politically, and morally. His trademark was the dry, almost robotic way he spoke, a rat-a-tat-tat of short sentences, a style that could be summed up by his favorite phrase: "Just the facts, ma'am."

Carly was too young to have seen *Dragnet* on-the-air. Her exposure to Jack Webb came from her grandfather, a retired cop who showed her episodes whenever she visited his place up in Big Bear. He thought it would teach her to respect the law and abide by a strict moral code. It didn't work out that way.

For whatever reason, Jack Webb made a strong erotic impression on her, completely rewiring her sexual synapses. All she had to do was watch Jack question somebody for thirty seconds and she was ready to fuck anything warm-blooded that was within reach. *Dragnet* was rarely rerun on TV so we had the whole series on video. That was my wife's porn stash.

I was thinking of Jack Webb on that fateful day for a couple of reasons. One, because I hadn't had sex with my wife in weeks and two, because Jack Webb's star on the Walk of Fame was right outside the building at Hollywood and Vine where I was stuck in traffic school for a speeding ticket.

I picked a traffic school run by a local comedy club and taught by a standup comic. I figured that a few laughs would make the eight hours of highlights from the California Vehicle Code easier to take. If I'd been smart, which I think I've already established that I'm not, I would have asked myself "How good can this standup comic be if the best gig he can get is in a traffic school class?"

There were two dozen of us traffic offenders crammed into a second-floor room in the Taft Building. That was twice the maximum room occupancy allowed by the fire department, at least according to the sign above the door that, in my boredom, I'd reread six times.

We all sat on folding chairs, except for a fat guy in an electric wheelchair with two red flags duct-taped to his seatback. The walls of the room were water-stained, and it smelled like a gym, maybe because the windows had been nailed shut since the days when Charlie Chaplin and Will Rogers had offices in the building.

The windows looked out on the old Broadway department store, which was surrounded by scaffolding because it was being converted into lofts. Big banners offered the opportunity to live at "the original address for glamour." Just below the banner, I could see a homeless guy urinating in one of the doorways. I wouldn't call that glamorous, but I'm not in advertising.

Our teacher was a comedienne named Irma, who introduced herself as a *yucky*, a "young urban comic." She was the only one who laughed at that. Everything about her drooped, from her eyelids to her ass, a sad fact made painfully obvious by the pink tank top and black tights she'd unwisely chosen to wear. She'd been teaching traffic school for a decade, though she was quick to point out that she'd just done a pilot.

"Me, too," said a twentysomething African-American woman in the back of the room. "Mine flew for Southwest Airlines."

That was the funniest joke of the day, maybe because it wasn't meant to be. The clueless twentysomething was apparently the only twentysomething in L.A. who wasn't trying to get into the industry and didn't know that a "pilot" was TV-speak for a sample episode of a proposed TV show.

Her name was LeSabre and she was a telemarketer for skin care products. I knew that because Irma started the day by asking everyone to introduce themselves, say what they did for a living, and how they got their ticket.

A lot of people got ticketed through the mail, nabbed by intersection cameras that caught them running a red light. LeSabre was one of them.

"I was in the intersection, making a left turn, when the light turned red," LeSabre said. "Everybody knows the rule is three cars."

"That's the accepted practice, but it's not the law," Irma said. "Like talking on your cell phone during sex."

It was a joke that made no sense and went a long way toward explaining why Irma was still teaching traffic school instead of starring in a sitcom.

The guy in the wheelchair was named Morris, and he fixed watches. His traffic violation was a D.U.I.

"You were drunk-driving?" Irma asked incredulously.

"In my wheelchair," Morris said. "I had a few too many beers and got ticketed weaving in an erratic and dangerous manner outside the boundaries of the crosswalk."

"And a cop wrote you up for that?" the guy next to me asked.

He had a deeply tanned, pock-marked face and wore a T-shirt with no sleeves, presumably so he could show off his muscles and the tattoo on his right arm of a big-boobed woman with hard nipples.

"What the officer did was ridiculous, but legal," Irma said. "Like guys who wear toupees."

Eight more hours of this, I thought. Kill me now.

"What an asshole," the tattoo guy said.

Morris nodded. "The judge took pity on me, knocked it down to a minor traffic violation, and let me come here to get it off my record."

"He should have thrown out the fucking ticket," the tattoo guy shook his head with disgust.

Irma turned to him. "And you are?"

"Titus Watkins," he said.

"What do you do for a living, Titus?"

"I'm in construction," Titus said.

"How did you get your ticket?"

"I got it driving in the car pool lane. Then the cop got me for crossing a single yellow line instead of waiting to exit at a broken white line. Then he cited me for not wearing a seat belt."

"How much was the ticket for?" asked Richie Nakamura, a six-teen-year-old who was cited doing fifty-miles-per-hour on a residential street in his dad's BMW.

"Twelve hundred bucks," Titus said.

"You must have done something to piss the cop off," Richie said.

"I did a few years in prison for armed robbery," he said. "After that, the cops shit on you forever."

Irma quickly turned to me, eager to change the subject. She asked me my name and profession.

"Kevin Dangler, I'm a writer."

"Books or screenplays?" Irma asked.

"Both," I said.

"Anything we would have read or seen?"

"An episode of *VIP*," I said.

"That show was cancelled five years ago," a lady behind me said. The bitch.

"Yeah, I know," I said.

"So what have you written lately?" Irma said.

"This and that," I said.

I still liked to think of myself as a writer, but the truth is, the only money I was making at it was as a reporter for *The Acorn*, which I don't tell people, because it sounds like a kid's magazine with a cartoon squirrel on the cover.

Actually, that would be a step up.

*The Acorn* is a freebie community newspaper in the Valley that covers the big stories that the *Los Angeles Times* and the *Daily News* are afraid to touch. Like the spat between the Las Virgenes Municipal Water District and the Triunfo Sanitation District over a proposal to share a water storage tank. Or the theft of a portable CD player and case full of John Denver CDs from the passenger seat of an unlocked Mazda 626. Those were my big stories that week.

Perhaps Irma, who probably spent a lot of time being ashamed of herself, sensed my shame. She dropped the line of questioning and asked me how I got my ticket.

I told her I was caught doing eighty miles-per-hour on the Ventura Freeway, and she moved on through the rest of the class, which included a stockbroker, a corporate safari booker, a basketball referee, a hairdresser, and a seventeen-year-old girl pulled over for text messaging while driving.

We had a ten-minute break at 11:00 and I practically ran out of the classroom onto Hollywood Boulevard. It was drizzling outside, but I didn't care. I needed air and I hoped the rain would wake me up.

The streets were virtually deserted, the wet weather driving the bums into alcoves, the hookers into their motel rooms, and the tourists into the trams at the Universal Studios tour. The black terrazzo sidewalks were shiny and slick, the water washing away the accumulated cigarette butts, dog crap, french fries, and chewing gum from the Walk of Fame.

I stood on Jack Webb's pink star, hands shoved in my pockets, and looked around. The Metrorail station was next door. The Pantages Theatre, a dive bar, a hotdog stand, and a donut shop were across the street.

Jack's star was near the entrance to a parking lot and beside what was once a phone booth, until the coin box was ripped out, the receiver was torn off, and people started using the post as a urinal. If having a star there was one of the rewards of fame, I was glad I was unknown.

I took a Krispy Kreme napkin out of my pocket, bent down, and wiped some dirt off the bronze letters of Jack's name. It was the least I could do, considering what Jack meant to my wife. I sensed somebody standing beside me. It was Titus, smoking a cigarette.

"So what's worse," I said, standing up, "prison or traffic school?"

I didn't really care, I was talking to cover my embarrassment at being caught buffing Jack's star. Titus snorted derisively. "This makes solitary confinement seem appealing. You aren't scared of me?"

"Should I be?"

He shrugged. "Everybody else in class is keeping their distance."

"Maybe they just don't want to get wet."

Titus flicked his cigarette butt on Jack's star. "Which episode of *VIP* did you write?"

I kicked the butt off Jack's star and into the gutter. Titus noticed.

"The one with the evil twin lesbian hit women," I said.

"You wrote that? Shit. That's my all-time favorite episode."

"You saw it?"

"*VIP* was big in prison," he said.

I motioned toward his tattoo. "Nice tattoo. Is she an old girlfriend?"

"Don't you recognize her?" he flexed his muscles creating the illusion that the tattooed woman's boobs were bouncing. "It's Pamela."

I studied the tattoo. Yeah, I suppose it could have been Pamela Anderson. It could also have been my wife.

\* \* \* \* \*

We spent the next two hours taking a multiple-choice traffic law quiz and going over the answers. The last question was: Is it permissible to have an open alcoholic beverage in a) the glove compartment, b) the back seat, or c) the trunk."

"The correct answer is 'c,' the trunk," Irma said. "Unless you're in it at the time."

We broke for lunch at 1:00 and were told to be back in forty-five minutes. Titus and I ended up at a pizza-by-the-slice joint that was next door to a sex shop. I thought about going into the shop and browsing. It was our fifth wedding anniversary on Tuesday and I still hadn't found anything for Carly. Maybe if I got her something kinky she'd think it was cute. Or not. Nothing I did seemed to please her anymore.

When I couldn't land another script assignment and had to take a job at *The Acorn* to pay the bills, she was disappointed in me. That disappointment turned into resentment and was edging toward hate. She was talking about leaving me and "jump-starting" her life. I'm not Dr. Phil, but I think it was a whole lot easier to be disappointed in me than in herself.

I wanted her to love me again. I wanted to save our marriage. I just had no clue how to do it.

"You want to stop by the sex shop before we go back?" Titus asked between loud slurps from his extra-large Coke.

"Why do you ask?"

"The way you looked at the place when we walked past it."

"My fifth wedding anniversary is coming up," I said. "I can't figure out what to get my wife."

"What's she do?"

"She's an actress," I said.

He nodded as if he should have known. "Have I seen her in anything?"

Carly was the TV queen of female discomfort. Sweaty armpits, vaginal itch, irritable bowels, awful breath, menstrual cramps, she's been afflicted by all that and more in commericals, only to be cured by some miracle product. It wasn't exactly the acting career she dreamed of, and for some reason, it was my fucking fault.

"Not unless you like watching commercials for feminine hygiene products," I said. "She's only been in one movie."

"Give me the title," he said.

"*The Endless Spiral.*"

"Was that the thing with Christopher Walken as a pimp?"

"Yeah." I was amazed he'd seen it. The movie wasn't released theatrically, and instead of going straight to video it went straight to obscurity.

"Was she the girl Christopher Walken finger-fucked in the taxi?"

Yes.

"No," I said.

That taxi scene was supposed to be Carly's big break. We'd been dating for a few months and she got the part the same week I sold my *VIP* script. We were certain our careers were on the verge of taking off. So we got married, put our money into a house, and waited for the next big break to come our way. Five years later, we were still waiting.

"That was a hot scene," he said.

"I'll be sure to let her know," I said.

"How could you let some guy finger-fuck your wife?" Titus asked.

"It was Christopher Walken and they were acting."

"That looked like a finger in her twat to me," Titus said.

"It was a stunt twat," I said.

He shrugged and took a bite out of his pizza. "No wonder you're thinking of buying your wife a dildo for your anniversary."

\* \* \* \* \* \*

For the next two hours, Irma told more awful jokes and gave us more wisdom from the Vehicle Code. We were released for another ten-minute break at 3:15.

I went back outside to check on Jack. It was dark: grayer and wetter on Hollywood Boulevard than it was before, but Jack hadn't changed.

I once asked Carly what it had been that turned her on about Jack Webb. She didn't know. My theory was that he was so rigid that he was phallic, a penis in a cheap suit. His face certainly looked like a scrotum. The rhythm of his speech was like the primal beat of fucking. The more he talked, the more he verbally humped her, the closer she got to coming.

Jack Webb was a definite mood-killer for me. So while Carly watched Jack, I'd watch her. I'd get excited by her excitement, her wide eyes, her trembling lip, her quickened breathing. God, it had been a long time since I'd seen that. Lately whenever I suggested bringing out the *Dragnet* tapes, she'd just give me this look like I was the most pathetic creature on earth.

"You got a thing for Jack Webb?" Titus stood beside me, smoking another cigarette.

"No," I said.

"Then why are you hanging out around his star and keeping it clean?"

"My wife is a big fan."

"No shit?"

"He gets her hot," I said.

It's amazing the things that you'll tell a complete stranger, especially one that you'll never see again. I think I said it to make fun of Carly, to make her seem as pathetic as she made me feel lately.

But Titus didn't react the way I thought he would. He mulled over what I'd said for a moment, flicked his cigarette into the street, and blew out a stream of smoke.

"Then that's what you ought to get for her," he said.

"We have all the *Dragnet* episodes."

"I'm not talking about the show. I'm talking about that," he tipped his head towards the star.

"You're kidding," I said.

"Why? You think anybody is gonna miss it? We're talking about Jack Webb, not John Fucking Wayne."

And with that, he turned and walked back into the building.

* * * * * *

I thought about what he'd said for the next two hours. The stars were imbedded in terrazzo and concrete on a public street. And not just any public street, but the Walk of Fame, right at the corner of Hollywood and Vine, one of the most famous intersections in the world.

The theft wouldn't exactly be a slick, precision operation, either. He would need a jackhammer to get that star out of the sidewalk.

It was a stupid, insane idea.

But it was just the kind of grand romantic gesture Carly would never have expected from me. Hell, I would never have expected it from myself. It would make her see me in a whole new light. It might save us.

* * * * * *

The class ended promptly at 5:00. Irma handed out our completion slips for the traffic court and discount tickets to a comedy club where she was appearing.

I caught up with Titus outside. He was standing by Jack Webb's star, studying it, casing the joint.

"Were you serious about what you said?" I whispered.

"Hell yes," he said.

"Why would you do that for me?"

"Because you're gonna pay me a thousand bucks and I need the money, otherwise the check I wrote for my speeding ticket is going to bounce and I'll be in real deep shit."

"Deeper than if you get caught stealing that star?"

"We aren't gonna get caught," he said.

"We?"

"It's a two-man job, Kev. Besides, you want to be able to tell your woman that you did this for her, not that you hired somebody else."

He had a good point. "But it can't possibly work."

"Why not?"

"Because we're going to be out in the open, on the Walk of Fame, making a huge amount of noise."

He shrugged. "There are crews out here at night all the time working on the sidewalk, especially now with that building being renovated. We'll be in and out in twenty or thirty minutes. All it takes is the right tools."

"You have the tools?"

"I work for a big construction company," Titus said. "I can get a van with all the stuff we need, no problem. They'll never miss it. Anybody who sees us will think we're a work crew installing cable or something."

I looked down at Jack's star. Stealing it was a ballsy thing to do. It would make me a ballsy guy. Somebody risky. Edgy. Unpredictable. Willing to risk it all for the woman he loved.

The star was the ultimate symbolic embodiment of Jack Webb. If Carly had it, she would possess him as no other woman could. Not only that, the star would be imbued with the danger and allure of crime, which is sexy all by itself. It would be a tantalizing secret that only the two of us shared, drawing us closer together.

"Let's do it," I said.

*   *   *   *   *

Monday was the longest day of my life.

It's hard to concentrate on reporting crap like the debate over the selection of delegates for the Las Virgenes/Malibu Council of

Governments and League of California Cities. It's even harder when you're only a few hours away from pulling off an incredible heist.

I didn't know exactly how the caper was going to go down, but the plan was already in motion. Titus was picking me up in front of my place at midnight and then he'd tell me what to do.

Somehow, I made it through the council meeting and wrote my story for *The Acorn*. When I got home around seven, Carly had already eaten dinner and was sitting in a tanktop and sweats at her vanity in the bedroom, studying her lines for a hemorrhoid commercial and practicing expressions of glorious relief in the mirror.

She was a natural blonde with blue eyes you could drown in. She had a band of freckles across her nose that gave her face a childlike innocence that contrasted sharply with the sensual delights promised by her curvacious body.

I came in behind her and kissed her slender neck. Her pained, cursed-with-hemorrhoids expression returned and she looked at my reflection.

"How's it going?" I asked.

"Do you think Jennifer Aniston ever had to portray rectal itch?"

"She doesn't have your range," I said.

"I don't have her bank balance."

"Not everything can be measured with money."

"Name one thing that can't," she said.

"My love for you," I replied.

She rolled her eyes. "Is that the kind of stuff you're writing in your novel?"

"Read it and find out for yourself."

"I think I'd rather work on my rectal itch," she said, dropping her gaze back to her script.

I wanted to tell her what I was going to do for her that night. I wanted to impress her. But I controlled the urge.

I left, closing the door behind me, and went to the kitchen. I made myself a frozen pizza, read the paper, and swiped the thousand dollars in emergency cash we kept hidden in the freezer.

After dinner, I went to my office. The tiny room was filled with books, magazines, DVDs, and about seven hundred manuscript pages of my unfinished novel, an epic tonepoem about the nature of human existence and two lesbian hit women. I'd been working on it for three years.

For the next couple of hours, I worked on the novel some more. I was actually on a roll, for the first time in months, when I had to stop writing at midnight. I checked on Carly. She was asleep in bed. I crept out of the house as quietly as I could.

Titus was parked out front in a Katz Construction Company van. I got inside. The van smelled like an ashtray. He was wearing a bright orange jumpsuit. I wondered if it reminded him of prison.

"You up for this?" he asked.

I nodded.

"Good, because I need the money and I wasn't leaving here tonight without it."

I didn't like the violent implications of that remark but it also thrilled me. He was a dangerous guy. I was a dangerous guy. We were going to do a dangerous thing.

I gave him the cash. He stuffed it in his pocket, reached behind him, and handed me an orange jumpsuit like the one he was wearing and a pair of mud-encrusted work boots.

On the way to Hollywood, he explained how we were going to get the star out. It sounded pretty simple. I started to believe that we were really going to do it.

\* \* \* \* \* \*

Titus parked the van at the curb in front of Jack Webb's star on Hollywood Boulevard. We set up saw-horse barriers on either side of the star to keep people away, not that there were any around. The street was cold, dark, and deserted. We setup some work lights, powered by a generator in the van. When Titus flicked the lights on, it was as if someone was shining a spotlight directly on us.

"Turn them off," I said. "We can be seen from blocks away."

"So what?"

"It's like were standing on a stage," I said.

"I need to be able to see what I'm cutting."

"Aren't the street lights enough?"

"Use your fucking head. Would a real construction crew work in the dark? No. They'd want to see what they were doing. Besides, it's not the lights that are going to attract attention." He leaned into the van and pulled out the Makita cordless circular tile saw with a diamond blade. "It's this."

I was starting to have second thoughts, and I think he could see it on my face.

"Grow some balls," he said. "There's a spigot in the parking lot by the ticket booth. Go hook the hose up to it."

I took out a hose from the van and walked over to the rusty spigot. I attached the hose, turned on the flow of water, and walked back to the sidewalk.

"Your job is to keep the concrete and terrazzo wet while I do the cutting," he said. "Think you can handle that?"

I nodded.

We both put on goggles and gloves and he got to work. The noise was even louder than I expected, echoing up and down the empty canyon of buildings along Hollywood Boulevard, rousing the bums who'd been sleeping in the alcoves and doorways.

The bums yelled at us, but I couldn't hear what they were saying over the noise of the saw. After a couple of minutes, they either shuffled away to quieter spots or retreated into the darkness from which they came.

The cutting didn't take long at all, but even after Titus shut off the saw, the sound still rang in my ears. I washed away the remaining dust from the sidewalk. He'd cut a clean square that left about four inches of terrazzo around the star.

I set the hose down and Titus leaned into the truck to swap the saw for the hammer and chisel he'd need to chip away at the cut he'd made, get underneath the star, and lift it out.

That's when I saw a black-and-white police car cruising down the boulevard toward us.

"Ignore 'em," Titus said. "Go roll up the hose and bring it back here."

I turned my back to the street and did as I was told, but I knew the police car would stop, the cops would get out, and they would ask us questions we couldn't answer.

While I was gathering up the hose, I heard Titus hammering away. The cops had driven right by. I was never more relieved in my life.

I tossed the hose in the van, got a tire iron, and jammed the teeth into the gap in the cement Titus had made with the hammer and chisel. I jimmied up the star. Titus slipped his gloved hands underneath, then I dropped the tire iron and joined him. Together we lifted Jack Webb's star out of the street and set it carefully on the floor of the van.

The theft took less than half an hour.

* * * * * *

I didn't sleep that night. I was too keyed up. On Tuesday morning, our fifth anniversary, I woke Carly up with a kiss.

"Go away," she mumbled.

"It's our anniversary," I said.

"I'm not in the mood."

"I have a present for you," I said. "I think you're going to like it."

She looked at me suspiciously, like she was afraid the present was in my pants.

"It's in the garage," I said.

That piqued her curiosity enough for her to throw back the sheets and put on her bathrobe.

"You're wearing what you wore last night," she said, regarding me with a sideways glance as we padded down the hall to kitchen and the door that led to the garage.

"Uh-huh," I said.

"Did you ever come to bed last night?"

"Nope," I said.

"Aren't you mysterious," she said.

"More than you know," I opened the door to the garage, turned on the light, and motioned her inside.

She looked past me at my old Toyota Corolla and her old Honda Civic.

"I didn't get you a new car," I said.

"Obviously," she said.

"I got you something better" I crouched beside a tarp on the floor.

"What is it?"

"Something no one else on earth has but you," I said. "Something as special and unique as you are to me."

She groaned. Before she had a chance to say something cutting that she'd regret later, I whipped off the tarp to reveal Jack Webb's star.

I'd buffed it up, so the star practically glowed in the dim light.

The look on Carly's face was priceless. Her jaw dropped and her eyes widened in shock.

"Is that—" she began.

"Uh-huh," I said, rising to my feet.

She started to smile. It was devious and delightful. "How did you get it?"

"I stole it from the Walk of Fame," I said. "For you."

She ran into my arms and mashed her lips against mine in a furiously hungry kiss. I lost my footing and we tumbled onto the star.

*  *  *  *  *

Carly had a thirst that couldn't be slaked. She fucked me three times, right there in the garage, on top of Jack Webb's star, and then we went back into the bedroom for more.

We didn't talk until hours later, lying in bed, bruised and scratched from rolling over the rough edges of the star and the concrete floor of the garage. We were dirty and sweaty and exhausted.

"I want to know how you did it," she said, her voice raw from her moans and squeals and shrieks.

I told her. Of course I embellished the story a lot. I built it up into a elaborate scheme that took weeks for me to meticulously plan and execute, that involved recruiting expert drivers, stone masons, and electronics experts. The heist itself was a carefully choreographed operation that required clockwork precision, special tools, and cutting-edge technology.

And I did it all for her.

It was the most imaginative writing I had done in years. Already, Jack Webb's star was having an unexpectedly positive influence in other areas of our lives.

When I was done with the story, she gave me another deep kiss.

"It's the best gift anyone has ever given me," she said.

Me, too, I thought.

* * * * * *

The big question was what to do with the star now that we had it. Carly wanted to put it the shower floor in our master bathroom. That way, she could see the star every day and it would be out of sight of any visitors we might have. But I knew there was another reason she wanted it there. We had a hand-held showerhead that she occasionally used for wicked purposes.

But installing the star in the shower was beyond our home improvement skills, even though we had the Home & Garden channel on our cable lineup. Of course, we couldn't just call someone out of the phone book to do the job, not unless we wanted to risk getting reported to the police.

I told Carly not to worry about it, to leave everything in my capable hands. If I could assemble a top-notch team of criminal talent to steal the star, I could certainly find the right person to remodel our shower and keep our secret.

"Sure, I can do it," Titus told me over the phone. "No problemo."

"What will it cost me?"

"Another grand," he said.

This was becoming a very expensive present. I'd have to work a lot of overtime at *The Acorn* to sustain our cash flow, but it was worth it.

"Okay," I said. "But if my wife asks how we met, tell her you were part of the talent I recruited for the score."

"The score?"

"Make sure she understands that I was the mastermind of the operation."

"Sure," he said. "You're a criminal genius."

* * * * *

It took three days for Titus to put the star in the bottom of the shower. I was very pleased with his work. So was Carly.

We spent hours in the shower, making love in positions I'd only dreamed about. We were reconsumating our marriage on the altar of Jack Webb.

Two weeks after the caper, I was still working long hours at *The Acorn* to make up for the two grand I'd spent on Carly's anniversary present. On that particular day, I'd volunteered to cover the Calabasas Planning Commission hearings on a controversial new building complex. The debate was likely to stretch into the wee hours, so I talked my editor into letting me go home and take a shower.

I immediately sped home, imagining the carnal delights that awaited me.

When I rounded the corner onto my street, the first thing I saw was a Katz Construction van parked in front of my house.

The only thing I could figure was that all of our furious coupling had shaken loose some tiles around the star and Carly had called Titus to come fix it.

I opened the front door and was about to announce myself when I felt the humidity in the air, the kind that comes from running a hot shower for a very long time. Carly couldn't get enough of Jack.

And then I heard the bedsprings squeaking. Rythmically.

Our bedroom was at the end of a short hallway. The door was wide open. As I approached, I saw Titus's naked back, my wife's hands clutching his pale, white buttocks as he pounded into her with animalist grunts.

I stood there for a good minute or two before Carly noticed me.

I met Carly's gaze, which was defiant and unapologetic. She didn't give a damn. She was jump-starting her life.

"I always knew stealing the star wasn't your idea," she said. "You aren't man enough."

Titus looked over his shoulder at me and sneered. A muscle flexed in his arm and the tattoo woman's boobs seemed to jiggle.

"I want a divorce," she said.

This wasn't the way it was supposd to go. I stole Jack Webb's star for her. I'd been betrayed by her. By Titus. By life.

I turned and walked away. The bedsprings immediately started rocking again. Carly moaned. Titus grunted. Something snapped in me.

I picked up the brass table lamp by the couch, marched back into the bedroom, and whacked Titus on the head with it as hard as I could. Blood spattered on Carly's chest and she screamed.

I dropped the lamp, grabbed the pillow beside her and covered her face with it. I placed all my weight against the pillow, smothering her. Divorce granted.

When Carly finally stopped moving, I placed Titus's limp hands on the pillow, picked up the bedside phone and called 911.

"Oh my God, you've got to help me!" I wailed.

"Calm down, sir," said the female operator in a robot monotone.

"He was raping her," I wailed some more.

"Are you in any danger?"

"No, I don't think so," I said. "He was on top of my wife, he had a pillow over her face and he—"

"The police are on the way sir," she said. Her monotone was comforting. Familiar. Almost arousing. "They will be there in four minutes."

"He was attacking my wife and I hit him, I hit him hard. There's blood everywhere."

"I understand," she said. I knew why it was familiar. She sounded like Jack Webb.

"I can't talk anymore," I said. "I can't breathe."

That was true. It was beginning to dawn on me that I'd just murdered two people, one of whom was my wife. My chest felt tight.

"Please stay on the line," she said.

I hung up because I had one more thing to do, and I couldn't take a chance that I might be sidelined by a heart attack before I got to it. I went into the bathroom, put the sticky-plastic mat over Jack Webb's star, and closed the shower curtain.

I sat on the edge of the bed, clutched my chest, and waited.

\* \* \* \* \*

It was a simple case, really. I came home and surprised an intruder in my house who was holding a pillow over my wife's face and raping her. I smashed the bastard over the head with a lamp but I was too late to save my poor, sweet wife.

Everyone knew I loved my wife, that we were happily married, and that we'd just celebrated our fifth wedding anniversary. My coworkers, my neighbors, and even my wife's family stood solidly behind me. Not that they needed to, because the cops never doubted my story. Nobody did.

Why should they?

All anybody had to do was look at Titus, an ex-con with a big-boobed woman tattooed on his arm, and then look at me, a law-abiding citizen and devoted husband.

There was always the remote possibility that the police would discover that Titus and I were in the same traffic school class together, but I wasn't concerned about that. It would have looked like Titus was a deranged sicko who followed me home and then stalked my wife before he raped and murdered her.

The only thing that worried me was what would happen if the cops stumbled on Jack Webb's star in my shower. But they didn't. All the action was in the bedroom and that's what they concentrated on.

The tightness I felt in my chest right after I murdered my wife and Titus passed before the cops showed up. I think it was stress or maybe acid reflux. In any other circumstance, I would have taken a Pepcid and not given it a second thought

The homicide investigation lasted two, maybe three days, and that was it.

I felt no remorse. I was certain that the only reason Titus helped me steal the star was so he could fuck my wife. He used the erotic power of Jack Webb against me. That made it justifiable homicide as far as I was concerned.

Carly wasn't any better. She knew what she was doing when she invited Titus into bed. She wanted to humiliate me and she succeeded. There are some cultures where women who commit adultery are stoned to death. Looking at it that way, things could have ended a lot worse for her.

I was sad, of course, and deeply depressed for days afterward, but I felt a whole lot better after I received $250,000 from Carly's life insurance company, $75,000 from the State Crime Victims Fund, and $150,000 from a studio that optioned my tragic story for a TV movie. I was even hired to write the script.

The truth is, I'm happier now than I've ever been. And I owe it all to Jack Webb's star, which has given me a thought: He's buried in Forest Lawn Cemetery in Hollywood, plot #1999. I wonder how hard it would be to steal his tombstone?

*Dick Lochte wears two hats—writer and critic—
with equal aplomb. Not satisfied with penning
two different series about P.I.'s—very different
from each other—he has of late been collaborating
in legal thrillers with Christopher Darden, who
prosecuted O.J. Simpson. Here he brings back his
most famous P.I., Leo Bloodworth, in a story of
modern-day Hollywood and religion—sort of.*

# Devil Dog

*by Dick Lochte*

That Tuesday morning, I was parked
along a quiet oak-lined residential street
in West L.A., sipping a tall cup of good
but overpriced black coffee, the earbuds of a tiny MP3 player firmly
in place, listening to Dinah Shore singing the Johnny Mercer classic
"Blues in the Night," a rendition so heartfelt it never fails to send a
chill down my spine. Not coincidentally, I was also keeping a half-
lidded eye on a Spanish-style bungalow a few lots away.

It was a comfortable-looking house, nestled in shrubbery and
separated from the tree-buckled sidewalk by a well-tended lawn.
It had been painted recently: ivory-colored stucco with a red front
door and shutters that sort of matched the faded red-tile roof. I
was appreciating the music and speculating on how much paint my
place would take when Joe Addis finally decided to greet the day
and get mobile.

The guy was built like a speed swimmer, tall, thin-waisted with broad shoulders and a small head that he shaved to the scalp. Where the swimmer look fell apart was a black mustache-and-beard combo bushy enough to slow Aquaman down to a crawl. The beard surrounded a face with close-set eyes separated by a nose long enough to get in the soup. He was wearing what passed for business garb in L.A.: Ray-Bans, baggy denims, and a dark full-cut jacket over a black T-shirt.

Before he could shut his front door, a fierce-looking cocoa brown mastiff tried to leave with him. The mutt was weirdly silent while Addis used his right leg to push him into the bungalow and slam the front door on him. You can bet I made mental note of the dog.

My name is Leo Bloodworth, sole proprietor of the Bloodworth Detective Agency, in business in scenic downtown Los Angeles continuously since 1982. I was on Addis at the behest of the television personality Pierre Reynaldo. I assume you're familiar with Pierre since he's all over cable news day and night, hobnobbing with actors, politicians, and other sociopaths, and hosting specials of a spectacular if not always genuine nature. Wavy black hair. Swarthy but clean-shaven. Wears bow ties and bright suits and a smug expression that any right-thinking viewer would want to personally slap into sadness.

In recent years there's been a fine line separating television news from bullshit. Pierre has more or less erased that line— and grown rich doing it. He lost some of his loot in a libel suit a few years back, and since then, he's thrown a few bucks my way to check out information coming from less than reliable sources.

He was hoping to use most of the current questionable material in a special on Satanism in Southern California (tentatively titled "The Devil in Paradise"). So far, I'd spent the better part of a week doing follow-ups, with less than positive results. The surfer dude who'd claimed to have seen Beelzebub and a dozen of his minions hanging ten at Rincon wasn't sure if the vision had occurred just before or just after he'd chased a fifth of Jack Black with a crack cooler. The pharmacist in Redondo Beach who'd been arrested, according to one news report, for engaging in Satanic practices, turned out to be nothing more than a twisted horndog who'd been supplying his female customers with birth control, diet, and pain pills in return for them letting him kiss and lick their feet. The Prince of Darkness aspect had been his insistence on bathing those feet in something he called Lucifer Lotion, a combination of vanilla extract and codeine cough syrup.

Such was the state of devil worship in our corner of paradise.

This was not the sort of reality Pierre wanted. He took that report in, scowled, threw an air punch that was about as sincere as one of his editorials, and said, "That leaves us with the Addis asshole."

According to one of his cop sources, a neighbor of Joe Addis had called in a complaint that she had observed him and others prowling around his place wearing black robes and hoods, mumbo-jumboing. It was not something the police rushed to investigate, the practice of one's religion in one's home not being a crime just yet. And the woman, who called herself J. Roberts, was a frequent complainer—usually about loud parties past curfew and other "sinful" acts. Still, a uniform had been sent out. He'd reported back that though Addis had a "thick accent of some kind," had seemed "a little flaky," and had "one big mother of a dog," he saw no evidence in or around the premises of "devil worshipry."

That satisfied the law, but not our Pierre, who was growing more and more desperate for evidence that Satan was still alive and well.

"Okay, Leo," he said, "it's up to you, amigo. Make this very special show happen. Bring me something I can use. Money is no object."

Those magic words I don't hear every day. I told him I would do my best.

My first move had been a visit to J. Roberts, who lived next door to Addis in a bungalow evidently designed by the same architectural hand as his. But she wasn't quite as house-proud. While his lawn looked nice and neat, hers was sprinkled with patches of uncut grass that resembled an alopecia victim's scalp. The bungalow needed a few coats of paint and some serious rescreening.

The woman who answered the door could have used a little upkeep, too. She was tall and lanky, with watery brown eyes and dull brown hair combed with fingers if at all. She was wearing rumpled faded-blue bib overalls over an aqua-green T-shirt that, as far as I could read around the bib, invited all to "Feel the Rapture." She wore no lipstick, no makeup of any kind. But there was enough red paint left on the toenails of her sandaled feet to suggest there had been a time when she might have cared about such things.

"Miz Roberts?"

"Yes?" Something fat and furry scooted across the hardwood floor and wound itself around her ankles. A yellow and white tabby, much better kempt than its owner, who was too engaged in giving me the fish-eye to respond to its arrival.

I told her my name and that I'd like to talk with her about Joseph Addis's suspicious behavior. I did not identify myself as a member of the LAPD, but I did nothing to discourage her from that assumption.

"I got the impression you cops figured I was fantasizin' about him calling up the Devil," she said, more weary than angry. "Like there's no evidence of his Satanic presence over there in Iraq, either."

She noticed the furry critter, scooped up the cat in one bony arm and stood with it licking her chin. "She's my widdle girl, Sheba is," J. Roberts said, rubbing her cheek against the cat's. "Just won't leave her mommy alone."

Her large brown eyes shifted to me, suddenly suspicious. "Something happen to change your mind about Addis?"

"My mind is like Ralph's supermarket," I said, "always open. I read your statement and I was hoping I could ask you a little more about what you saw."

"Why not?" She moved aside to let me enter a small, surprisingly neat living room. The walls were bare except for a large framed portrait of Jesus Christ hanging over the mantle.

"C'mon back to the kitchen," she said. "Lemme sign off."

The kitchen smelled of coffee and toast. It seemed to be the hub of the house. Its pale green linoleum was worn in spots near the entryway and beside the sink where a dishwasher thrummed. A wooden table occupied the center of the room, places set for two diners. There were three wooden chairs.

The fourth was supporting J. Roberts, who sat at a small table against one wall, still holding the cat in one arm while using her free hand to peck at the keyboard of a computer. She was signing off from a website that identified itself as The Truth-Seeker Network.

"With you in a minute," she said. "Coffee's on the stove, if any's left. Cups in the cabinet."

The electric range was from the '50, squat, square, with burners on either side of a cooktop. It triggered a faint, pleasant, youthful memory that I didn't bother to pursue. A ceramic coffeepot rested on one cold burner.

I found a cup, poured a couple of inches of thick black tepid coffee and took it to a place at the table that had not been set for dinner.

A gauzy white curtain with three green stripes at the bottom was doing its best to minimize glare near the computer. Its mates were all open, brightening the room and giving me a clear view of Joe Addis's bungalow and rear yard. No activity visible.

In a few seconds, J. Roberts joined me, dragging her chair over. The cat was on its own, lapping at something gooey in a white plastic bowl on the linoleum floor near the sink. I made a big thing of removing the MP3 player from my pocket and pressing its side, as if I had a clue how to record what she was about to tell me. The fact was, it took the kid who gave me the gizmo for my birthday nearly an hour to show me how to plug it into the office computer and transfer my songs onto it. Neither she nor I had been all that anxious to explore its other uses, like recording conversations.

"Fancy," J. Roberts said, squinting at the tiny silver device.

"I'm a big believer in using the latest technology," I said. "Why don't you tell me what you saw that night over at Addis's?"

She wrinkled her nose. "Man's unholy. Him and his devil dog."

"I'm sorry. What?"

"That giant dog of his. I'm sure he uses it in his black arts. Never barks. Never makes a sound. Unnatural." She shivered. "A few weeks ago, the devil dog was in our back yard, digging up my vegetables. Don't know how he got past the fence. Barry went and told the freak to take care of his animal or he'd shoot it. Barry would, too. Barry's like me. We're cat people. Got no feeling for dogs, whatsoever."

"Barry's your husband?"

"Baby brother," she said. "I never married. Took care of my sainted father till he passed away, must be nine years. Take care of Barry now."

"Can you tell me exactly what you witnessed Joseph Addis doing the night you mentioned in your complaint?"

"I'll do better than that." She got up and went to the smaller table where she punched a few computer keys. Eventually, the printer beside the computer spit out a sheet of paper.

"I keep a diary," she said, handing me the sheet.

The excerpt was from a Saturday, three weeks before. At approximately 10 pm, Roberts and her brother, Barry, had observed Addis and two other men, all dressed in black robes, moving through the bungalow next door. Eventually, the lights had been turned off in the bungalow, replaced by the glow of candles.

"That seemed curious behavior to me and Barry," she wrote. "So we went outside and stood by the fence out there where we could hear better. Addis and his unholy brethren were speaking in the profane language of Satan. This is too much for good Christians to abide."

The diary entry ended there.

"I'm not sure I understand what you mean by 'language of Satan," I said. "What were they saying, exactly?"

"It would take one of Satan's followers to decipher it," she said. "And Addis had this shiny thing he was waving around, some kind of weapon. The other two sinners were on their knees, babbling like crazy men in that devil language."

"Then what happened?" I asked.

"They just kept on doing that."

"Umm," I said. "No blood, chickens with their heads chopped off?"

"There was nothing like that. You mocking me?"

"No, ma'am," I said. I was a bit let down, getting a mental image of Pierre Reynaldo's wallet being folded and put back into his pocket.

"I do have something I didn't have when I went to the station," she said. "From last week. I took them with a new little camera they gave Barry at the studio. He builds sets and they needed something done in a rush, so he spent his own time last weekend and they gave him a camera."

She played with the keyboard some more and the printer spun out another sheet. This one contained six color snapshots of Addis wandering in his rear yard with his dog. He was wearing a long black robe and a scowl and seemed more than ready to summon up dark deeds.

"Well? Does that look like a son of Satan, or what?"

"Could I keep this?" I asked, thinking that it would definitely be something Pierre would want to see.

Before she could reply, we heard the front door open and a male voice say, "Yo, Jules, I'm home early. McGuire's back got hurting him, so they closed down for the day and sent every—who the heck is this?"

He was a guy about my size, six-two or -three, maybe a pound or two lighter and twenty-five years younger. Same dull brown hair as his sister. A couple of days' growth of beard. Wearing a khaki cap, bill backwards, a paint-stained brown workshirt, denims that were powdered with sawdust, a utility belt weighed down on the right by a ball-peen hammer, and pale brown boots that were made for stompin'.

"This is Detective Bloodworth, Barry," his sister said. "It's about the Unholy."

"Detective, huh?" He scowled at me. "He show you a badge?"

"No, he didn't."

"I don't carry a badge," I said, folding the print-outs and shoving them and my MP3 player into a pocket. "I'm a private investigator."

Barry Roberts took a threatening step toward me. "Why you bothering my sister, Jack?" he asked, right hand resting on the hammer hanging from his belt. "You pay him any money, Jules?"

"N-no."

"And you're not gonna," he said. "Get moving, Jack. I see you around here again, you're gonna feel my boot up your be-hind."

\* \* \* \* \* \*

Pierre Reynaldo was encouraged by the photos of Addis in basic black. "I smell success, Leo," he said. "Get me more."

And that's why I was in my car, waiting, when the bearded and bald Mr. Addis slid into a battered white Yugo and took off in a plume of exhaust thick enough to send the clean-air arrow into the red zone.

I quickly finished the pricey coffee, and when the Yugo was half-way down the block brought the Chevy to life. I exchanged the car radio for the MP3 player, since the batteries don't last forever and I hate to get stuck on a stake-out with only my thoughts to occupy my time.

The Yugo took me on a journey from West Los Angeles through the morning traffic along Wilshire to Fairfax, then over to Holly-wood Boulevard, finally coming to rest in an empty metered space along Vine.

I drove past, then pulled to the curb and watched the subject in the rearview. When he entered the Good Life, a flash bar a few doors down from Hollywood Boulevard, I turned off the engine and bought a temporary piece of the street, too.

Then I tucked the earbuds into place and fired up the MP3 player.

The temperature was still in the low eighties and it was pleasant sitting there, listening to Frank Sinatra singing the bejeezus out of the Mercer tune "Midnight Sun," self-amused to be doing so in the shadow of the Capitol Records building, which the composer had built and the singer's albums had helped to finance.

After another three or four Mercer tunes, I got a little curious about what Addis was up to. I locked the headset and player in the glove compartment and headed for the Good Life.

It was cool and dark inside. A sound system was turned down so low the music was more like white noise. When my eyes adjusted to the change from daylight, I was looking at a barroom of moderate size, all black and chrome, black-and-white photos on the walls of performers like Elvis and the Rolling Stones. The small tables and chairs looked sad and empty. To my right was an onyx bar with the silver outline of a martini glass visible through the stools. Behind the bar was a long mirror and above the mirror a sign spelling out in cursive blue neon: "It's Martooni Teem."

At the far end of the room was another blue neon sign over an arched portal. This one read: "Club Caviar." It was accompanied by a blue neon arrow pointing up.

There were three men in the room, none of them Addis. They looked like brothers. Big beefy boys in their late twenties to early thirties, curly black hair, ugly as gargoyles, skin the color and texture of partially mashed potatoes. Dressed alike in white shirts and black trousers.

The oldest was behind the bar. He headed my way with a pasted-on smile. "Yes, sir. What you have? Apple martini?" He had a Slavic accent.

Trying not to think too much about how awful an apple martini might taste, I asked, "You the manager?"

"Sure, I'm manager," he said, prompting a snicker from one of the others. "So?"

"Douglas Furshaddle," I said, offering my hand.

"So?" he repeated, ignoring my hand.

"I represent the CNCV," I said.

"The what?"

"The Council of Northern California Vintners. I've been visiting some of the better clubs in the Hollywood area, telling them about our champagne and—"

"Not interested," he said.

"But if you have just a minute or two …" I continued to scan the room, trying to figure out where Addis had gone and what might have drawn him there. Probably not apple martinis.

"You don't hear so good." The bartender reached for something under the bar. It looked like a kid's baseball bat.

"Whoa, at ease, Vlad," the youngest of the three said without a trace of an accent. "As you can probably tell, my brother isn't who you want to talk to. Our father deals with salesmen."

"Great," I said. "Is he here?"

The young man glanced back at the arched doorway. "He's busy," he said. "Come back later."

"Will do," I said and turned to go.

"Hold on a minute," the third man said. "You say California champagne?"

I nodded.

"Don't bother to come back," he said without any emotion. "Our customers don't go for domestic."

"They would be if they tried our champagne," I said.

"Good-bye, Mr. Furshaddle. Peddle your pisswater elsewhere."

\* \* \* \* \* \*

Addis lived The Good Life for another twenty minutes. When he exited, he was followed by a stocky, gray-haired man who was patting him on the back and grinning like a monkey.

Addis returned the smile, said something, and the two men hugged.

The old man went back inside the club. Addis watched him go, then headed for the parked Yugo. He was no longer smiling. In fact, he looked troubled.

I kept some distance between us as I trailed him back to his bungalow. He went inside. I waited for a few minutes to make sure he was settled before daring to drive to the nearest gas station washroom to get rid of the aftereffects of the coffee I'd been drinking all morning.

I'd returned the washroom key to the cashier and was heading for the Chevy when a pretty, very dark-skinned woman in a business suit fell in beside me. "Hi," she said.

"Hi," I replied. "Nice day, huh?"

"Could go either way," she said.

We arrived at the Chevy. She seemed to have something on her mind.

"Can I help you?" I asked.

"Maybe," she said. She opened the rear door and slid in.

"Hey," I said. "What's going on?"

I realized then that another woman was already in the car, on the passenger seat. This one was white and not so pretty. She was holding a .45 in her left hand, pointing it at my chest. "Get in, Mr. Bloodworth."

With a sigh, I slid behind the wheel and closed the door. "What now, ladies?"

"Place both hands on the steering wheel, Mr. Bloodworth," the woman with the gun said.

The black woman leaned forward and reached over my shoulders to prod my chest for a weapon that wasn't there. I could have head-butted her, but her white sister would have shot me dead and then where would I be.

"No weapon," I said.

The white woman slid closer, jammed the gun in my ribs and felt around my waist, then down my legs. "Clean," she said. She rested the gun hand on her lap, the barrel pointed away. I took that to be a gesture of trust, so I relaxed a little.

"What are you up to, Mr. Bloodworth?" the black woman asked.

Locking eyes with her in the rearview mirror, I said, "You first."

"Fair enough," she said. "We work for the government."

"Oh, please don't tell me Homeland Security," I said.

The white woman chuckled. "No need to get offensive," she said. Her free hand slipped inside her jacket and withdrew a leather folder. She flipped it open, exposing a colorful shield on which a goose took flight against a bright rising sun and a whale leapt from the sea.

"You ladies are with Fish and Wildlife Service?" I asked, not quite believing it.

"F & WS, Division of Law Enforcement," the black woman said. "I'm Agent Andrews from Division One in Portland. Agent Calibrese is from the local office in Torrance. Joseph Addis is assisting us in an investigation. So, why are you following him?"

"Since you know who I am—from my license plate, I'm guessing—you probably know how I earn a living."

"Are you working for the Sogorskys?" Agent Calibrese asked.

"Never heard of 'em," I said.

"Wrong answer," Agent Calibrese said, covering me again with her weapon.

"Are they part of the men-in-black crew?" I asked.

"The men in black?" Agent Calabrese said. "You mean from the church?"

"Is that what they call it? A church?"

"What else?" Agent Andrews asked.

"I don't know," I said. "Do Satan worshipers have churches?"

The two agents exchanged glances. Then Calabrese started making a sound like a kid imitating a machine gun. Her version of laughter.

Andrews kept her amusement down to a crooked smile. "You think Joseph Addis is a Satanist?" she asked.

"That's what I'm trying to find out," I said. "He and some other guys have been seen running around his house wearing these black outfits, mumbling incantations."

Calabrese was shaking her head. She had tears in her eyes. "He can't be making it up," she said.

"You've been following the man because you think he's got this black mass thing going?" Andrews asked. "You interested in selling your soul or something?"

I wondered if that's what I was doing, working for Pierre Rey naldo. I said, "No. I'm gathering material on devil worship in Southern California. So I'm following up a tip I got on Addis."

"This guy is priceless," Calabrese said between ack-ack-acks.

Andrews was no longer even slightly amused. "An hour ago, we saw you go into the Good Life. What were you doing in there?"

"Addis was inside there awhile. I got curious about what was going on."

"What *was* going on?" Andrews asked.

I told her about the three guys in the bar who looked like brothers; that Addis was probably upstairs in a room they call the Caviar Club, talking with the owner; that a few minutes after I left the club, Addis showed up on the sidewalk with an old guy that I assumed was the club owner.

"I'm guessing they're the Sogorskys?" I said. I was hoping for a confirmation or a denial, but I got neither.

"We've wasted enough time here," Andrews said to her partner. "For the record, Mr. Bloodworth, Joseph Addis is not a devil worshiper. Quite the contrary. So strike him from your list of things to do. If I see you anywhere near him again, I guarantee you will wind up in a small steel-and-cement room for a long, long time. Am I clear?"

"Like crystal," I said.

I watched the two agents march to a black Infiniti and take their leave with a squeal of tires.

Then I started my engine and, driving a bit slower than they, headed to Pierre with the bad news.

*  *  *  *  *  *

His reaction surprised me. Instead of shouting or throwing a fit, as he'd done in similar situations, he just sat behind his massive black oak desk, lost in thought.

A couple of minutes of that and he shouted for his assistant, Luna, a handsome Latina with a steel-trap mind I would put up there with Stephen Hawking's. "See what you can find on the name 'Sogorsky' and the Good Life bar on Vine Street," he told her.

He watched Luna depart, then said, "She hates me, you know."

"Doesn't everybody?" I said.

He laughed.

"I didn't think you'd be so cheery about losing another devil worshiper," I said.

"I'm getting a feeling this might be just as good. I sense something . . . unique. Fish and Wildlife. What's their franchise, anyway?"

"I think they go after bear hunters," I said. "Fish poachers."

"What do you suppose they're doing with our Addis?" he asked.

In just a few minutes, Luna brought us the answer in the form of hard copies of Internet info. One set for Pierre, one for me.

"You get the picture, Leo?" Pierre asked when we'd finished perusing the pages.

I told him I did.

Luna made it clear enough. First, there were copies of a "sogorsky.com" website announcing to the world that they, Russian nationals all, in addition to having "one of the nation's most popular nightclubs, located at the historic crossroads of Hollywood and Vine," were "among the Pacific Southwest's leading importers of smoked salmon, foie gras, and truffles."

There were newspaper accounts concerning the threat of sturgeon extinction leading to a recent worldwide ban on wild-caviar production. And, clever lady that she is, Luna added a news item about the president of an import company in Miami being convicted of smuggling the salty eggs into this country. The investigation had been conducted by the U.S. Fish and Wildlife Services Law

Enforcement Division in conjunction with U.S. Customs and the Food and Drug Administration.

Pierre wiggled his eyebrows, his indication of extreme interest. "The Sogorskys are smuggling caviar," he said. "And this Addis jamoke is somehow involved."

"I think you'll find the answer to that on page four," I said.

He flipped to the page. "Russian Orthodox Church . . . problems with funding." He scanned the article. "I didn't bother reading . . . oh, I dig, the caviar thing again. "

The news item started out by explaining that perestroika had put a lot of Russian Orthodox churches back into operation without providing the funding to keep them going. So some church officials eventually felt the need to get in bed with questionable "donors."

The article took its own sweet time getting to the current news: thirty-two Russian priests were accusing the very powerful bishop of a diocese along the Ural of an assortment of moral and legal failings stemming from way back at the start of perestroika. Among them was his cooperation with a gang of caviar poachers whom he'd given a free pass to cast their nets into the diocesan waters.

"And I should be interested in this because . . . ?" Pierre asked.

"Agent Andrews told me that Addis was helping them. She also said he was the opposite of a Satan worshipper. He speaks with a thick accent, sports a big furry beard, and wears black robes. What does that tell you?"

"So he's a Russian Orthodox priest," Pierre said. "Big whoop."

"Let's say he was this bad old bishop's contact man on the West Coast. Like his fellow priests back home, he gets religion and decides God isn't smiling on this smuggling thing. So he blows the whistle on this end of the operation, which happens to be run by the Sogorskys."

"It's not Devil worship," Pierre said, begrudgingly, "but it's something. Presented properly, this Addis might just turn out to be a major heroic figure." He raised his hands as if positioning letters on a marquee. "Father Joe Addis, Environmental Champion."

He shouted for Luna.

"Get me Joseph Addis on the phone. You got a number for him, Leo?"

I gave Luna the phone number.

She was back in a minute. "Not there," she said. "I left a message to call us."

"Go to his place, Leo. When he shows, bring him here."

"The guy's in the middle of a federal criminal investigation," I said.

"So? How's talking with me gonna interfere with that?"

"I was thinking more of *me*," I said. "Agent Andrews promised that if I showed up in his vicinity, she'd toss me in the clink."

"That's why I hire lawyers," he said.

"I'm not that fond of jails."

"Not even for a grand each day you spend inside?"

\* \* \* \* \* \*

What with pulling a few twenties out of a nearby ATM and washing down a beef stromboli with a Moretti at Bruno's, it was nearly three o'clock before I arrived at Addis's bungalow.

There was no sign of the black Infiniti sedan that agents Andrews and Calabrese has been using earlier. No sign of anybody watching Addis's house. That made some sense, if Addis was elsewhere.

But his battered Yugo was parked in front of the bungalow.

I eased the Chevy toward the curb. With the engine idling, I dialed the bungalow's number. And got his answering machine. So he was out somewhere being chauffeured. He had to return home sometime.

I killed the engine and prepared to wait. I wondered if Andrews had just been blowing smoke with that threat of arrest. I wasn't breaking any laws I knew of. But if she did arrest me, Pierre's legal scoundrels would work their magic.

And if they dragged their feet, I'd be collecting a grand a—

An unpleasant sound interrupted my dream of short term wealth. I lowered the window to get a better fix on it.

It was the whimper of an animal in pain. Coming from Addis's bungalow.

As I got out of the Chevy I heard another whimper. It wasn't coming from inside the house. I headed toward a gate that led to a rear yard along a shoulder-high thick bush that separated Addis's property from the Roberts'.

I paused at the gate, studying the area before opening it. Back in the yard, Addis's brown mastiff lay on its side, its heavy breathing causing its massive rib cage to rise and lower.

The animal whimpered again.

I was still a little nervous about sharing a yard with him. "Hey," I yelled.

The mastiff tried to raise its huge head, but hadn't the strength.

I opened the gate and moved toward the wounded dog.

I could hear its ragged breathing now, along with the whimpering.

It was in seriously bad shape. The back of its head was pulpy. There was blood on his muzzle and on his front paws. I wondered if it was his or if he'd gotten a piece of the bastard who'd walloped him.

I didn't think there was much that could be done for the poor critter, other than putting it out of its misery. I took out my cellular with the idea of letting the West L.A. ASPCA make that decision. I was waiting for Directory Assistance to provide me with that number when I happened to look in the direction of the bungalow.

The back door was wide open and just a few feet from it, Joseph Addis was sprawled on a brick walkway, looking pretty damned still. I stared at that open door, wishing I'd been one of those guys who loves the feel of a gun on his hip.

There were enough windows to give me a pretty good view inside the bungalow. Nothing seemed to be stirring.

I moved to Addis's body. His skull had not been as sturdy as the dog's. The walkway bricks beneath his ruined head were coated with thickened blood. Just on the odd chance he might still be alive, I pressed fingers against his neck searching for a pulse.

Finding none, I backed away, eyeing the open door, half expecting some crazy yahoo to rush through it waving a bloody lead pipe.

The dog's whimper had grown so faint I could barely hear it as I double-timed it through the gate. In front of the bungalow, feeling a little less vulnerable, I dialed 911. A female took down the information without batting a verbal eye. She said the officers who'd be arriving shortly would decide what to do about the wounded dog.

She also suggested that, should the perpetrator still be in the vicinity, I was to take no action that might place me in jeopardy.

Like I had to be told.

* * * * * *

The blue-and-white arrived with sirens blaring, as though the officers were hoping to chase off the killer rather than confront him. Through the Chevy's rear window, I saw J. Roberts at her window, gawking at the uniformed cops as they exited their vehicle. This was better than TV.

The pale, freckled officer looked to be in his early twenties. His dark-skinned partner had about ten years' seniority on him and was calling the shots. He asked me a few quick questions about the situation in the back yard, ending with, "You didn't see nobody moving around in the house?"

I told him I didn't.

"Okay, Mr. Bloodworth. You say you wore the blue, so you know the drill. Detectives are gonna wanna talk to you. Just sit tight. We'll take it from here."

I watched them move to the open gate, arming themselves, then heading toward the rear. They'd know what to do about the dead man. But the dog might pose a problem.

Not mine, any more.

* * * * *

Before too long more uniformed cops arrived. And plain clothes detectives. And technicians. The media would get there eventually, but Agent Andrews beat them to the scene.

She arrived in a Crown Vic, with a guy in a smartly tailored suit and tinted glasses. His face was the shape and color of a bruised tomato. It looked like he and Andrews were arguing. When she saw me, she started toward my car. He wasn't finished whatever he was saying. He called to her. When she didn't respond, he shook his head and moved off to where the action was.

"Where's Vlad Sogorsky, Bloodworth?" she asked, getting into the car beside me.

"Which one is he, again? The bartender, right?"

"The bartender who broke Agent Calabrese's wrist with his little baseball bat."

"Aw, Jeeze. How's she doing?"

"Better than Father Addis," she said. "Here's what I want, Bloodworth. I want you to have been lying to me earlier today. I want you to be working for the Sogorskys. Because then I could offer you some kind of deal, maybe a slightly reduced sentence, if you put me in Vlad's direction."

"Look, lady, the only thing I'm guilty of is letting that poor animal in the yard continue to suffer."

"An LAPD tech just put the sad old thing to sleep." she said. She sighed in frustration. "What the hell are you doing here, Bloodworth?"

"Waiting to give the detectives a statement. I discovered the body and called it in."

"So I hear," she said. "What I want to know is why you're still here. If you had been involved with the Sogorskys you'd have run, right?"

"Definitely," I said.

"Damn, I've got nothing," she said. "This has been a total screw-up."

"What happened to the surveillance on Addis?"

She gave me an angry look. "That's your doing," she said.

"Mine?"

"Our plan had been to hang tight and wait for the Sogorskys to get their next shipment. Then we'd net them, the shippers, and the smugglers, and reel them all in. But you spooked us. Calabrese and I believed your Devil worship story, but the man in charge of the operation, Agent Hidalgo of Customs—that's him over there," she pointed to the bruised tomato face, who was shouting at one of the LAPD cops, "he called us amateurs for cutting you loose.

"He said we couldn't take the chance you wouldn't tip the Sogorskys. So we had to move on them immediately before they could clean house."

"And that left Addis out here all by his lonesome," I said.

"We didn't know Vlad would slip out of the net and come here and do this."

"Why did he come here?" I asked. "Especially if he was on the run?"

"Either he thought Father Addis betrayed the family and was looking for vengeance," she said, "or he was looking for help from his priest. Either way, something set him off and he used his baseball bat again."

She was looking so miserable, I said, "Would a witness to the murder help?"

"Don't kid around."

I pointed in the direction of J. Roberts who was still at her window. "She doesn't miss much. You might want to suggest to Agent Hidalgo that he talk to her."

"Hell with Hidalgo," she said, opening the car door. "Come on. You can introduce me to the lady."

As we walked to the Roberts house, I overheard Hidalgo calling one of the LAPD detectives a jackass. "They've shot people for less," I told Andrews.

"You make my mouth water," she said.

J. Roberts took her time answering the bell. She opened the door just a few inches and asked, "Yes?"

"Hello, Miz Roberts," I said. "Leo Bloodworth, remember? With me is Special Agent Andrews. She'd like to talk to you about the trouble next door."

"W-what about it?"

"Can't we come in?" Agent Andrews said.

"Might as well let 'em in." The voice was clearly her brother's.

He was standing in the living room, looking a little less like a workman and more like a slacker without his utility belt. He'd also exchanged his paint-stained T-shirt and Levi's for a pair of rumpled khaki slacks and a gray warm-up sweater with the Warner Bros. logo covering most of the front.

He gestured toward me with his stubbled chin. "I know Bloodworth isn't official," he said to Agent Andrews. "You got some real tin you can show me, brown sugar?"

Scowling, agent Andrews held out her badge.

"The beaver patrol, huh?"

"I'm a federal investigator, Mr. Roberts," she said. "With full arrest power. You may want to keep that in mind."

"Okay, lady, what do you wanna know? But make it fast. I got things to do."

Agent Andrews turned to the sister. "Have you been home all day, Ms. Roberts?"

Before J. Roberts could reply, her brother Barry said, "We went over to the Westside Pavilion around noon. Ribs at Roma's. Caught the new Mel Gibson on a three-dollar matinee. Weird flick, all those dudes wearing white powder. Nothing like 'Passion of the Christ.' Anyway, we just got back maybe an hour, hour and a half ago. Right, Jule?"

His sister nodded obediently.

"Then I guess you didn't see anything unusual next door?"

"Heck, there was always something unusual over there. The dude was a nutcase, queer for Satan."

"He was a Russian Orthodox priest," Agent Andrews said.

Barry Roberts blinked, clearly surprised. "Get serious," he said. "What about that black robe? And the goofy-looking hat?"

"It's what they wear," Andrews said, "when they pray to what I suppose is the same God you pray to."

"Oh, Barry," J. Roberts said. "A priest."

Barry Roberts looked almost as shaken as his sister. "I thought he was some kind of . . . well, never mind what I thought. It don't matter anyway."

"Well, thank you both for your cooperation," Agent Andrews said. "I'm sure the homicide detectives will want to talk with you, too."

"We'll tell them same's we told you. We weren't here when the dude . . . when it went down."

"Where's your cat, Miz Roberts?" I asked.

She blinked and shifted her eyes to her brother.

"Sheba's outside somewhere," he said.

"They have this nice big cat," I said to Agent Andrews. "Sweet old tabby."

J. Roberts's eyes were moistening.

Barry moved quickly to her side, put his arm around her. "You're upsettin' Jule," he said. "You better leave now."

"I'm surprised to hear Sheba's outside," I said. "Especially since Jule told me that the cat never left her alone."

She was weeping now. She pulled away from Barry and leaned against a wall, her body shaking. Agent Andrews approached her, placed a hand on her arm. "What's the matter, ma'am?"

"You two are the matter," Barry Roberts said, moving between the agent and his sister. "All this stuff going on. The cops. You coming here with all your gosh-darned questions."

"I bet Sheba's in the back yard," I said, ignoring him. "Now that the big dog next door is dead and can't get through the fence, I guess it's safe for her to be out there."

Agent Andrews turned to me, a puzzled look on her face. "Bloodworth, what in the world are you –"

Barry Roberts had moved behind her and used his left arm to place her in a choke hold. Pulling her back against him, he yanked her weapon from its holster. Then he tossed her aside.

"You nosy son of a buck," he said, aiming the gun at me. "Just won't let it alone."

"The cops will figure it out anyway," I said, talking fast, hoping to distract him from pulling the trigger. "They'll discover it's cat blood on the dog's muzzle. They'll find the hole in the fence. Once they're here, it's just a matter of checking out that ball-peen hammer of yours and the clothes you were wearing earlier."

"That devil dog killed Sheba," he said, holding steady on the gun.

"Tore the sweet baby apart. In our own back yard. Right in front of our gosh-darned eyes." He was crying now, too. "Even after I cracked the darned dog's skull, it still crawled back through the fence."

"The dog's dead now," I said, hoping to calm him a little. "You did what had to be done."

"You got that right," he said. He inhaled deeply and noisily through his nose and blinked away a tear. "That . . . foreigner. I don't care if he was a priest. He brought his devil dog into our neighborhood. Killed our little Sheba.

"Still, I didn't mean to do him any harm. If only the dog had died in our yard, I'd never have gone onto another man's property. And if he hadn't come out of his house to try and stop me from killing that hellhound . . .

"I been a good, God-fearing Christian all my life. Now I'm a murderer. Standin' here with a gun in my hand."

He held the weapon out. "Here, take this thing."

I didn't wait for him to change his mind.

\* \* \* \* \* \*

"I haven't heard any 'thank-you-Pierre's for putting your mug on our newscasts last night," the TV entrepreneur was saying at brunch the next morning. We were at his "special" table at Farmer's Market on Fairfax, within shouting distance of a group of usually rowdy and frequently funny screenwriters who seemed to enjoy sending insults his way.

"I'm not sure publicity is a good thing in my game," I said, polishing off the remnants of what had once been eggs-over-easy with corned beef hash.

"Maybe not the Tony Pellicano type of publicity," Pierre said. "But you're a hero. Even the black girl—what's her name?"

"She's a woman. Evelyn Andrews."

"Whatever. Even she says you broke the case. Not the LAPD dicks or the Customs guy, Hidalgo, which is how the *Times* played the story."

"Speaking of the *Times*," I said, "I read they caught Vladimir Sogorsky on the 405, heading for Mexico."

"He's agreed to cooperate with Customs, so they're pulling in the whole smuggling operation," Pierre said. "A twenty-million-dollar business, can you believe it? Fish eggs. Anyway, it's a happy ending for everybody but Addis and his dog."

"And Barry Roberts," I said.

"He'll walk," Pierre said. "They can't get a murder case to stick out here. And there's sure to be one cat lover on his jury. Know why his sister calls herself 'J. Roberts'? Her first name is Julia. Julia Roberts. Can you imagine what that musta been like for her, walking around with that name, with a mug like hers?"

"Pierre, there's stuff I should be doing," I said. "If there's a reason you're buying me brunch, maybe we ought to get to it."

He gave me a half smile. "I was thinking you might wanna come up with some pages for me."

"I'm sorry, what?"

"The CW network's looking for a crime-adventure show with broads. Something different. This Fish and Wildlife Service is a whole new franchise. You've done some writing. Put together a series synopsis for me. Shouldn't take you that long."

"I don't know, Pierre," I said. "I've written fiction, but TV . . . I don't know."

"Use the Sogorsky story, punch it up with some gunplay and car chases, only make sure you copy far enough away we don't get sued. Dawn will love the fighting-for-the-environment angle, and I know Les is always looking for something a little different."

In Hollywood, hope is the thing with residuals, not feathers. I looked at the screenwriter's table. The guys there seemed relaxed and happy. And wealthy. I recognized one of them—a mystery novelist who at one time had been called the next Raymond Chandler but who'd given it up for movie gold.

"Would it be okay if I wrote it like a short story?" I asked.

"Geeze, Leo, how long you been livin' out here in La-La? Haven't you learned by now that in TV it's not the writing that matters, it's the selling. Write it any way you want. Just give me some paper with words on it. I'll take it from there."

*Gary Phillips works in both the prose and graphic novel arenas. His best known creation is California P.I. Ivan Monk. He has also written about Las Vegas courier Martha Chainey. However, it's his recent anthology of drug-themed stories,* The Cocaine Chronicles, *perhaps, that really illustrates how Phillips works on the edge. There's really no telling what he's going to come up with next. For it is sex, drugs, and rock n'roll underlining the following story, in which he introduces a character who embodies the notion, "What if funk master Rick James had lived and got wise?"*

# Where All Our Dreams Come True

*by Gary Phillips*

His arthritic knee caused Terry Haze to groan as he moved onto his side in the bed. This to ogle his girlfriend, Betty Abaya, who was standing and shimmying out of the funky sweats she slept in.

"What time is this thing?" In her cut off T and panty, she stood in profile to the mirror over the dresser, her hand patting her still-flat stomach.

"Two o'clock." He yawned and stretched. "They figure it might get some play on the late afternoon news."

"And who's on the program?"

"Besides Nina?"

"Yeah, besides that stuck-up ho," Abaya snorted. "Oh, sorry, stuck-up old ho."

Haze chuckled, shaking his head. "Remember Dan Scott?"

She looked over at him, searching her memory. "He played the cop with the eye patch in that show, *Street . . .* " she trailed off.

"*Street Heat,*" Haze finished for her. "He'll be there, and the son and daughter of Dallas Reeves, who played the female gunslinger in those movies."

Abaya bent over to search in the dresser for clean clothes. Haze enjoyed the view. She straightened up, clutching garments and shaking them at him as she talked. "And why the hell aren't you on the program, Terry? They got a goddamn statue of you in there too."

Haze sat on the side of the bed, massaging his knee. "Maybe I don't want to remind anybody of the me then."

Abaya sat beside him. Her lavender-nailed fingers gripping his unshaven jaw, she made kissy face. "You were fine, honey. Had all them groupies lined up backstage to take your pick. Two at once sometimes, huh?"

"Even three sometimes." He scratched graying whiskers. There were too many gaps from those years, his memory robbed by the infamous duo of booze and coke. "Of course that's ancient  history."

"Shit changes, baby." She bounded up to take her shower.

Haze proned on his back. What if he just gobbled down a couple of Vicodin and let the day mellow away? "No, I suppose not," he lamented, sitting up again.

"Hey, pops," Abaya called from the bathroom, the water going, "think you can handle going a round in the morning?"

Haze was already out of his boxers and tossing off his tattered T with a fading Daredevil on it, and damn near slipped on the tiles, he was so eager.

"Careful now," Abaya teased, pushing open the glass door to let him in.

Haze stepped under the invigorating spray and into her embrace, gingerly.

* * * * *

"Is it too much to ask that we have some quality water in here? What is this shit?" Nina Venis complained, holding the offending bottle aloft.

"I'm afraid that's all we have, Ms. Venis," Julie Whitten answered in a measured tone. "The good news is, there's plenty of it." She regarded Venis the way orderlies eyed one of their charges they routinely cajole to take their meds. "Three minutes, people," she announced and walked out of the makeshift green room.

"Who the fuck does Miss Thing think she's talking to?" Venis demanded of the room's occupants and the universe.

Haze eschewed saying 'a has-been,' which would have been cruel and not quite accurate. It was true that Nina hadn't had a number on the charts since the greatest hits CD five years ago. But she did all right with her revival show off the Strip in Vegas, and a few of her disco tunes had been redone and used as background jingles for hamburger and feminine hygiene commercials.

"Relax, Nina, want some Percodan?" Dan Scott asked her, checking his face's tan lines in the mirror.

"I'm clean and sober, baby," she declared proudly.

"Aren't we all," Elmira Reeves Franco said.

"Amen," Haze added.

"I still don't get why you've got to hold Nina's hand for this, Terry," Aldo Reeves said. "She worried one of the aging funkateers gonna rush up and break her hip by making her do the Bump?" He again looked longingly at the cigarette Julie Whitten had forbidden him to light.

"You don't know what you're talking about, Aldo, and let's leave it at that." With a disgusted look on her face, Venis had some of her supermarket-brand water.

A young man with spiky hair and a Bluetooth earpiece stuck his head in the room. "If you please, folks. The audience awaits."

"Swell," Venis grumbled.

"Show business is my business" Dan Scott said, erecting a practiced grin. One after the other, with Haze taking up the rear but Venis in his sights, they filed out of the room. It had once been used to repair the resin re-creations of actors and musicians, and the occasional president, at the misnomered Hollywood Wax Works.

Blogs, video games, or simply all things traditional had to give way to the new, whatever it was, and the Works was now closing after more than sixty years in operation. It wasn't even in Hollywood per se, but in the Los Feliz area at the foot of the Griffith Park Observatory. In its time, it was the largest such attraction in the United States, boasting more than three hundred minutely detailed plasticine figures in sets and scenes from movies, TV, and concerts.

Haze laughed dryly as he walked past himself from more than twenty-five years ago. Hands on Lycra-clad hips, Jheri-curled hair down to his shoulders—which he'd augmented with some tastefully woven in extensions in those days—eyelashes, hoop earring in one ear, studded V-top over his muscular frame, and his Gibson electric guitar slung across his chest, the King of Party Funk was indeed one bad ass mutha.

Julie Whitten, the outgoing manger and director of the Works, was making some remarks to those gathered in the front reception area. For the occasion, what remained of the staff had placed the statues of the participants in here, though Haze wasn't scheduled to make any remarks. The crowd was mostly those in their forties and fifties, with a sprinkling of younger people. Electronic and print media was also present, capturing the end of yet another middlebrow cultural icon.

"It is with sadness that we bring you here today," Whitten said, "the last day of this wonderful palace of recreation."

The lone security guard on duty, an older gent with a beer gut, crept behind Haze, giving him the up and down. Haze noted this but was doing his own calculations of potential threats in the audience. There was the lanky kid with the three rings in a row under his bottom lip and the overweight woman in a tiger-stripe-print skirt much too tight for her heavy hips talking into her iPod. Like he had any idea what a nut who would send Nina a severed rat's head would look like—a rat's head with a torn piece of music sheet in it.

The sheet was from "Club Freak," one of Venis' biggest hits. The one about which over the years she'd been unable to shake the talk that the song was not just sweetened via the mixing board, but that another woman's voice had been overlaid as well.

Whitten finished her remarks and Dan Scott stepped to the mic. A man with a mini-cam stepped forward and Haze glared at him, frowning. As there was no stage, the participants were on the same level as everyone else, and even given his six feet plus, there was no way to see everybody. Having once been stabbed in the stomach by a disturbed fan, a woman who'd written him repeatedly begging Haze to father a baby with her, he didn't dismiss the threat against Nina as the cops had. Of course it didn't help that she was a drama queen and effortlessly turned people against her.

"Damn, but I looked good then, didn't I?" Scott joked, a hand on the shoulder of his double holding a Colt Delta Elite pistol and wearing a pin-striped suit, silk T, and deck shoes over sockless feet. The woman in the tiger dress shouted, "You're still my blue plate special, Dan." She then started mumbling into her iPod again. Moving behind her was a woman with oversized dark glasses and hip-hugger jeans that tickled something in Haze. She was a handsome fortysomething, maybe a former groupie, he considered.

The son and daughter of Lady Gunhawk, the character their

mother, Dallas Reeves, played, gave their heartfelt comments. When it came to Nina Venis's turn, as she was not one to be upstaged, she broke into an impromptu a cappella rendition of another of her disco hits, "Fever and Sweat." Her voice had lost some of its range, but being an experienced singer, she knew how to give the right emotional shading on the proper phrasings. The applause was genuine. She bowed and gave her remarks.

Julie Whitten closed out the ceremony. "While the Works will no longer be a reality, I am very pleased that many of our creations have and will find homes among other museums and private collections. And so now, please enjoy our refreshments, and I believe our guests will be available to answer questions from the press." There was polite applause. Venis, scampering to the envy of an NFL running back, shouldered past Dan Scott zeroing in on the representatives of the media. She was also not one to pass up an opportunity, Haze mused, keeping pace with her.

After the questions and chatting and hanging around, the afternoon was on its last legs. Whitten came over to Haze. "Did you know that your statue is going to the Riverhead Casino in Vegas? Victoria Degault, the owner, asked for it specifically among some others."

Haze had to search the rabbit warren of his brain. "The last time I played there I got in a fight with my rhythm guitarist on stage and I walked off in the middle of a number." He didn't add that he was coked to the moon, and the then-owner of the casino got in his face and they almost came to blows.

Whitten said, "It's for this nostalgia wing they're putting together. They might ask you there for the opening."

And so it was that Haze could now look forward to ribbon cuttings at malls, and keeping tabs on fading divas.

"Linda's going there, too," Whitten continued, "but not the other statues from her tableau." The Venis exhibit included her and two of her band members in a setting that recreated a famous concert of hers broadcast on VH1's *Remember the Legends*.

"What's going to happen to the statues that aren't sent elsewhere?" he wondered.

Whitten looked forlorn. "We'll hold an online auction for them and the memorabilia that hasn't already been bought. When that's done, what's left will be, well, recycled."

Haze was gazing at Christopher Lee as Dracula, arms wide, eyes red, about to swoop down on a terrified virgin in bed. "Wow," was all he could say, inwardly glad that his statue had a destination. It was weird imaging his stand-in melting in a pile of other figures casually tossed into a blast furnace.

"Is it alright that I take this home?" Venis was carrying a Fender Stratocaster guitar.

Whitten made a face. "Which exhibit did you take that from?"

"Mine," Venis said, "it was Larry's." Larry Barker had been her lead guitarist and lover for a while. He'd died after sustaining head injuries when he lost control of his Porsche on Pacific Coast Highway. He'd been trying to get away from the repo man.

"Instruments like this guitar are to be given to school music programs," Whitten informed her.

"This was Larry's ax," Venis insisted. "His old lady donated it."

"I'm aware of that," Whitten said. "It's going to the music department at Fairfax High, where he went to school. In fact, I believe they're going to put it in a case with items from other famous students who went there."

"I'll buy it," Venis countered.

"Sorry, Nina, but I promised the school." Whitten reached for the guitar and Venis took a step back with it.

Damn, now Haze was going to have to regulate his own client. "Give the nice lady back her guitar, Nina."

"I knew you'd try some shit like this." The woman in the oversized sunglasses stepped over.

"Take it easy, Dee." Her voice clicked, and he recognized Larry Barker's widow.

"Damn that, Terry," Denise Barker said. "This chick always has to have her way and she's not going to this time."

"Fuck you," Venis yelled. "I was closer to him than you ever were."

"That right?" Denise Barker reached into her handbag and Haze was on her.

"Oh shit, oh shit," Venis panicked, gripping the guitar by the neck with both hands. She turned violently and collided with the food folding table, upending it.

"Good grief," Whitten blared, invoking Charlie Brown.

Haze had grabbed hold of Barker's wrist. She'd been taking out a digital camera. This was apparently to document Venis bogarding her old man's guitar.

"Sorry," Haze apologized, letting go of her. Whitten and the lone security guard were getting a protesting Nina Venis to her feet.

"You should be," she said. "Why are you helping this tramp anyway, Terry?"

It beat sitting around polishing his platinum records, he reasoned. Looking away, he caught sight of a man quickly heading out. It registered because the woman in the tiger-print dress was reacting to him. She'd gotten Dan Scott to pose with her. Another woman, about Haze's age, in hot pants of all things, was taking the picture.

"Where you going with that?" Tiger Print shouted.

The man started to run and Haze took off after him as did the security guard. As the man headed toward a side exit Haze hoped his bad knee didn't lock up. The trio dashed past Laurel and Hardy frozen in that famous bit where they attempted to maneuver a piano up a series of endless steps in Echo Park, a dour Bogart as Sam Spade holding the fake Maltese falcon before a sultry Mary Astor as

Brigid O'Shaughnessy, and the governor of California clad in a loin cloth, a barbarian battling himself as a cyborg.

"Hold up," the security guard yelled from behind Haze. He wasn't sure if the rent-a-cop had a gun or if he was yelling at him or at both of them. And then a shot boomed and the hand of Chuck Norris as Walker, Texas Ranger, blew apart right beside him. Haze halted and put his hands up. The escaping man was through the Star Wars set, reached the fire exit side door not too far behind Chewbacca, and was gone. The alarm whooped.

"Don't try shit, ya goddamn hair-on fiend."

"I didn't—" Haze began.

"Shut the fuck up and get your chicken-stealin' black ass on that ground or this time I put one through your spine." The guard was darker than Haze. "I know who the hell you is. Had my eye on you the whole goddamn time."

Haze did as commanded, wincing as his knee chose that moment to give him trouble. He kneeled at the feet of a leather-suited Halle Berry as Catwoman in stilettos, holding a whip. Any other time, he would have been happy to be in that position.

Whitten ran up, shouting at the guard. Then Venis and Denise Barker arrived, and the shouting and finger pointing and accusations went round and round. This stopped when the cops came, and Haze was brought in for questioning.

"Show me your titties, I'm Terry Haze, bitch." Detective Rosavitch guffawed. "Didn't you say that shit from the podium to Aretha Franklin at a Grammys telecast?"

"Not exactly," Haze said, fidgeting in the interrogation room at the Hollywood substation. It was airy and well lit, sterile as a doctor's surgical prep room. "But that's the spirit of it, unfortunately."

"And you were high then, right?" the other one called Edwards added. He reread something from a file he'd brought in and closed the folder. "That's why you go by H-a-z-e and not H-a-y-e-s, your actual name?"

"It's all about the show, officer. I'm not high now and haven't been in more than a decade."

"Hoo-rah," Rosavitch chided, sitting across from the suspect. "Let's go through it one more time, and this go-'round, tell us who your accomplice was who stole that football from the wax museum."

"Did you not hear me when I said I want my lawyer?" Haze said. "You laughing too loud?" He sat back, folding his arms. "And stealing a prop like that is a misdemeanor, petty theft or something, isn't it? Why you two sweating me?"

"That was the Super Bowl-winning ball Rexford threw, homeboy, as if you didn't know. It's valued at eight grand, a felony we're gonna lay on you, brah." Rosavitch triumphantly sucked a tooth.

The stolen football had been in the hands of a suited-up Jason Rexford in classic QB action. He was a local boy who went on to be a popular pro for the L.A. Barons.

Edwards said, "You need to come clean, Haze."

The former master of funk glared at him.

"You've got a good hustle with these music types, don't you?" Edwards asked, using another tact. "Diet-pill-dependent, stressed, out signers, or coked-up record producers come to you when they won't or can't go to the law. You know that world and can move in and around it, taking care of this or that indiscretion."

Rosavitch jumped in. "Like today, getting to do some glorified gophering for Nina Venis. And hell, I wouldn't kick her off my jock, she looks pretty good for her age."

"You're not meant to play the sympathetic role, man," Haze declared. "Y'all got any bottled water around here?"

It was their turn to glare at him. Not too much later, Betty Abaya arrived with Haze's lawyer, criminal defense attorney Parren Teague.

It took another half hour of wrangling, and then Haze was outside the police station talking with the two who'd come to get him.

"Want me to make a call to Ivan?" Teague asked. He was referring to a private investigator who did occasional work for him named Ivan Monk.

Haze stood with his hands in his back pockets, Abaya had an arm around his waist. "Thanks, Parren, but I doubt if there's anything to investigate. Some hardcore sports fan took advantage of the closing ceremony and made off with the prize he wanted. Or it'll show up in some online auction and they'll bust him."

"Probably right."

They shook hands and he departed. Abaya and Haze walked to her car parked a few blocks away on Hudson.

"Nina didn't even bother to see about you, did she?"

"Don't start, baby."

"Some friend."

"That's Nina," Haze said.

"Uh-huh," she muttered derisively.

"Let's get something to eat, I'm starving," he deflected.

"Where you want to go?"

"How about Madam Wu's on Western? We haven't been there in a while."

"Okay." In the car, heading north on Hudson, Abaya turned east on Hollywood Boulevard, heading toward the restaurant. At Vine, they passed one of the older buildings still remaining on the Boulevard. The area had been going through a revitalization, and not much of bygone Hollywood was left. Though for many, it never existed at all.

Abaya glanced over at the building, a hard look on her face. "That's where Empire Films used to have their office."

Haze put a gentle hand on the back of her neck. Abaya was from California's Central Valley. Her parents, her dad Filipino and her mom Guatemalan, were immigrants who'd worked in a fruit packing plant. She'd been a wild teenager and ran away to Hollywood. Meth and a Rasputin-like boyfriend got her into the porn business, doing the do for the Empire outfit run by twin feuding brothers. Eventually one of the brothers shot and killed the other one over money, and Abaya finally got out through rehab, where she and Haze met.

"Hollywood's not about the movies or the music business," she was saying, "it's a fuckin' rat maze run by designer label sadists. Your reward for getting through to the other side is a stale piece of cheese and a bus pass."

Haze had nothing to add to that.

The next day, after Nina Venis had ignored his calls and Abaya had bugged him to collect the money Nina owed him, which he'd use to pay Teague's bill, Haze drove to Nina's place in Ladera Heights.

There wasn't an answer to his knock, but her car was in the driveway. Climbing onto the green plastic garbage bins L.A. residents had for lawn cuttings, Haze got over the gate to the backyard where there was a pool. Off that was a sliding door. The curtain was pulled back and he could see Venis in a robe lying face down on the floor. Busting out the glass didn't seem like a good idea but he was able to get in through the unlocked back door to the kitchen. Probably the way whoever put Venis on the floor had gone.

He felt for her pulse and turned her over. She was conscious, a bruise was turning colors on the side of her swollen mouth, soon to match her purple-black eye. He got her to the couch.

"What happened?" He asked her. "Want some water?"

"Vodka." It was two-forty in the afternoon, but she had just been assaulted in her own home. Haze got her a belt from her wet bar and she took a healthy dose.

"I'll pay you double—no, triple—to get it back," Venis said, her good eye focusing and orbiting toward him.

"What?" he asked.

"The football," she answered imprecisely. And then, after another swallow, she explained it to him.

On the move, Haze used Venis's money—heeding his girlfriend's advice, he got her to pony up an advance—to hunt down Wesley Hodges, the boy toy she'd been shacking with, and who'd stolen the football ostensibly for her. And who'd fallen out with her, knocking her about to underscore their parting. Hodges, as in so common a story as to be cliché, had come to town to get into the music business as an R&B crooner. He did some backup singing for Venis in her Vegas show, and from there began sharing her bed.

Haze talked to Hodges's female agent. Using Venis's name and creatively suggesting she was heart broken about Hodges's sudden disappearance, he got from the middle-aged woman, who also thrilled to the company of younger men, the names of a few other struggling singers and musicians who knew Hodges. For a mere $85 paid to one of these cats facing an electricity cutoff, Haze got to a fellow named Clete who frequented the Hollywood Park Casino. The casino and the adjacent racetrack were not in Hollywood, but miles south in Inglewood, a small municipality next-door to L.A., where the Lakers used to ball in the days of Magic and Kareem.

"Can't tell you where the boy is," Clete said over mouthfuls of his tri-tip sandwich in the food court of the casino. This was after Haze slipped him a gratuity. "But I do know he's into Freddy Famous for some ducats. 'Bout fifteen or twenty grand, I understand."

Farush Famouz, known affectionately as Freddy Famous, was a gangster and loan shark who owned a nightclub in West Hollywood. He'd been an early investor in Empire Films.

"Gambling?" Haze asked.

Clete chuckled. "Hodges borrowed money to shoot a music video from one of his songs. It was so bad, even with girls shaking their booty all up in it, BET wouldn't put it in rotation."

Haze drove by a happening eatery on Sunset that Famous frequented. He parked, and through the window saw the sixtyish man sucking on a sugar cube he'd dipped into his glass of tea. He was having lunch with a woman who could be either a girlfriend or daughter, as Haze knew he had grown children. His hand on the door, an idea came to him, and Haze left, hoping the gangster hadn't spotted him. But if he had, Famous would probably not recognize him now. The last time they'd had face time, one of Famous's boys was holding a pry bar next to his head, the grease from his processed hair mixing with his sweat.

It was Betty Abaya who provided Haze the most cogent information. "I heard from a friend at one of the entertainment shows that Hodges has been shopping a video of Nina Venis in her underwear snorting blow on camera, bragging about how she put it over the Grammy Committee when she won for 'Club Freak.'"

"Admitting she didn't do all the singing on that song."

"Yes. He's got a couple of offers, but not the kind of money he wants, it seems. Nina's not exactly new news, you know."

While he tried to figure out how the hell that video wound up hidden in the football, Haze set up a meeting with Hodges through one of the musicians who knew him. They met in the dead of night at Krazy's Armenian roasted chicken joint on lower Santa Monica Boulevard near the hospital. A hooker Haze wasn't sure was a woman was in the back booth with a large man in an even larger Darth Vader T.

"How much Nina give you, home?" Hodges hadn't come with backup. Why should he, Haze estimated. He was some twenty years younger and twenty pounds of muscle more than the older man. What did Hodges have to worry about?

"Thirty thousand," Haze declared.

"Shit. It's worth more than that."

"No it isn't. *Entertainment Daily* only went as high as twenty."

Hodges looked past Haze, then back at him. You tryin' to make me small like you, Haze? I've got a future."

"This ain't about you and me getting all Brokeback, Wesley. This is about business. Nina had to hock her Grammy to raise the money. You want the best deal for the tape or not?"

Hodges assessed that. Then, shaking his head, he said, "Hollywood."

"Where all our dreams come true." Haze summed up.

Hodges was paid and Haze got the digital videotape that Larry Barker had shot when he and Venis were being drug silly. Years later, Venis, having gotten clean and worrying about history's view of her, sought to get the tape back. Larry was dead and the wife was no fan of Venis's. She wasn't going to use the tape to blackmail her; she wanted it keep it to spite the other woman.

Several years ago the two of them, along with others, had been at the installation of the Venis MTV exhibit. Fearing that Venis might hire somebody to break into her house, Denise Barker had brought the tape, with the idea of hiding it in her husband's donated guitar. It was also her way of playing a private joke on the self-centered singer. Denise Barker would have done this before, but the guitar had been in the possession of Larry Barker's brother, who didn't get along with his former sister-in-law.

Hollywood was all about its precarious relationships.

At that ceremony, Barker's widow didn't get a chance to get the tape into his electric guitar due to needing a screwdriver and the time to do so. But as they were near the Rexford quarterback exhibit, making a slit with her nail file wasn't too tough on her way to the bathroom. It helped that the football had been stuffed with foam so there was no air to let out. Venis had spied Denise Barker do this. But as long as Hollywood Wax Works was open, Venis didn't have the wherewithal to break into it after hours, she let it be—until the impending closing.

But lust is a capricious thing, and once he'd taken the tape, Wesley Hodges's lust for the big time took over. He concluded there was more to be made from selling the tape than any chance his career had of being Nina Venis's bongo boy. Probably he was correct in that assessment.

"Who sent the rat?" Abaya asked him as she and Haze cuddled in bed.

"Denise did," he said. "She wanted to see if she could scare Nina away, 'cause she looked to get that tape back, too. But that clown of a security guard, in between scowling at me, was so hyped up, he actually was doing good job of keeping a watch on everything. Denise didn't have a chance to snatch the tape."

"But Nina's business with the guitar was to cause a distraction?"

"Yep, so her boyfriend could get the tape, that is, just grab the football itself." Haze started to fall asleep.

"Aren't you worried about Hodges?"

"Nope."

"Terry." She thrashed to rouse him.

"Baby, he's already split town. He might come back if Freddy kicks off, but in the words of Warren Zevon, I'll worry about that when I'm dead."

"The song is 'I'll Sleep When I'm Dead.'"

"That, too."

"He could have made a dupe of that tape."

"Then Nina will have to pay for her sins," Haze said.

"As we all will."

"Yes, dear." Haze had paid Hodges with convincing-looking movie money. Abaya, who worked in a post-production house, had gotten it from a prop man she knew. When Hodges settled his debt with the fake bills, and Famous discovered this, Haze knew Hodges would have to go on the run.

She bumped him again. "How come Nina went to all this trouble about that tape? So what if it came out now that her song was augmented by another singer? It's not like people would stop going to her shows, is it?"

"She hopes to make it into the Rock and Roll Hall of Fame. If this came out, it would kill that chance. And she wants that bad. Real bad."

Abaya was silent, then said softly. "I don't know, Terry. I'm one to talk, but wouldn't that be kind of cheating if she did get nominated?"

He exhaled audibly. "I made a copy."

She murmured, "There is hope for you."

He pulled her closer. He hummed a lullaby of Hollywood, where you could reach for anything, and if you were lucky, your empty hand came away with its fingers still attached.

*Percy Parker specializes in short stories. It's
something he does very well. His work has appeared
in numerous anthologies and he's a regular in*
Ellery Queen's Mystery Magazine. *His one novel,*
Good Girls Don't Get Murdered, *is out of print
but worth searching for. Here he introduces P.I.
Vince Thorn, who is trying to grant the dying wish
of a man who wants Vince to solve his murder.*

# Letter from a Dead Man

## by Percy Spurlark Parker

f you're reading this letter, then I've been
murdered."

The check had fallen out of the letter
as I'd taken it out of the envelope. I would've taken a look at the
check right away, but I'd caught the word murder in the letter and
read the first sentence, then continued on.

"I'm putting a lot of trust in you, Mr. Thorn," the letter went on
to say. "You can cash the enclosed check and forget all about me,
and my murderer will most likely never get caught. But I'm hoping
you won't allow that to happen. After the other night at Gilhouley's I
got the impression that regardless of your ups and downs, you were
a man of your word. I'm counting on that integrity now.

"There are three people I seriously suspect of wanting to murder me. Two of my clients: Masta Bling because he wants out of his
contract and that's not going to happen, and Allan Clark because he

doesn't think I'm paying enough attention to his fading career. But first and foremost there's that bitch of a wife of mine, Mona. She, most of all, has me sleeping with one eye open. I let myself be fooled at first. But it's becoming more and more apparent that she married me only for my money.

"You may be asking yourself why I didn't send the letter to the district attorney. Frankly, I don't have much faith in our public officials. If they couldn't keep O. J. and Robert Blake behind bars, what chance would there be of their finding my murderer? I'm begging you, Mr. Thorn, as one solitary drinker to another, don't let the person who murdered me get away with it."

The letterhead read Prime Talent Productions, and from the address, they had offices in the Capitol Records building. The letter was from the desk of Jonathan Wallace, president and chief executive officer, and was signed simply, Jon.

Payment was a cashier's check, drawn on the First National Bank of California for ten thousand dollars and made out to me, Vincent Thorn, signed, full name this time, Jonathan B. Wallace.

If he'd just hit me with the name, I might've been scratching my head for some time trying to come up with a face. But the part about Gilhouley's and the solitary drinking locked it in for me.

Gilhouley's was a dive by anybody's standards, wedged between a pawnshop and a costume jewelry store on Hollywood Boulevard. It may have been two, three weeks ago. Wednesday, I think, around one a.m. or so. I was holding down my usual spot, back counter two stools over, minding my own business, knocking back Crown on the rocks with a water chaser. I must have been on my third Crown, still nursing my first chaser, when he came in.

Seven-eight-hundred-dollar suit, from the looks of the cut. He took a moment to give the place the once-over. There wasn't much going on in the joint that night, and we happened to be the only blacks in the place. He came down to my end of the bar, nodded, and sat down, leaving an empty stool between us. Fisher, the bartender, had followed him and took an order for a double scotch and soda.

He was an older guy—not ancient, but older than my thirty-seven. He was beginning to go bald but his barber was working hard to try to hide it. Dark complexion, heavy eyebrows, clean-shaven, just about completed the picture.

He lit up a fat cigar and downed half his drink before turning back to me. "Man, nothing like a good stiff drink after busting your balls all day. I just had to stop in and have one or two before heading home."

I'd nodded in agreement.

"Music business, that's my racket. I cover the whole package. Record promoter, agent, producer, you name it. Been at it over twenty-five years. Shit ain't getting any easier either. I been up in my office going over things with some of my talent. Label deals, song selections." He paused long enough to take another swallow of his drink. "What about you, friend?"

"I come here for the solitude."

He shrugged. "I can respect that. Me? Running my mouth is a big part of my business. I'll probably go to my grave flapping my jibs."

"Feel free to flap," I said, not about to share my story with him.

I'd been a cop once. Three years ago I'd shot my partner in a drug bust. Sheer carelessness, too eager to put a drug dealer away, or Mark's not announcing himself when he came into the room. The review board had called it an accident. I'd played it over in my head hundreds of times and I still wasn't sure where to place the blame.

I wasn't much good after that. Mark and I had been more than just partners on the job; we were close friends, almost brothers-in-law. His sister and I had been dating for about eight months. I'd begun to think she was going to be the one. But my quick trigger finger had put an end to all of that. I left the force and Crown Royal and I got to know each other really well.

A little over a year ago, my old training officer looked me up. He'd retired from the force and had started a small detective agency operating out of the Taft Building, one of the tourist stops at Hollywood and Vine.

He read me the riot act. Told me it was way past time I got my head out of the bottle. I didn't give him much of an argument, I guess I'd been waiting for someone to come and grab me by my collar. So, I became a gumshoe, checking out wayward spouses, tracking down folks who move and conveniently forget to give their creditors their new address. For the most part it'd been a positive step, although Mark's death was never that far from me. And occasionally, like that night, it had me sitting in my favorite spot at Gilhouley's, drinking alone.

"Remember Allan Clark? I got him under contract. It's a crime. Can't get him anything but a few 'oldies' gigs now and then."

Clark had a string of number one hits back in the mid-eighties. I could remember doing some of my first horizontal mumbo on the backseat of my old man's Chevy, listening to him on the radio.

"You like rap? Personally I hate the crap. But it's hot now. If you're black and want to make money in the music biz, that's where you got to be."

I didn't agree, but I wasn't about to tell him that. I hadn't come to Gilhouley's for any conversation.

"I got Masta Bling under contract. Ever hear of him? Bastard's real name's Fred Diggersby, but he has to have a rap handle. He's been doing good numbers, but he's going to turn the corner with this next CD. He's going to come out of it a millionaire."

He'd gone on like that for about a halfhour, throwing in a few jabs about his no-good wife. I still wasn't in the mood for conversation, but I'm always out to earn a paycheck. I get a weekly salary from the agency, but any business I generate on my own works out to an eighty/twenty split.

"If you're so worried about your wife, I may be able to help you there," I said, sliding one of my business cards across the counter to him.

"Private detective, uh, no shit."

"I could check things out for you. See if she's knocking boots with anybody. Get you some solid grounds for divorce. If that's what you want."

"You guarantee you'll get the goods on her."

"If it's there it's there. I won't make anything up."

"Don't tell me you're an honest man."

"I try."

"I like that," he nodded, taking my card and putting it in his shirt pocket. "I'll let you know."

After another swallow of his drink he got back to talking about the music business.

I hadn't heard anything else from him until now. Not that I'd actually thought about him anyway.

The letter and envelope were neatly typed, which could easily be handled these days by anyone with a thumb and a word processor. Today was Tuesday. The letter had a Victorville post mark, mailed this past Friday in the p.m. I recalled there being a news story about some record executive committing suicide about a week or two ago. I hadn't paid much attention to it then and couldn't say if the letter was from the same guy. One thing though, if it was him, he sure as hell didn't mail the letter himself.

We have a three-person operation here. I say person because, beside the boss, Chuck Rimherst, and myself, Bea Fitzgerald is the third P.I. in the agency. Our offices are lined up in a row with Chuck's taking up the middle and largest space. Doris Smith is the lone receptionist. She sits out front and directs traffic.

"Chuck tied up with anybody?" I asked Doris, as I stepped out of my office.

Looking over her shoulder she shook her head, her short gray curls bouncing slightly. "He just finished a long-distance call."

I knocked on his door and went in when I heard his graveled, "Yes?"

He was a whale of a man, appearing even more so sitting behind his desk. He'd always been big, standing a good six foot four and packing a couple of hundred–plus pounds. But he'd added nearly a hundred more since leaving the force. His silver-gray hair contrasted with his heavily jowled sun-drenched complexion.

"Got a minute or two?"

"Sure thing. What's up?"

I handed him the letter and the check, and flopped down in one of the chairs in front of his desk.

He read the letter with a grunt and a nod, and ended with a low whistle as he looked at the check. "Nice to get unexpected presents. I believe our ex-brothers in blue have already done your work for you, Vince. Here." He handed me back the check. "Might as well put this in your bank account and call it a day. Oh," he added with a smile, "and don't forget my twenty percent."

"What'd you mean my job's already been done?"

"The guy's wife was arrested this weekend. Saturday, I think. Don't you keep up with the news?"

"I try not to."

"I see." He reached for the phone, dialed, then engaged in a moment or two of small talk before he asked, "Say, who's handling the Wallace case? Yeah, that one. Pepe and Brewster. Either one of them around?" He paused, drumming his fingers on his glass-top desk.

"Brew, you old fart. What's going on?" He broke out in loud laughter that rocked his head back and shook his whole body. "Say, hear you got the Wallace beef. Uh-huh. Well, one of my people got a letter today you might want to see. I can fax it to you." He went into an explanation, then a long paused as he listened, mixed in with a "no kidding" or two. "Okay, Brew, I'll fax the letter over to you right now, kiss Helen for me."

He got up, went over to the fax machine, wrote a quick cover-note and stuck it and the letter I'd gotten into the machine. When he came back to his desk he was breathing somewhat raggedly. He hit his chest a couple of times with his balled fist, belched, and sat back down. "Take the check to the bank, Vince. Brew feels they pretty much got a lock on this Wallace woman.

"Apparently she tried to make it look like a suicide. When the cops arrived, he was sitting at his desk at home. Gunshot wound, right temple, close range. Gun on the floor by his right hand. But the lab couldn't find any gunpowder residue on his hand. The wife had been at a concert. She says she found her husband dead when she got home. Time frame says she was home in time after the concert to killed her husband and then call the police. It was her gun and both of their prints were on it."

"They find any residue on her?"

"Brew says no, but then she could always change clothes, the husband couldn't."

"Motive?"

"Besides the usual husband and wife BS, they were business partners. There been reports of some heated arguments lately. Brew says the autopsy found a brain tumor. If she'd waited six months or so the tumor would've done the job for her. So, I repeat, deposit the check."

* * * * * *

I got as far as the sidewalk, just standing there watching the traffic, trying to decide what I should do. Hollywood and Vine. For people who don't see it every day, the mention of the intersection conjures up thoughts of Hollywood's heyday. The glamour and glitz, big cars and movie stars. Well, most of the glamour is gone these days, and you don't have to look too hard to find the rust on what's left.

The Taft Building, where our offices are located, sits on the southeast corner of Hollywood and Vine, fronting Hollywood. Directly across the street is the Equitable Building, and next to it the Pantages Theatre. Throw in the Hollywood Walk of Fame, and, Capitol Records Tower just north on Vine, and you've still got enough for the tourist to gawk at, even though they have to mingle with the whores and the homeless to do so.

Every so often the city's fathers make some pronouncement about cleaning up the area, restoring it to its glory days. It generally last about fifteen minutes.

The light changed and I started up Vine toward the Capitol Tower. Wallace had paid me. I had to do something although I wasn't sure what it should be.

"Hey, how's it hanging, Vince?"

"What's up, Skin?"

That's what we called him back in high school, Skin, short for skinny. I'd forgotten what his real name was. I'd run into him a few months ago in front of a restaurant east on Vine asking for handouts. He wasn't as tall as I remembered from high school, or maybe I'd just caught up with him. But he was still skinny as hell, the fattest thing about him being the stubble on his sunken cheeks. I've seen him a number of times since and I guess I've become an easy mark. I'm not sure why, maybe seeing him reminds me of how close I came to becoming him.

"You wouldn't have a couple of bucks on ya, Vince, would ya?"

There was a grayish pallor to his dark complexion, a hollowness in his eyes. "I'll give it back to you this time, I promise."

"Sure, Skin." I dug a couple of dollars out and gave it to him.

"You the man, Vince," he smiled with yellowed teeth. "You the man. Ya know, I talk you up a lot. I tell everybody I know this big-time P.I."

"Thanks for the publicity, Skin."

"No sweat, Vince. I'll keep steering as much business your way as I can."

The walk up to the Capitol Tower was pretty much uneventful from there except for a couple of hookers who gave me an open invitation with a nod. I'd smiled back and kept going.

Prime Talent Productions had offices on the third floor of the weathered white stacked-pancake-looking structure that was the Capitol Tower. I guess it was suppose to represent a stack of records, but it had never struck me that way.

The walls of Prime Talent Productions were lavender in color and filled with framed album and CD covers. The receptionist sat at her desk with her back to two unmarked doors. She had seen her best years go by but she was still quite striking. Her dark, close-clipped curls flattered her full lips. Her make-up was done with a practiced hand, no one part overshadowing an other.

I handed her one of my business cards.

She read it and looked up at me. "Yes, Mr. Thorn, what can I do for you?"

"Frankly, I'm not sure, Miss…" She wore rings on both hands but nothing on the ring finger.

She hesitated. "Campbell."

"Yes, Miss Campbell. Have you been working here long?"

"I was Mr. Wallace's receptionist for twelve years. Why do you ask?"

"Frankly, I'm not even sure why I came." It was true. When I left my office I hadn't planned on coming here. Standing on the corner, I'd seen the Capitol Tower and just headed in this direction. Now that I was here I didn't know what I expected to find.

She shifted some papers on her desk. Lying next to the phone were a couple of travel brochures for Las Vegas.

"Planning a trip?"

She picked up the brochures, tried a smile that vanished too quickly. "Some girlfriends and I drove over there this past weekend. They thought it would do me some good after all that's been going on around here. We stayed off the Strip at the Rio, caught a couple of shows."

"Help any?"

She shrugged. "Not really. It was nice of them to try, but when someone you've known for twelve years is torn out of your life, it's not that easy to get over."

"Yes, I can imagine," I said. "Coming up in the elevator, I wasn't sure if anyone would be here."

"With the exception of the day after Mr. Wallace's death, it's been business as usual." There was an unmistakable bitterness in her tone.

"I don't understand. Was there another partner beside Mrs. Wallace?"

"No, it was just the two of them."

"But isn't she—"

"Out on Bail. From what I understand she was arrested Saturday morning, and released late Saturday afternoon."

"Sounds like she had a lawyer on speed dial."

"Could be, I don't know for sure. I was in Las Vegas, I got everything secondhand. Anyway, she's out and she's moved into the big office," she said, nodding to the door behind her on her left. "She's in there now with one of our clients."

It was easy to tell she wasn't too pleased with the situation. I had the check in my wallet, and the letter in my inside coat pocket. I took the letter out and handed it to her. "I got this in the mail today. You wouldn't know anything about this by any chance?"

She took the letter from me, taking her time reading it. When she was finished she looked up to me. "He hired you to find his murderer? But, how? I don't understand."

"I'm puzzled also. That's his signature?"

She studied the letter again. "If he knew you well, or was in a hurry, he'd sign his correspondence that way. Yes, I'd say it was his."

"Had he ever expressed to you any fears that someone might want to kill him?"

She shook her head. "No. But as far as the letter accusing Allan Clark, he was in Maine at his daughter's wedding when Mr. Wallace died."

"Which leaves Masta Bling and Mrs. Wallace."

"Yes," she said, then added, "Mr. Wallace and his wife had some pretty heated arguments in the past few weeks. I took it as artistic temperament. Maybe I was wrong."

"Police are saying he had a brain tumor. Was he under a doctor's care?"

"I've heard the reports, but I can't believe it," she said, but she'd hesitated before answering. "He seemed perfectly normal to me."

"Are you sure about that, Miss Campbell?"

I waited for her reply. She looked away, then back to me.

"He confided in me that he was having a problem. But he said it was a small tumor and the doctors had caught it in time. He asked me not to tell anyone."

"And you didn't?"

"Of course not. After twelve years he had complete trust in me. I would never violate his confidence."

"I see," I said, taking the letter back. "If you don't mind my asking, what's your gut feeling about all this? Think the police are on the right track?"

Another paused. "I wouldn't venture a guess. But personally, I didn't think he should've married her in the first place, nor made her a partner."

"Why so?"

"She was too young for him, their ideas clashed."

"Did the business suffer?"

"I'd say it was heading in that direction. Maybe it wasn't noticeable to everyone, but I could see it. My opinion, you understand?"

"Thanks for being candid."

She nodded.

"You know, I'm really still kind of fumbling along. But I guess, since she's here, I should speak to Mrs. Wallace. Do you know about how much longer she'll be?"

"I don't know why you can't interrupt her. She's in there with the other person mentioned in the letter, that Masta Bling."

She buzzed through on the intercom saying there was a detective here to see the both of them and was told to send me right in.

It was evident that Mona Wallace hadn't had the chance to truly make the office her own. The room reeked of masculinity, from the oak-trimmed walls, and the cigar humidor on the desk to the fully stocked bar that took up four feet on the far corner. It was a power room. A room built to impress, maybe intimidate at times. The willowy blonde standing behind the desk didn't quite fit. She was somewhere in her early twenties. She had pale blue eyes hooded by long dark lashes, prominent cheekbones, and a wide inviting mouth. A double string of marble sized pearls adorned her long neck. The pocket on her spotless white blouse hadn't lain flat since it came off the hanger. I didn't know what she saw in Wallace, but I knew damn well what he saw in her.

"Mrs. Wallace?"

"What do the police want with me now." For such a pretty mouth the words came out with a vile edge.

"Yo, ain't Five-O done enough already? What's with all this harassment shit?" Masta Bling added his two cents standing in front of the desk decked out in a baggy Jean outfit. He was wearing enough gold to fill a show window, including about a half dozen gold teeth. Bald, bearded, and black, he was probably a solid two hundred even without the jewelry.

"Relax. I'm not the police."

"But Wilma said . . . " she stopped, took a breath. "I told Jon to fire her long ago. As soon as I get things straight around here, she's going to go. Just who are you, anyway?"

"Yeah. What the hell you bust up in here perpetrating for . . ."

Masta Bling started toward me, and when I didn't back up he stopped.

"The name's Vincent Thorn. I'm a private detective. And Mr. Wallace hired me to find out who murdered him."

Masta Bling took a step back this time. "What . . ."

"That's impossible," Mona said, frowning. It didn't do much to diminish her looks. I couldn't think of anything that would. She had probably been cute from day one, and now as a woman she was pretty damn close to gorgeous. "How could Jon hire you when he's dead?"

As a reply I handed her the letter. "I got this in my morning mail."

She started reading, stopped long enough to sit in the high-back leather chair behind the desk, then continued to read shaking her head as she went along. "This is ridiculous," she said, throwing the letter back at me.

"Evidently the police don't think so."

"I didn't kill Jon. The police can't prove I did. They're so far off base it's silly. How do you think I made bail so quickly? They've got a hell of a weak case. Everybody knows it. My lawyer says we stand a good chance of not even going to trial."

"So, you're claiming your husband killed himself?"

"He had to. I don't have any other answer." She shrugged.

"That's the way it plays out, man," Masta Bling added. "Jon wasted his self. End of story. If Mona had stayed for the concert's after party like I wanted her to, Five-O would've never looked her way."

"So, it was your concert she went to that night?"

"We played the Forum. Me and my dogs tore the place up."

"One of the biggest part of my job is to support my clients whenever I can. Jon and I were both supposed to've gone, but he said he had a headache. I didn't believe him. He never understood rap anyway."

"And you do?"

"Exactly. That's what I brought to the partnership. I'm responsible for signing Freddie, er, Masta Bling with the firm. Moving some other things in a new direction. There was a nearly twenty-year difference in my and my husband's my ages, Mr. Thorn, and just as big a difference in our musical ear."

"With all the differences, how did you two ever hook up?"

A sly smile crept across her wide mouth. "He had a cute young thing on his arm, and I had a guy who was savvy in the workings of the music business. Off the path with what was going on these days, sure, but he still had contacts, he knew people."

"I didn't hear any mention of love."

She shook her head, the smile still there. "The marriage worked for us."

"They were a cool couple," Masta Bling snapped. "Don't try to twist it all up."

"I'm just trying to make some sense out of this for myself."

"I didn't kill my husband, Mr. Thorn."

"Right. That's what you've said. He killed himself. Why?"

"Why?" She repeated. "Who the hell knows why? Maybe it finally got to him that he was out of step with what's going on these days. Maybe that tumor they found had something to do with it. He'd been kind of moody off and on."

"Maybe he was concerned about you and Masta Bling wearing the same shade of lipstick." It was something I had to mention.

Masta Bling automatically grabbed a tissue from the desk and did a thorough job of wiping his mouth. A day late and a dollar short, as they say. I'd noticed the rose-red shade of Mona Wallace's lipstick adorning the right corner of his mouth when I first came in. A casual peck between male and female associates . . . maybe. A more meaningful embrace between a man and a woman, most likely.

"I think we're finished here, Mr. Thorn," she said.

I couldn't have agreed with her more.

The last thing I got from Wilma Campbell before leaving Prime Talent was the name of Jonathan Wallace's lawyer, a Mr. George Truskin. As luck would have it, his office was on the tenth floor of the Equitable Building almost, directly across Hollywood from my squat four walls.

I caught him on his way out.

"I'm sorry, young man. I'm just running down to the cafeteria for a quick bite, and then I've got an appointment I must keep."

He was tall and looked fit, with a lot of wavy white hair and a slightly darker mustache. His voice was a deep, rich baritone, his eyes a cool gray. I imagined he could be very convincing in a courtroom.

"Mind if I share a table with you? I won't take up much of your time. It's about Jonathan Wallace. I'll even pop for lunch."

I don't know if it was the mention of Wallace's name or the free lunch, but we wound up at a small table in the busy cafeteria.

I showed him the letter, gave him time to read it, then said, "Someone sent me the letter, and it wasn't Wallace. I'm thinking a friend or a lawyer. Maybe both."

He nodded with a mouthful of turkey on rye. Chewed a bit. Swallowed some black coffee. "I've been Jon's lawyer for a number of years. And you're right in your assumption that we were friends. But I had nothing to do with mailing you that letter."

"Any ideas in that regard?"

He shook his head. "None."

"You wouldn't be defending Mrs. Wallace in this matter, would you?"

"I'm not a criminal lawyer, Mr. Thorn. Although I happen to believe Mona had nothing to do with Jon's death."

"But wouldn't she have the most to gain by his death?"

"Maybe yes, maybe no. Its not that cut and dried."

"He had a will?"

"Of course, but I can't discuss the contents with you."

"What about Mona playing footsie with Masta Bling?"

No reaction. I couldn't tell if he'd known about them or not. "If that in fact is the case, Mr. Thorn, it's none of my concern." He stood up. "Thanks for the lunch, but I've really got to go now."

I sat at the table finishing my coffee and hamburger, trying to figure out just what the hell I had. A check for ten thousand dollars, eight after Chuck's twenty percent. It should've been enough. To hell with trying to get all the questions answered.

As for the people mentioned in the letter, the idea of Allan Clark sneaking in from his daughter's wedding in Maine, then making it back there to cover his alibi, was pretty far-fetched. Likewise, for Masta Bling. I suppose he could've ducked out of his after party, killed Wallace, then made it back without anyone noticing. But that would be a hell of a stretch in probability.

It came down to Mona being the likeliest one in the bunch. She was having an affair with Masta Bling. She'd only married Wallace to get a foot in the door of the music world. The cops already had her pegged for the murder. There was nothing I could add of a concrete nature. It was time to stand back and let the police do their job. If they couldn't prove her guilty, maybe she was innocent after all.

I saw Skin standing in front of my building as I was crossing the street. I tried to avoid him, but he came up alongside me and matched me stride for stride.

"Hey, Vince, how ya doing, man. Say, you wouldn't have a couple of dollars on you, would you?"

"You already caught me once today, Skin. Remember?"

"Huh? Oh yeah. I kind of forgot. Money slips through my fingers real fast sometimes, you know? Hard to keep up with it."

"Yeah, well, not right now, Skin."

"Come on, Vince. Don't be like that. You can spare a buck or two. With all the business I keep sending your way, you gotta be rolling in the Benjamins. I tell everybody they can catch you at your office or Gilhouley's most nights. You gotta be cashing in on some of that."

Skin stopped abruptly, his face crunching into a frown. "What? What'd I say?'

I guess he was reacting to the fact that I had stopped and was staring at him. I could only guess what my own expression was looking like.

"Everything's okay, Skin," I said, pulling some cash out of my pocket and giving it to him. I'm not even sure how much it was, but a big grin pushed the frown away, and he broke into a run yelling, "Thanks, man" over his shoulder.

I turned back to the Capitol Tower.

\* \* \* \* \* \*

Wilma Campbell was still sitting at her desk when I returned to Prime Talent Productions.

"Oh, Mr. Thorn," she said looking up. "You've just missed Mrs. Wallace and that Bling character."

"That's alright, Miss. Campbell, I came back to see you, anyway."

"Yes?" There was just the slightest quiver in her voice.

"I wanted to give you the opportunity of coming to police headquarters with me. It'll be better than if they have to come get you."

"I-I don't understand."

"I think you do." It had all been there for me to see. I just had to open my eyes and take a good look. "The letter I received was mailed from Victorville. I should've caught it sooner. Driving through Victorville is the most direct route from here to Las Vegas. I'm sure if the ladies who went with you were asked, they'll say it was your idea to make a quick stop there."

She swelled up a bit, nodded, and leaned back in her chair. "Okay, I'll admit it, I mailed the letter. Mr. Wallace asked me to in case of his death."

"Wasn't it just a little more than that, Wilma?"

Skin had slapped me in the face with it. The problem I was having was I'd been looking at Wallace as the victim. It began to make sense when I thought of him as a willing participant. Whether Skin had told them separately or together, once or a dozen times, Wallace knew I frequented Gilhouley's, knew a little about my pass. He'd mentioned in his letter about my ups and downs. I hadn't shared any of my history with him. And he hadn't come to Gilhouley's for a drink. The bar in his office was stocked better than most liquor stores. He'd came there to meet me. To set the plan in motion.

"Wallace knew that the tumor was killing him, didn't he? Did he hate his wife so much he wanted to frame her for his murder?"

"The little tramp, she didn't deserve him." There were tears in her eyes now.

"You cleaned up afterward, made it easy for the police to jump to a conclusion of murder." It was a statement; the big question came next. "Did you shoot him, or did you watch him kill himself?"

"No, no. He wanted me to, but I couldn't do it!" Her shouts were mixed with tears. "He put a glove on and covered his shoulder with a towel. I couldn't watch. I turned away. He said I was the one he should've married, and then . . . " She buried her face in her hands, crying openly.

I let her go on for a few minutes until she seemed to've cried herself out, then together we went down to police headquarters.

It felt good being in a squad room again, taking in the copness of the place, if I can make that a word. I got a pat or two on the back, a thumbs up here and there.

I wasn't sure what was going to happen to Wilma. It all depended on how hard the district attorney would press things. It wasn't an election year, so there was a chance it might not go too badly for her.

On the way back to the office I deposited Wallace's check, minus Chuck's twenty percent, of course.

All in all, the results may not have gone the way Wallace had intended. But I'd done what I was hired to do.

*Paul Guyot is a veteran TV writer who is just now
entering the arena of mystery/crime short story
writing. He had a story in last year's anthology
Greatest Hits and will appear in an upcoming
Michael Connelly anthology Burden Of The Badge.
This is his third short story, featuring a P.I. named
Hooker, and damned if it doesn't read like an episode
from the heyday of TV P.I.'s. I LOVED that stuff!*

# Barry of Hollywood

*by Paul Guyot*

I t's not as if Barry O'Brien had been a
friend of mine.

We'd met on what's known as the
WCT—the West Coast Tour—a golf minitour I played on a few
years back. Barry had a knack for long drives and short love affairs.
We were paired in subsequent tournaments—both of us choking
badly—and thus ended up together subsequently bars in, with subsequent shots of tequila. The only thing Barry did better than drive
his golf ball was drink his tequila, and he could drive the hell out of
a golf ball. We were asked to leave the bar at the Temecula Creek,
and were told to leave the one at Hansen Dam. Memories, sure. But
nothing to form a friendship over.

\* \* \* \* \* \*

Forest Lawn Memorial Park seems better suited for a championship golf course than it does a cemetery. Set on hundreds of acres of lush, softly rolling hills, it overlooks both the Warner Bros. and Disney studios. Barry was being laid to rest on a nice little hill near a willow tree. If he'd been to sit up and look out of his casket he could've seen Mickey Mouse.

There were about eight people at the gravesite, and that was counting the priest, or minister, or whatever he was. I leaned against the willow tree and watched Barry being lowered into the ground. I thought, *You're in a helluva bunker now, O'Brien.*

"What are you doing here, Hooker?"

I turned and saw Randall Manupolo's hulking figure standing behind me.

"Grieving," I said, holding his envy-colored eyes. Manupolo was one of the few Samoans I'd ever met, and the only one with bright green eyes. Pushing fifty now, he stood just over six feet but still carried the armored-car body that had made him an All-American guard at USC. He'd been drafted by the Broncos, but bad knees ended his career before it really began. He took his criminal justice degree to the LAPD and turned out to be just as good a detective as he was a pulling guard.

"Bullshit. You'd have to have a heart to grieve."

I let the remark slide. People began to move away from Barry and his bad lie.

Manupolo stuck a Newport between his lips and fired it up. I watched his eyes follow Edgar Lopez-Barry's caddie—who was holding hands with a beautiful Latina girl. They climbed into a battered Nissan pickup.

I turned toward the short, fat man approaching us.

"About time you got here, Hook," said Teddy Hard-on. He looked at Manupolo with some surprise. "Hey, you're the detective played for the Trojans. Something wrong? Something going on with Barry's death?"

Manupolo blew smoke at Teddy and said, "You the one responsible for this heartless prick being back in town?"

It took Teddy a moment to decide how to respond. Finally, looking more at me than Manupolo, he said, "There's a few questions regarding Barry's insurance and such. Hooker's the only private investigator I know."

Manupolo took another long drag, set his shoulders, and fixed me with a stare. "Don't fuck around in my city, Hooker. You're not even supposed to be here."

"No problemo, Detective," Teddy said. "It's all good. Just dotting i's and crossing t's." But Manupolo was already gone.

"Guy's probably juiced on steroids," Teddy said, wiping his face with his hands. "Come on, I'll buy you lunch. We'll go to Kwan's. Be like old times. I'm driving the maroon Park Avenue over there. Donation from McCoy Buick." He slapped my back and waddled down the hill. I glanced back at the last place Barry O'Brien would ever be, and followed Teddy.

\* \* \* \* \* \*

Kwan's is a tiny Chinese restaurant just down Pico Boulevard from the Rancho Park golf course, site of two of the fourteen tournaments on Teddy Hard-on's WCT. The players often end up at Kwan's after their rounds.

Teddy squeezed himself into a red booth. A young Chinese girl brought us grease-stained menus and asked if we wanted something to drink. We both ordered Tsingtao. After she left, Teddy laid out the situation.

He told me Barry O'Brien had been having a decent year on tour—four tournaments so far, in the money in three of them, including a third place at Yorba Linda. From what I remembered of Barry's game, that was a career.

"He'd really improved his putting," Teddy said, like he knew what I was thinking. "Might have even won this year."

"Then why take the header?"

"Exactly. He didn't jump off that building. You know it and I know it."

"I don't know anything, Teddy."

After the waitress had taken our order, Teddy told me that the cops had investigated and ruled it a suicide. Teddy had then taken it upon himself to get Barry's things in order. It made sense. To a lot of guys on tour, Teddy is the closest thing to a father figure. An abusive, passive-aggressive, stupid father, but a papa nonetheless. He told me how he had come across a life insurance policy Barry had taken out a year ago. It was for a million dollars and listed a sole beneficiary: Maria Lopez.

Daughter of Edgar Lopez, Barry's caddie.

Teddy told me Barry had been dating Maria Lopez for the past year. Only her.

Playing good golf, dating only one woman? This was not the Barry O'Brien I remembered.

Teddy said he asked Maria about the life insurance policy and the girl said yes, Barry had told her he'd done it, but she thought he was just being "funny Barry."

Ha ha.

"And the policy doesn't pay off for suicide," I said, stating the obvious.

"Yep."

"Did Manupolo look at Maria? First rule of murder is follow the money."

"The cops looked at all of us," Teddy said. Then his eyes narrowed. "But I don't think they looked hard enough at Edgar Lopez. He was pissed about Barry and Maria."

"That's a little obvious," I said. "If it wasn't the person benefiting from the policy, an angry father is the next obvious choice."

"What are you, getting lazy, Hooker? You want to solve it before lunch is over?"

The waitress brought our food, and before I'd even pulled apart my chopsticks, Teddy had a mouthful of beef lo mein, and a chin full of sauce. He explained that he wanted me to prove Barry was murdered so that Maria could get the money she's entitled to.

I stared at Teddy and said, "You don't do anything for other people unless there's something in it for yourself."

Teddy gasped—ugly, considering he had yet to swallow the lo mein. "How can you say that after all I've done for the players on my tour?"

"The players are the last people you think about. You sponsor those tourneys to get in tight with all the golf-playing CEOs, getting yourself free cars, free trips, whatever you can get." Before he protested I added, "Your payouts are some of the lowest in the country, and your entry fees some of the highest."

Instead of objecting he shoveled in more food.

"You think if you get her this money, she might—what—let you score your own hole-in-one?"

"You're disgusting," he said. "Maybe I'm just trying to turn this tragedy into something positive. Make Barry's death mean something."

I nearly choked on my Kung Pao.

"For real, Hook. If I prove he was murdered, then Maria gets her dough, and the WCT gets some major pub on account of one of my players was a martyr. You know, like that chick Joan of Arc."

Barry of Hollywood.

"So it's not sex you're after, it's money. You want to exploit Barry O'Brien's death until you've squeezed every last penny out of it."

He shrugged.

"I don't know if I want to help you do that."

"Sure you do," he said. "Because you're a broke motherfucker. You've been trying to walk away from this shamus gig for years, but you can't. If you were doing *anything* on that dog of a tour in Missouri, you wouldn't be sitting here. I bet you're hitting your irons okay, driving straight, but you get within fifty yards of the green and everything goes to shit."

The players called Ted Harden "Teddy Hard-on" because he had this knack for coming on like a stiff prick. Not only was he a tight-ass bastard when it came to money, he had an annoying habit of telling the truth. What pissed you off most about him was his God-damn honesty. I told him, yes, my short game was currently non-existent.

We talked golf for a few minutes. Teddy can't play worth a damn, but he understands the game as well as Tiger Woods.

As we were leaving, I asked him for the numbers and addresses of all involved in the O'Brien case, and if Barry had any family. Teddy said the WCT was Barry's family.

"There's a Travelodge in Hollywood," he said. "Got you a room there. Need anything else?"

"A car."

"Take public transportation."

Teddy Hard-on.

"Get me something from one of your sponsors. I'm not doing this without a car, Teddy."

\* \* \* \* \*

The next morning I sat in a Hyundai Accent waiting to turn north on Vine from Hollywood Boulevard. As I waited for the boulevard traffic to break, I looked up at the Taft Building. I imagined Barry that night. Tossing himself twelve stories down to the Holly-Wood Walk of fame. Teddy said he landed right between the stars of Vladimir Horowitz and Spike Jones—a place as metaphoric as it is geographic.

Teddy figured the reason Barry was at the Taft that night was because Maria Lopez worked for some company there. At least that's what Teddy had heard.

What Teddy Hard-on didn't know was that Barry had been on the roof of the Taft before that night.

He'd been up there with me.

* * * * *

Monty White was a lowlife with busts for robbery, possession, and passing bad checks. He was convicted of assault on a police officer with special circumstances.

The so-called victim was a detective named Ezra Quartermous. "EQ," as he was known, gave mesmerizing testimony about arriving at White's place to question him about some bad checks. EQ said the smaller man "went berserk" and attacked him with a tire iron. The detective was forced to defend himself and shot White in the thigh—purposely sparing his life.

After the trial, White's mother hired me to prove that her son was innocent. It didn't take me long to discover that what happened was White had walked in on Ezra Quartermous giving White's wife the old high hard one. The detective was actually the attacker wielding the tire iron, and it was Mrs. White who shot her husband in the leg—aiming for his head.

My investigation resulted in White being freed, Quartermous going to jail, and the city of L.A. being sued for millions.

The following week Barry and I ended up paired at Teddy's Braemar tournament, and as we putted out on the eighteenth green, there was Randall Manupolo.

He gave me a choice—leave LA for good, or have every cop in the city out to get me.

Easy choice.

* * * * *

I showed a fake Water & Power ID to the sixtyish security guard manning the lobby of the Taft. He was listening to the Dodgers getting beat and barely glanced at it. I took an elevator that smelled like disinfectant and old fish to the twelfth floor, then the stairs up to the roof. I looked out over the city and remembered the only other time I'd been up there.

It was my last night in L.A., the Monty White debacle having sealed my fate. Barry and I had missed the cut at Braemar, and, after too much tequila at the Frolic Room, we'd ended up here with a bucket of balls and a pair of 7-irons Barry had stashed on the roof.

Barry claimed he knew someone who worked inside the building, and that's how he was able to gain access at two in the morning.

We were standing there, looking out over the city when Barry said, "Los Angeles. City of Angels."

"Yeah," was all I could manage in my Cuervo-induced haze.

Barry then told me how his father used to take him up to the Hollywood sign to look out over the city. He said his father used to tell him that you could see the angels hovering over the city from up there.

It was the first time Barry had ever shared anything the least bit personal with me. But before I could start to think maybe there was more to him than big drives and drunken adventures, he added:

"Let's drill those fucking angels in their celestial heads."

We began hammering 7-irons into the night. After a couple of broken windows and one car alarm, two of LAPD's finest appeared on the roof, informing us that we were already in trouble for trespassing and vandalism, and if we happened to hit some pedestrian on the head and they died, it'd be manslaughter. Barry curing the older cop's slice was the only reason we were spared a ride in the back of their cruiser.

I moved some crates and saw the two 7-irons still there. I grabbed one and took a couple of swings.

I smiled. Maybe Barry had been more of a friend than I thought.

I walked over to the north side of the building and look down at Hollywood and Vine. I don't know how long I had been up there when I heard the security guard's voice.

"I called the power company, sir, and they have no record of sending anyone here."

I turned and saw he had his hand on the butt of his Beretta. But he wasn't being aggressive, probably hoping I wasn't there to jump like the last guy.

"Yeah," I said, setting the golf club down. "Sorry about that. Name's Hooker. I'm a private investigator. You know about the jumper last week?"

"Sure," he said, his hand still on the butt. "I'm the one who called it in. I was in that little convenience store when I heard the splat." His hand fell away from the gun. "So, what's an Eye doing looking at a suicide?"

"That's the other thing," I said. "He was a friend of mine."

I watched his shoulders drop just a touch. He took a step closer to me.

"That's gotta be rough," he said. "Was he an out-of-work actor or something?"

"No," I said. "A golfer."

"Oh," he said, then took a couple of steps and peered over the edge. "Must have been a pretty bad one."

I asked him, "Is Triumph Trading Corp still in the building?"

"Sure."

"Who runs it, you know?"

"Can't say that I do. But there's a couple of real lookers there. Brunettes. One smart, one dumb. Your friend have business with them or something?"

I shook my head. Said I just saw the name in the lobby, sounded intriguing. He knew I was lying, but didn't push it. I liked this guy.

"What's your name?" I asked.

"Kowalski, Duane. Philly PD, retired."

\* \* \* \* \* \*

My next stop was the home of Edgar Lopez, Barry's caddie. Lopez was looking at the back end of his fifties, naturally bald, with a thick, compensating mustache. He had been around the mini tours as long as I could remember. He was a good caddie, though he occasionally struggled with reading greens. He lived in a small two-bedroom place just off Sunset Boulevard, in the shadow of Dodger Stadium. A rusted dryer dominated the tiny front yard, and a small brown dog was sprawled on the stucco porch. The dog disappeared under the porch as I approach.

"Jimmy Hooker. ¿Que pasó?" Edgar said as he opened the tattered screen door and stepped onto the porch. "Is Carpie with you?"

"No, he's back east, caddying for some young Asian phenom on the women's tour."

"Whatcha doin' back in L.A.?" he asked, glancing around the yard. For the dog, I assumed.

"Barry's funeral."

His eyebrows formed two-thirds of a triangle. He started to say something, but I saw him change his mind.

"So, you back in the game? Need a looper?"

"No. Just doing some work for Teddy Hard-on."

"What kind of work?"

"Teddy has me looking into Barry's death. He thinks it may not have been a suicide."

A look streaked across his face just for an instant—like lightning from a faraway storm—and I watched him wipe it away with his hands.

"You mean, like somebody killed him?" he asked, his eyes looking down and to the right—usually the sign of a lie.

I nodded.

Edgar looked around. "Who does he think did it?"

"Don't even know if it's true. I'm just checking things out. Do you know if Barry was into anything that could have gotten him killed?"

Edgar's lips tightened, and he said, "You know about him and my little girl?"

"Yes, I do."

Edgar nodded and focused on a spot in the yard. After almost a moment he said, "He corrupted my Maria."

"How?"

"She was planning on going to college. Gonna study that psychology stuff. Then Barry got his hands on her, and she didn't give a damn about college no more. Talking about getting married to him. O'Brien and my little girl? Bullshit."

Edgar's cheeks had flushed. He opened and closed his hands.

"No one's ever good enough for a father's little girl," I offered.

"What would you know about it, Hook?"

"Nothing."

He nodded again. The dog appeared and Edgar picked it up. I

decided to hold back asking about the life insurance policy. I'm not sure why. "Where's Maria? I'd like to talk to her." Edgar didn't answer me. He just kept hugging the dog. "Edgar?"

"*Sí*, yes. Talk to Maria. But Hooker. Don't make her cry. She has cried enough."

\* \* \* \* \* \*

I got lucky and found a parking spot on Hollywood Boulevard in front of the Pantages Theatre. Ricky Martin was performing there in two days.

Triumph Trading was located on the ninth floor of the Taft Building, next to a limo service. I entered and almost immediately came knee-to-wood with a desk. Behind the desk the office opened up, but you could hardly tell due to the floor-to-ceiling stacks of boxes, cabinets, and assorted knick knacks.

Maria Lopez was twenty-three, thirteen years Barry's junior. She was sitting behind the desk in a tight white top that seemed designed to bring attention to her breasts. She stood up when I introduced myself, and I saw that the white top stopped just above her navel, while loose-fitting jeans started a few inches below.

She came around the desk, and due to the lack of space—or maybe not—she brushed against me as she led me out the door.

\* \* \* \* \* \*

"Mr. Hooker, that whole life insurance stuff is, like, not something I'm trying to get my hands on, or whatever, you know? Teddy thinks I should have it."

We were sitting in a dark booth in a near-empty restaurant on the northeast corner of Hollywood and Vine. Maria had a latte, I was on my second iced tea.

"Obviously Barry wanted you to have it."

She looked out the window toward the Taft, but I had the feeling she was looking a thousand miles away.

"We were gonna get married, you know? I mean, we hadn't set a date or nothing, but we talked a lot about it. Barry wanted to be a daddy, have kids, all that."

It was hard to believe she was talking about the guy I once watched dance on a bar wearing nothing but cowboy boots and a sombrero. "What about your father? Did Barry ever talk to him about you, or maybe the life insurance policy?"

A curt laugh escaped her throat. "Barry and my father did *not* talk."

"Edgar was his caddie. They were together for years."

"Yeah, but when my father found out about Barry and me, he freaked, you know?"

"No, I don't."

"Huh?"

"What do you mean he freaked?"

"He like, smacked me around, said he was gonna kill Barry. You know, freaked."

"How did he find out?"

"Um, after the October tourney at Brookside, he caught us making out."

"If he was so angry, why did he keep caddying for him?"

"My father's old school, you know? Said he had a commitment to honor or some shit."

"Your father told me you had planned on attending college but changed your mind after you and Barry started dating."

"My father don't know me," she said. "The whole college trip was his deal, not mine. College can't teach me nothing I don't already know."

Uh-huh.

A tinny electronic reggae tune started playing somewhere. Maria pulled a paper-thin cell phone from her pocket. She looked at the caller ID, then opened the phone and said, "Call ya back." She closed the phone and made a production of slipping it into her back pocket. Her top rose and I stared at her golden-brown stomach and the bottom edge of a lavender bra. She caught me and didn't seem to mind.

"Do you think Barry killed himself?" I asked.

"Yes," she said.

"Why do you think that?"

"I don't know how well you knew him, but he liked to date lots of women, you know? My father used to tell me stories. Said one time Barry was running between two women at the same freaking time. One upstairs, one downstairs."

I hid a smile. I'd been there, and witnessed Barry literally running up and down the stairs at the Rancho Bernardo Inn. Lyla upstairs, Carol downstairs.

Maria stared into her drink. A waiter came by and asked if we were okay. I said yes. As the waiter left, tears began to roll from Maria's eyes. But she never lost control of her breathing, her voice never cracked.

"I broke his heart," she said.

I waited.

"I was cheating on him. Believe that? He was the wild ladies' man and shit, and it was me who ended up cheating."

"Why?"

She wiped her wet cheeks and gave a half-hearted shrug. "Why does anyone? I'm screwed up. I had this great guy, and it wasn't enough. I knew Barry was a player and all, so I guess I needed to prove to myself I was hot to someone else, you know?" She stared off again.

* * * * * *

Back at the Travelodge, I showered and called Teddy. I asked if he wanted to grab some dinner, go over what little I had so far. He told me he couldn't—he was on his way to schmooze some potential sponsor at a Beverly Hills restaurant—but we should have breakfast in the morning.

I fell back on the bed and stared at the ceiling. I was pretty convinced Barry didn't kill himself, but it was nothing more than a feeling. I had zero evidence. I thought about ordering some pizza and watching pay-per-view, then realized the Travelodge didn't offer pay-per-view.

I needed to make some kind of move but had no idea what. Private investigation is nothing like golf, except for the fact that if you don't do it regularly, you get rusty.

I thought about Edgar. Maria said he'd hit her. I thought about Maria. She seemed like your typical twentysomething—thinking they've got the world by the balls, but in reality they don't have a clue.

* * * * * *

One of the new Volkswagen Beetles was parked in the driveway of Maria's tiny Burbank two-bedroom. I settled into my Hyundai and tore the wrapper off a PowerBar I'd purchased on the way over. I had no idea what I could possibly learn sitting outside Maria Lopez's home, but it made me feel like a proper P.I.

After about thirty minutes, a maroon Buick pulled up, and I watched Teddy Hard-on hop out, and bounce up to the house. Maria opened the door, greeted Teddy with a long kiss, and led him inside.

It's funny how one little move can completely turn things around.

I guess private investigation actually *is* a lot like golf.

* * * * * *

"No, she's the smart one," said Duane Kowalski, confirming my suspicions. I was showing him a picture of Maria Lopez.

"Have you ever seen this guy before?" I asked, showing a photo of Teddy and Barry. "The fat one."

"Yeah, maybe. What's going on, Shamus? They have something to do with your friend's jump?"

"I'll be back later today, tell you all about it," I said as I hustled out of the Taft Building. I was late meeting Teddy at Rae's Diner in Santa Monica.

* * * * * *

"You look like shit," Teddy said as he stuffed a forkful of pancakes into his mouth.

"I was out late following a lead."

"Really? What kind of lead?"

"I found out someone's been lying."

"Who?" he asked without hesitation.

"I'm not sure yet. But you're right—Barry didn't kill himself. I just have to find out who did it, and why. But I think it all centers around Maria Lopez."

"See? I told you. It was Edgar, wasn't it?"

"I don't think so," I said.

"But he was really pissed about her and Barry. Said he was gonna kill Barry."

Teddy just sliced into the woods.

"Why didn't you tell me Edgar said that?"

"Huh? I did."

"No, you didn't. Who told you Edgar threatened Barry?"

"Maria. She used to say he hit her and stuff."

I nodded as if considering this. Teddy downed the rest of his chocolate milk.

"No," I finally said. "It wasn't Edgar. Maria was seeing someone else, and I think that's who pushed Barry off that roof."

"Someone else?"

I stood up, and said, "I'm going to find out who killed Barry. That's the job you hired me for."

"Where you going?" Teddy asked.

"Back to Hollywood and Vine. The security guard at the Taft Building has some information for me."

"What information?"

"I'll let you know."

\* \* \* \* \* \*

I found Duane Kowalski on the floor behind his guard podium. He was bleeding badly from the back of the head. A good sign, actually. When there's no blood, the wound can be a lot worse. I still felt guilty. I had baited Teddy into going there, but figured I would beat him. I guess a Buick moves faster than a Hyundai.

As I bent down to see if Kowalski was still conscious, I heard Teddy Hard-on's voice say, "Get in the elevator, Hooker."

I turned and saw him holding a Beretta. Kowalski's Beretta.

We stepped onto the elevator.

"You think Maria Lopez is going to stay with you after she gets the money?" I said as we rode up, then laughed for emphasis.

"Shut up," was all Teddy could manage.

The doors opened to the twelfth floor and we headed for the stairs to the roof. I wasn't worried. I knew Teddy was an amateur when it came to crime, and I figured I'd have plenty of opportunity to take the gun when we got onto the roof.

As we stepped out, I saw Maria Lopez, holding an internal-hammer Smith & Wesson Airweight.

Now I was worried.

"Where is the security guard?" Maria asked Teddy, in a voice I hadn't heard before.

"Downstairs. I cracked him on the back of the head."

Maria opened and closed her eyes, like she was dealing with a toddler. "Go and get him, you idiot."

"Yeah, but—"

"Now."

Teddy reluctantly went back down. I took a step toward Maria, but she leveled the gun.

"Please do not make me shoot you, Mr. Hooker."

I held my hands up, and said, "That whole street attitude you gave me—the double negatives and 'you knows'—nice touch."

Maria glanced at her watch, shot a look toward the stairs.

"It must be rough dealing with a moron like Teddy, huh? And having sex with him? Wuff." I shuddered.

"Move toward the ledge," was all she said.

"So, Barry tells you about the policy and then, what, you lure him up here and push him off—or did Teddy do it?"

Maria just stared. And it hit me.

"Wow, did I have this figured wrong," I said. "I thought you and Teddy concocted this together. But it was all you, wasn't it? You offed Barry, then cuddled up next to Teddy when the cops were so quick to say suicide."

Maria remained silent and the Airweight remained rock steady.

"Where the hell is he?" she said, looking at her watch again.

"Give him a break. He's a fat slob dragging a hundred and sixty pounds of dead weight up a flight of stairs," I said.

The door opened and Teddy stumbled out, blood soaking his golf shirt. I expected to see the cavalry in the form of Duane

Kowalski appear next. But it was Randall Manupolo holding the Beretta and his service piece.

"Where have you been?" Maria said.

"Traffic," the Samoan muttered, and kicked the writhing Teddy Hard-on away from the door.

"Why'd you shoot him?" Maria asked. "I thought we needed him"

"Not anymore," Manupolo said, glancing my way. "This heartless prick showing up was a gift from God."

Manupolo walked over, stood an inch from my face and said, "You've fucked up my city for the last time."

"You two meet during the Monty White thing?" I asked, indicating Maria. "She's a little young, isn't she?"

Teddy screamed, "Maria!"

It was like a bad scene from *West Side Story*.

"Shut up, Teddy," she said.

"You said you loved me," Teddy said between moans.

Maria Lopez bit her lip. "What do we do, baby?" she asked Manupolo.

"Same plan, different mark. Instead of Harden, we put the murder on this guy. It's better. He was jealous of O'Brien, jealous of his game, of you, the whole deal."

"What about Teddy?"

"Hooker killed him."

Manupolo pulled a Newport from his pack and as he went to light it, I grabbed the 7-iron and swung.

If Randall Manupolo's head had been a golf ball, I would have sent it a mile. Instead it made a sound like a meat tenderizer hitting an eggplant. The big man dropped to one knee, and I took my mulligan. He went down all the way.

Maria was too shocked to remember she was holding a gun. I grabbed it and just for the hell of it, smacked her across the face.

I heard sirens and figured Kowalski had regained conscious-
ness.

* * * * *

After nearly six hours at Hollywood Division, wherein Maria
Lopez gave a full confession—well, full in the sense that she said
she was forced by Manupolo to do everything—I caught a cab back
to the Travelodge, then to LAX.

Edgar Lopez called me and said Teddy Hard-on was out of surgery and going to make it. Randall Manupolo was still in surgery.

Edgar told me Manupolo had been around his daughter lately, but he figured it was because of the investigation. He asked me
where he went wrong as a father. I asked him what would I know
about it.

I hung up and closed my eyes.

Time to go.

Go home, go to hell, go anywhere.

Anywhere but Hollywood and Vine.

*Gar Haywood has written hardboiled, crime, and cozy, and he's written for television. My personal favorites are his Aaron Gunner novels. This story, however, ranks right up there with my favorites of his work. It's a clever tale, as well as a commentary on the TV and movie business.*

# Moving Pictures

*by Gar Anthony Haywood*

D anny Floyd's first clue that he'd picked the wrong man to write screenplays with was his partner's name: Farrel Johns. Did that handle not say all there was to say about the fool's pretentiousness, or what?

Danny's second clue that Farrel was a loser was his "bible," or the book he constantly referred to as such: *Adventures in the Screen Trade* by William Goldman. William fucking Goldman? The old fart who wrote *Butch Cassidy and the Sundance Kid* ten thousand years ago? Goldman didn't have a thing to teach Danny, but Farrel hung on his every written word; his dog-eared copy of *Adventures* was always close at hand, and a quote from the book was never more than two hours away, no matter how insipid or unfunny.

Standing on the corner now, waiting for Farrel to pick him up so they could make good their escape from the slime pit of broken promises that was Los Angeles, Danny wondered how in the hell he'd managed to tolerate the fat boy's hot air for all of the last eighteen months. And how a writing team with as much promise as theirs had somehow done nothing of any interest to the Hollywood press beyond committing a stupid murder.

*  *  *  *  *  *

Farrel Johns was one of those film-school monkeys who thought every inch of celluloid shot in black and white was a "classic," a masterpiece to be viewed and deconstructed over and over again until you could recite every line of dialogue in your sleep. He studied old films and the long-dead geezers who'd made them as if God were going to test him on the shit come Judgment Day. If it weren't for the fact he could knock out a 110-page first draft in nine days, and pitch a story in three acts to perfect strangers with seamless precision, Danny would never have befriended him, let alone driven out to California with him to try and sell screenplays together.

But the truth was, Danny had needed the help. He was an idea man, a story machine who could crank out spectacular, perfectly structured movie premises any studio exec would salivate over—but that was as far as his abilities went. A junior-college dropout of twenty-four, Danny's grammar was for shit and his spelling was pathetic, and his pitching skills were even worse. Danny told a story out loud like a man performing Shakespeare with rocks in his mouth. To ever realize his dream of becoming a big-money, A-list screenwriter, Danny didn't think he needed film school nor an appreciation for movies so much as five minutes older than he was—but he was fairly certain he was either going to have to learn how to *write*, or hook up with somebody who could.

When he'd first met Farrel eighteen months ago at Barndance, the only annual film festival their native Kansas City ever hosted, Danny wasn't sure the portly twenty-two-year-old with the baby blue eyes had the goods he was looking for. Farrel was a nerd's nerd, polite and soft-spoken and too quick to smile just to be nice. But then Danny overheard him pitching one of his scripts to a couple of female junior production execs in a bar, hitting every beat right on the nose, and despite the fact his story was dumb and pedestrian, his telling of it was a marvel of charisma and salesmanship, precisely the kind of performance act that could sell one of Danny's ideas in a heartbeat if he could ever get it into the office of an actual yes-man.

Farrel hadn't taken easily to the idea of partnering up with Danny. It had taken Danny two weeks to bring him around. But come around he eventually did, because he'd suffered enough rejections to know he had serious limitations of his own, and the logic of combining forces with someone who actually knew the difference between a great story and a trite one proved too much for him to deny. Within three weeks of meeting each other, they were gone, having ditched the mundane lives they had in Missouri—two single guys in dead-end jobs with families they rarely saw—for the promise of stardom in the City of Angels.

Throughout the drive to California, Farrel had run his mouth about William Goldman says this, *Citizen Kane* did that, yadda-yadda-yadda. RKO, Humphrey Bogart, *Strangers on a Train*, *Mildred Pierce*, Bette Davis, Scorsese and DeMille and Ford and Hawks and Capra and on and on and *fuck*, it never stopped! That had been Danny's chance right there to jump ship, to recognize Farrel for the old-school, wanna-but-never-will-be schmuck he was, but Danny hung tough, determined to give their partnership at least six months before dumping Farrel like a ballast bag from a hot-air balloon.

"You need to know this stuff," Farrel had said at one point, finally aware of the disdain Danny had for his preoccupation with cinematic trivia.

"What stuff?"

"Classic movies. Film noir. People like Orson Welles and Federico Fellini, Kubrick, Cassavetes, Billy Wilder—"

"Why? Who gives a fuck? Nobody's making those kinds of movies anymore, so why do I need to know about 'em?"

"Because you're writing in a vacuum if you don't. How can you write a script no one's ever written before if you don't know what's already been done?"

"I know plenty about what's already been done. I've seen the *Matrix* trilogy six times, and both *Kill Bills* twice apiece. Everything relevant to the industry today I've seen a million times on DVD."

"And by that, you mean you've seen everything post–*Star Wars*."

"*Star Wars*? Man, gimme a break. I'm talking about everything post-*Tron* and the birth of CGI. Prior to that, movies were nothing but 'moving pictures.'"

The two of them went around and around like that for months, Farrel touting the significance of one slug-paced, Technicolorless "classic" after another, Danny blowing both him and the movie off. That they managed to produce two feature specs and land an agent after being in Los Angeles less than four months was a minor miracle, but it was also a testament to the wisdom of their having joined forces. Disparate thinkers or not, they were two halves of a decent screenwriter that together formed a whole, and the proof was in the work they produced, and the moderate attention from industry people it had quickly received.

Perhaps if they had landed a different agent, that attention would have eventually led them down the road to triumph rather than tragedy. But the agent they came to sign on with, and eagerly so, was Rob Venatore at the Horizon Agency, a smooth-talking rodent in the form of a Yale grad, and that had ultimately been their undoing. After representing them for less than a year, Rob took the pair right to the brink of a seven-figure deal . . . and then dropped them as clients before it could be consummated.

Farrel was incredulous. Danny was spitting blood.

* * * * * *

"He left? What the fuck do you mean, he left?"

"I mean I called him at the agency this morning, and they said he no longer works there. He's moved to Barrows and Stern. He's been there since Friday."

"Barrows and Stern? Without telling us?"

"Yes."

"But he took us with him, right? And the Dreamworks deal?"

"No."

"Then we're still represented by Horizon."

Farrel shook his head, blue eyes flitting this way and that.

"What the fuck are you telling me, Farrel?"

"I'm telling you we just got screwed, Danny. We no longer have an agent. Rob went to Barrows and Stern without us, and nobody at Horizon wants to take us on."

"Even with the Dreamworks deal on the table?"

"It's not on the table anymore. Apparently, the gig went to somebody else. Somebody at Barrows and Stern."

Farrel waited for Danny to put two and two together.

"Oh, wait," Danny said, suppressing a twisted laugh. "You aren't trying to say it went to another one of Rob's clients?"

"I just got off the phone with Susie Emmons. She said she was sorry, but they decided to go with somebody more experienced in comedy: Mark Haskell Smith. it'll be in all the trades tomorrow morning."

"Mark Haskell Smith? Who the fuck is Mark Haskell Smith?" Danny threw the TV remote control across the room like a javelin, watched it disintegrate against a wall in their apartment, missing by inches a window they'd never be able to pay for.

They were in deep trouble. They were behind in their rent two months and counting, and the only ride they had between them was Farrel's old Chevy Caprice, the limping gas guzzler they'd driven out to California that kept threatening to choke on its own exhaust fumes and expire at any moment. The Dreamworks rewrite job Rob had put them up for had been their last real chance for survival, the closest they had ever come to serious money and Writers Guild cards, and now, like their agent, it was gone just like that.

"He can't do that," Danny said, seething.

"Who?"

"Rob, you dumb shit. Who do you think I'm talking about?"

"Hey, it's already done. There's nothing we can do."

"The hell there is. That Dreamworks deal was ours, he can't just take it away from us like that."

"Yes, he *can*. Jesus, Danny, haven't you been paying attention to how things work out here? People like us get reamed every day, it goes with the territory. It's like William Goldman said—"

"Fuck William Goldman. Fuck him, and you, and all the other ancient has-beens you're constantly going on about. If it weren't for you and your Golden Era of Hollywood bullshit, we wouldn't be in this mess, we would have sold something months ago."

"Me?"

"That's right. The year is two thousand and six, Farrel, not nineteen forty-four. Nobody cares about *the Big Sleep*, or *Some Want It Hot*, or *North By Northwest*, or any of that other boring crap you hold in such high esteem."

"You mean 'like.'"

"What?"

"It's *Some Like It Hot*, not 'want.'"

"*Like, want*, it doesn't matter. What matters is that nobody goes to the movies today to think, Farrel. They go to see hot sex, fast action, and cameras constantly in motion, boom, boom, boom! And if you haven't figured that out yet, you're the one who hasn't been paying attention, not me."

Danny went to the door and yanked it open. "Let's go."

"Go? Go where?"

"We're gonna go see our fucking agent and get that writing gig back. Come on."

"What?" Farrel laughed at the absurdity of it. "How the hell are we gonna do that?"

"If he gives us one word of shit? By showing him what a real 'reaming' feels like, that's how."

\* \* \* \* \* \*

"You guys have been looking for me all day? Really?"

Rob sat at the dining room table of his home in Los Feliz, opening his mail and examining each piece as if Danny and Farrel weren't even there. After five hours of going ignored by phone, and chasing after him from one end of Los Angeles to another, they'd finally just camped out in front of his crib and waited for him to show up. He hadn't seemed happy to see them on his front porch, but neither had he seemed particularly troubled by the intrusion.

"Get off it, Rob," Danny said. "You know we have. Just like you know why."

"Fellas, I'm sorry. I really am. But I had an opportunity to move to a larger, more prestigious agency, and I could only take so many clients with me. What can I say?"

"You can say you're a prick, and that we're better off without you."

"Done. I'm a prick, and you're better off without me."

He inserted a silver letter opener into another envelope, slit it open without showing either man the courtesy of his gaze.

"And you're going to leave us a little parting gift to make up for your unforgivable behavior," Danny said.

"Of course I will. Name your price. How about tickets to the next Lakers game? They're playing the Kings, I believe."

"We had something a little more substantial in mind," Farrel said, so incensed by the man's casual indifference that he was actually following Danny's lead now.

"Such as?"

"The rewrite on *Summer Smackdown* for Dreamworks. That was our gig, and we want it back."

Rob didn't laugh, but he did make a face of mild amusement. "Excuse me?"

"It was all set up, Rob. The job was ours," Danny said. "You wanna walk, walk, but you aren't gonna take that deal with you."

Their agent took a deep breath, set himself to dispense some sage advice. "Danny. Farrel. I like you guys. Really. That's why I initially took you on. But the Dreamworks deal was no more 'yours' than any of the dozen others I put you up for. Susie Emmons thought your pitch was great, but— "

"But what, Rob?"

"But she wasn't going to give you the job. You weren't quite what she was looking for."

"What does that mean?" Farrel asked.

"It means your stuff's not fresh enough. You make too many references to pictures nobody's ever heard of. There, I've said it. Are you happy?"

"What the hell are you talking about?"

"You guys are too old-school, Farrel. MGM doesn't exist anymore, all right? So when you walk into a room and say your script is a darker, more intense version of *Out of the Past*, nobody knows what the fuck you're talking about, number one, and number two, nobody would give a rat's ass if they did. You guys are supposed to be screenwriters, not film historians."

Danny glared at his partner, said, "Did I tell you?"

"Oh, hey, it's not all on him," Rob said. "You've got problems of your own. This obsession you have with originality, for instance. Is that an Oscar category I've been missing all these years, or something? Who cares if something's been done a thousand times before? If an exec says he wants act two to end with a killer hiding in the back seat of a lady's car, put the fucker in the back seat. What's so hard about that?"

"It's not the way I write," Danny said, feeling his anger starting to slip away from him.

"No. It's not. And therein lies the rub, doesn't it, boys? You write the way you write, and nobody in this town much cares for it. Which left me in a rather uncomfortable position when the time came to decide who to take with me to Barrows and Stern, and who to leave behind."

"Fuck your uncomfortable position. It wasn't so uncomfortable that you couldn't give our *Summer Smackdown* rewrite to Mark fucking Haskell Smith!" Farrel said.

"Again, it wasn't your rewrite. And I didn't give the gig to Mark, Susie Emmons did."

"After you put him up for it."

"I'm his agent. It was my job to put him up for it, same as it was to put you two up for it. You guys wanna make this personal, but there was nothing personal about it. It's business. Mark sells, you don't. That's simple math, not malice."

"We need that deal, Rob. Our careers are over if we don't get it," Farrel pleaded, indignation melting.

"There's nothing I can do, Farrel. It's a fait accompli."

"Please!"

Rob shook his head.

"The man said 'please', Rob," Danny said.

"I heard him. And I feel his pain. But what do you want me to do? Turn back the clock like Robert Taylor in *The Time Machine*?" He turned to face Farrel directly and grinned. "You see, Farrel? Some of us actually do know a thing or two about the classics, huh?"

Danny was about to slap the smile off the bastard's face when Farrel beat him to it, snatching the letter opener off the dining room table and plunging it into their former agent's throat. Danny immediately leapt back to avoid the spray of blood, aghast, but Farrel didn't flinch. He just stood there watching Rob spasm in his seat, the expression on Farrel's face as devoid of emotion as a fresh patch of concrete.

"Jesus Christ!" Danny cried. "What the fuck did you do that for?"

"It was *Rod* Taylor in *The Time Machine*, not Robert," Farrel said. He looked down at Rob, finally a dead man grown still, and added, "Rod Taylor, you asshole."

Danny didn't bother asking any more questions. He could see that his writing partner was all the way gone, so far beyond the edge of sanity that trying to talk to him now would be like asking a tree for driving directions.

He shoved Farrel out of the house and they started to run.

\* \* \* \* \* \*

Inevitably, the shock wore off and Farrel came to terms with what he'd just done.

"Oh, my God. Oh, myGodmyGodmyGod," he said, sitting in the passenger seat of the Caprice as Danny drove.

"We've gotta get out of L.A.," Danny said. "Like immediately."

"Hell yes, let's go."

"They're gonna know it was us. We were running around looking for the sonofabitch all day."

"Yeah, yeah."

"How much money have you got?"

"What, you mean on me right now?"

"I mean period. On your person, in the bank, whatever. How much?"

"All told? Maybe a little over a hundred, maybe a little less. Jesus Christ, I killed somebody!"

"That's it? A hundred?" Danny shook his head, chuckling to keep from crying.

"I suppose you've got more?"

"Are you joking?" He took one hand off the wheel to dig in his pants pocket, tossed a small wad of bills at the man beside him. "Here, count it."

Farrel did. "Twenty-eight dollars. We are so fucked!"

"There's only one thing we can do with that kind of money, and that's buy gas."

"Drive as far and as fast as this piece of shit will take us and don't stop. Right. Only . . . " He turned sheepish.

"Only what?"

"Only we can't go together. They'll be looking for two men fitting our descriptions. We're gonna have to split up, Danny."

"Split up? How the hell can we do that?"

"We divide all the money fifty-fifty and go our separate ways. Otherwise, we're as good as dead."

"Okay. Whatever. But the Caprice comes with me."

"Say what?"

"You think I'm gonna try walking out of L.A. while you drive? That's bullshit, Farrel."

"All right, all right." Farrel nodded, conceding the point. "But we should split up for a while, at least. Until we've got all the money together and all our shit out of the apartment. The longer we ride around together like this, the better our chances are of getting busted."

"But they aren't even looking for us yet."

"We don't know that for a fact. You said yourself, the minute they find Rob's body, we're the first people they're gonna start looking for."

Danny didn't like it, but Farrel was insistent, so he agreed to let his partner drive the Caprice to their apartment to gather their things while he took Farrel's ATM card to the bank to clean out his checking account. Farrel wasn't going anywhere without his money, and the money was no good to Danny without a car, so it seemed like a plan that was foolproof against betrayal.

As it turned out, what it wasn't foolproof against was a change of heart.

Farrel was supposed to pick Danny up in thirty minutes in the parking lot of a minimall behind Farrel's bank, but he didn't show up. After fifteen minutes, Danny was entertaining thoughts of committing a murder of his own when his cell phone rang, his writing partner's cell number appearing in the phone's caller ID window.

"I can't come. They're looking for us now," he said, his voice barely audible.

"What? Who?"

"The police. They've already found him, I just heard a news report on the radio."

"Then come and get me and let's get the hell out of here!"

"That's no good. We can't hook up again so close to the apartment. I'll have to pick you up somewhere else, in about an hour."

"Where? And how the fuck am I supposed to get there?"

"I don't know, let me think. I've gotta get off this phone, Danny, I think there's a cop right behind me."

"Farrel!"

"Okay, okay. I'm gonna talk in code, just in case somebody's listening."

"What?"

"Two P.I.'s, Robert Culp, the hotdog stand on Hollywood and Vine. Grab a bus and I'll pick you up out front in an hour. I've gotta go, they're pulling up right alongside me now."

"Wait! Robert who? What hotdog stand? Farrel!"

But Farrel had hung up.

Danny couldn't believe it. The man was insane. Even at a time like this, the only language Farrel knew how to speak was old movies. They were running for their lives, every minute counted, and now Danny had to hop a bus or spring for a taxi to get to Hollywood and Vine, so he could look for a hotdog stand he didn't know the name of that had apparently been in a movie starring Robert somebody that he'd never even fucking seen.

He cursed out loud like a homeless person too long in the cold and went to find a bus stop.

\* \* \* \* \* \*

When he arrived at Hollywood and Vine less than fifty minutes later, he wasn't at all surprised to find that the hot dog stand wasn't there. Not on the corner, not a block away in either direction—the fucking place just wasn't there.

By now, he was sweating bullets, his mind making a police cruiser out of every dark sedan that rolled by, and he couldn't keep a straight thought in his head. He wasn't easily frightened, but he sure as hell was frightened now. Had he gotten the intersection wrong?

Had Farrel said Hollywood and Vine, or just something that sounded similar? Hollywood and Gower, maybe? Yesterday, Danny would have been certain one way or the other, but yesterday, he hadn't been complicit in the act of one man plunging a letter opener into the goddamn throat of another.

He tried to call Farrel, but his cell phone battery was dead. An SUV stopped for a signal at the curb beside him, and through its open windows he caught a snippet of a radio news report on Rob's murder. Something about a girlfriend finding his body, and two suspects at large. The announcer was about to name them when the SUV pulled off, leaving Danny to wonder just how terrified he should be.

There was still no sign of Farrel, and Danny wasn't crazed enough yet to try leaving L.A. without him. His partner had guessed wrong about his estimated worth—all he'd had in his bank account was $44 and some change—and that wouldn't buy Danny a seat on a bus that would take him any farther than Fresno. Farrel's Chevy was his only real hope of escape, and Farrel came with the ride, so Danny had to find this fucking hot dog stand he was supposed to be standing out in front of, fast, before his partner gave up waiting him and hit the highway alone.

Farrel had said it had been in a movie about two "P.I.'s," as in "private eyes," plural. And it starred somebody whose first name was "Robert."

Danny scanned the street, spotted a Blockbuster video sign on the north side of Hollywood Boulevard, and started running.

The kid at the counter was a long-haired freak, bearing every mark of a tuned-out dork except for braces on his teeth.

"Robert who?"

"I don't know. That's what I'm trying to find out. Two P.I.'s, eating at a hotdog stand near Hollywood and Vine. I need to find the stand." Danny was getting tired of repeating himself.

The kid looked at a list of names on his computer screen. "Robert Blake?"

"That might've been it."

Now the kid ran a history of Blake's movies. "Oh, right. You must be talkin' about 'Busting.'"

"Busting?"

"Yeah." He walked around the counter and Danny followed him as he weaved his way through the racks of tapes and DVDs. Eventually he stopped, reached up to pull down a VHS case with two men on the cover, bursting through a hole of some kind, one flashing a badge, the other a gun.

"Robert Blake and Elliott Gould, two P.I.'s bustin' a drug dealer in L.A. I seen it once, it's pretty cool," the kid said, skimming over the film's story synopsis on the back of the case.

"Great. So where'd they eat? The hot dog stand?"

"Pink's. Where else?"

The kid said it like that was all the explanation necessary, oblivious to the fact that Danny was a vegan who had never heard of the place.

"Pink's. Where?"

"You've never been to Pink's? Dude."

Danny took the gloves off. "Where the fuck is it?"

The kid blanched, shrugged. "La Brea and Melrose. Next door to a flower shop, you can't miss it."

"La Brea and Melrose? It's not on Hollywood Boulevard?"

"Nope. It's on the west side of La Brea, just north of Melrose. You need directions?"

Danny left the dumb shit standing there and fled.

The intersection of La Brea and Melrose was a good two miles away, and he ran every inch of the distance. He didn't have time to wait for any more buses. He found Pink's right where the kid said he would, on the west side of La Brea next to a florist shop, but Farrel wasn't there, either. There was what appeared to be a crowd of sixteen hundred people standing in line out front waiting to order, and not one of them was the man Danny had been praying to see.

Danny had been loitering here ever since, going on an hour now. He didn't know what else to do. Goddamn Farrel Johns. A million aspiring screenwriters in the world, and Danny had chosen to partner up with a walking encyclopedia of useless cinematic history. A damn lot of good all that knowledge was going to do the fucker now, Danny thought. Unless his eventual cellmate was equally deranged, having total recall of the entire cast and crew of *Double Indemnity* was going to do nothing whatsoever to keep him from becoming somebody's bitch in the Big House. Watch and see.

Another dark sedan caught Danny's eye, rolling to a stop in a no-parking zone right in front of him, and this time he didn't flinch. He was tired of flinching. Two uniformed cops stepped out of the car and started toward him, and he found out he was also too tired to run.

They asked if his name was Daniel Floyd and he nodded his head, an inexplicable sensation of relief coming over him from head to foot.

That was Show Biz.

\* \* \* \* \*

Meanwhile, sitting in a holding cell at the Hollywood Division of the Los Angeles Police Department, Farrel Johns was feeling anything but relieved. He'd fucked everything up. Whatever chance he and Danny had of getting out of Los Angeles before the hammer fell had been blown the minute he'd told his partner to meet him at a hot dog stand that didn't exist anymore. He'd cruised the corner of Vine and Selma a dozen times before the realization dawned on him that not every building you saw in a movie that had been shot in 1972 was still standing more than thirty years later.

Fuck.

He hoped Danny made it out okay. His freedom wouldn't last, of course, but he wasn't a murderer. Danny's only crime was being in the room when Farrel had lost his head and killed Rob Venatore, so he deserved every minute outside a cage like this one he could get.

Farrel broke down and wept, thinking about the life awaiting him in prison. A famous Jimmy Cagney line from "*White Heat*" immediately came to mind:

"Top of the world, Ma. Top of the world!"

* * * * * *

On his lunch break, the kid behind the counter at Blockbuster told his manager about the crazy guy who'd come in asking about Pink's in an old P.I. movie starring Robert Blake.

"Two P.I.'s? That wasn't 'Busting,'" Phil, his manager, said.

"It wasn't?"

"No. 'Busting' was about two Vice cops. Haven't you seen the movie?"

"I thought I had."

"The guy must've been talking about 'Hickey and Boggs.' And that was Robert Culp and Bill Cosby, not Robert Blake. I guess you never saw that either?"

Andy, the kid, shrugged his shoulders. "I guess not. It's good, huh?"

Phil shook his head disapprovingly. "You call yourself a future director. How're you ever gonna make a movie if you don't know this stuff?"

"Puh-lease. 'Hickey and Boggs'? Robert Culp? Who the hell is Robert Culp?"

He picked up his sandwich and left the lunch room to eat outside, not wanting to hear the same old argument for the hundredth time this month.

Some people thought every movie with a plot was a goddamn classic.

# AUTHOR BIOS

MAX ALLAN COLLINS has been called "the master of true-crime fiction" by both *Publishers Weekly* and *Chicago* magazine, his Shamus Award winning Nathan Heller series and the *New York Times* best-selling graphic novel, *Road to Perdition*, prime examples. In recent years he has moved into independent filmmaking, including Eliot Ness: An Untouchable Life and the anthology DVD *Shades Of Noir*, which includes his documentary *Mike Hammer's Mickey Spillane*. He lives in Iowa with his wife Barbara, with whom he has collaborated on one son and three novels.

MATTHEW V. CLEMENS is coauthor of the regional true-crime best-seller, *Dark Water* and has published numerous short stories, many of them in collaboration with Max Allan Collins. Working as a forensics researcher and coplotter with Collins, Clemens has contributed to numerous tie-in projects for the hit TV series, *CSI: Crime Scene Investigation* and its spin-offs *CSI: Miami* and *CSI: Ny.* The team has produced ten novels, most of them *Usa Today* best-sellers, as well as jigsaw puzzles, video games, and graphic novels. He and his wife, Pam, a teacher, live in Davenport, Iowa.

**MICHAEL CONNELLY** is the author of the award, winning series featuring LAPD Detective Harry Bosch. He is a former president of the Mystery Writers of America. *The Lincoln Lawyer* won the Shamus Award for Best Novel of 2005. His most recent book is *Echo Park*.

**TERENCE FAHERTY** is the author of the Shamus Award–winning Scott Elliott private eye series. His latest Elliott book, *In A Teapot,* was published by the Mystery Company in 2005. Faherty also writes the Owen Keane series, which last year won the Macavity Award and was nominated for its second Edgar Award. He is currently working on a new Scott Elliott novel, *Dance in the Dark*.

**LEE GOLDBERG** is a two-time Edgar Award nominee whose many TV writing and/or producing credits include *Martial Law, Diagnosis: Murder, The Cosby Mysteries, Hunter, Spenser: For Hire, Nero Wolfe, Missing* and *Monk*. He's also the author of *My Gun Has Bullets, Beyond the Beyond, Successful Television Writing, The Man with the Iron-On Badge,* and the *Diagnosis: Murder* and *Monk* series of paperback originals.

**PAUL GUYOT** has worked in Hollywood for years. He is an award-winning television writer/producer whose credits include *Snoops, Felicity, Judging Amy,* and pilots for Fox, Warner Brothers, and TNT. He lives in Missouri, where he tries not to let writing interfere with his golf and fishing.

**GAR ANTHONY HAYWOOD** is the Shamus and Anthony Award–winning author of ten crime novels: six in the Aaron Gunner series, two in the Joe and Dottie Loudermilk series, and two standalone thrillers written under the pen name Ray Shannon. Gar's written for both the *New York* and *Los Angeles Times*, and for such television shows as *New York Undercover* and *The District*. He is presently gathering material for his seventh Aaron Gunner novel, and is nearing completion on CEMETERY ROAD, the first standalone thriller that will be published under his own name.

**STUART KAMINSKY** was the recipient, of the Mystery Writers of America's Grand Master Award in 2006. He is the author of the Toby Peters, Porfiry Rostnikov, Abe Lieberman, and Lew Fonesca series.

**KEN KUHLKEN**'s novels are *Midheaven*, chosen as finalist for the Ernest Hemingway Award for best first novel, *The Loud Adios*, *The Venus Deal* and, *The Angel Gang*, all Tom Hickey mysteries, and *The Do-re-mi*, from Poisoned Pen Press. In addition to the novels, he collaborates with Alan Russell on the continuing saga of their book tour adventures. And his shorter work has appeared in *Esquire* and dozens of other magazines, most frequently in the *San Diego Reader*. His stories have been honorably mentioned in *Best American Short Stories*, and he received a National Endowment for the Arts Literary Fellowship.

**ROBERT S. LEVINSON** is the best-selling author of the standalone thrillers *Where The Lies Begin* and *Ask A Dead Man*, as well as the Neil Gulliver and Stevie Marriner series of mystery-thriller novels, *The Elvis And Marilyn Affair*, *The James Dean Affair*, *The John Lennon Affair*, and *Hot Paint* (The Andy Warhol Affair). His short stories appear often in *Ellery Queen's Mystery Magazine* and *Alfred Hitchcock's Mystery Magazine*. He's been voted an *Ellery Queen Readers' Award* for three consecutive years. His freelance writing includes four years as an art columnist and critic for *Coast* magazine, as well as features for the *Los Angeles Times West Magazine*, *Rolling Stone*, *Westways*, *Los Angeles Free Press*, *Written By* magazine, and *Los Angeles Magazine*. He is currently at work on a thriller blending rock and roll, rap and revenge in the underbelly of the music industry. He resides in Los Angeles with his wife, Sandra. Website: www.robertslevinson.com.

**DICK LOCHTE's** popular crime novels include *Sleeping Dog*, which won the Nero Wolfe Award, was nominated for the Edgar, the Shamus, and the Anthony, and was named one of the 100 Favorite Mysteries of the Century by the Independent Booksellers Association. His bimonthly column, Mysteries, that appeared for nearly a decade in the *Los Angeles Times*, earned him the 2003 Ellen Nehr Award for Excellence in Mystery Reviewing. Lochte, who lives in Southern California with his wife and son, is also an award-winning drama critic and has written screenplays for such actors as Jodie Foster, Martin Sheen, and Roger Moore.

**CHRISTINE MATTHEWS** is the author of the Gil & Claire Hunt series. Her sixty plus short stories have appeared in publications such as *Deadly Allies Ii*, *Ellery Queen's Mystery Magazine*, *Lethal Ladies*, *For Crime Out Loud I & Ii*, Mickey Spillane's *Vengeance Is Hers* and *Till Death Do Us Part*. Three of her stories have been chosen to appear in collections of *The Year's Finest Stories*. The most recent was

"For The Benefit of Mr. Means," from *The Mammoth Book of 1920's Whodunits* (Carroll & Graf, 2004). She is the editor of an anthology called *Deadly Housewives*, published by Avon/Morrow, which features 14 stories by some of the top female writers in the field today.

**PERCY SPURLARK PARKER**, like a number of mystery writers, had the honor of his first work of fiction being published in *Ellery Queen's Mystery Magazine*, in 1972. The following year he introduced mystery fans to Big Bull Benson, a black gambler and hotel owner who traverses the mean streets of a city not unlike Parker's native Chicago. *Good Girls Don't Get Murdered*, Benson's one outing in novel form, has become a cult classic. Parker and his wife of forty-eight years, Shirley, live in Las Vegas, where he divides his time between the slot machines and the word proccessor.

**GARY PHILLIPS** writes crime and mystery stories in various mediums. His latest efforts include the *Partisan Mandate*, a thriller, and *Culprits*, a graphic novel for Dark Horse Comics. Visit his website at: www.gdphillips.com.

**BILL PRONZINI** a full-time professional writer since 1969, has published sixty-six novels, including three in collaboration with his wife, the novelist Marcia Muller, and thirty in his popular Nameless Detective series. He is also the author of four nonfiction books, nineteen collections of short stories, and scores of uncollected stories, articles, essays, and book reviews; and he has edited or co-edited numerous anthologies. His work has been translated into eighteen languages and published in nearly thirty countries. He has received three Shamus Awards, two for Best Novel the Lifetime Achievement Award (presented in 1987) from the Private Eye Writers of America; and six nominations for the Mystery Writers of America's Edgar Award. His novel *Snowbound* was the recipient of the Grand Prix de la Littérature Policiere as the best crime novel published in France in 1988. His mainstream suspense novel, *A Wasteland of Strangers*, was nominated for best crime novel of 1997 by both the Mystery Writers of America and the International Crime Writers Association. And his young-adult short-short, "Christmas Gifts," was the recipient of the Paul A. Witty Award, presented by the International Reading Association for the best YA short fiction of 1999.